Radiomen

Radiomen

ELEANOR LERMAN

THE PERMANENT PRESS
Sag Harbor, NY 11963

For information, address:
   The Permanent Press
   4170 Noyac Road
   Sag Harbor, NY 11963
   www.thepermanentpress.com

Library of Congress Cataloging-in-Publication Data

Lerman, Eleanor—
   Radiomen / Eleanor Lerman.
       pages ; cm
   ISBN 978-1-57962-383-8 (hardcover)
       1. Human-alien encounters—Fiction. 2. Cults—Fiction.
   I. Title.

PS3562.E67R33 2015
813'.54—dc23   2014035886

Printed in the United States of America

"Hi there. What's your name?"

"My name is Laurie."

"Laurie. And something with a P."

"Perzin."

"Yes, I knew there was a 'z' in there, too. Well, hi, Laurie. Thanks for calling in. Do you have a question you want me to address tonight?"

I didn't, really, or maybe I did when I started to make the call, but I couldn't remember what it was. I don't think I had actually expected to get through to the psychic who was answering questions on this station, way at the end of the radio dial. The show originated from somewhere in the city— some outer-borough outpost, probably not unlike my own neglected neighborhood—but it was syndicated nationwide.

"What's your question, Laurie?" the psychic asked again.

It was late, I was tired, and I'd drunk half a bottle of wine: something Australian with an animal on the label. Maybe a kangaroo or some kind of bat. In any case, at the moment, I didn't really have an idea of what was bothering me so I was about to say the first thing that had come to mind, maybe ask some dumb question about work (like there was really anything to ask; I was a bartender and every night at my job was pretty much the same), but the psychic spoke again before I even got a word out.

"Hmm," she said. "This is kind of strange. Usually, I get a feeling—a strong impression—about some incident or event related to a question I'm asked but . . . well. You haven't even asked anything yet and I already have something. This really is strange," she repeated.

"Strange how?" I switched the telephone receiver from one ear to the other as I heard the psychic draw in a breath.

"Well, I'm being presented with an image, so let me tell you what I see. There's a room in an apartment building. No, more like a boarding house. That's the sense I'm getting, a boarding house. The room is kind of bare, but there's a cot in it, a table and chair, a gas ring on a counter next to the sink. And there's a window on the far wall; I can see through the window that it's nighttime. The sky is full of stars."

Then the psychic paused. She seemed to be waiting for some response from me—perhaps a confirmation that I knew the room she was describing. I said nothing.

Finally, she continued. "Okay, then. Here comes the strange part. There's a . . . a figure, I guess I'd call it. Him. A figure sitting on the cot. I can see him, sort of, but I'm not sure how to describe him to you; he's . . . hmm. He's just a kind of shadow. I mean, I only seem to be able to see him in one dimension. He's gray and flat, featureless. But . . . wait. Wait. He sees me. Yes, I'm sure he sees me. And because he knows I'm watching, he's . . . he's putting his index finger up to his lips—I mean, where his lips would be if I could see his face—like the way you do when you're signaling for someone to be quiet. Now he's doing something else. I can't quite see . . . oh yes. Wait. That's what it is: he's pointing to the fire escape outside the window. There's something important out on that fire escape. Hmm," the psychic said again. "He seems very agitated. I don't quite know what to make of all this. Do you?"

"It's pretty weird," I replied, deflecting her query.

"Do you know who . . . that figure is?" the psychic persisted. She seemed to have forgotten that she was the one who was supposed to be answering questions, not asking them.

"No," I lied. "I have no idea."

~ 6 ~

I imagine that must have frustrated the psychic along with whatever audience was listening to this late-night radio call-in show. It could have been a dozen people or teeming hordes of fans of the supernatural. I had no idea, really, but found myself trying to picture some selection of them: stoked on caffeine or cocaine, lonely or restless or just unable to sleep, listening to this program on some old boom box sitting on a shelf or a silver sliver of metal tucked in their pocket, broadcasting straight into their skulls through a pair of headphones. I possessed neither of those devices; instead, I was listening on a complicated contraption I thought of as a radio since it picked up a wide range of AM, FM and shortwave stations, though it was really something that my uncle had built for a different purpose. It was a Haverkit, a receiver assembled from parts made by a company that was no longer in existence. My uncle, Avi, had used it to listen to the telemetry signals broadcast by satellites—the signals ground controllers use to track an orbiter's path around the globe—which was a hobby of his. Actually, it was his passion. According to family lore—the little that existed of it, anyway—he had always liked building and fixing radios, an avocation that baffled his parents. He had been a dedicated amateur radio enthusiast from as far back as anyone could remember, earning his amateur radio broadcaster's license when he was a teenager. But with the launch of the first Sputnik satellite in 1957, his focus had honed in on building receivers that could pick up satellite transmissions, which in the early days of satellite launches were primarily broadcasts of information they sent to their ground stations reporting on their position, velocity and temperature. The radio I had was the most sophisticated, and probably the last device that Avi had built. When you attached a special antenna to it—a kind of inverted metal pyramid, hollow inside—you could also listen to the faint hiss of radiation given off by celestial objects such as the moon and stars in the neighborhood of the night sky that was visible to observers on Earth. I hadn't seen that antenna since I was a child, but I didn't miss it because I had enough problems listening to the radio without any special attachments. Mainly, it was sometimes difficult to tune because it was so sensitive that it reacted to changes in the ionosphere, which is one of the layers of Earth's atmosphere. Avi had explained to me why that was: during the day, when sunlight hits the ionosphere, many of the atoms in this layer of the atmosphere lose their electrons and turn into ions, which are not good conductors of radio waves. But when it's dark, this transformation of atoms into ions is halted and the ionosphere becomes a far better reflector of radio signals. So much so that sometimes they can travel hundreds of miles farther than during the day. Sometimes they can even circle the globe.

I thought of asking the psychic if she knew anything about that, but I figured she wouldn't. And since I wasn't giving her anything to help her connect me either to the room she had described or the strange figure in it, the psychic quickly cut me off. "I'm afraid that's all we have time for," she said. "I have to take another caller. Thanks for tuning in, Laurie. Bye now."

"Bye," I said, and clicked off my phone. I sat on the couch for a while after that, without the energy to get up. Finally, I did, steadying myself on my feet and then directing myself to the bedroom, where I pulled off my clothes, got under the blankets and fell quickly asleep. That was the way—that night, at least—I managed not to spend even a minute considering the psychic's question. Did I know who the shadowy figure was? Well, maybe. Maybe he was the radioman, which was the only way I had ever described him to myself. And maybe I even knew *where* he was, since I was pretty sure that I recognized the room that the psychic had described: it was Avi's, his cot-in-the-kitchen of a small railroad flat my family used to rent in a summer boarding house in Rockaway Beach, a peninsula that stuck out into the Atlantic Ocean at the end of Queens. But I hadn't been there for—what? Almost forty years? Since I was a young child. So what was the radioman doing there now—if *now* had any meaning in this peculiar vision, sitting on Avi's bed? As far as I knew, I had only met him once. And even then, it was only in a dream.

II

The next day, I slept even later than I usually did. When I finally got up in the early afternoon, I badly wanted coffee. I was still barely conscious when I dragged myself into the kitchen and poured water into the coffeemaker. I waited for it to brew, doing nothing, thinking nothing, just listening to the noise of the day banging away outside.

Luckily, since I worked nights and slept during the hours when most of the rest of the city was at work, my bedroom was in the back of the building I lived in so it was relatively quiet. But my living room faced a busy street lined with body shops, car parts wholesalers and other automotive repair services. Some of them also carried on some kind of black-market operations that involved lots of hurried loading and unloading of big trucks late at night. (They were smuggling cigarettes from the Midwest Indian reservations, one of my neighbors said; another thought electronics were involved.) Occasionally, coming home from work on the last late-night bus to make the run from Kennedy airport, where I did my bartending, to where I lived at the far end of Queens, I'd have to walk around a Diamond Reo or a Peterbilt with a forty-foot trailer parked right up on the sidewalk, close to the buildings, with only its running lights on and its engine idling. If a giant truck that took up half the block could be inconspicuous, that seemed to be the intent; like you wouldn't notice it, or shouldn't, if it snuggled up to the iron gates drawn across the entrance to a row of garages. Sometimes I'd see a couple of men loading or unloading boxes from the back of one of these trucks. They went about their business efficiently, without making too much of a racket—I had to admit that. The morning was another story.

Six days a week, from early in the morning until around seven in the evening, the noise that penetrated into my front room was pretty impressive, even with the windows closed tight. The neighborhood I lived in was often referred to as automobile alley because the car repair businesses lined the streets for about ten blocks in every direction except south, where the grassy inlets and salt marshes of Jamaica Bay jutted up against the boundary shores of the borough. My building, an old brick high-rise with a couple of dozen apartments, had the look of a relic from better days that had been marooned here, all by itself, when sometime in the past the neighborhood was gradually taken over by the men and machines who fix smashed cars. But its location was exactly what kept the place affordable for me. I had thought of moving from time to time, but where would I go that would be any better for what I could manage to pay?

When I finally had enough caffeine to wake me up—halfway, anyway—I wandered into the living room and sat down on the couch. I meant to turn on the TV and watch the news on one of the cable channels, but that's when the previous night decided to come back to me. I had help in the way of some visual props: facing me on the coffee table was the near-empty bottle of wine I had decided to relax with when I came home from work and, of course, the radio, a big, clunky black box that while missing its exotic pyramid antenna still had a utilitarian directional antenna attached. I liked to fiddle around with the radio in the same sort of way I liked to surf the web—I'd just tune up and down the various bands to see what I could find. I enjoyed listening to people talk out there in the dark—the ham broadcasters relaying gossip to each other, boats anchored in the shipping channels, pilots guiding their planes home to the airport where

I worked or to the smaller landing strips out on Long Island and in New Jersey. Once in a while, I tuned into the atomic clock, installed on a military base in the foothills of the Rocky Mountains. Ceaselessly, second by second, it declared the exact time in a stern, robotic voice that, late at night, could easily be mistaken for the voice of doom. I could also pick up international programs, and one of my favorites, when I could find it, was an American expat living in Chile who read e-mails and letters from people who had picked up his broadcast. He said hello, they said hello back. I'd sent the guy a postcard, once, that I'd bought at the airport—a picture of the Statue of Liberty photographed on a sunny day—and waited for two weeks afterward for him to say hello to me. When he finally did, it seemed like an accomplishment, like I'd made a connection or closed a circle.

I actually had listened a number of times to the program I'd tuned into last night. For a while, the big topic up for discussion on the show had been the increased sightings of UFOs that had coincided with 9/11, and the theory that the terrorist attacks had alarmed "the aliens"—people on the radio talked about aliens like it was a given that we were being visited by other-worldly beings on a regular basis—to the point where they might be considering some form of direct intervention in the affairs of our quarrelsome little planet. But many months had already passed, and since nothing like that had happened (that we knew of, anyway, as the occasional caller liked to point out), the discussion had turned to other looming dangers and esoteric mysteries, like a ghost hunter who had described his experiences with the angry dead and various self-described "out-world" archaeologists who discussed the Sphinx-like formation that formed the supposed "face" on Mars. But I had never actually called in when they opened the phone lines for questions. I still couldn't figure out what had possessed me to phone in last night—boredom, maybe, or the effects of the wine. But whatever, I certainly hadn't expected anything like what I got: a stranger's voice describing a room I hadn't been in for decades and a shadow that I had met in a dream. It was bizarre. Inexplicable. As was the fact that the shadow was pointing to the fire escape—as if I needed to be reminded about what had happened out there—that is, what had happened in my dream. I had never forgotten it but I also hadn't thought about it in what seemed like eons, and I wasn't sure there was any point in thinking about it now. And if there was anything I was really good at, it was finding ways to avoid what I didn't want to think about. That's what the radio was for, and my computer, and the TV. Besides, there were a couple of things I had to do before I left for work in the late afternoon, like go to the supermarket, which was a long hike from my building. So, I decided that buying groceries was more important than dwelling on my late-night encounters with weirdness in radio land. I got dressed, plopped a baseball cap on my head, and headed out the door.

By the time I got home, showered and pulled on clean clothes, it was time to get to work. I locked up my apartment and walked a few blocks past the body shops and garages to where the sidewalks ended at the road that fronts the marshland at the edge of Jamaica Bay. The bus I had to take to get out to Kennedy airport followed a route along the bay, winding along the back roads past more garages, junkyards and small factories until it turned onto the Grand Central Parkway where the driver could finally hit the gas pedal and join the traffic speeding toward the airport and then on to the city, beyond.

There was a chain-link fence near the bus stop where I waited that prevented access to the reedy wetlands beyond. The waters around here had once been an oily morass but were better now, after years of clean-up efforts. In the spring, there were often egrets standing along the shoreline, looking like white handkerchiefs blown in with the breeze, and even the occasional heron or cormorant. But it was winter now and the migrating birds had not yet returned. The appearance of the gray water lapping against the rocky shore was dulled by cold; the leafless trees planted along the street side of the fence looked skinless, barely alive.

When the bus arrived, I got on and took a seat among the other workers on their way to put in their hours on the night shift at various service jobs at JFK or the hotels around the airport that cater to the traveling public. We all knew each other—not by name, but recognized one another from this daily commute, though no one exchanged a greeting. At this time in the afternoon, we were generally the only people who used this bus route: maids, cleaners, cooks, clerks, mechanics, waitresses, bartenders, and other low-rung personnel, with our identity cards hung around our necks. Except for the clatter of traffic and the airplane engines screaming overhead as we got closer to Kennedy, we rode together in silence, disembarking singly or in small groups as the bus finally entered the airport grounds and made the rounds of the terminals.

I worked in the oldest terminal, in a sports bar that's part of a regional chain called The Endless Weekend. Our motto, printed on our napkins and on the black tee shirts we were required to wear with black jeans was, *We Party All the Time.* (I sometimes entertained the idea that I had been hired for this job less because of my bartending skills, though I did have those, than for the fact that I was dark haired and dark eyed, which fit in with the color scheme some corporate manager somewhere had picked out for the hired help.) We had five high-def TVs in the bar and they were all tuned to either a game of some sort or a sports-talk program; those were the rules and there were penalties for breaking them if any of the supervisors who did random spot checks of our operations found that we had tried to fiddle with the preset channels. In the bar, where there were no windows, it was always meant to be some version of a boozy, neon night where serious drinking was celebrated and team rankings were debated with unbridled fervor.

Five nights a week, on a rotating schedule, I was the bartender at The Endless Weekend, working with just one waitress. We used to have more staff but the company had downsized the workforce when the travel industry took a nosedive after September 11. I had worked at this same bar for a couple of years but the waitresses tended to come and go. In the past year or so, many of them were laid-off flight attendants whose lives had been upended by the problems that the airlines were experiencing. Bankrupt airlines—particularly a few notable regional carriers—had looted the employee pensions, sold their computers, their furniture and even their planes, and left their workers with little to fall back on. It was a sad story that I had now heard over and over from more than half a dozen women who had thought of themselves as professionals with good jobs that provided both decent benefits and serious responsibilities but had to face the fact that, in the end, once the world of work stripped their résumés down to the essence of what they did, potential employers thought of them as waitresses. A woman handing you a beer and a napkin, whether on a plane or in a dive bar on some lonely road, was a waitress. At The Endless Weekend, the main skill required for this job was that you could stand on your feet eight or more hours a day, smile even at idiots, and fit the jeans and tee shirt. It was supposed to be a big secret and, of course, completely illegal, but if you wore anything larger than a size ten, you'd never get the job.

I tried to be sympathetic every time I heard this tale of woe from a new waitress—and I was—but only to a point. It was hard for me to really empathize with the loss of something I had never had, like a real career. For me, bartending was just one more in a series of similar jobs I'd had after I graduated from high school. That was in 1972, an unsettled time of international crises, abundant Acapulco gold and disco music invading all the radio stations. I had no close family ties anymore and no idea of what to do with myself, so I joined the vestiges of the wandering tribes of kids in vans who had headed to California, then up to the Pacific Northwest, and then, finally, dispersed to rural communes to wait for the revolution that everybody already knew was never going to come. I had lived in Canada for a while, in Alberta, and then in rural upstate New York, but plains and mountains were not my thing; if I couldn't see water and know the ocean was nearby, I felt trapped. The edges of the country, the coasts, were better for me; I liked the feeling of being able to sail away if I needed to. Not that I was going anywhere anymore or knew the first thing about sailing in any real sense; it was just an idea I had, something dating back to my traveling days. Given a few minutes notice, I thought I could still throw some shirts in a backpack and head out. Where didn't matter as much as the fact that I could just *go* if I had to. If the need arose.

Eventually, I made my way back to New York—home was home, no matter how rough a start it had offered—and had found work in restaurants and shops. I worked cash registers, managed a kitchenware store, even fired pottery in an old warehouse on the far west side of Manhattan for a while and then delivered packages on a bike I navigated through the New York City streets, keeping myself just a level or two above an existence that involved real deprivation. It did occur to me now and then that I should go back to school, though for what I didn't know. I paid attention to those ads that came on TV late at night, offering the chance to enroll in a school that taught sound engineering or how to be a medical assistant or a pastry chef, but I couldn't picture myself doing any of these things. I just wasn't a mainstream person; I knew how to manage at the margins of the system but I just couldn't quite push myself up onto even the lower rungs of the middle class, where I suppose I should have been at this point in my life, at the tail end of my forties. It was the same with the relationships I'd had—boyfriends, girlfriends—things just seem to come apart without my really understanding why. I didn't stick to things, I drifted away from people. At least, that had been my pattern for as long as I could remember.

My current job, which I had more or less lied my way into (though I had worked at enough restaurants to have picked up some bartending skills and learned more as I went along), was actually one of the longest I'd had. A lot of that had to do with changing times. There just weren't that many jobs available anymore for someone with the kind of post-hippie-jack-of-all-service-trades résumé I had, so for once, I was playing it safe and not even looking around for another job. Having already survived a round of staff reductions at The Endless Weekend, I was just more or less keeping my head down, my mouth shut, and serving drinks with an ever-present smile, as instructed by the supervisors who also dictated our all-sports-all-the-time TV fare. They were in charge; I just did what I was told to do. At work, they—the supervisors, the corporate bosses I never saw—more or less owned me, and I understood that. I didn't like it, but there wasn't much I could do about it. I needed to pay rent, I needed to buy groceries, and so I needed to work.

Tonight, at The Endless Weekend, ice hockey season was underway, so while watching the money on the bar, keeping my charge receipts in order, and generally trying to pretend that yes, indeed, this was the place where a perpetual party was going on, where every guy was a hunk, every gal a babe, and every conversation sparkled with wit, I worked on through the hours of a game that was interrupted by a bench-clearing fight and then went into overtime. I knew that because part of my training for this job had involved being instructed that it was my responsibility to keep track of the action displayed on the TV screens. People wandering in at the middle of some game would often ask about the score and we were supposed to be able to tell them. I guess it made the bar seem like more than it really was: a destination instead of just a stopping-off point in a journey elsewhere. So, I kept an eye on the hockey game as well as an international soccer match playing on one of the screens. The see-sawing score in the soccer game paid off with a nice tip when a South African fellow (I didn't even have to ask; I had become an expert at accents) stopped in for a couple of shots and wondered if I knew what was going on. Sure, I said. And I did.

The night manager, who was responsible for this bar along with several others around the airport with different names but owned by the same parent company, came by just after midnight to start checking the receipts and bundling the cash into the safe for collection by an armored car service. Around one A.M., when he was finished and we had helped to clean up, I was free to head back home. I was looking forward to doing nothing much at all until I had to come back to the airport tomorrow night.

The terminal was a sleepy place at this hour of the night. The TSA people were around, of course, drinking thermos coffee and eating sandwiches they had packed at home because the restaurants were all closed—and they couldn't really afford to buy the overpriced, overpackaged stuff they sell in those places, anyway—and there were always a few cops strolling around with their big dogs that you weren't supposed to pet. The cops were friendly and I knew most of them by name, just as I knew their dogs, but even as I said hi, I could see the German shepherds watching me as I passed by, sniffing the air.

As I was walking through the terminal, I was stopped by someone else I knew to say hello to, the driver of one of those electric carts that the airlines use to transport disabled passengers. He offered me a lift so I took a slow ride with him, sitting in the seat beside him as the car beeped its way down the long airport corridors lined with lighted panels advertising great places to visit and things you'd want to take with you on your dream journey: fabulously expensive luggage, extravagant jewelry, and sunglasses that cost more than the moon.

I left the airport through a service exit that let me out near the cargo bays used by the food-service companies. There were a couple of refrigerated trucks parked in the bays, but I didn't see many people around except for a pair of security guards. I showed them my ID badge and they let me continue on my way.

The cargo area led me to a parking lot for the food-service employees; it was almost empty at this time of night, but because it had electric fencing all around, I had to pass through the entry gate, which meant showing my badge to another guard. After that, I was back on a municipal street, though you could hardly call it that: there was a narrow grass verge along the edge of the parking lot and on the other side of the two-lane road that ran past this back end of the airport, a long stretch of tangled marshland. Beyond, there were briny estuaries that freshened with the tides and fed into the deep-water bay. The landscape presented much the same vista as the bus stop where I waited on the first leg of my journey back and forth to work.

The night had turned out to be colder than I expected and I had on the wrong kind of jacket. Shivering, I tried to distract myself by picking out the constellations overhead—the stars Castor and Pollux were easy to spot in Gemini, as was Orion, with the three sisters in his belt, a nebula wielded as a sword and his hunting dogs chasing him through the black sky. From the many nights I had waited here for the bus, I knew how to follow the progress of these starry markers across the seasons as fall turned to winter and then to spring when they disappeared below the horizon until the year changed over again.

When the bus finally came, I found my usual seat in the back and settled in. A while later, as I was nearing my stop, I became aware of a little jingly tune, muffled but clearly audible, that was coming from my shoulder bag. It took a few seconds for me to register what it was, and then I thought. *My phone? Really?* Who could possibly be calling at this hour of the night?

I pulled out the phone and said hello. In response, a man spoke to me. "Is this Laurie Perzin?" he asked.

"Who are you?" I demanded. I wasn't going to identify myself until I knew who was on the other end of the line.

"This is Jack Shepherd," he said. His voice had an impatient, ironic edge to it. And even at this late hour, he sounded full of energy.

Suddenly, the name and the voice fit together. Now, I knew who I was talking to. "Oh," I said. "*Up All Night.*" That was the radio show I had called into last night. Jack Shepherd was the host of the program. I was going to ask him how he'd gotten my number, but then I remembered that when I'd initially dialed into the show, a taped message asked me to leave my contact information while I waited to speak to the guest on the radio. I assumed it was to call back in case someone in the call-in queue was disconnected. So that was the answer to that question—but a much more important one was why he was phoning me at all.

"What do you want?" I asked.

"I thought you and I could have a chat," Jack Shepherd said.

"A chat? It's after one in the morning."

"Yeah, well, I thought since you were a listener you were probably also a night bird. I mean you called in around this time, so I thought it would be okay to call you. Besides, I had a guest cancel on me, so the first hour of the show tonight is a taped segment, which means I'm not on live for a while and to be honest with you, I'm kind of bored. I was trying to figure out what to do with myself when it occurred to me that the perfect thing would be to call you up. And I'm right about the night bird thing, aren't I? You don't sound like I woke you up."

"You know what?" I told Jack Shepherd. "I'm on a bus right now and it's not the best place to talk. I should be home in a little while. I'll call you back then."

I didn't give him a chance to try to persuade me to stay on the line—I just clicked off the phone. I couldn't imagine what Jack Shepherd wanted to talk to me about, but the first thing that came to mind was that he was trying to pull some kind of a scam. Someone I had never met was calling me in the middle of the night, sounding just a little too familiar, I thought, a little too chatty; that seemed pretty suspicious to me, no matter who he was. And who *was* he, anyway? Some guy filling up the overnight hours by talking to every weirdo with a theory about how the government was concealing the truth about alien abductions or a method for decoding the secret messages hidden in the geometry of the Great Pyramid. I might call him back and I might not, but I wanted to think about it first.

When I got home, I opened another bottle of wine. This one had a laughing frog on the label. (What can I say? I just pulled these things out of the discount bin; I didn't spend a lot of time worrying about who made them.) Outside my window, I heard a truck pull up across the street. Its air brakes heaved a long sigh and then the street was quiet again, except for the occasional thud of a crate hitting the sidewalk. The smugglers were at it again.

I let the truck's arrival distract me for a while, but once the noise outside settled down, I started thinking about whether or not I should return Jack Shepherd's call. His number was in my phone, so all I had to do was hit a button or two. But I was still hesitant. What if my first instinct was right and he was trying to trick me in some way, tell me I wasn't on the air when I really was and then involve me in some kind of embarrassing conversation? I had just about convinced myself that must have been his motive when my phone rang. I knew, even without looking at the number, that it was him again. I didn't want to answer the phone but it's very hard for me to just let a phone ring without picking it up. It sounds too much like it's yelling at me.

I said hello and Jack immediately started talking. "Okay, so you didn't call me back. Or maybe you were going to and I'm just jumping the gun."

"You're right," I told him. "I wasn't going to call."

"Well then," Jack said, "you would have missed out on some interesting information. That is, if you're Avi Perzin's niece."

I listened to a kind of faint crackling in the phone—more background noise generated by the universe, I imagined—pinging from cell tower to cell tower across the river of night. On the other end of the connection, Jack Shepherd was listening to me breathe.

"Are you still there?" he asked.

"Yes. And yes, Avi was my uncle. How did you know him?"

"I had him on my show a couple of times. That was a lot of years ago—a lot—but he was an interesting guy. He made an impression."

"Avi was on your show?"

I couldn't think of why that would be. The last time I had seen Avi, I was still a child and I remembered him as a tall, lanky man, awkward and shy. The only member of my family that I knew of who had any kind of higher education, he had spent his life teaching science at a community college in the Bronx. When I was young, I was with him a lot of the time because my mother had been diagnosed with lupus soon after I was born, and with my father away all day working, Avi, who seemed to spend as much time at home studying and grading papers as he did teaching, often ended up as my caretaker. We all lived in the same apartment building in the Bronx, so at least a few times a week, my mother would send me up a couple of flights of stairs to Avi's apartment. It was there, on wet afternoons and cold evenings with the heat banging in the radiators, that Avi told me about things like the properties of the ionosphere and about how radio and television waves could drift out into space and keep on going for an unimaginably long time (so that I envisioned people on other planets being able to watch episodes of my favorite cartoons if they could just reel them in with the right antenna).

My mother died when I was around eight and then my father had a falling out with Avi, who was my father's younger brother. A cousin later told me that as far as she knew, the argument was about nothing much and mostly one-sided—my father was just angry at everyone after my mother passed away. My father remarried not long afterward to a jealous woman who didn't want him to reconcile with his brother, and so prevented that from happening. We soon moved to New Jersey, which I hated; I was lonely and angry myself after I lost my mother, and the dreary, down-market landscape of the suburb we lived in made me feel like I was spending my days pacing a cage I had to escape. I had little contact with my uncle after that, though I did know that he had never married, never moved from the Bronx or changed teaching jobs, and died of cancer in his forties. There was nothing in this biography that I thought would suggest he'd be a suitable guest for a radio show devoted to strange occurrences and unexplained phenomena, but I was wrong. It turned out there was a lot I didn't know about Avi.

"I used to invite him on pretty regularly," Jack continued. "And once or twice he mentioned you—I mean, he mentioned that he had a niece named Laurie. When you called in last night, I thought I remembered that—after all, how many Laurie Perzins can there be?—so I went through my files. I don't have the tapes from shows I did that long ago, but I still have my notes, and I realized I was right. One of the last times Avi was on my show, he talked about you. Well, not on the air—but afterward. He talked to me."

That would probably have been when I was a teenager and already long gone from Avi's life, so I was still puzzled. And, though I didn't want to give this guy Jack Shepherd the impression that I was all that interested in what he was saying, the truth was that I was very curious. "Why?" I asked. "Do you remember what he said about me?"

~ 23 ~

There was a pause before Jack Shepherd answered. I got the feeling he was constructing the right way to answer me. Finally he said, "Yes, actually. I do."

But that's all he said. He was going to make me work for the answer—or at least pretend that's what I was doing. "Okay," I said. "You got me. What did he tell you?"

"He said that once, when you were a child, you told him you'd had a kind of close encounter. With someone you called the radioman."

Instantly, I was aware of all kinds of internal alarms going off. I framed my response cautiously. "That's interesting. Do you know what he meant?"

"You mean *who*, don't you? And my guess would be he was referring to the same guy who came through to Raven-ette last night. The psychic I had on—that's her name, in case you didn't catch it."

"Maybe what she's psychic about is people's dreams, because that's the only place I ever saw . . . that thing. Him. The radioman. I must have told Avi about it." I didn't remember doing that—in fact, I didn't remember ever telling anyone about the shadowy figure but it was possible. Anything was possible, right?

"Well, you were a little kid," Jack continued, mildly enough. "I guess it was easy to convince yourself that you had a dream. Sometimes, though, dreams can be like screen memories. You know, images, pictures, that screen out things you might not want to think happened to you in real life. Like an alien encounter."

The idea seemed ridiculous to me. "Please," I replied. "What are you suggesting? That I met ET? He wasn't anything like that."

"Okay," Jack said. "Fine. Definitely no cute guy with a glowing finger. But that still leaves me wondering about something. Why did you call him the radioman?"

I didn't answer this question, preferring to ask one of my own. "Why was Avi on your show? You still haven't explained that to me."

"You really don't know?"

"I have no idea. If you want to tell me, fine. If not, I'm hanging up."

"You're kind of cranky, aren't you?" Jack said.

"I'm tired," I told him. "I've been working all night."

I realized that, despite my resolve to be careful, the conversation had taken on a bantering tone that wasn't exactly unfriendly. Maybe I just couldn't help myself; working in a bar, you get used to talking to people you just met as if you'd known them for years. But Jack Shepherd seemed to have adopted a similar attitude. Perhaps because he'd known Avi, he thought he knew me. But nobody really knew me. If I had a mantra, that was it. Nobody knew me.

"Night's the best time to work," Jack said. "It sharpens the focus, don't you think?" The focus on *what*, he didn't say. But he did, finally, start to talk about Avi. "So," he began. "Avi Perzin. You know he was interested in tracking satellites, right? Well, it seems that at some point, he went to a conference of amateur radio guys—hams, mostly, but also satellite trackers—and he heard someone give a presentation about a strange phenomenon that seemed related to satellite launches. Apparently, from the time that the Soviets launched the first Sputnik, people who were tracking satellites could hear the telemetry signal that the orbiters broadcast on the frequency that was given out to the public—the Soviets, in particular, always liked to do that; they especially liked amateur radio operators to track their launches because that provided independent verification of their feat—but they also could hear another, faint pinging on a different frequency. At least, the ones who were playing around with what amounts to homegrown radio astronomy, like your uncle. You do know he was doing that, right?"

I remembered the hollow, pyramid-shaped antenna, the hiss of celestial radiation. "I guess so," I admitted.

"Well, when these amateur astronomers monitored the Watering Hole, that's where they'd hear this ghost signal, which is what they started calling it. Whenever a satellite was pinging on its advertised frequency, there would almost always be what Avi liked to call 'whispering at the Watering Hole' as well."

"What's the Watering Hole?"

"Remember *Star Trek*? Maybe a better term would be a hailing frequency. Literally, it's the frequency band on the radio dial between eighteen and twenty-one centimeters, which are the wavelengths of hydrogen and the hydroxyl radical—wait, don't tell me: that's more than you want to know, right? So let me put it this way: both of those are essential elements of water, and water, most scientists think, is not only necessary for life on Earth but for any kind of extraterrestrial life as well—if it exists. So for radio astronomers, that's always a critical frequency to monitor for any signals that extraterrestrials might be beaming our way to let us know they're out there. The idea is that those frequencies would be known to any living beings, so it's a starting point where everyone could gather and say hello."

"I don't understand," I said. "If people expected to hear an alien signal in that frequency range and suddenly, they did, wouldn't everyone have gone crazy? I mean, *contact,* right?"

"Right—except the signals were going the wrong way. They weren't coming *from* space, they were outbound, from Earth going *into* space. Unfortunately, nobody could ever pinpoint where, exactly, they were being broadcast from or figure out what their real connection was to orbiting satellites. Eventually, they became just one more weird, unexplained phenomenon. Some people thought they weren't anything more than a sophisticated hoax. In any event, no one has heard any ghost signals for years now. But they were still being picked up by satellite trackers when your uncle was alive, and he was always fascinated by them. He never let it go. Mostly, because of what had happened to you."

"You mean because I told him about my dream?"

"That's your story and you're sticking to it, right?"

I let Jack's sarcasm just roll on by, along with his remark. "So you had Avi on your show to talk about these ghost signals?"

"He was obsessed with them. I assumed that's why he never moved, never changed jobs—he wasn't really interested in anything else but pursuing the truth about those signals. You can still hear them on the Internet—did you know that? You can hear Sputnik's original telemetry signal and a recording of its ghost, along with most of the satellites that were launched afterward, as well, both by the Soviets and the United States." Suddenly, Jack took the conversation in another direction. "So tell me," he said, "what's out there? On the fire escape."

"What do you mean?"

"You know, the fire escape. Ravenette told you that the figure she saw was pointing to the fire escape. What's out there?"

"Nothing," I replied.

"Okay. I guess I have to frame the question exactly right to get you to answer me. So here goes: *Who* is out there?"

"Just me," I told Jack Shepherd. "Me."

Of course, I was lying again.

III

*W*ho is out there?

Well, I thought, as I clicked off the phone and concluded my conversation with Jack after managing to tell him nothing more than I'd already said, maybe I wasn't totally lying when I said, *Just me,* because the honesty of my answer depended on whether or not what happened to me on the fire escape was or was not a dream. Maybe Jack Shepherd wanted to suggest that it was a screen memory—a term I had never heard before—but I wasn't even going to waste a minute considering that as a possibility. I'd simply had a strange dream, and I couldn't remember a time when I thought it was anything else. Still, that didn't stop me from staying up for another hour or two, trying to remember everything I could about that night. Most of my childhood only came back to me in bits and pieces—it was not a happy time and I don't seem to have much of it tucked away in memory—but the night I met the radioman was an exception. I remembered almost everything about it.

When I was young, there were four adults who formed the core of my family: my mother and father, my Uncle Avi, and my grandmother, the mother of my father and uncle. My grandmother, who lived with my parents, was an immigrant from Ukraine. My father was a factory worker and my mother a housewife. Avi, the college boy-turned-professor was the only one who had not only pursued an education but also had an avocation—his fascination with radios and satellites—that seemed both highly technical and beyond comprehension to his relatives. Because of these things, he was considered to be an eccentric and something of a genius. Perhaps he was both or neither; I have no real idea.

One important thing I do know about Avi was that his teaching salary, small as it may have been, made an important contribution to maintaining the one annual tradition that everyone in my family valued: spending our summer vacation in Rockaway. Once a year, Avi drove our belongings out to the beach in his car, where the adults shared the cost of renting a few rooms in a boarding house called the Sunlite Apartments. It was an old, run-down brick building with white fretwork around the outside balconies, an effect that made me think of a collapsing wedding cake. Inside, there was a warren of tiny apartments with shared bathrooms at the end of each hallway. Even pooling their resources, being able to afford a few weeks at the beach was a stretch for my family, but Avi contributed to the cost of the rent by doing repairs. Among a building full of factory workers on vacation, most of them in the garment trade, and most refugees or the children of refugees from Eastern Europe, my uncle Avi—Professor Perzin, as our neighbors called him—was the only one who knew how to repair the boiler or patch the ancient wiring in the building that was always causing someone's hot plate to overheat or make the dim hall lights sound like they were sizzling. There were a few tenants who lived in the building all year, and the landlord would sometimes pay Avi to drive out to Rockaway in the winter when it was necessary to have something fixed.

Avi was the only person in the family who *could* drive, or who had ever owned a car. He was fond of Impalas, long-nosed cars with bench seats in the front. One unseasonably cold March night when I was six, he stuck me in the front seat of the latest Impala, a gold-colored vehicle that, to me, looked as big as a boat, then loaded a homemade radio receiver in the back and drove us out to Rockaway. On the way, he said he had two purposes: first, to fix a blown fuse that had knocked out the electricity for the winter residents of the Sunlite Apartments; but once he got that done, he promised me that he and I were going to be able to use the radio to listen to Sputnik 10, the newest entry in the Sputnik series. This one had just launched and would be passing over the east coast of the United States that night. The space race between the USSR and the USA was in full swing, and though we were catching up—the United States had actually sent a satellite named Explorer I into orbit just a few months after the first Sputnik was launched in 1957—the Soviets kept sending up more Sputniks, like a relentless, endlessly replenishable army of night fliers. Each time one returned to Earth, another was launched, outward bound into space. In school, our teachers were still using the launch of Sputnik as a goad to spur us on to paying more attention to our lessons and growing up to become smart people who could beat the Soviets at their own game. I don't think I was particularly impressed by this argument—nothing anyone ever said in school energized me very much—but I was interested in the idea that you could listen to Sputnik's successors, Soviet and American, on the radio. I had the idea that I might actually hear them speak.

In hindsight, I could guess, now, that there was yet another reason we went to Rockaway that night: my mother was often in a lot of pain and welcomed any excuse she could find to get me out of the house so I wouldn't have to see how sick she was. And as usual, Avi was my babysitter. He didn't seem to mind and I was excited by the idea of going on an unplanned trip, into the night. Why not? I was a kid. Any change in the daily routine was interesting.

In any event, once Avi and I got to Rockaway, I was struck by how different the community was in the winter: the streets were deserted, the rows of bungalows and boarding houses mostly shuttered for the season. And the cold seemed more biting because the sand swept around my feet by eddies of wind felt as sharp as the scrape of a whisk broom.

Avi parked in front of the building, which also looked very different to me; its wedding-cake cheeriness had vanished, as if I had only imagined how welcoming the Sunlite Apartments seemed in the summer. Now, most of the windows were dark and the building itself had a squat, grim appearance. I thought it looked a little frightening.

In the basement, Avi pretty quickly got the fuse fixed and the lights back. Then he led me up the stairs to the top floor, to the one small room he occupied during our summer getaway. The only apartment he had the key to, it faced the backyard and had no balcony, but there was a fire escape right outside. Once we were inside, he opened the window, lifted me onto the rusty metal flooring of the fire escape and climbed out after me, carrying the radio equipment in an old milk crate. The cold, clear air out by the ocean, he explained, was a good place for radio reception, and like thousands of other shortwave radio operators around the globe, we were going to tune into the new Sputnik's telemetry broadcast frequency, which had been published in all the amateur radio enthusiasts' magazines.

As much as I understood of what he was saying, there was something else about this particular Sputnik that was on my mind that night—my uncle also told me that it had a dog aboard and I was wondering if it was scared.

Out on the fire escape, Avi told me to sit down, to be careful and not to move around too much so I wouldn't accidentally slip between the railings and fall the five stories down to the yard. I was so bundled up in corduroy pants, a sweater, a jacket, a knit hat and mittens that I could barely move anyway, so I did exactly as I was instructed.

I remember that the sky looked really close to me that night and it was easy to identify the animals and hunters and dipping cups made out of stars. I kept imagining that I could see one of the stars moving slowly across the sky, guessing that it might be Sputnik 10, but Avi told me it was unlikely that we would actually be able to pick out the dim, reflected luminescence of the satellite.

After a while, Avi got his radio receiver assembled and attached the pyramid antenna, affixing it in what seemed to me like an upside-down fashion, with the narrow end fitting into the radio and the wide mouth open to the sky. He twisted the antenna this way and that as he listened to what sounded to me like nothing more than static coming out of the receiver's speaker. And then, all of a sudden, Avi said, very softly, "Listen, Laurie. There it is."

I really had expected to hear a faint, tinny voice—syllables spoken, perhaps, with the inflection of a robot. Or perhaps the barking of a dog. Instead, what I heard coming out of the radio receiver was a tinny, echoing beep.

I probably would have been a little disturbed by the eeriness of the sound except for the fact that Avi seemed so enthralled by it. To him, I guess, the metallic pinging was the equivalent of *Greetings, Earthlings,* and he was thrilled to have been able to tune into this salutation from outer space. We listened for a few minutes and then, all of a sudden, the radio went silent.

Frowning, Avi started fiddling with the tuning dial, trying to find the satellite signal again. I remember hearing voices coming out of the radio; someone was chattering in a language I didn't recognize, and that was followed by music and more voices as Avi continued to turn the dial—but the heartbeat-like beeping sound we had been listening to remained elusive.

Finally, Avi glanced up toward the roof. There was a set of metal stairs that led up to the roofline, but they were rusty and doubtful looking. There was even one spot where a bolt was missing, allowing one or two of the ladder-like rungs to wrench themselves away from the brick wall. Avi frowned again, and then said, "Laurie, I have to go fix something."

He explained that he had to go up to the roof for a few minutes, but he didn't want me to try to climb the rickety steps with him. I guess he was equally concerned about leaving me alone five floors above the ground because he took off his belt, pulled it through one of the loops on my pants, then worked it around the railing and fastened it, so that I was now, effectively, belted to the fire escape. Once again, he told me to stay still and started to climb toward the roof.

So there I was, all alone, with the night sky clamped down on the earth like a star-filled hat and some tinny, foreign music playing on the radio. At that point, I did start to get a little scared, overcome with the kind of thoughts that made sense to a six-year-old: What if Avi didn't come back? What if I got stuck on the fire escape forever? What if it got colder and colder and I started to freeze? And what if Sputnik 10—now lurking silently somewhere above my head—was more dangerous than its predecessors and started to do something evil like shoot bullets down at defenseless children who were sitting on fire escapes when they probably should have been home in bed?

Of course, Avi returned very shortly and the radio was once again broadcasting what had now become a familiar electronic pinging sound. We listened for a while longer and then Avi packed up the equipment. Soon, we were back in the Impala, heading home.

And that would have been that, except for the fact that almost immediately afterward—beginning while I dozed during the car ride home—I had a dream that in the weeks and months that followed, even years, repeated itself over and over again. In the dream, just after Avi climbed the ladder to the roof, someone else climbed up from what I thought was the floor below, or maybe even from the yard. Someone? What else should I call him? He—it—was a flat, gray figure, featureless, dim, hard for me to see. And yet, I *could* see him; I was sure of that. I watched as he came up the fire escape stairs and then walked over to the radio. But first, he turned toward me and raised his hand so I would pay attention as he extended one finger and brought it close to the oval shadow that was his face, a gesture that I understood as clearly as if he had spoken. *Shhh,* he was saying. *Don't speak.*

And so I didn't. I watched as he knelt down and made some adjustments to the upside-down pyramid antenna and then turned one of the dials. I understood those actions, too, because they were just what Avi had done: he was adjusting the radio's reception and tuning in a specific frequency.

Then, when it appeared that he was satisfied with his work, he knelt down and put his head close to the radio's speaker. The foreign voices and the music were gone now and I could once again hear the metallic pinging of the satellite, but it sounded somewhat different—a little fainter, maybe; each ping just a little farther apart. A moment later, just as quickly as he had bent down, the radioman, as he had now become in my mind, stood up and without making any other sign of recognition that I was still there, turned and disappeared back down the fire escape stairs.

Only it occurred to me, now, as I lay on the couch, that maybe I had the sequence of events wrong. I didn't like that idea because of its implications, but what if the dream about the radioman hadn't come to me *after* we drove home from Rockaway but rather, while I was still tied to the fire escape by Avi's belt? Meaning, what if it really happened in the few minutes that I was alone, under the stars, with the radio? Could I have fallen asleep so quickly, and awakened when Avi came back?

That possibility alone wasn't disturbing; what was, was the alternative: that it wasn't a dream. At the edges of the scene—the shadowy figure disappearing down the stairs—I was sometimes able to identify additional shreds of recollection, bits of conversation with Avi during which he, too, knelt down to listen closely to the radio's speaker and then asked me if I had moved the antenna or touched the dial. If those bits of memory were real and not something I had added in over the years, then either the dream extended further than I had allowed myself to remember or the conversation had actually taken place. And if it had taken place . . . well, then maybe Jack Shepherd was onto something. But that was too much to think about, too new an idea to add into a scenario that I was comfortable with. At least, comfortable enough so that at the moment, I simply didn't want to think about it anymore.

I was always making resolutions not to stay up all night after I got home from work, and I decided now to try to enforce some self-discipline on that score and go to bed. My intentions were good but didn't quite pan out. I did get myself as far as the bedroom but that's where my laptop was, so I found myself turning it on and carrying it over to the bed. I sat down, opened a browser and looked up the Sputnik launches. I quickly came across a list of them all and the information for number ten noted that it had made one orbit of Earth and carried a wooden dummy representing a person and a real, live dog, just as Avi had told me. Interestingly, the cosmonaut Yuri Gagarin, who was soon to become the first human being to journey into space, had been the one who named the dog and the name he gave her—Zvezdochka—meant "little star." But had she survived her flight? I remembered, again, how as a six-year-old, I had wondered if the dog in the satellite was frightened. Scrolling down the web page, I saw that there was a grainy, black-and-white image that had been transmitted from the satellite during flight: it was Zvezdochka, looking, I thought, wide-eyed and curious as the capsule that held her flew through the stars.

But again I wondered, had she survived? I read farther and finally found what I was looking for: a few sentences that described how, at the conclusion of the flight, *the satellite was recovered successfully with the dog, alive and well, inside.*

I wasn't sure why, but I felt a real sense of relief that Zvezdochka's travels through the starry void had ended not only without any harm coming to her, but probably with a well-deserved pat on the head from Yuri Gagarin, as well. I felt comforted by that. I felt like, for a while, it would be okay to let go of the things that were bothering me. To lie down and go to sleep.

∽∾

BUT WHEN I woke up late in the morning, the question Jack had asked me was still on my mind: *Who is out there?* My answer hadn't changed—it remained, *Just me*—and the best way to leave it at that was to let the question fade away, much as the dream had until Jack Shepherd brought it up again. So, I decided to get myself out of bed and go through my usual routine—coffee, shower, cable news, and then off to work—as a way of putting some distance between myself and any possible strange, stray thoughts that might have been provoked by my conversation with Jack. But as soon as I threw off my blanket, I realized that it was freezing in my apartment. And I didn't hear steam banging in the radiators as it usually did in the morning, which meant that there was no heat in the building, and not for the first time this winter.

I bundled myself into a pair of jeans and a sweater, threw on a coat and went out into the hall to knock on my neighbor's door. I wanted to be sure that the problem wasn't just in my apartment before I started making phone calls to try to get the heat turned back on.

My neighbors were nice people, though I was never sure how many of them there were. The core group was a mother and father—he drove a taxi, she worked in a convenience store—and a whole bunch of small children. There was also an ever-changing cast of relatives and friends who came and went and, I assumed, also lived in the apartment from time to time. They were Africans, though I had never quite sorted out which country, exactly, they were from. I knew that some of them—the parents, certainly, and probably some number of the relatives—were illegal, and because of that, they would never complain about anything that went wrong in the building. But as soon as the mother opened the door, it was clear that they, too, had no heat because she was also wearing her coat, and the baby she held in her arms was wrapped in a heavy blanket.

"No heat again?" I asked.

The mother shook her head. From where I stood in the hall, I had a view of the kitchen, and I could see two small children, each wearing layers of sweaters, sitting on the floor near the stove, which was the only source of warmth in the apartment. With them was a dog, a small, thin creature the color of dust that I had occasionally seen being walked by one or another inhabitant of the apartment.

"I'm going to call the landlord," I said.

"No, no, no," my neighbor said. "We wait. Wait."

"If we wait, no one will do anything," I said. "Don't worry. I'll call. I'll complain."

"No, no," she said again, looking frightened.

"It'll be okay," I said. "I promise." I pointed at the baby in her arms. "Baby will get sick," I said, and then gestured at the children. "Too cold for everybody."

I felt bad about the way I was communicating with her—I thought I sounded like a condescending idiot, but I didn't think she spoke much English, and I was doing the best I could. When I went back to my apartment, I pulled a small space heater out of my closet, which I had bought last winter when we didn't have heat for nearly a week, turned it on so I could warm up a bit and started my telephone campaign. *Avi*, I thought as I started dialing, *instead of how to listen to satellites, why didn't you teach me something useful, like how to fix a furnace?*

I didn't really know anyone else in the building, though I thought many of the other tenants also were undocumented, so I might be the only one in the whole place who would register a complaint about the lack of heat. Which is exactly what the landlord's wife told me when I got her on the phone, as if accusing me of lying about the fact that the temperature in the building had fallen to a level I described to her as arctic. She said she'd tell her husband "when he got home," which could have meant a few hours or even a few days. He wasn't a very pleasant man and he always did everything he could to delay any needed repairs. So, my next call was to the city's heat emergency hotline, where I demanded some help. I told the woman I was speaking to that I had complained about this problem numerous times before, and if she would just look up the record for my building, she would see how often we went without heat. That hardly seemed to diminish the windy sigh of boredom in her voice, but I knew from experience that once I called, someone from the city eventually would show up to make repairs if the landlord didn't do it himself.

I started toward the bathroom to take a shower and then I remembered that of course, if there was no heat, there would be no hot water. I was already angry about how cold it was in my apartment, and the realization that I couldn't even take a shower made me furious—and then it made me want to cry. I knew that my reaction was all out of proportion to the actual situation, but being without the basic creature comforts like heat and hot water always rattled me. I think it made me feel like I was responsible, somehow—like I wasn't able to do the one really important thing I had been in charge of from the time my mother died: taking care of myself. Maybe I didn't do it all that well and maybe, even when I did, things tended to hover right around the barely managing level, but it mattered to me that at least I kept myself housed and fed and strong enough to deal with whatever came my way. The fact that I had to heat up water on the stove in order to wash myself and walk around my few small rooms wrapped in my winter coat seemed like evidence that I was failing at something very fundamental about maintaining the quality of my life, and I didn't like it.

I left the house as soon as I could. I'd be early for work but at least it would be comfortably warm in the airline terminal, and I could just sit around for a while, watching the planes take off until it was time to start my shift. I was halfway down the block, heading for the bus stop as I picked my way through the smashed-up cars parked all over the street, waiting for service at the repair shops, when a thought occurred to me—a small idea with a little bit of light around it that managed to float up through my anger. I hesitated for a moment, but then turned around and went back to my apartment.

I found two long extension cords, plugged them into each other, and then into my little heater, which I carried next door. I knocked on my neighbor's door again—what was her name? Sassouma, I thought, or something like that—and again, when she answered, she had the baby in her arms.

"Here," I said, offering her the heater. She shook her head, but I persisted. We had lived next door to each other for years and she had, occasionally, asked me for little bits of help, like reading something that came in the mail or filling out school forms, so I knew she wasn't worried that I might want to extract money from her or something like that in return for the use of the heater. I had already figured out that what would concern her would be the cost of the extra electricity. These little electric heaters were helpful, but they were energy vampires, and when you're on the kind of budget that people in this building no doubt lived on—myself included, though I was probably better off than most of my neighbors— things like that mattered a lot. "I'm going to work," I said. "I don't need it. And look." I pointed to the extension cord, which was snaking out of my apartment, under my locked door. "My electricity," I said. "I'll make the landlord pay me back." That, of course, was never going to happen, but Sassouma seemed to think I had it in me to work this miracle, and she finally took the heater from me, saying *thank you, thank you.*

I thought that doing something nice for someone else— something that would burnish my karma and make me feel like I really *was* managing well enough to be able to be generous to my neighbor—would make me feel better, and it did, but for just a little while. By the time I got to work, my unhappy mood had returned.

I bought a newspaper and a sandwich, and then settled myself into a seat near a gate that wasn't currently in use. Nearby, nervous people were waiting for an outbound flight to Los Angeles. Even months after the terrorist attacks, a feeling of dread always seemed to hang over the airport, unless, of course, you were in The Endless Weekend, where as far as we were concerned, *It* had never happened, so I deliberately sat facing away from the anxious passengers, looking out the glass walls of the terminal. Spring was late in coming this year, and the afternoon was still dull and wintry. I watched the big planes taxi out on the runways and lift off into the hard sky, turning as they climbed over Jamaica Bay, headed either out over the ocean or inland, toward the far coast.

It did help a little to be warm, and then, when I started my shift at the bar, to be busy. Some nights everyone seemed to be drinking beer, and some nights I seemed to be on continuous cocktail duty. For whatever reason, this turned out to be a Jack Daniel's night, which meant fewer quiet drinkers and contemplative travelers and many more raucous guys hooting and hollering at the TV screens. One of the cable channels was showing the rebroadcast of a British soccer game, and even that had its loud fans. As flights were announced and customers came and went, I just kept refilling the shot glasses. For the first time in what seemed like forever, I was surprised by how quickly the night went; when the manager showed up to cash out my register and help me close up, I hadn't yet even glanced at a clock.

But the night's frantic pace caught up with me once I was on the bus, and I felt exhausted. I dozed more deeply than usual as we traveled along the Grand Central Parkway and then turned onto the deserted residential streets, coming fully awake only when the bus driver called out, "Hey, bartender! Isn't this your stop?"

I was still feeling a little blurry when I unlocked the front door of my building, but then the cold hit me. I had completely forgotten about the heat problem, but now it seemed to be icier inside than outdoors. At least there was a hand-lettered sign taped near the mailboxes explaining that the boiler needed parts and would be fixed by the day after tomorrow. I didn't know if the landlord had left it or workmen from the city, but either way, it was a good-news, bad-news situation for me because, while at least I knew that someone was working on the problem, my electric heater, as I saw when I went upstairs, was still in my neighbors' apartment. It was too late at night to ask for it back and besides, my supposedly rising stock of karma would surely plummet somewhere below zero if I did that. So, I went inside, kept my coat on, and tried to get my mind off how cold I was by watching TV.

A couple hundred cable channels—more?—and there was still nothing on that I seemed to be able to pay attention to. I didn't feel like listening to Jack Shepherd tonight, or fooling around with the radio, so I picked up my laptop and wandered around the Internet for a while. Eventually, even that began to bore me. Maybe being cold was making me restless and unable to concentrate. Finally, I decided to go through my mail, which was piled on my coffee table; at least I could sort through the bills I had to pay and start on that chore. But almost the first thing I came across was a letter—or what looked like an actual letter, addressed to me in someone's handwriting. I didn't recognize the writing and there was no return address. That was peculiar enough, but the envelope, too, was unusual: it was a deep sapphire blue, a rich hue that didn't look like anything you'd find in a greeting card store, for example, or anywhere else that I could think of.

Maybe because of that, I had a kind of creepy feeling about this strange piece of mail, but when I finally opened it, what was inside seemed pretty mundane: it was a flier, printed on blue paper the same rich color as the envelope, offering a "Free Psychic Reading by Ravenette, World-Renowned Psychic." At the bottom, in the same handwriting as was on the envelope, the world-renowned psychic had penned me a decidedly melodramatic note—*Dear Laurie: I hope you'll come to see me. Live on the radio wasn't the best place for me to tell you all that I see.*

When the phone rang about twenty minutes later, I had a feeling I knew who was going to be on the line, and I was right.

"Laurie?" Jack Shepherd said. "Can I talk to you for a few minutes?"

"Are you ever really *on* the radio?" I asked him. "Or are all your shows taped repeats so you can spend your time on the phone with me?"

"Hey," he said. "I'm just calling to say hello. I kind of enjoyed our chat last night. It was interesting."

"Maybe for you."

"Uh-oh," Jack said. "You're annoyed with me. I have to tell you though, I'm not sure why."

"That Ravenette person," I responded. "The so-called psychic. Did you give her my phone number or anything like that?"

I hadn't been asked to leave my home address on the tape when I'd called into the radio show, but even I knew that on the web, once you had some information about an individual, even just their name and phone number, it was pretty easy to ferret out everything else about them that you wanted to know.

"No," he told me. "Why are you asking?"

"Because she sent me a flier and I'm wondering how she got my address."

"She's a psychic."

"Very funny." My impulse, at that moment, was to do something dramatic, like tear up the flier—and do it close enough to the phone so that Jack could hear me—but I didn't. I just folded it up and put it back into the envelope it came in. "She's just trying to drum up business," I said, having decided that the "free" reading would somehow undoubtedly end up costing me tons of money.

"I don't know if that's all there is to it. She did ask for your number," he admitted, "but I didn't give it to her. Cross my heart." He almost seemed to be playing the injured party, but that didn't last long. Just a few moments later, he reverted right back to the personality I had gotten acquainted with in our last phone call: the guy with a lot of questions to ask. "To be honest with you, even though she sort of cut you off when you were on the air, later she did seem like she really wanted to talk to you some more. Like there was something specific she wanted to tell you—or maybe ask you. Do you have any idea what that might be?"

He was baiting me, and I knew it. "I thought we went through all this last night. There is no more." I hoped I sounded definitive.

"Okay, fine. But if you do decide to see her and if there is something else to the story, something you'd like to share, maybe you'll come on my show?"

"Something else like what?"

Now, on the other end of the phone, there was only silence, but in that silence, I imagined that I could hear Jack Shepherd thinking, calculating. Ravenette, apparently, wasn't the only one who had something she wanted to tell me—so did he. He was just trying to figure out how long I would stay on the line and listen.

"Well," he said, "when we talked the other night, you didn't really give me a chance to chat with you about what

~ 43 ~

Avi told me. What he told me about you, I mean—you and the radioman. But I've never forgotten it, because it was so strange."

Jack paused for a moment waiting for a reaction from me, but I didn't intend to give him one. I said nothing. I just listened. Finally, he continued.

"Avi said there was a night he had you with him when he drove out to Rockaway, to the building where you used to spend the summers. He fixed some electrical problem and then took you out onto the fire escape to listen to a satellite broadcast, but then he had to leave you alone for a few minutes. He said he used his belt to secure you to the railing so you'd be safe and when he returned, you were right where he'd left you and you couldn't have reached the radio. But when he went back to it, he noticed that the frequency had been changed from the point on the dial where he remembered leaving it. Now, it was tuned to the Watering Hole. Someone had not only changed the frequency, they had turned the horn of plenty in the right direction to pick up signals on that band."

Jack paused there for a moment. I stayed on the line, but I still wasn't saying anything, so he kept talking.

"Do you understand what I'm saying? When Avi left you, the radio was receiving . . . I think he said a music station from Finland. He had lost the Sputnik telemetry signal and had been tuning around to try to get it back. But then he left—just briefly, he said. Very briefly. When he came back, it was tuned to the Watering Hole frequency, and on that frequency, it was picking up some sort of sound—similar to the ping of the telemetry signal, but not exactly the same. That was the first time Avi ever heard the ghost signal for himself. He said you told him that a man who looked like a shadow—you called him the radioman—had 'changed the station.'"

I finally found my voice again. "Avi must have gotten mixed up," I said.

~ 44 ~

"Your uncle didn't seem to me like the kind of person who got mixed up about anything," Jack replied.

That sounded like a challenge and it made me angry. "So is *that* the ploy? Is that what this is all about? I'll bet you arranged with your friend Ravenette to get me to come see her so she can tell me more made-up stuff that will convince me to come on your show and talk about my childhood visit from a little green man. Are you that desperate for people to talk about crazy things?"

"First of all, I've never even met the woman before; she's just someone with a lot of celebrity clients and a reputation for being good at what she does, so she filled up some air time for me. Second, I don't ever, knowingly, put anyone on my show who's making up a story and I don't participate in hoaxes of any kind."

"Okay, fine. I'm still not going to see her."

"So don't go," Jack said. "Don't find out what really happened."

"As if she could tell me."

"Apparently she *did* tell you," Jack said. "At least part of the story, anyway. Think about that, will you?"

I was getting really pissed off now. Who *was* this man to be meddling in my life like this? Or at least trying to, because that's what it felt like. I was about to hang up when it occurred to me that he'd said one thing—*one*—that I was interested in and if he felt free to ask me all sorts of questions, then I had one for him.

"What's the horn of plenty?" I asked. I had never heard Avi use that terminology.

"It's an antenna. It looks sort of like a metal cone, or maybe a better way to describe it is that it resembles a cornucopia—a horn of plenty. It's the kind of antenna that an amateur would need to tune into the Watering Hole. Back in the sixties, they used to be huge; no one had built one small enough to transport from place to place that actually worked. Your uncle Avi was the first."

So he meant what I had thought of as the upside-down pyramid antenna. Great. I had a new piece of knowledge. And now, as far as I was concerned, case closed.

"That's it?" Jack said. "That's the only thing you're curious about?" He sounded exasperated. "You're really not interested in anything else?"

"Not if we're going to have this same conversation every night, no."

"All right then," Jack said. "Fine. I have to get back on the air anyway."

We hung up on each other—I think we were competing for who could do that first, but it's hard to tell when you're on a cell phone, since there's no receiver to slam down—and then I turned the TV back on, but still couldn't seem to follow the story line of any show I happened upon. I read for a while, but couldn't concentrate on that either. Finally, I tried to get to sleep, but it was so damn cold in my apartment that even wrapped in a cocoon of blankets, I was too uncomfortable to doze off. I got out of bed, went into the kitchen and turned on the stove, staring into the glass door of the old, grimy Hotpoint as if it were a fireplace. At least it warmed me up a little.

It was now about three A.M. I remembered reading somewhere that this was the hour when the majority of people who otherwise seem perfectly healthy tend to drop dead. Fantastic. This is what I was thinking about in the middle of the night, in my cold apartment, with the sound of some giant truck motor outside making my windows rattle. Maybe I could think about that, instead? What might they be smuggling tonight? Tires? DVDs? Fake designer handbags?

But smuggled goods didn't seem very interesting at that moment, because I had suddenly started thinking about that sapphire blue flier again. When was it that I had called into Jack's show—just a night or two ago? How, then, had Ravenette managed to get that piece of mail to me so quickly? Unless the postal service had suddenly become efficient and reliable—which maybe it was in some residential neighborhoods of the city but certainly not here, in automobile alley where the mailman seemed to only stop by when he was in the mood—it was surprising that I had gotten her communiqué in anything less than a week. But why was that even bothering me? I wasn't sure, but it was.

Still wrapped in a blanket I had carried with me from my bed, I padded out to the living room and found the flier and the envelope it had come in still sitting on my coffee table. I picked up the envelope and realized that it did not have a stamp on it. Earlier, though it had obviously registered in the back of my mind, I must have initially overlooked this oddity because I had been so taken by the fact that the mail was hand addressed. What that had to mean was that Ravenette, or someone she had sent to my building, had not only gone to the trouble of hand delivering this flier, they had somehow opened my mailbox and put it inside. I didn't even know how long it had been waiting for me, since I never bothered to collect my mail on any regular basis. For all I knew, she—or some minion with a set of lockpicks—could have crept over here later on the same night I spoke to her on the radio to leave me this seemingly innocuous flier. But why? Why was it so important to her?

It was certainly possible that she was just trying to bilk me out of some money by sucking me into becoming a repeat client for her supposedly psychic readings—I knew how that went; I'd seen psychic scams exposed enough times on TV—but okay, fine, I could sort of allow some grudging admiration for being creative about that, even if Jack Shepherd was somehow involved. What I couldn't get over, though, was all the trouble she, they—whoever—were going to in order to entice me to schedule a psychic reading, *if* that was really what this was about. If Ravenette had my address, then she also had my phone number; she could just as easily have called, or sent the flier through the mail like anyone else would have. This complicated business of hand delivering her message, of breaking into my mailbox—because that's what had to have happened—was meant to be some kind of message to me beyond the invitation in the flier, but what? Was I supposed to feel that I was being stalked? Or courted? The whole thing was bizarre.

Of course, there was also the fact that she knew about the radioman. It did seem possible, now, that Jack had told her Avi's story, but on the other hand, there was no way they could have known that I was going to call into the radio show that night and have been prepared to repeat the story to me. Jack's joke aside, I didn't care if she really *was* a psychic— the idea that she could predict a random telephone call was ridiculous. So the more I thought about all these events, the stranger they all seemed.

I was never going to do anything because I was prodded to. Push me one way and I'd be sure to go another, so Jack Shepherd could call me a dozen times and he would never get me to do anything he seemed to be angling for. I would not revisit the circumstances surrounding my dream or make an appointment to hear what else Ravenette "saw" for me just so I could satisfy his curiosity. But as I sat by the stove, wrapped in my blanket, I began to focus less on Jack and more on the fact that Ravenette not only had described the radioman to me, she told me he was pointing to the fire escape. She didn't know any of the details of the story, but she was close enough to make it very difficult for me to simply dismiss what she had told me as some sort of fluke, a random guess that she happened to have gotten right.

One by one, like nails being pulled from a great, dark wall, dawn was beginning to remove the stars from the sky. I was still really cold, but tired enough that I felt like I could finally fall asleep. I didn't head right off to bed, though—not yet. I sat by the stove for a while longer, still trying to think things through.

Strange, strange, strange. No matter how many ways I tried to examine the stream of events that led from Jack to

Ravenette to the invitation proffered by the blue flier and then added in what I now knew to be Avi's belief that my dream was real, then *strange* was the only description I could come up with. (Maybe breaking into my mailbox was also a little threatening, but my well-developed ability to ignore things I didn't want to worry about helped me lock that idea away for the time being.) To my surprise, I wasn't as repelled by all of this as I probably should have been. In fact, I felt a sort of compulsion to see what was going to happen next—if I *let* anything happen. I could, for example, simply throw away the blue flier. Or, I could wait a few hours and call Ravenette. Not because Jack said I should but because, simply, left to make my own decision, I was beginning to think that maybe I wanted to. *That* was an interesting development, one I attributed to the fact that whatever it was inside me that for so long now had opted for playing it safe—every day in every way—was granting me a one-time pass. Or perhaps I was just being contrarian, which was a character flaw I was secretly proud of. Another explanation I could offer myself was even simpler: I didn't have to go to work later, and it was clearly going to be another cold day in my apartment. I wondered if, in her place, Ravenette had heat.

~IV~

I did manage to sleep for a few hours, and when I got up in the middle of the morning, I called Ravenette without even giving myself a chance to reconsider my decision. She sounded pleased to hear from me and told me I could come to her place in the afternoon. She gave me an address in Manhattan, and we chatted amiably for a moment or two about which subway line I should take and where I had to change from one train to another.

It was still cold in my apartment, but I did hear faint banging coming from somewhere downstairs, so it seemed like someone was indeed trying to fix the boiler. My neighbor, Sassouma, knocked on my door later in the morning, cradling the baby in one arm and carrying the heater in the other. She also had her purse and a diaper bag, so it looked like she was going to work at the convenience store and taking the baby with her, but I knew there were always other people in the apartment, including her other children, who would be home after school. I told her to keep the heater until we were sure the radiators would be working again. "I'm going out anyway," I told her. "No problem, no problem."

I left my apartment earlier than I would have if I were going to work, and decided to walk to the subway. It was a long way—maybe fifteen blocks down a stretch of Queens Boulevard, which was as wide and nearly featureless as a highway. There were six lanes of traffic here, all crowded with speeding cars headed toward the city—a distant mirage of gray skyscrapers huddled under a gray sky—or outward bound for the suburbs of Long Island. The few built-up areas that I did pass included the occasional rooms-by-the-hour motel and a used car lot or two sandwiched between old, brick apartment buildings that looked weary and blank-faced as their windows stared into the steady March wind. It was a cheerless walk, but the exercise warmed me up. I felt like my bones had been frozen and were finally beginning to thaw out.

By comparison, the subway ride was relatively short; it took me maybe half an hour to arrive at a stop that let me off near the edge of Chinatown, in a neighborhood that was transitioning from factory buildings and fire-trap tenements that had been partitioned into tiny rooms for immigrant workers into million-dollar-plus loft spaces for the monied hipsters moving down from Soho to take over the blocks around Canal Street. When I found the address Ravenette had given me, it was in one of these repurposed buildings. The structure resembled a pile of dark concrete whose colonnaded façade had been stripped bare and refurbished to emanate a steampunk look that someone must have felt represented the aesthetic of early twentieth-century manufacturing even better than the name of the long-departed box-making firm still chiseled above the entranceway.

I rode the elevator—an iron cage that was another remnant of the past, though the ceiling was now crisscrossed with thin tubes of neon lighting that changed color as you rose from floor to floor—which let me out directly into Ravenette's loft. If I had expected anything like a gypsy-themed parlor featuring tasseled shawls and tufted chairs, I was apparently in the wrong place. The loft gleamed. An expanse of polished wood the color of honey swept off into a living area that featured low couches attended by small side tables made of what looked like highly polished steel. Here, on one of the couches, perched Ravenette, who rose to greet me.

Just like the loft, she was not what I expected. At least she *was* a brunette (I mean, "Ravenette"—come on), but she was also movie-star pretty: tall, thin, green-eyed and with the look of someone who is carefully sculpted, from the perfect tangle of long hair that brushed her arms to the pale pearl tones of the french manicure on the hand she extended to me as she ushered me into the living area. One thing about this woman that was not evident to me, however, was her age; she could have been thirty-five or fifty. It was impossible to tell.

Ravenette offered me coffee, and when I said no thanks, she went to a cabinet, brought out a bottle of white wine, and poured two glasses. I took a few sips—it was a lot better than anything we served at The Endless Weekend—and waited for her to lead into the reading she had promised me. Drinks were always nice, but they weren't what I was here for.

Finally, she settled herself on a chair that matched the color of the couches, a kind of sea-foam hue that served to heighten the intense green of her eyes. She leaned back, placed her arms on the wide arms of the chair, and fixed me with a steady stare. I kept on waiting for her to say something.

When at last she did, her voice featured a different tone than I had heard from her before, and her whole attitude seemed to have shifted; now, she was serious, almost stern. I began to suspect that the genial personality who had been trotted out to appear on the Jack Shepherd show had been put away in a trunk somewhere, like a costume, and now the real Ravenette had taken over. This person did not exude cheeriness, or invite questions. This one spoke in a commanding voice, and she had some unpleasant things to say.

"All right," she began. "Now I'm going to tell you what you need to know. First of all, you're lucky—very lucky that you and I met because you need help and I can give it to you, but only if you understand that this *thing* you see in your mind, which transferred itself to me, to my mind when you were on the telephone, isn't what you think. This shadow that seems animated and alive is not in that state, not at all. It is, in fact, what is known as an engram. It is a false memory, an encapsulation of pain and loss that you have chosen to represent in this way. And it has been with you so long that it has actually caused a change in your neural tissue, which accounts for its persistence. In other words, the cells of your brain have altered themselves to accommodate this false memory, which is harming you. It has harmed you all the days of your life since it first formed. You have to kill it, get rid of it, or you will never progress. You will be stuck in your current state and no advancement of your presence on Earth and no progress for your spirit beyond this realm will be possible."

"What?" That was all I could think to say to this astonishing declaration. "What?"

I really was stunned. My presence on Earth? My spirit? Please. Those were code words that led into New Age territory, and I'd been through all that, explored just about all the alternative belief systems that had been popular at the tail end of the hippie years when I was young enough to be interested. But I wasn't interested anymore. I had sat in enough communal halls, meeting house basements and crash pads to have heard more than I ever wanted to about the care and feeding of my spirit, aka, my soul. And I had heard it from more gurus, protogurus and their followers than even I could remember. That was certainly not what had drawn me here—to listen to a lecture about how to ensure my progress in the great, mystic beyond. Conversations about that kind of thing were vastly unsatisfying because they led nowhere, unless you could will yourself into the mindless acceptance of what always ended up being the equivalent of some fanatic's drug dream, and I could not. Did not want to.

I suddenly felt very foolish. I had been drawn into the orbit of what I was just about ready to bet was some cult follower who used whatever real psychic ability she had (and *that* was still debatable) as bait. I was sure that was the case;

in fact, some parts of the litany she was intoning sounded familiar, and not in a good way.

"Did you hear me, Laurie?" Ravenette said, leaning forward. "The engram must be neutralized."

Engram. That was it—that was a word, a concept I had heard somewhere before. Thinking about this, I didn't respond to Ravenette but she wasn't bothered by my silence; she just kept on talking, and her intensity only seemed to increase.

"Your spirit is imprisoned by this engram and it must be freed. There is only one way that can be done. We can help you do it."

"We?" I said. She suddenly had my full attention. "Who are *we*?"

But I didn't really need her to answer. The image of the sapphire blue paper floated through my mind and I knew the answer for myself.

"The Blue Awareness," I said.

"Yes," Ravenette responded. She seemed pleased that I had identified her as a member of this group.

"No thanks," I said. I placed my wineglass on her steel table and stood up to leave.

"You haven't heard me out," Ravenette complained. "I have so much more to tell you."

"Oh, I'm sure you do," I said. "But the Blue Awareness is just not my thing."

"How do you know?"

"I ran into you guys when I was a kid. I was living in the Haight and someone brought me to a Blue Awareness Center. Absolutely not for me."

"Maybe you were too young to understand what we're really about. We can help you."

"I don't think so. But I will give you this, I'm impressed. A psychic recruiter—that's pretty good. Still—no thanks. I'll just get going."

I was trying to seem offhanded about getting myself out of Ravenette's loft, but I was actually a bit alarmed. When I was maybe nineteen, I had sat through an "Introduction to Awareness" session that one of my friends had taken me to at an Awareness Center in downtown San Francisco and I vividly remembered their fondness for blue banners, brochures printed on blue paper, even blue clothes—though judging by Ravenette's fashionable black pencil skirt and satiny silver blouse, perhaps they had eased up on that particular rule of the road. I also remembered that even back in those years, the Blue Awareness had seemed a little crazy to me—which was really saying something, because, at the time, I had not been exactly the most stable person myself. If I remembered the general outlines of their ideas correctly, they believed that we, the human race, had forgotten our true nature. We thought we were just higher-order animals that had evolved from lower forms, but that wasn't the case. We were, in fact, descendants of an alien race who had traveled to this planet for purposes that were only revealed to those who had attained the highest levels of Awareness. You had to pay increasingly escalating fees as you progressed through the levels, and as you did, you were also granted access to the different centers and retreats they had established around the country. If all this sounded like the basis of a science fiction story rather than the spiritual movement that the Blue Awareness claimed to be, there was a reason for that: the group had been founded by a man named Howard Gilmartin, who was a not-very-successful author of science fiction tales before he became the revered mentor of the Blue Awareness devotees. When I had first encountered them, they already had a substantial number of followers, but in the ensuing decades, the movement had become popular abroad and total membership had risen into the millions, or so they said. I came across articles about them from time to time, or saw some movie star talk about them on TV, since the Blue Awareness had become the religion du jour with celebrities. But there also had been a number of exposés written about the group, accusing it of being a well-funded cult that practiced and promoted violence against anyone who left them. They also, apparently, refused to admit that Howard Gilmartin had died some fifteen years ago, though his son, Raymond, was recognized as the titular head of the Blue Awareness. I had thought they were creepy at the "Introduction" meeting and had never gone back; after this session with Ravenette, I thought they were even more creepy.

I turned to walk back to the elevator, but as I did, Ravenette said, "I'm at the Second Level of Awareness. If you know anything about the movement, you know that's a rare achievement."

I actually knew nothing about how the Blue Awareness divided up the levels of esoteric knowledge they supposedly imparted to their followers, but I could imagine that if First Level was the be-all and end-all of Awareness, then being Second Level was probably a big deal.

"Well, I'm sure you're very proud of yourself," I said. "But I'm still leaving."

"Why did you come at all?"

I decided I'd reply with Jack Shepherd's quip. "You're the psychic," I said. "You tell me."

That didn't go over very well. Ravenette narrowed her green eyes and said, "You have no idea what you're dealing with. You've stepped into the Wild Blue Yonder and you don't even know it."

"You're right about one thing. I have no idea what you're talking about."

She continued as if she hadn't even heard me. "No one can be exposed to the knowledge in the Wild Blue Yonder without the proper preparation. But at some point in your life, you were somehow exposed to elements of that knowledge and it was too much for your spirit to deal with—which explains why you created the engram. That shadow man. And it's blocked your path, it's kept you stuck at the bottom rungs of even this meager life you're living."

So now we had come full circle, and were back to the place where Ravenette was going to unblock my psyche and free my soul to find its true path through life, blah, blah, blah. Listening to all this was making me angry; I felt like I was being played. "Look," I said, "I think all this Blue Awareness stuff is fake. Fake and crazy and I don't want to hear anymore about it, okay? Enough."

"You don't even want to try the Blue Box?" Ravenette said, sounding suddenly sly. "If you went to a session at a Center, I'm sure they explained how helpful it can be in neutralizing engrams. It's a long process, but generally people seem to feel better—less depressed, for example—even after one session." Now she rose and walked over to a nearby cabinet, from which she removed something shaped like a shoebox and covered with muslin wrapping. From the way she held it, I could tell that it was heavy in her hands.

She returned to the couch, put the object on the table in front of her and removed the wrapping. What I saw looked, indeed, like a blue metal box with a voltage meter on it. Attached to it by wires were two metal canisters, small enough to grip with your hands. At the Introduction to Awareness meeting I'd gone to years ago, they had presented a slide show that included pictures of a Blue Box and a description of how it worked: you gripped the metal canisters while discussing the circumstances of how your "engram" had evolved—or how you thought it had. During the discussion, the Blue Box directed a tiny electrical current through the wires, supposedly allowing the Aware to measure changes in your body's electrical resistance. According to the doctrine of Blue Awareness, the resistance corresponds to the "mental mass and energy" of a person's mind while they sort through the problems caused by their engram. Seeing the box and listening to this explanation had made me laugh; it was also the point at which I'd walked out of the meeting.

"The process involved in using the Blue Box is called scanning," Ravenette told me. "Usually, we only conduct scans at an Awareness Center, under the most strictly supervised conditions. But at my level, I'm allowed special privileges. We can try it out now, if you like."

"Don't be ridiculous," I told Ravenette. "I used to play with one of those when I was a kid."

She looked shocked. "That's impossible," she told me.

"Well, I don't think so, because I have one at home."

At least, I thought I did. I had moved around a lot, but the gadget I was thinking of had been with belongings I'd kept in my father's house until he passed away, which was around the time I moved back to New York and retrieved my things. The device was another artifact of my Uncle Avi's life. When he died, there was no one but my father—no other relative or close friend—to go through whatever possessions he left behind. I was a teenager then, and I had gone to Avi's apartment with my father, who was feeling a great deal of remorse about his estrangement from his younger brother. They had reconciled when Avi had gone into the hospital to be treated for liver cancer, but the disease had run its course quickly and the two brothers had very little time left to spend together.

The day my father and I spent cleaning out Avi's place after he died was very sad. The apartment—the same one Avi had always occupied, in the same Bronx tenement where I had lived with my parents—was now pretty shabby. It consisted of just a few dim rooms with very little furniture but lots of books, papers, and a closet full of radios, parts of radios, and all kinds of equipment related to radios: antennas, coils of wire, transistors, vacuum tubes, soldering irons and anything else that might be used in building a radio receiver. Also stuck in with all this stuff was a black, shoebox-shaped device that I remembered from my childhood. If you plugged it into an outlet and held onto the canisters attached to it by coils of wire, it made your hands tingle. I used to play with it when Avi was babysitting me. He was always telling me to be careful with it, but even as a small child, I had the impression that it was something like the joke-shop buzzer some kid in my class had—when he concealed it in his palm and shook hands with you, it gave you a mild jolt. As far as I could see, the only difference among the device in Avi's apartment, the Blue Box depicted on the long-ago slide show I'd seen at the Introduction to Awareness meeting, and now, the one Ravenette was holding, was the color and the fact that Avi's was made out of Haverkit parts—the name was clearly stamped on the outside casing—just like his radio. In the apartment, I had asked my father if I could have one of Avi's radios— the same receiver he had brought with him to Rockaway to listen to satellites—which was on a table in the living room, not stuffed in the closet with the other equipment. It was the era when FM stations were just beginning to switch over to broadcasting rock music and all I had was a small transistor radio; I thought that with Avi's receiver, I could not only get better reception, but maybe listen to stations from other cities, too. Maybe I was being insensitive, thinking of the radio as a boon to my ability to groove to the Beatles and the Stones instead of mourning Avi, but I don't think I was feeling much of anything in those days, except sorry for myself. I was already a wild kid, depressed and angry, cutting school whenever I could and sneaking out at night to hang out with my friends and get high. In any event, my father said that I could take the radio, so I put it in a carton and, on a whim, took the joke-shop box with me, too. Maybe at the time it seemed like some kind of memento of my childhood, but not then—and certainly not now—did I even entertain the idea that it had the power to do anything other than let you feel the sensation of a tiny electric current traveling along your fingers.

"I don't believe you," Ravenette said. "You can't possibly have a Blue Box."

"I don't care whether you believe me or not," I told her. Then I smiled as widely as I could. "But I really do have one."

"You must have stolen it somehow," Ravenette asserted, sounding furious.

"I didn't," I told her, "but you can think what you like." I wasn't in the mood to tell her anything personal about myself, which meant I certainly wasn't going to mention Avi and how I had acquired my version of a Blue Box. At the same time, I couldn't resist the impulse to piss her off just a little bit, since it made me feel like I was getting back at her for tricking me into coming here, so I added, "It's just a toy."

"That," she told me, "is an insulting thing to say. And very stupid."

There seemed to be an ominous ring to that last remark, but I decided not to engage her any further. Who knew what an enraged psychic cult member might say to me next. Or do. There was nothing in it for me to hang around and find out, so I finally did turn around and walk out. I rang for the elevator, which luckily came almost immediately, but just after I stepped in and turned around, I saw that Ravenette had hurried after me so that she could slam the elevator door shut in my face. She glared at me through the iron grillwork as the ornate cage began to descend.

Shortly, I was back on the sidewalk, feeling like I was trudging along the grim, gray edge of a lost afternoon. The anger toward Ravenette that had energized me when I was in her loft was leeching away again and I felt . . . what? *Hollow* was as close as I could get to describing my state. I couldn't figure out what was bothering me since I thought I had given as good as I'd gotten in terms of arguing with Ravenette over that damn box, but I didn't feel like I'd achieved anything. In fact, I felt exactly the opposite: like I had lost something, but I had no idea what.

I kept walking for a while until I came to a subway. I went down to the platform and, looking around, realized that my surroundings seemed familiar. The slab walls were cracked and grimy, letters were missing from the tile plaques that spelled out the name of the stop, and filthy water, leaking from eternally broken pipes, was pooled around the train tracks. But even though the station had probably not looked quite so dismal when I'd last been here, I knew exactly where I was. By random chance, I had found myself in one of the older stations that served as a hub for several different subway lines—a place where I had waited with my parents to change from one train to another when we were on our way to Rockaway. The routine, for our family, was that Avi drove to Rockaway in his Impala with my grandmother in the seat beside him and the rest of the family's belongings packed into the trunk, with the overflow stashed in the back seat. My parents and I met them after riding the subway, specifically the A train, for the longest distance possible to cover, point to point, on the entire system: from the northwest Bronx to the end of the Rockaway Peninsula.

I was still feeling edgy and out of sorts. I didn't really want to spend the rest of what felt like an endless afternoon sitting around in my cold apartment, but I didn't have anyplace else in mind to go, so I left my next move to fate. If the E train arrived first, the line I needed to take to get home, then that was where I was going. But if the A train did, I was going to get on it and ride, once again, to the end of the line.

No train at all came for quite a while. But finally, leaning over the edge of the platform, I saw a pair of bright yellow headlights appear in the tunnel. As they came closer, I could hear the screech of steel wheels against the steel track and feel the great, sighing wind that precedes a train as it pulls into the station. As the first car finally emerged from the darkness, I saw the round, illuminated circle above the conductor's cab framing the letter "A."

I got on and found a seat in a middle car. It was a long ride out to Rockaway; about an hour and a half as the train plowed along, first crossing under the East River into Brooklyn and then making what seemed like every stop in the borough before heading into Queens. Eventually, the train emerged from underground and became an elevated line, traveling along tracks that ran above old immigrant neighborhoods where you could peer into the windows of apartment

buildings as your car rushed past someone's kitchen, someone else's empty living room looking bleak and lonely in the
middle hours of a gray afternoon.

When the train left Queens, it made a hairpin turn around
a bend in the track, and began heading toward Rockaway.
After a while, it crossed over a trestle bridge that spanned
Jamaica Bay, where I could see, in the distance, planes coming
and going from the airport where, on most any other day, I
would be just about arriving for work. Once it traversed the
bay, passing by a line of ruined bungalows built on a crumbling pier, the train turned east to follow the shoreline of the
narrow peninsula. Now, outside the window, I could see the
Atlantic Ocean. The water was the dull color of graphite, and
when the doors opened at the first station near the beach, I
could hear the waves; there was not much surf today, so the
ocean sounded like it was mumbling to itself as it rolled a few
choppy breakers toward the shore.

I couldn't even count how many years it had been since
I'd set foot in this place. Though I had heard about how badly
the area had declined, decimated by changing times, I was
still not prepared for what I saw as the train rolled on. My
parents' working-class generation had been grateful to be able
to afford a few weeks in a boarding house by the shore, but
when the children of that time—most of them anyway, not
counting me—grew up into monied professionals, they were
off to the Caribbean or the Hamptons for their summer fun;
some gritty peninsula at the end of Queens was not exactly
high on their list of vacation spots. There had been an effort
at what was termed "urban renewal" sometime in the 1970s,
but that had only resulted in most of the summer bungalows
and boarding houses being torn down before the city ran out
of money and its planners walked away, having built nothing
and leaving behind mile after mile of empty lots, some with
the remnants of building foundations looking like jagged concrete teeth rising out of the sandy soil.

I got off the train at the stop where we had always disembarked, Edgemere Avenue, and found myself on a deserted platform in what felt like the middle of nowhere. The late afternoon sky was like a lead ceiling; the wind off the ocean stung my face and hands with tiny seeds of salt. I went down the stairs, listening to my footsteps clanging on each metal step. There was no one in the booth near the turnstiles, no one in the street below.

In fact, there was hardly any street at all. What I remembered as a broad sidewalk fronting a strip of stores—a dry goods emporium that sold hats and hair bands and bathing suits; a drugstore with a lunch counter; a small grocery—was now just an array of cracked concrete blocks bordering a vast, weedy lot. The intersecting street ran straight toward the boardwalk and the beach. It used to be crowded with bungalows on one side and multistory boarding houses on the other, but now, all I could see was a kind of flat, sandy plain that had been taken over by tall brown cattails and strewn with broken glass. In some places, clumps of trees had taken root so that what used to be a block of bungalows instead looked like a small forest. It occurred to me that this deserted area was not exactly the safest place to be, but I wasn't ready to leave yet. After a few moments of looking around and trying to acclimate myself, I started walking up the street toward the boardwalk.

I walked the length of one block and then another. On either side of me were dense stands of trees, denuded by winter and blackened by damp. Even if spring suddenly forced itself past the cold weather that seemed, this year, to be refusing to give in to the seasonal rotation of the planet, it appeared that these bare branches, buffeted as they were by the wet salt wind blowing off the ocean, were going to have a hard time coming to life. Still looking around, I kept on walking, trying to judge, from memory, exactly where our old boarding house would have stood.

And then, to my great surprise, there it was: the Sunlite Apartments. At first I was almost willing to believe that what I was seeing was really just a projection of my memory. Maybe I just *wanted* it to be there and so it was, ready to fade away in the blink of an eye. But I blinked, and it was still there, partially hidden beyond the blackened trees. The slate pavers that used to form a walkway leading from the sidewalk to the building's front door were long gone but the structure itself, a brick box, five stories high, trimmed with faded wedding-cake fretwork around its broken balconies, still seemed to be at least partially intact. From what I had seen so far, it was the only building for a mile in each direction that was still standing.

So. Now I was here, in an abandoned neighborhood, on a gray afternoon, with the invisible sun drowning in the ocean as the hour raced toward evening and the wind blew sand down the empty street. But why was I here, what did I want? I felt like I had been on automatic pilot ever since I'd left Ravenette's loft, drawn to this place by some feeling, some huge, gaping hole that had suddenly opened up inside me that I thought I could fill by coming here. But why? The best I could do was trace my lemming-like journey to this abandoned building to the sense that something was waiting for me here and I, in turn, for it. *Him.* Him. Was that what I expected? What I had wanted Ravenette to reconnect me with—the shadow on the fire escape that, for my entire life, I had been claiming was just a dream? Well if so, why did I think I'd find him here, in this shell of a building, this old ruin where Avi once took me to listen to the raspy beep that was the sound of satellites signaling their ground stations? That was something like forty years ago. What a ridiculous idea it was to think that even a shadow man might be found in the same spot where, decades ago, he had listened to the radio with a child.

But thinking that I was being an idiot didn't deter me from taking a few steps into the trees to try to approach the building. There was a tangle of roots and broken branches underfoot and my way was partially barred by a dense growth of brambles. I got just close enough to look toward the back of the building and see that the fire escape was still there—rotted, rusted, missing many of its steps, but still attached to the building. Gazing upward, I could see the part of the fire escape where I had sat, waiting for Avi to return. In his place had come a shade, a stranger, who had raised his finger to make me hush while he tuned in . . . something. Ghost signals whistling in the universal darkness, perhaps—that is, if Jack Shepherd was to be believed.

I stood there for a while, looking up at the fire escape, waiting for something to happen. To see something that, of course, it was impossible to see again. But still I kept looking until I knew that there was no point anymore. It would be evening soon, and too dark, too cold, too lonely to hang around here any longer.

And so I turned back, heading for the train. But finally, I could at least do something that I had been unable to do for most of the afternoon—give a name to what was bothering me. As I walked quickly down the deserted street, listening to the fading sound of wind and waves, I knew what I was feeling. I knew exactly. I had seen nothing; nothing had happened. And because of that—precisely, unquestionably because of that—I was disappointed.

V

As the train rattled back along the trestle bridge that crossed the bay, I could see a few thin streaks of gold along the horizon where the sun was displaying the rays of light it had been barred from presenting all day because of the heavy cloud cover. These remnants were gone in a few minutes and the sky began changing itself into its nighttime regalia, complete with blurry stars and a crescent moon.

As we rode along, something changed inside me as well: the feeling of disappointment I'd been so easily able to identify turned black and ugly and boiled itself back into an angry state. That didn't really surprise me; I was pretty good at turning an uncomfortable feeling I couldn't do anything about into one that I could. Disappointment was depressing and hard to get rid of; anger could be directed outward, at somebody. It could be wielded. It could be used.

There was a half-hour ride ahead of me on the elevated tracks before the train descended into its subterranean tunnel, which meant that I was able to get a cell phone signal. I was alone in the train car, though I don't think the company of other people would have stopped me from pulling my cell phone from my shoulder bag and dialing Jack Shepherd. I needed somebody to be mad at and since I'd already taken my shot at Ravenette, I decided that the next person on my list was Jack.

I didn't expect him to pick up the phone himself, since I assumed that the number I found in my cell phone—the number he'd called me from, twice—was his studio. I thought he'd have a secretary or a producer or whomever they had at radio shows to screen for inappropriate callers and calm down crazy people. But after just a few rings, there was Jack, saying hello in his deep-toned radio voice.

"It's Laurie Perzin," I said, and then I hurried on before he could even acknowledge me. "Why didn't you tell me that your girlfriend was a member of the Blue Awareness?"

"Who are you talking about?"

"Oh, come on. Don't pretend you don't know. Ravenette."

"Wow," Jack said. "You're kidding. Well, for the record, I barely know the woman. And I certainly had no idea that she was Aware."

I didn't want to listen to him; I just wanted to keep on telling him why I was upset. "She set me up. She wanted me to come to her place so she could give me a recruitment pitch. Apparently, my engrams are out of whack. I need a lot of treatments with that idiotic Blue Box thing because my neural tissues are withering away even as we speak." Listening to myself repeat this stuff only made it sound even more like lunacy. "You wanted me to go see her—don't tell me you're not involved in this."

"I'm going to have to tell you that because it's true. But I also have to say 'wow' again. She seems to have gone to a lot of trouble to try to recruit you—if that's what she was up to. I mean, I'm sure you're a fascinating person and all that . . ."

I cut him off quickly. "What's the Wild Blue Yonder?" I demanded.

Suddenly, there was silence on the other end of the phone. The train was now rolling through a long strip of marshland. On the far horizon, I could make out the lights of the control tower of Kennedy airport again, but outside the train windows there was nothing but tall grass and cattails.

"She told you about that?" Jack asked, finally.

I barely registered his actual words, but the sound of his voice set me off again. "And that stupid Blue Box. I told her I have one at home and that when I was a kid, I used to zap my stuffed animals with it. The whole thing is idiotic."

"She told you about the Wild Blue Yonder and you told her you had a Blue Box."

"Yeah?" I said, tuning him in again. "So?"

"So a couple of things. Let's start with I'm pretty shocked that she mentioned the Wild Blue Yonder to you. Awares are usually very secretive about that."

"So you *do* know about this."

"I know about the Blue Awareness," Jack said. "Over the years, I've had some people on the show who left the Awareness, and they've talked about the various levels you have to reach in order to find out about the different principles that guide their beliefs. As I understand it, you have to be pretty high up to be introduced to the Wild Blue Yonder. Ravenette must be . . . what? Fourth Level? Third? Did she tell you?"

"Second," I said grudgingly, annoyed with myself for ratcheting down my emotions to a state where I felt reasonable enough to answer this question.

"Huh. That's pretty impressive. None of the people I interviewed had actually risen high enough in the group to know a whole lot about the Wild Blue Yonder, but I've . . . well, I've found other people to ask. And of course, you can find all sorts of information about it on the Internet—on sites devoted to debunking the Awareness. But most of the information seems to be wrong." Then, unexpectedly, he started to chuckle. "Boy, Ravenette must have been really pissed off when you told her that you had a Blue Box. Nobody is supposed to have access to one of those things except trained Awareness scanners or very high-level Awares."

"I told her it was a toy. She reacted like I'd said something sacrilegious."

Jack suddenly stopped laughing. "You did," he said in a voice that now had an undertone of a warning in it. "To people who are Aware, their beliefs are a religion. And they're very serious about that. Maybe more than you realize." Again, he fell silent. I was still feeling combative, but there was something about his silence, this time, that made me keep my own.

Finally, Jack said, "Can I ask you a question? Where on earth did you *get* a Blue Box?"

"Avi built one—well, something like it—out of Haverkit parts. I got it after he died."

"I thought so," Jack said.

"What do you mean, you thought so? *You knew* about the box? I mean, that Avi built one? How?" Just then, the train shuddered to a halt and the doors opened. A few passengers stepped into the car, which made me look out the window to see where we were. We had passed through the strip of marshland and were back on the section of the train's busier route. "Shit," I said, before Jack had a chance to answer me. "We're going to be in the tunnel in a few minutes."

"You're on the train?" When I said yes, Jack had a suggestion for how we could continue the conversation. "Look," he said, "why don't you come by here? We'd have more time to talk. The story's a little complicated, anyway."

"Where's here?" I asked.

"Brooklyn," Jack told me. "That's where my studio is."

He gave me more specific directions, but it would have taken at least another hour—and changing twice, to two different subway lines—to get to his place. As much as I wanted to hear whatever story he had to tell me, I was running out of steam and I just didn't feel up to any more traipsing around. Eventually, we worked out that I would come to his place at the end of the week. He repeated the directions to his studio, and I wrote them down.

By the time I finally got back to my own neighborhood, the garages were shut and the black market guys had returned. A sealed trailer without any markings but sporting some very serious chains looped through its back doors was parked across the street, waiting for someone with the right key to show up and unlock it. I didn't even give this set-up a second glance; I just let myself into my building and went inside.

It took me a few moments, but as I walked up the stairs I realized that the building wasn't freezing anymore; it seemed like the heat was finally back on. The fact that this minor miracle had, indeed, taken place, was confirmed when I reached my apartment and saw my portable space heater sitting outside my door. There was a note taped to it, a white sheet of paper with a child's drawing of an animal on it, which I assumed was meant to be the dust-colored dog that belonged to the children of my neighbor, Sassouma. The dog had been drawn with a big smile on its pointy face and above its head, in child's writing, were the words *Thank you.*

I carried it inside, took off my jacket, made myself comfortable on the couch and turned on the TV. I started to channel surf, not much caring what was on. I was ready to watch anything mindless. Anything at all.

THE NEXT few days continued to be chilly so I was grateful that the boiler had been repaired and we had heat in the building, even though the landlord kept it turned on only during the minimum number of hours required by the city to make his tenants' life bearable. Day after day, I slept later than I should have and then tried to get myself ready for work, knowing that I should be rushing around but managing, mostly, to just wander aimlessly from room to room. Finally, I'd bundle myself into my jacket—swearing that next year, I was going to buy myself a heavier coat—and wait for the bus under a sunless sky, feeling gloomy and tired. It was as if my experiences with Ravenette and then in Rockaway—unsettling as they ultimately were—had at least drawn me out of my usual routine, a change I hadn't known I'd wanted. But now that

I was back to my everyday schedule of home, airport, bar, home, a blue mood seemed to have descended, and I couldn't shake it. On top of that, I found myself eating too much junk food and having bad dreams.

By the end of the week, on the day I was supposed to meet Jack Shepherd at his studio, I didn't even feel like going. But for once, I had risen when my alarm clock buzzed instead of shutting it off. I showered, made coffee, and after that, all that was left to do was sit around the apartment until it was time to go to work. I was feeling too bored to do that and restless, as well, so before I even thought much about it, I was dressed and out the door. Once again, I made the long trek down Queens Boulevard, got on the subway and began the long ride to Brooklyn.

Jack's studio was in a distant neighborhood, like mine, where the subway stations were far away from just about anywhere people actually lived. So, once I got out of the train, I had to walk for about fifteen minutes. My route led me through blocks of sagging tenements and grim bodegas into an industrial area that had been built up around the riverfront. As I headed west, past warehouses and manufacturing plants, most long abandoned, I could see the skyscrapers of lower Manhattan, looking like tall glass sticks poking at the heavy clouds massed above the oily waterway that separated Brooklyn from the lower Hudson Bay. To the north, this old shipping channel led into the East River; to the south, it met the grimy Gowanus Canal, which I imagined was contributing to the rusty smell in the air. Finally, I found the address I was looking for on a narrow street that led down to the river, ending at the skeletal pilings of a collapsed pier.

Above the entranceway of the building I wanted was a sign that said *Up All Night Productions,* which was what Jack had told me to look for. He buzzed me in to a cavernous lobby, dim and silent enough to have served as a bank vault. I took the elevator to the top floor, where, at the end of the hallway, I finally found Jack Shepherd's home base.

When Jack opened the door, I had the feeling that I had seen him somewhere before, but that wasn't really the case. He just had the familiar look of an old hipster: a little overweight and sporting both a goatee and a black turtleneck. He was, I thought, somewhere in his sixties, a little older than I had guessed, but not all that much.

"So," he said, "you found your way here."

"It wasn't so bad," I told him, which was true. I liked these out-of-the way neighborhoods better than the glitzy parts of New York; it was like finding old, hidden parts of the city that got left out of the tourist guides. The walk had actually lifted my mood a little. I felt less like I was stuffed full of gripes and complaints.

Jack spent a few minutes showing me around what turned out to be a primarily one-man operation; he said that an assistant sometimes came in at night, but that was about it. The studio he broadcast from was a room with a glass wall; inside was an automated phone deck, a couple of microphones, computers, and a lot of electronic equipment bristling with dials and lights. Jack explained that the show was syndicated to stations across the country, transmitted to them via an online digital feed. There was also an antenna on the roof of the building that provided an over-the-air broadcast. He told me that he actually interviewed many of his guests on a digital phone line that sounded live, but when he did have someone in the studio, he brought them here by car service and sent them home the same way. To get home himself, he didn't have far to go; he lived on a lower floor in this same building, from which he had been doing his show, he said, for longer than he could remember. Before that, he explained, he had originated the program at a small Midwestern station where he was also the evening drive-time DJ; but late-night talk about ghosts, aliens and the supernatural had proven to be so popular that he'd been able to move to the larger East Coast market and eventually set up his own studio and sell the program nationwide. That, years ago, was what had brought him to New York.

Jack ushered me into his office, where there was a desk, another computer, and floor-to-ceiling shelves filled with books. CDs and DVDs were stacked in piles around the desk, along with a wide variety of magazines and other periodicals, most of them having to do with UFOs, spiritualism, astrology, and other subjects that might offer ideas for his show. I took a seat on a couch in front of one of the bookcases, but before Jack joined me, he offered coffee, sandwiches—maybe snacks? When I said no thanks, he grinned at me.

"You're holding out for a real drink?"

"Too early," I told him.

"Not for a beer," he said.

He disappeared somewhere and came back shortly with two bottles of some microbrew with a picture of the Brooklyn Bridge on the label. I noticed that he also had a brown accordion folder with him, bulging with papers. He didn't say anything about that to me as he settled himself into a chair.

During his short absence, I'd picked up one of the magazines, which featured a story about poltergeists. It was still in my lap when he handed me the beer and it prompted me to begin our conversation by saying, "So, ghosts and ghoulies. What got you involved in all that?"

He shrugged. "Like I said, I was a DJ for a lot of years. A lot. There were a couple of different jobs before that— nothing really important except for four years I did in the army. Straight out of high school. I was a ham—an amateur radio enthusiast—from the time I was a kid, so they sent me to the Signal Corps. I was assigned to the radio shack on a base in Germany and I guess that's when it started; sometimes the pilots would see odd things when they were flying. Occasionally, I'd pick up some chatter about some weird thing they'd seen or picked up on radar, but when they landed, if you asked them about it, they'd clam up. As far as the Signal Corps was concerned, there were no UFOs or anything like that, so making a report about seeing anything unusual—unless there was a possibility that it had some military importance—was seriously discouraged. *I* wasn't discouraged, though. I was fascinated. But so was someone else," Jack continued. "Do you know who Howard Gilmartin is?"

"Sure," I said. I took a sip of my beer and decided it wasn't all that great. Or maybe it was and I just wasn't used to the taste; at the bar, we never stocked microbrews, just the standard labels, so the few times when I was out somewhere and had a beer, I tended to buy what I served. Jack must have seen my reaction, so he offered to get me something else. I said no, but he insisted.

"Let me get my hosting duties over with," he said, "and then I'll tell you the Blue Awareness version of the creation story."

"Which will get us to the Wild Blue Yonder?" I asked, reminding him what I really wanted to know.

"Eventually," he said.

He put the brown folder down on the floor and left the room again, returning with a can of Miller Lite.

"Better?" he asked, as he handed it to me.

"Better," I told him.

He settled back into his chair and then he began to explain.

Jack told me that Howard Gilmartin had also been what he called a radioman, though he had served in the navy, in World War II, years before Jack's time. Gilmartin—much like Avi—had been a dedicated amateur radio operator when he was a boy. Probably because of that skill, when he was drafted into the service he, too, had been assigned to a radio shack, but his post was on a carrier that fought its battles in the South Pacific. On this ship, it was the custom to name different areas where the crew worked: they ate in the Pineapple Lounge and showered in the Tiki Hut. But the sailors who manned the radios and radars had a different idea about what to call the place where they spent their days and nights;

because their main job was to track airplanes, both their own and the enemy's, they had dubbed their workspace The Wild Blue Yonder.

Jack continued his story. Radar, he said, was still a relatively new technology at the beginning of the war, when Gilmartin had been drafted, but on the carrier he became fascinated by it and was training to become an operator. One night, someone told him to climb the tower where the radar was positioned to clean off some debris, and that's when he saw what he thought was another crewman standing on a platform under the radar array. But it wasn't. It was, instead, exactly the kind of figure that lived in my dreams—or my memory—the same one that Ravenette had described to me. Flat, gray, featureless. Standing on the platform next to the radars. Gilmartin froze, momentarily unable to believe what he was seeing, but as he watched, the shadow figure leaned against one of the radar dishes and pushed it, slightly changing its position. Apparently, without even thinking about what he was doing, Gilmartin moved toward the figure which, finally noticing him, turned toward him and emitted a sound that Gilmartin later described as somewhere between a growl and a high-pitched hiss. Painful to listen to and clearly unfriendly. Dangerously, aggressively unfriendly. The sound somehow emanated from within the shadowy figure that had no face, no eyes or nose or mouth, snaking outward like radio static carried on the damp night air. Shocked, Gilmartin climbed down the tower and ran into the radio shack.

Maybe he was going to tell the other crew members what he saw, maybe not. But when he entered the shack, the other technicians were already dealing with a mystery of their own: the radars were registering strange signals, too faint and on the wrong frequencies to indicate that they were pinging off any real, physical target. Possibly they were echoes or some malfunction of the equipment. They were about to send Gilmartin back up the towers when they suddenly faded away. Having had a few minutes to think about how his fellow crew members would have reacted to him confessing that he had encountered some kind of alien being readjusting the positioning of their radars—and that might be the cause of the weird signals they were receiving—Gilmartin decided to keep quiet. That was the only time in his entire life that Gilmartin ever saw the shadow figure or personally encountered the phenomenon of what later came to be called ghost signals.

"Does any of this sound familiar?" Jack prodded. Well, of course it did. When I admitted as much, Jack said, "So do you want to go on trying to convince me that your friend on the fire escape was a dream?"

My reaction was to try to make light of the idea. "At least he must have liked me better because he didn't hiss at me."

That made Jack laugh. "Yes, I'm sure he liked you better. Even an alien could tell that Howard Gilmartin was an asshole from the get-go."

"You know," I said to Jack, "I went to a Blue Awareness introduction session when I was . . . well, back in the hippie days, in San Francisco. They explained how Howard Gilmartin had founded the Blue Awareness but they never mentioned anything like the story you just told me."

"No, of course not," he agreed. "Because that would make Gilmartin sound like a coward. Instead, when he got out of the service and started writing, he turned the story around. In his version, the alien—whom he describes as looking like a shadow—is hostile to him at first, but Gilmartin is able to create a rapport with him. Apparently, somehow the alien senses that Gilmartin is not your everyday human: he's a superior being. Smarter, stronger, a highly advanced version of your everyday homo sapiens. Anyway, over the course of the next few days, the shadowy alien returns again and again to Gilmartin's radar station and has a lot of long conversations with him—only in the stories, the radar installation is somewhere in a remote desert area of the southwest instead of on a navy ship and the Gilmartin character is the lone operator stationed at this post, where he works for a secret government agency. Eventually, he quits because the higher ups at the agency don't believe him when he reports his particular close encounter with this strange being, or the information that his visitor revealed to him, which is that humans are actually the descendents of an ancient alien race who deliberately placed us on this planet long ago. It seems that over the course of time, we lost our collective memory about our real origins. Somewhere in our recent history, however, the aliens began returning to remind a small, select group of individuals that we have just taken on these shell bodies to accommodate the conditions of living on Earth. As the stories progress, the Gilmartin character learns more and more about the plans that the aliens have for these special humans: they are the ones destined to become the first people to be made 'aware' that they are the aliens' seed and that they have to reclaim their true nature, which is, more or less, to join the master race of beings who run the universe. That's where the Blue Box comes in. It's a device that the alien gives the Gilmartin character to help him and the people who will follow the movement he establishes to develop their consciousness, rid themselves of their human nature and remember their alien identities."

"That doesn't sound at all like why Ravenette wanted to hook me up to that thing," I told Jack. "Just the opposite, really; she was trying very hard to convince me that the shadow on the fire escape was nothing more than a damaged engram, or something like that. She wasn't exactly inviting me to join the ranks of the exalted."

"Well, sure," Jack replied. "Because the way she must see things, a non-Aware can't possibly have had an encounter with a member of the alien race. Gilmartin's son, Raymond, is running the organization now and he's the one who took his father's ideas—and his lousy science fiction stories—and turned them into what he says is a religion. And from what I understand, one of their sacred tenets is that no one—no one—other than Howard ever actually saw or spoke to the alien. With the possible exception of you, of course. Am I right?"

I didn't respond one way or the other, but Jack didn't seem to care. "What Awares aspire to by studying the principles of Blue Awareness," he continued, "is to eventually achieve a true understanding of the Wild Blue Yonder which, as far as I can make out, symbolizes for them all the knowledge that the alien supposedly shared with Howard Gilmartin. When they reach that goal, they will finally get to meet their alien creators once again. I can't imagine it would sit well with a Second Level Aware like Ravenette that she hasn't reached nirvana yet, but somehow you have—and you don't even seem to take it seriously. I suppose she wanted to hook you up to that box and get you to tell her why the radioman was so interested in you. You, specifically."

"I never said he was," I pointed out to Jack. "She did."

"And I'm telling you that she wasn't happy about it."

"What about the ghost signals?" I asked. "Are they part of Blue Awareness theology?"

"That's part of what's revealed when you're ready to face the Wild Blue Yonder which, of course, only happens after you've been thoroughly worked over by the Blue Box and cleansed of all your bad engrams. Which is where an interesting connection between Howard Gilmartin and Avi Perzin comes in. Your Avi Perzin."

That was a surprising development. More than surprising—bizarre, I thought. Bad enough that I had stumbled into an involvement, however tenuous, with the Blue Awareness; what were the odds that before me, Avi had, too? Apparently, I was about to find out.

"Just like in his stories," said Jack, "in real life, Howard Gilmartin felt that he was the only person who took the ghost signals seriously enough—except, of course, for Avi. At some point after he'd begun writing his tall tales, Howard read an article about the ghost signals that your uncle wrote for some scientific journal. I gather there was some contact between them—letters went back and forth for a while. And it seems that somewhere along the line, the two of them met in person. Howard must have shown Avi the Blue Box, or maybe just some early prototype. Either way, that turned out to be a very bad idea, at least for Howard, because whatever your uncle believed about ghost signals and aliens, in his heart of hearts, he was a scientist. And he immediately recognized the Blue Box for what it really is: a simple Wheatstone Bridge, a device for measuring electrical resistance dressed up as a kind of lie detector for the soul. As a matter of fact, in 1969, the FDA sued the Blue Awareness for, essentially, practicing medicine without a license by claiming that they could actually cure a variety of afflictions by subjecting members to Blue Box sessions designed to cleanse their spirits of disabling thoughts and ideas. Avi was one of the scientists who provided the FDA with a brief to support their claims. But he did more than that: he actually built a Wheatstone Bridge and demonstrated that it had no healing properties whatsoever. That's the primary reason that now, Awares have to be careful to say that they use the Box only for 'counseling.'"

"And?" I said, because there was something in his voice when he mentioned Avi that made it clear to me there was an *and* coming. Maybe not unless I prodded him, but it was definitely there.

"Well, okay," Jack said. "I did make you come all this way so I might as well get to the rest of it, since I feel a little responsible. Maybe a little more than that, because I pushed so hard for you to go see Ravenette. Maybe she would have just let it go, the coincidence of seeing the radioman when she tuned into you, or whatever the hell it is she does—but telling her you had a Blue Box was probably going too far. Laurie," Jack said, leaning forward and adding a clearly discernible emphasis to his words, "these people can be vindictive. Dangerous. They are also not averse to using violence. People have been beaten up. A reporter who wrote an exposé a couple of years ago received mail tainted with anthrax. I'm telling you all this because I want you to be careful. Please."

I had read about some of these incidents, but it was very hard to think of them as having any real relevance for me. "You're serious?"

"I am. I just don't like that she even mentioned the Wild Blue Yonder to you. That's in the vicinity of saying 'if I tell you, I'll have to kill you.'"

"Okay," I said. "So that sounds really crazy." And then something else occurred to me—something even worse. "You aren't implying that the Blue Awareness killed Avi, are you? Because he died of cancer. I don't think there's any question about that."

"They may think they were responsible. It would fit in with Howard Gilmartin's ideas that the body can be destroyed because the mind's ability to defend itself against destructive forces from within and without can be severely compromised by diseased engrams. That's how the Blue Awareness views most illnesses, both physical and mental—as manifestations of damaged engrams. Some of the Awares also think they can *cause* illness—maybe even kill a person—by deliberately misusing a Blue Box. You hook it up to someone you want to harm and reverse the energy flow or something like that. That's more secret lore from the Wild Blue Yonder, though it seems Raymond—Gilmartin's son—may have been the one who added that particular tenet to Awareness doctrine. He's even more—well, shall we say, extreme?—than his father ever was. So do I really have to tell you that there's no end to what true believers like that are capable of? I think we can agree that someone who's reached the Second Level of Awareness is the definition of a true believer. I'll take the responsibility for bringing you two together but I don't want to be responsible for you getting hurt."

Jack asked me if I wanted another beer and I said no because I had to leave, soon, to get to work. But he said he thought he'd have one, so he left the room again and returned a few minutes later. When he sat down again, I pointed at the brown folder, which was still sitting on the floor.

"So what's in the folder?" I asked.

He smiled. "If I tell you, I have to kill you."

"Nice," I said sourly.

He laughed, and then tipped back the bottle of beer. After taking a long swallow, he put down the beer, lifted the folder from the floor, and tapped it with his finger. "What's in there," he said, "is the real secret of the Wild Blue Yonder."

"I can't wait."

Jack ignored my sarcasm. He tapped the folder again and said, "I'd heard so much about the ghost signals, first from Avi and then from one particular Awareness defector who actually knew Howard Gilmartin, that I decided to see what I could find out about them. Avi tried before me using the Freedom of Information Act. But the material he got didn't really shed any light on what the ghost signals were. All Avi received were redacted reports and transcripts of conversations in which all sorts of people were speculating about what the signals could be. There was one interesting thing though: during World War II, there were a couple of reports of these kind of signals being registered at radar installations—which does track with Gilmartin's experience on the ship—and then nothing until Sputnik was launched. After that, they turned up fairly steadily, always associated with satellite telemetry, until they completely stopped."

"When was that?" I asked.

"In 1972." Jack gave me a curious look. "Why? Are you thinking there might be some connection to Avi?"

"How could there be? That was a year after Avi died."

Jack shrugged. "Well, it seemed like anyone wanting to delve any deeper into the ghost signals was going to hit a brick wall—except for the fact that just a couple of years ago, the government expanded the Freedom of Information Act to include sources that had been off-limits before. So I made a request. I asked for information about the ghost signals that had been heard from the time of World War II up until 1972. And this is what I got."

Jack pulled a thick sheaf of papers from the file and handed them to me. I paged through them but quickly realized that I'd never be able to extract any real meaning from them. Most of the pages were covered with equations of some kind and electrical diagrams. There were a number of memos from various government agencies, including the air force, as well as pages of correspondence, but most of these had whole sections blacked out.

"What does all this mean?" I asked, handing the material back.

Jack took the pages from me but instead of slipping them back into the folder, he held onto them, as if he weren't yet ready to tuck them away. "It means," he said, "that I think whatever he, or they, were doing . . ."

I interrupted him right there. "They?" I said. "Who's *they*?"

"The radioman," Jack said. "Or maybe radio*men*. The ghost signals are not originating from just one ground source on Earth—they jump around a lot, but there are clearly multiple sources. Maybe your friend is alone here, maybe not."

"Please stop calling him my friend."

Jack shrugged. "Well, even if we assume he's the only one here—at least now—he must have started out trying to somehow use radars to broadcast the signals, but they didn't work very well. Once the Soviet Union and the United States started putting satellites into orbit, they worked a lot better—until, for some reason, they didn't anymore."

"Use them for what?"

"I can only give you my best guess about the answer to that question, so here it is: the satellite telemetry signals are broadcasting to stations on Earth so their movements can be tracked and coordinated. Nobody wants their satellite to bump into anybody else's, to put things very simply. So everybody on Earth is listening for signals coming in to us. Even the various groups like SETI, the Search for Extraterrestrial Intelligence, which is listening for possible alien hailing signals—you know, *Hello Earthlings, here we are*—is expecting to hear signals coming toward us, from far away. But the ghost signals are—were—completely different. Whoever was sending them started using satellites, the Soviets' and ours, as a sort of hi-tech trampoline; they were bouncing their signals off our hardware. And as I told you already, they're pinging them outward. The signals originate on Earth and are going out into space."

This sounded very much like Avi's explanation about how the same TV signals that brought me my Saturday morning cartoons could travel out into space, journeying on through the solar system for unimaginably vast distances—so much so, that I had a hard time taking Jack seriously. Objectively, I understood that he was describing something decidedly strange and seemingly inexplicable—what were the aliens broadcasting, and why?—but it was hard for me to shake the image of a stream of electronic pulses, formed into the cartoon shapes of dancing mice and wise-cracking bunnies, slowly drifting past the nearest planets on their way to the asteroid belt and beyond.

"Of course," Jack continued, "as most researchers eventually concluded, the real likelihood was that these signals were some sort of artifact of regular, Earth-linked communications systems. Our planet, along with the layers of the atmosphere around us, is blanketed with electronic chatter that's growing exponentially every minute of every day. Millions of people using billions of devices—from incredibly complex military systems to homemade, hand-cranked radios—are sending and receiving broadcasts of all kinds, all the time. It's impossible to even begin to estimate the volume of all these transmissions or pin down the kind of anomalies that so much atmospheric noise might cause."

"So that's the big reveal?" I asked. "That's what you find out in the Wild Blue Yonder? There's a lot of unexplained atmospheric noise around us?"

"No," Jack said. "Not exactly." Still holding onto the sheaf of papers, he said, "Everything I just told you adds up to the conclusions that most reasonable people would probably come to after reading all this Freedom of Information material. But that's not what a top-level Aware learns when he is taken into a locked room and allowed to read Howard's last story, one that has never been published. In that story, the alien reveals to Howard that the ghost signals are really homing beacons and that he is part of an advance contingent sent here to assess whether the time is right to help humans recover their memory of who their real ancestors were. The homing beacons will help guide other members of the alien race—the descendants of our original alien ancestors—through the vastness of the universe, back to ours."

"Why do they need the help? Because they lost their interstellar map?"

"You think you're being funny, but actually, you're sort of right. Wherever they come from—this universe, or some other—apparently, it's not so easy to get from *there* to *here*. In the distant past, they used to be able to find their way here by homing in on the life force of the humans who still retained a memory of them. But now—well, now, the only guides they have are the Awares, but there aren't enough of them. Hence—homing beacons."

There was something so deliberate about the way he told this story that made me wonder if he might believe any of it, and so I asked him that. I wouldn't have been surprised if he'd reacted scornfully, but he didn't. Not exactly.

"Look," he said, "I believe that the Blue Awareness is a cult and like any cult, I tend to think they're a little nutty. Maybe a great deal more organized—even respectable, and certainly a lot larger than most—but nutty, all the same. But then you come along and you, who have absolutely no interest in anything about them, seem to confirm at least one part of their creation story. I think that's interesting."

"I don't."

"Really? Then why are you asking me all these questions?" I wanted to reply with some snappy answer, but I wasn't fast enough. Jack quickly started in again. He said, "Some of *my* questions would be answered if I could just understand what was happening on the fire escape. Or at least, what you think was happening. Was your radioman adjusting the signal of a homing beacon? Was he doing something else entirely? And whatever he was doing—what was the reason? Are you really sure you don't know? Because when you called, I was hoping that if I told you all this and then we talked some more, if you did know something, or remembered some detail . . ."

I rose to my feet and gave Jack Shepherd what I intended to be a poisonous look. I was suddenly beginning to feel the same way I had in Ravenette's loft: like I was being manipulated to serve someone else's agenda. I was getting sick of it; I felt like I had been suckered into playing head games that I didn't understand and absolutely did not like. Until I had called into Jack's damn radio program, worrying about aliens—real, imagined, or otherwise—was not high on my list of fun things to do and as of this moment, it was going right back down to the bottom of the heap.

"There is nothing. I've told you that. Nothing to remember, no details to add. So maybe now the best thing to do would be to just stop bothering me about all this. Okay, Jack? Just leave me alone. You, that crazy Ravenette and all the aliens from here to . . . Vulcan!"

Well, Vulcan might not have been the wittiest thing to come up with, but it did seem to resonate with Jack—though not in exactly the way I would have wanted—because he lifted his right hand, separated his fingers and gave me the Vulcan high sign.

"Live long and prosper," he said with a grin. He was trying to make amends by being amusing, but I was having none of it.

"Fuck you," I said. And then I got up and walked out.

Once I was on the street, for the first few moments, I was so hyped up that I couldn't even remember where I was. Grim buildings leaning down toward me, a broken chain-link fence, the dull clang of a buoy rocking in the salty current of the nearby river; my head finally cleared and my breathing calmed down. Of course. I was in Brooklyn, a million miles away—or so it felt—from where I had to be in an hour and a half: back at the airport, back at my station behind the bar. It was just a job, just the normal thing I did night after night, but right now, it felt like a lifeline. Enough with shadows and mysteries. Maybe, for a brief while, I had been intrigued by the idea that somewhere, somehow, there was something else besides the regular routine of my daily life waiting to be revealed to me. But now, I didn't know who I was angrier at, myself or Jack—or maybe even Avi—for making it seem possible that there was. It was clear to me that there wasn't. Was not. Period. End of story.

And that was what I kept telling myself as I tried to find my way back to the train.

VI

Two trains later plus a ride on the AirTrain monorail to the airport, I finally got to work. I was late, which made the afternoon bartender mad at me since he had to work an additional half hour for which he was going to have to fight to get paid, so the evening started out a little on the tense side. Plus, it must have been take-the-last-flights-out-for–big-business-meetings-in-Europe night, because the bar was packed with guys who didn't have enough miles or points or clout or whatever to get into the first-class lounges, so were getting drunk at The Endless Weekend before flying off to London or Zurich or wherever else it is that thirty-something-year-olds go to help the masters of the universe keep the rest of us broke and begging for crusts of bread, so to speak. This is the kind of crowd that requires lots of service but leaves small tips, so I was not in the best frame of mind while the Knicks pounded up and down the floor of the Garden on three of the TVs in the bar, a pair of British soccer teams hammered each other on a screen in the corner and a rebroadcast of a Jets game was showing on the big flat screen right above my head. It was noisy, it was frantic, I cut my finger slicing limes (and in violation of all the health and safety rules, just ran it under cold water, did not apply antiseptic or a Band-Aid, and went back to work) and by the end of the night I was worn out and ready to kill the first person who gave me a reason to. Luckily, no one did; the manager showed up on time, checked out the register, and helped me lock up. Then, feeling even more exhausted than I usually was after eight hours on my feet, I stalked out of the bar and headed for the bus.

As I waited, I saw that Orion was getting lower in the sky, a sign that, despite the chilly weather, spring was bound to come and send the great hunter and his star dogs to roam the night on the other side of the globe. Other than that, my mind was a blank, or maybe I was deliberately trying to keep it in that state. I didn't have the energy to think about anything, not a thing.

I thought I would doze on the bus, but couldn't. I felt too tired to sleep, too weary to really relax. So instead, I watched the traffic passing by—cars on the highway, planes in the sky; they filled the night with lights. I just absorbed the images and the sounds, and let myself be carried home.

When I finally pushed open the front door of my building, I noticed a small pile of mail with my name on it lying in a corner of the outer lobby. That was our exasperated post-man's solution to the problem of me picking up my mail with even less regularity than he delivered it; once the tiny box couldn't hold any more of the junk it was usually stuffed with, the postman just dumped the rest on the floor. I would have liked to kick the PennySavers and credit card offers out the front door, but then I'd probably get grief from the super for making a mess, so I picked up the pile on the floor, emptied my mailbox as well, and carried everything upstairs.

After I changed into a tee shirt and sweatpants and poured my usual glass of wine, I started going through the mail. I had been avoiding my mailbox like the plague since I'd gotten that communiqué from Ravenette and tonight the weirdness continued: in with the unwanted magazines, newsletters and other junk was an expensive-looking ivory-colored envelope with my name and address typed on the front. I don't gen-erally get *anything* addressed to me, personally, on fancy stationery, so once I realized that the return address appeared to be from a law firm I knew, instinctively, this couldn't be good news.

And I was right. There was a letter inside, typed on the same heavy, ivory-colored stock, but I had to read it twice to grasp what it said because the message was so . . . well, bizarre. Crazy. I mean, the language wasn't crazy—just the opposite; it was clipped, precise and to the point—but the message was decidedly outrageous. It was from a law firm called Robinson and Reynolds and the letter was signed by someone named Henry Robinson, Esq., writing in his capacity as counsel for Raymond Gilmartin, who was referred to as the "Chairman of the Board of the Religious Technology Center of the Blue Awareness." After imparting this information, the letter went on to say that it had recently come to the attention of Mr. Gilmartin that I was in possession of a Blue Box. Blue Boxes, Henry Robinson, Esq., stated, were religious, i.e., "devotional" items sacred to the Blue Awareness and, as such, should be returned to the church, specifically to Mr. Gilmartin, who in the second reference to his exalted personage, was described as the "paramount ecclesiastical authority" of the Blue Awareness. This return of said devotional item should be carried out, stated Mr. Robinson, "forthwith."

The letter seemed so ridiculous to me that my first reaction was just to stuff it in the garbage and forget about it. To begin with, what I had was not really a Blue Box. Further, what were they going to do if I did not—*forthwith*—get in touch with Mr. Robinson and arrange for the handover of this sacred item? That is, if I could even find it.

I got up off the couch and went into my bedroom, where I rummaged around in my closet for a while. Somewhere in the back, I found what I was looking for: a battered old valise with leather straps that had once belonged to my father. Inside were the few things I always wanted to keep, but had no real use for, including some costume jewelry of my mother's, a couple of photo albums, and assorted other mementos—including the "toy" that I had taken from Avi's apartment after he died. The supposed Blue Box. Since I had never explained to Ravenette how I happened to have this device—and since she was obviously the person who had reported to the Chairman of the Board of the Religious Technology Center of the Blue Awareness, and/or his representatives, that I had a Blue Box—she must have really believed the accusation she'd leveled at me: that I had somehow stolen the thing or otherwise acquired it in some devious manner. I still didn't think it was any of her business, but I also had the feeling that the only way I was going to stop her and the chairman from hounding me about this was to write back to Mr. Robinson and explain to him that I was not in possession of a sacred religious object but rather, as I now knew, a simple electronic device that my uncle had built himself.

Even so, I expected to be obsessing about the attorney's letter for the rest of the night, which was going to make it even more difficult for me to unwind. But that turned out not to be the case. Having come to the decision to write back and, essentially, just say *fuck off* (actually, to say that for the second time in one day, which might have been a personal record, but maybe not) made me feel a lot better than I had since I'd left Jack's studio. I took myself off to bed and slept soundly until late the next morning.

And when I woke up, I had what I thought was a great idea: instead of writing back to the Blue Awareness attorney myself, why didn't I get my own attorney to send an equally snotty letter to Mr. Robinson, Esq.? That would certainly help me feel a lot less like I was just letting myself be victimized by all these crazy people. And I knew just where to find an attorney without too much trouble; every day, as I rode the bus to the airport, I passed a strip mall where there was a storefront lawyer's office. There was a sign in the window advertising the fact that the attorney, whose name I couldn't recall at the moment, was an immigration specialist, but I imagined that even so, I could get him to write a letter for me. I already knew what I wanted to say; I just wanted the message to come from someone who could also put "Esq." after his name.

I looked up the attorney online and found that his name was Victor Haberman. I called, explained what I needed to the receptionist (saying I wanted to respond to a letter I'd received about the disputed ownership of a piece of property) and was told that, indeed, Mr. Haberman could help me with that. I made an appointment for the following afternoon.

The next day, I left earlier than usual and rode the bus only as far as the strip mall. Though the weather was milder than it had been for weeks, the lawyer's office was close enough to the airport for even light gusts of wind to bring with them the strong odor of jet fuel. Still, there was enough sunshine to suggest that maybe the season was finally going to change itself from winter to spring. A clump of bushes bordering the parking area outside the storefronts was beginning to display some ragged greenery and it felt good to be able to shrug off my jacket as I crossed the parking lot without feeling like I was going to freeze.

Inside, I gave my name to the receptionist, a bored-looking young woman sitting at a metal desk with nothing on it but a calendar, a phone and a computer that she stared at once in a while, tapping a few keys with a decided lack of enthusiasm. I settled myself into a chair and, since there wasn't a magazine or newspaper around to read, passed the time watching the sunlight and shadows drift across the parking lot that divided the strip mall from the highway beyond.

After a while, the phone on the receptionist's desk buzzed. Without even answering it, she pointed me toward a door at the end of a short hallway behind where she was seated and told me that Mr. Haberman was now ready to see me.

Victor Haberman turned out to be a slightly overfed middle-aged man with a very businesslike air about him. However, in contrast to his receptionist's barren terrain, Mr. Haberman's office was something of an organized mess: there were papers everywhere—on his desk, in piles on the floor, in boxes on the sagging couch shoved up against a wall. It occurred to me that perhaps people just got off the airplanes landing half a mile away and showed up in Haberman's office asking for help with their immigration status, and that all these papers were really piles of problems and woe.

Haberman shook my hand and then fitted himself into a big, tired-looking leather chair waiting for him behind his desk. I sat opposite him, facing a window that framed a view of the highway. From this vantage point the sky looked white-washed; in the distance, I could see the control tower at the airport, a pale monolith that had the misleading appearance of being empty, abandoned.

"So," Haberman said, folding his hands in front of him on the desk, "what can I do for you? You said something about a property dispute? That's really not my field but if it's a straightforward issue . . ."

"It is," I interrupted. "At least, I think so. It's not really about property—I mean, not land or anything like that. It's about an electrical device my uncle built."

Hearing that, Mr. Haberman looked interested; maybe he welcomed a change from his usual cases. He stood up, took off his jacket, and draped it across the back of his chair. When he was seated again, he leaned forward and said, "What kind of device?"

"Have you ever heard of the Blue Awareness?" I asked him.

"It's that celebrity religion, right?" Since I'd walked into his office, the attorney had kept a dour expression on his face that signaled he was a serious man doing serious work, but now, he almost smiled. "My daughter watches those enter-tainment news shows," he explained.

I said yes, and added what I knew that was relevant. "As part of the way you advance through the levels of their reli-gion, you go through a process they call scanning, which involves being hooked up to a contraption—a Blue Box is the name they use—that supposedly measures the resistance emanating from your body when you discuss experiences in your past. The memories of those experiences are called engrams. Anyway, my uncle built one of these devices. Now, an attorney for the Blue Awareness wants me to turn it over to them."

I showed Haberman the letter and, after he'd had a chance to read it, explained as much as I thought would be helpful, including how Avi had built the box as evidence for an FDA lawsuit. "I can't imagine why I would have to give it to them when it never belonged to them in the first place."

"Is your uncle still living?" Haberman asked.

"No," I told him.

"But you have the box?"

"I do. I've had it for years—since he died."

"Do you have any kind of proof that he built the device and didn't somehow acquire it from these people? Something relating to the FDA lawsuit, for example? That material should be part of the public record."

I thought immediately of Jack's thick file. I had no doubt that the kind of documents Haberman was asking for were in there somewhere. Still, I wasn't eager to get back in touch with Jack Shepherd right now.

"I know who probably has those kinds of documents," I told the attorney. "But is it really necessary for me to get them?"

"Is that going to be a problem?" Haberman asked, sounding a little suspicious.

"I'd have to talk to . . . a friend of mine," I explained. "He has a bunch of stuff he obtained through a Freedom of Information Act inquiry."

"Really?" Haberman said. "The Freedom of Information Act?" He picked up the letter again and studied it for a moment, as if it might have contained some hidden meaning he'd missed the first time he read it. "It's hard to imagine that ownership of this thing is such an issue. But I suppose if they view it as some sort of religious object . . ."

"There is one thing that might help. The box I have was constructed from parts made by a company that used to manufacture kits to build radios and equipment related to radio broadcasting. The parts are clearly marked with the company name."

"I don't think that's evidence enough to support your claim that it never belonged to anyone else—anyone outside your family. It could have been a prototype, for example. Or built by a member of the group for the purpose they state in their letter—a religious purpose. The problem is that you can't prove how it came into your possession." He frowned again. "It would be best if you could get me the backup material, and then I'll respond to them on your behalf. I'll need a small retainer up front."

He wanted $150. Since I'd expected to have to pay something, I'd brought my checkbook with me. I wasn't happy about having to spend so much money—including, he told me, another $150 once our business was concluded—but I wanted this issue dealt with and out of my life.

I left Haberman with the idea, not a promise, that I'd get the papers he wanted. I still wasn't sure if I was going to make myself call Jack. I knew that I didn't want to, but was debating with myself whether I should or not. It would mean telling him about this latest chapter in my unexpected and—well, bizarre, what other word was there for it?—run-in with the Blue Awareness. So far, all Jack had done was get me even more involved with them by pushing me to see Ravenette. Even if he couldn't have foreseen the consequences, I blamed him for the crap I was dealing with now. On the other hand, of course, was Haberman's insistence that he needed copies of the documents Jack had. As I waited outside for the next bus to come by, all I could think was *shit. Shit, shit, shit, shit, shit.*

That night, at The Endless Weekend, the waitress I was working with kept disappearing into the back to take calls from her boyfriend, which left me busier than I should have been. I didn't mind it all that much, though, because running back and forth between the bar and the tables kept me too occupied with keeping orders straight and customers' glasses full to obsess over what I should do. But some part of my mind must have been debating the question, because when the waitress finally decided to get back to work and try to earn some tips, I took a break to make a phone call of my own—one I would have bet another $150 that I would have ended up deciding not to. But I had come up with a plan.

Unfortunately, my plan—which was to ask for the copies but not exactly tell Jack why—had a very brief life span. I called him at midnight, when the various radio networks that syndicated his show took over the airwaves for about eight minutes for a news and weather update. I figured that would naturally limit our conversation. So, without mentioning anything about how unpleasantly our last meeting had ended, I simply asked him if he could fax me copies of the documents relating to my uncle's role in the FDA lawsuit.

"Why?" Jack asked.

"Because I'd like to have them."

"Why?" Jack asked again.

"Because I think it would be interesting to read them. Because I'd like to keep them with the Blue Box—I mean, the Wheatstone Bridge—I have. As a kind of record of Avi's work."

"Really?" Jack said.

"Really," I replied.

"You know what?" Jack said. "I don't think I believe you. From what you've told me, you've managed to get through your entire adult life without being interested in your uncle's work. And now all of a sudden, you want to compile some sort of record about this particular aspect of it? Why? What's going on?"

Even though I was not being honest about my motives, I was taken aback by what Jack had just said. He made it sound like I had no regard for Avi at all, which wasn't true.

Still, it made me feel bad—or maybe guilty. It was my father's choice to more or less sever his ties with his brother, not mine. When I was a teenager, I could have made the effort to get back in touch with him again, but I had been too preoccupied with my own problems to even think of that. It was something to regret.

I must have fallen silent for a moment, because the next thing I heard from Jack was a sharp question. "Are you still there?"

"Can you just please let me have copies of the papers?" I asked. "I saw a fax machine in your office and we have one here, too. I'll give you the number. Just send them over to me, okay?"

Maybe I sounded upset enough to make Jack decide to stop questioning me—or it could have just been the fact that the news broadcasts were about to come to an end and he had to get back on the air. "All right," he said. "I'll fax them over later. But if something's happened . . . has Ravenette gotten in touch with you again?"

"I haven't heard from Ravenette," I said, and hung up on him.

I half expected that Jack wouldn't send me the documents until I was more forthcoming about why I wanted them, but he did. Before we locked up for the night, I went into our back office just in case, and found that he'd faxed me twenty-some-odd pages of material pertaining to Avi's interactions with the FDA about the Blue Boxes. And, there was both a diagram—drawn and labeled in Avi's handwriting, which I was pleased to see that I still recognized—of the Wheatstone Bridge he had built as well as a photograph of the device. The photo was a copy of a copy, so it was somewhat grainy, but it certainly looked to me like the small, squat black box with the metal canisters attached to it that had spent a good part of its life packed away in my father's old suitcase.

I took the copies home with me and, on the way to work the next day, dropped them off at Haberman's office. He wasn't around, but the bored receptionist managed to will herself to engage in verbal communication long enough to tell me that she would see that her boss got the documents. When he sent off the letter to the lawyers for the Blue Awareness, she added, he'd put a copy in the mail for me, too.

The letter arrived a few days later. I read it and felt satisfied that it sounded formal, serious and final enough to get the attorneys for the Chairman of the Board of the Religious Technology Center of the Blue Awareness to leave me alone. I went off to work—I had a Friday to Tuesday shift to do— and managed not to think about Blue anything all through the weekend and on into the next week.

Wednesday morning, I was fast asleep when my phone rang. I felt like I had been ripped from the depths of dreamland and thrown back into daylight. I grabbed for my cell phone, which was on my nightstand, and as soon as I pushed the button to connect to the call, I heard what sounded like a man screaming.

And I was right. The man was Victor Haberman, and he was screaming at me.

"Get over here," he was yelling into the phone. "Get here right now!"

"Where are you?"

"My office! It's un-fucking believable."

"What's the matter?" I asked. Victor Haberman sounded like he was in a state of genuine panic.

"This is your fault!" he shouted. "I've called the police!" And then he clicked off the phone.

The police? That didn't sound good. I got out of bed, splashed my face with water, pulled on some clothes and called the local car service because I didn't think I had time to wait for a bus. Whatever was going on, I wanted to get to the strip mall quickly. Well, really, I didn't want to go there at all, but I knew I had to. Haberman had not even given me a clue about what had happened to his office that was freaking

~ 97 ~

him out, but since he was blaming me, it wasn't hard for me to guess just who was most likely to be involved.

At first, when I arrived at the strip mall, it didn't seem like anything worthy of causing havoc was going on. That is, until I stepped out of the hired car and started walking toward Haberman's office. It took a few moments, I think, for my brain to actually register what I was seeing: in the middle of the row of drab storefronts—a nail salon, a Laundromat, a sandwich shop—the plate glass window that fronted Haberman's office was obscured by wide smears of bright blue paint.

As I approached, Haberman came out the front door and, spotting me immediately, ran up to me and grabbed my arm. His face was red and he still seemed to be just as agitated as he'd sounded on the phone. His breath was ragged. In fact, he sounded like he was panting.

"Look at this!" was about all he could get out as he gestured wildly at the paint-smeared window. I looked again and saw that blue paint had been splattered on the front door, as well.

"Have the police been here yet?" I asked him.

He nodded. "Come and gone," he choked out. "They said vandalism. Just vandalism. Ha!"

"You don't think so?" I asked. I was being disingenuous, and I knew it.

"It's those nuts you had me write to!" he spit out. He was beginning to breathe a little better, but that only seemed to send him back into screaming mode. "Those Blue . . . blue lunatics. It has to be them, right? I mean, blue paint—I get the message. But I had no idea they'd do anything like this. Did you?" he said. Turning to face me directly, his face displayed an accusing glare. "Did you?" he repeated.

Did I? The only honest answer to that was both yes and no. But really, more *no*, because I simply couldn't have imagined that they would have responded with such vehemence. Despite what I saw as Jack's attempts to freak me out about what the Blue Awareness might be capable of, his warnings hadn't sounded real to me. Or maybe I had just assumed that whenever representatives of the Awareness felt moved to retaliate against someone for a perceived transgression, their actions would be confined to their own members. And I'd also thought that in a time when their most prominent spokespeople were athletes and celebrities and they ran ads on television inviting people to come to their introductory sessions to see how open-minded and inclusive they were, their days of acting thuggishly against those who angered them were past. Looking at the paint splattered across the front of the attorney's place of business, I had to admit that I had been wrong. The celebrities were their public face. What I was seeing here was their real identity. Behind the pretty people and the TV ads with soft voices speaking in comforting tones, there was still violence. And clearly, some sort of unfettered need to assert power over anyone who crossed them.

I hadn't yet responded to Haberman's question, so now he interrupted my thoughts by answering it himself. "They're angry at you, so they're taking it out on me."

"But it's such a bizarre thing to do," I said. It was, but that was the point, and I got it. What they had done was supposed to seem bizarre. Something like breaking a window would have been frightening, but this was both frightening and strange. I was getting the feeling that they liked strange. And why not? It was the same inclination they'd shown by breaking into my mailbox. *Strangeness* was at the root of Howard Gilmartin's experience with the radioman; he had transferred that sense of strangeness to his stories and to the religion that had grown out of them. And it still remained.

"I'm finished," Haberman said to me. "I don't want to be involved with this anymore. I'm going to give you half your retainer back and send them a formal letter explaining that I'm no longer your attorney. I don't need this kind of trouble."

"That's fine," I said.

"I can give you the names of some other lawyers. I think you need someone—a firm—that's used to dealing with situations like this."

"Like what?"

Haberman seemed perplexed by my question. "Like having a crazy religious group out to get you."

"I don't know if crazy is really the right word."

"This doesn't seem crazy to you?" Haberman said, gesturing at his ruined windows.

"It seems extreme," I agreed. "That's how they get what they want. Or keep what they have. Either they seduce you or scare you." I was thinking of Ravenette and her quicksilver change from my new friend, concerned with my welfare, to an angry foe. "Seducing didn't work with me so now they're going to try scaring me."

"*Try?*" Haberman exclaimed. "Try? This isn't working?" Again, he waved his hand in the direction of the blue-stained storefront. I found myself wondering if the bored receptionist was still inside, still tapping away at her keyboard, already having lost interest in the incident that had managed to temporarily interrupt what to her probably seemed like just one more endless workday.

"You know what?" I said to him, realizing I was as surprised as he was going to be by my answer. "No. Not really."

"Then you're the crazy one," he said. Angrily, he turned and strode away from me. As I watched him head back toward his office, I saw him pull out his cell phone, punch in a number and quickly start barking at someone else.

I stayed in the parking lot for a few minutes longer, staring at the long, ragged swipes of blue paint. To my eyes, the pattern formed a code I could easily decipher, and what it said was, *Watch out, Laurie. Don't play with us.* So Haberman was certainly right. I should have been scared. I *wanted* to be scared; that would have been the normal reaction to such a clear threat. But the more I stared at the blue paint splashed across the blank windows, the more I felt something quite opposite from fear. It was as if that one-time pass I had given myself when I got Ravenette's letter, the chance to take a break from the routine of my very ordinary, very as-basic-as-basic-can-get existence, was unexpectedly being renewed. And with it came wandering back all the wild recklessness I had drummed out of myself over the years in order to get some control of my life; that, too, was now making a case for its right of return.

In other words, while I knew that what I should have been doing was considering whether or not to go talk to the police myself, or at least mulling over the possibility of engaging a new lawyer—or maybe a bodyguard—I was, instead, thinking only one thing. And that was, *Go ahead. Bring it on.*

VII

Over the next day or two my feeling of bravura slowly faded, but I remained in an odd mood. I felt neither here nor there, drifty, unsettled. I spent a free afternoon at the movies and then a quiet, cloudy morning wandering around Central Park, remembering long-ago summer days when I would regularly skip school to be one of thousands of kids in rags and rainbow glitter dancing around at a Be-In on the Sheep Meadow. On the way, you used to be able to walk down the cobbled path to the zoo and buy pot or hash as openly as the pretzels and ice cream that vendors were now hawking from food carts. This particular morning, I bought nothing, but after walking around for a while, sat on a bench near the carousel, watching nannies take small children for rides on the painted horses.

My work shifts occupied the next week or so, and tired as I was every night when I got home, I did make myself check my mailbox with some regularity. All I ever found were the usual bills and junk mail; there were no further communications—written or otherwise—from the Blue Awareness or their lawyers.

Then, when my next day off from work came around, I started feeling even more like I was at loose ends. I thought about going to another movie, and even checked the paper to see what was playing nearby. I picked out something I thought I wanted to see, got dressed and was ready to go to a matinee when I decided no, that wasn't really what I wanted to do at all. In the back of my mind, I'd been thinking about another destination all through the long nights of mixing drinks, opening bottles of beer and catching glimpses of baseball players on the big screens in the bar that were now mostly set to follow the early games of the new season. I knew where I wanted to go. And really, I'd probably wanted to go for a long time. I wanted to go see Avi.

Though I had never been there before, I knew where he was buried. My father had arranged a kind of Egyptian burial for himself; he was interred in a cemetery out on Long Island with both his wives—my mother and stepmother—neatly tucked in beside him. But Avi, according to instructions he'd left in his will, was buried in the same cemetery where his parents were interred, which was in New Jersey. I hadn't gone to the funeral; it was during my crazy hippie kid period and not only was I committed to the theory that I didn't love, even *like,* anyone in my family, I certainly didn't believe in attending some bourgeois ceremony like a funeral. Still, though so many years had passed, I remembered the name of the cemetery and where it was: on US Route 1, near the town of Woodbridge, and I had a good idea of how to get there. That's one thing about working in an airport bar; if people aren't discussing sports or flight delays, they're talking about how to get from one place to another, and they always think that bartenders have the routes and schedules of every method of ground transportation catalogued in some bin in the back of their brains. Eventually, you do end up with a lot more information than you thought you ever needed about trains, car services, cabs and buses, but for once, all this miscellaneous knowledge served my own purposes. I knew there was a bus from the Port Authority terminal in Manhattan that would travel the length of US Route 1 all through the state of New Jersey. I called the bus line and found out that the bus did, indeed, make a stop near the cemetery and it left from the city every hour on the half hour.

I was on the eleven thirty bus. It was turning out to be a cold spring; the days featured changeable weather, skies laddered with clouds and windy gusts that felt like cold breath on the back of your neck. From my window seat, I watched as the bus passed through the Lincoln Tunnel and headed through the swampy outlands that surrounded the interstate roads connecting New Jersey to New York. Occasionally, I'd see a heron wading through an algae-covered pond or a hawk circling above the marshes. Later, as the bus headed deeper into Jersey, the scenery became more commercial: we passed a giant blue-walled Ikea, then endless outlet stores for shoes and carpeting and lawn furniture.

I had asked the bus driver to announce the stop for the cemetery and he did. A few moments later, I was standing alone at the edge of the far lane of a busy highway that swept through a landscape of blank, grassy hills. In the near distance, though, I spotted the entrance to the cemetery: an elaborate stone archway above a tall, wrought iron gate. After reaching the gate and passing through, I walked up a wide pathway toward an office building with smoked glass windows. The building itself was a modest structure, long and low, and fronted by a circular driveway from which a network of small, gravel roads and pathways led out into the vast green fields beyond. The graveyards.

I crossed a flagstone porch and entered the building, finding myself in a kind of hushed visitors' center. Forest green carpeting and walnut paneling dominated the space, though at its center was a counter, also of dark wood, with maps and pamphlets arranged along the top in small, discreet piles. The room seemed to be empty, but my arrival must have set off some bell in a distant office, because very soon a woman with carefully coiffed hair, wearing a white blouse and a gray skirt, appeared from somewhere down a side hallway to ask if she could help me.

I explained that I was looking for a particular grave, but wasn't sure exactly where it was located. "Avram Perzin." I said. "He's buried in a family plot, with his parents, Muriel and Louis Perzin."

The woman told me she'd have to consult the cemetery's records. She disappeared again, back down the hallway, but returned in just a few minutes. Picking up one of the maps on the counter, she unfolded it and showed me that it depicted how the major areas of the cemetery were laid out.

"Is your car parked outside?" she asked, with a pen poised above the map.

"I came on the bus," I told her.

She frowned, as if I had presented her with a problem she wasn't used to dealing with. "Then you're going to have a long walk," she warned me, but lowered the pen to the map and made a mark. Turning the map around to face me, she said, "Avram Perzin is interred in the Jerusalem Memorial Mausoleum. You follow this path—Monument Avenue—all the way past these burial society sections and then make a left when you reach King David Avenue. Go down the hill and that's where you'll find the mausoleum."

I found this information perplexing. "A mausoleum? You mean like . . . a crypt?" I didn't know how else to explain what I was thinking of, though even to me, it sounded like I was describing the location of a scene from a bad horror movie.

The coiffed head turned from side to side indicating a very clear *no*. "It's a beautiful space. There are niches for cremated remains. Avram Perzin is here," she said, pulling out another map that showed a grid divided into rows and rows of small squares. She made a mark on a square that was a few rows down from the top.

"You're sure?"

"Oh, yes," she told me.

Well, maybe this was just another one of Avi's eccentricities. There was something to be said, I supposed, for choosing to spend eternity inside where it was warm instead of outside, in all kinds of weather.

It occurred to me that I was thinking about the cemetery as a kind of hotel instead of the resting place for the dead when the woman who was helping me got my attention again. She made another mark on the map and said, "Muriel and Louis Perzin are buried on the other side of the cemetery," she told me. "In one of the memorial garden areas."

Though I didn't think I'd spend the time to hike over to another part of the cemetery today to visit my grandparents' graves, I thanked her and then left the quiet building, heading out on the path that she had indicated. It was actually a narrow, unpaved road, just wide enough for one car to drive down, and it led me through a landscape that was nearly silent, except for the occasional bird call or a gust of wind carrying with it the sound of the metallic growl of traffic on the distant highway. I proceeded down the path under a brisk sky that threw down more long shadows than shafts of sunlight, making the fields of graves marked by uneven headstones look lumpy and ungroomed.

I finally found the mausoleum, a tall structure of sand-colored marble fronted by monumental glass doors. Once inside, I had the momentary sense that I was in some stark marble temple that had been transported to New Jersey and reconstructed here to stand and brood in stoic silence through the centuries ahead. But of course, as soon as I remembered to consult my map and find my way down the marble halls, it was clear that the walls around me contained burial niches and the carved words on each niche were not ancient injunctions but the names of the deceased.

When I came to the south wall, I located Avi's name just where it had been marked on my map of grid lines and squares. There was a bench in the middle of the floor, and once I sat down, I was aware that there was some faint, somber music being piped in from speakers hidden somewhere in the ceiling. That was okay; in fact, it helped a little bit—it made me feel just a little less like I was in some distant outpost of the vast cemetery, all alone but for the remains of the departed. Except, of course, that's exactly where I was.

And with Avi. So now that I was here I had to ask myself, why? Really, why? Maybe the reason was simply that I was feeling guilty. I had probably thought more about Avi in the past few weeks than I had in years, and he deserved better than that from me, didn't he? He had loved me, he had been kind to me, and more than that, he had made time for me when nobody else had, or could. Maybe I had come here to honor his memory, to assure him, or some vestige of him— whatever atoms or essence of his spirit might still be hanging around—that he wasn't forgotten.

Or maybe it was something else. Sitting in the quiet, marble hall, staring at the rows of marble boxes, I forced myself to do a little personal inventory and had to admit that what I really wanted was for time and space to collaborate on a magic trick that would allow Avi to appear before me for a few moments—as a ghost or hallucination; either one would have been just fine with me—and explain to me what was going on. All this craziness about radiomen and aliens and mysterious broadcast signals. Cult leaders sending me threatening messages. Blue letters, blue paint, what was I supposed to do about all these things? All that they represented? And I had another question, too: what kind of a normal person had problems like this in their life? Probably no one—which wasn't all that surprising. *Normal* was something I had to admit I simply was not, at least by the general definition I would have applied to most other people I knew. And whose fault was it—maybe, besides mine—that I was not *normal*? Well, who else could I assign some of the blame for that to but Avi? After all, it was Avi who, night after night, tuned in the mysterious sounds of distant places and let me listen, who pointed to the infinite sky and said, more or less, *Who knows what goes on out there?* I had always thought that the source of my dissatisfaction with the life that I had been brought up to lead—finish school, get a job, start a family—had something to do with the loose, root-less wandering tribe of hippies I had attached myself to at a young age, and to the era itself, when revolution was in the wind, change was coming and who cared what the past had been because tomorrow was going to be different, new, with new rules or maybe no rules at all. But maybe that wasn't the problem with me, or not all of the problem. Maybe it was the fact that, intentionally or not, Avi had led me to believe that there was something really, really interesting going on somewhere just beyond the edges of what our eyes could see and that we should look for it, whatever it was, if we could. But I had no idea how to do that without him. I hadn't known when I was a kid and I certainly didn't think I was any better prepared now.

So, great. These were the conclusions I came to while sitting with the dead. I couldn't see any way that they were going to help me and I began to regret the fact that I had traveled so far for what seemed like such poor reasons. All I seemed to have accomplished was to remind myself of my own shortcomings. I could have saved myself a long trip by doing the same thing at home.

But just as I was about to leave, I heard a sound at the other end of the corridor, which branched off into another hallway that led to the mausoleum entrance. At first, I thought it was just footsteps echoing on the marble floor, but I soon realized that what I was hearing had a sharper edge than a footfall would have made: the sound brought to mind something clicking against the cold stone. And whatever was making that sound was heading straight for me.

I turned my head in the direction of the clicking sound and waited as it drew nearer. I couldn't imagine what it could be.

And then, suddenly, at the far end of the hall, I saw a thin brown dog, not much taller than the bench I was sitting on. It regarded me with a look of intense concentration, pausing for a moment before it advanced down the corridor. Now I knew that what I had heard was the sound of the nails on the dog's paws tapping against the stone floor.

As the dog drew nearer, I found myself riveted by its purposeful demeanor; it didn't seem lost, or out of place though surely, it had to be both. The dog continued to advance in my direction, but then paused once again to stare at me, tilting its narrow head sideways, as if it were considering some question that needed an answer before it continued forward.

At last, as if it had made a decision, the dog walked up to me, stood still for just a moment, and then seated itself beside me. Finally, and completely unexpectedly, it leaned itself against my leg. Now, it was facing in the same direction I was, looking toward the marble wall of burial niches. Tentatively, I put my hand on its head and gave it a sort of pat. The dog seemed relaxed but alert. His body was so close to mine that I could feel the slight rise and fall of his chest as he breathed.

I felt like I had crossed over into some sort of dream state. This morning, I was wandering around my apartment, not knowing what to do with myself and now, just a few hours later, I was sitting in a mausoleum, petting a strange dog who seemed to have a better sense of purpose than I did myself. Jack Shepherd suddenly came to mind and I thought, *Well, I should call and tell him about this. A dog has come to visit Avi.* Because that was what I was beginning to think. It didn't make much sense, but that was what occurred to me. I was here, working through a bunch of complex feelings about Avi, and about my own life. The dog, on the other hand, just seemed to be a visitor, some kind of quiet, neutral force that signaled the welcome end of my experiment in soul searching. And while he was here, to also stop for a moment and say hello to Avi.

Was that true? Well, really, what difference did it make? At the moment it was what I decided was true, and so I felt better. I sat on the marble bench awhile longer with the dog leaning against my leg. Eventually, I decided it was probably time to go. The bus back to the city came only once an hour and I thought I'd better try to make the next one.

But what to do about the dog? When I got up, he followed me like a thin, brown shadow as I headed down the marble corridors toward the glass doors. Before I went outside though, concerned that the dog might run away, I thought of calling the cemetery office to see if anyone knew who the animal might belong to. If not, I wasn't sure what I was going to do. If he was a stray, I didn't think I could just leave him here to fend for himself. On the other hand, I couldn't exactly buy him an extra bus ticket and offer him a ride to the nearest shelter. Or take him home. I actually considered doing that for a few moments. After all, his unexpected appearance in the mausoleum seemed like a sort of sign of something— either that or the beginning of a bad joke: *a dog walks into a cemetery* . . . Whatever it was, I didn't think I could just take off without doing something.

My problem was solved for me when I saw a young couple, trailed by two small, worried-looking children, walking through the field of graves on the other side of the gravel path that led to the mausoleum. Even through the glass doors, I could hear them calling, "Buddy! Buddy!"

I led the dog outside and waved my hand in the air, calling out to the family. The father heard me and turned in my direction. A moment later, they were all heading down a grassy slope that angled toward the path, picking their way between the gravesites as they hurried toward me.

The first to reach me was the father, who quickly bent down and put a collar and leash around the dog's neck. Then, as the rest of his family caught up with him he explained that they were on their way to visit relatives in Pennsylvania and had stopped along the way to put some flowers on his mother's grave. They had left the dog in the car with the window only slightly cracked so he could get some air, and none of them could imagine how he had both slipped his collar and managed to escape from the car. As I accepted everybody's thanks for returning their beloved Buddy to them, I didn't mention the even stranger problem of how the dog had managed to get into the mausoleum. Those were pretty heavy glass doors and they didn't open automatically; you had to pull them open in order to enter. Buddy, it seems, had acquired either one of two skills: the ability to open doors or to pass through them, like a ghost. I would have given money either way.

With some final thanks, the family started to walk away. But Buddy, it seemed, wasn't ready to go. He turned around to face me and then sat down on the ground, stubbornly refusing to move. Dad tugged on the leash, but the dog wouldn't budge. He just kept looking at me, as if we hadn't yet finished whatever business he had come to carry out.

So, since the situation was becoming a little embarrassing— I didn't want the family to think I somehow *wanted* the dog to refuse their efforts to get him to come with them—I walked over to the dog and once again gave him a pat on the head.

"Go on," I said to him. "It's okay. I get it."

Get *what*? I had no real idea of what I meant but it somehow seemed like the right thing to say. And apparently, the dog thought so too because he immediately stood up, turned around, and let himself be led away. One of the kids turned back once to wave at me, but the dog just kept on trotting briskly along in the other direction. His business with me was finished and now he was ready to continue on his way.

~VIII~

I kept meaning to call Jack and tell him about the dog, but I never quite got around to it. I was pretty much over being angry with him and was, in fact, a little embarrassed about how I'd behaved. I always did seem to overreact when I thought someone was trying to manipulate me, or finesse me into doing something—a holdover, I suppose, from my younger days when the worst thing you could do was cooperate with authority. Well, Jack Shepherd didn't have any authority over me—I knew that, of course—and it really wasn't his fault that I had gotten involved with Ravenette and the Blue Awareness. It was my own. Jack had encouraged me to see her, but I'd made the decision to do that all by myself. I was the one who had allowed myself to delve into things I knew nothing about: lost ideas, old mysteries, strange dreams. No one had forced me to do that. At some point, I was going to have to call Jack and apologize for placing the blame on him for everything that had happened. After all, he had even given me the documents I needed for the attorney, and I hadn't exactly been Miss Lovely during that conversation, either.

These were my thoughts on my way home from work a few days after my visit to the cemetery. I was feeling a little lighter, a little less mired in my own craziness. I seemed to have let some of my darker thoughts depart from me along with the thin brown dog who had walked away. I was looking forward to getting home, plopping myself on the couch and watching a movie or maybe a late-night reality show. I was in the mood for a program about supermodel talent wars or something else on that sort of high intellectual plane.

But that was not to be. When I walked up the stairs of my building and got to my landing, I was shocked to see that my door was open. It was just slightly ajar, but even that was frightening because I never left the apartment without locking up. As I pushed the door open, my hand was trembling. Badly.

Inside, the scene that confronted me looked as unreal as a movie set. The apartment was in shambles. Everything I owned seemed to have been strewn around. Closets and drawers were open and their contents dumped on the floor; even the cabinets in my seldom-used kitchen had been raided and the few pots and pans I owned had been swept from the shelves. It was a scary scene—very scary, and maybe that was the real intent of the invasion because it was quickly apparent that nothing seemed to have actually been taken; even my laptop and television, the only objects that might have had some street value, were still here. I continued to think that nothing had actually been stolen until I walked into the bedroom and saw that my father's valise, which had been in the closet, was now sitting open on my bed. The old family photo albums it held along with some personal mementos, like my sixth grade autograph book and a stuffed cat with glass eyes that my mother had given me, were still inside. But the Wheatstone Bridge—the erstwhile Blue Box—was gone. As soon as I saw that the valise had been searched, I knew it would be. The only surprise was that the searchers hadn't left some sort of calling card behind: another smear of blue paint, maybe, or a blue handprint on the wall.

I pulled out my cell phone and, without thinking, dialed Jack's number. I got a recording at the main number of the studio but the day I'd visited him he'd given me his personal cell phone number in case I got lost, so I hung up and dialed again. I got voice mail on his cell, too, but I left a message—and once I clicked off the line again, I couldn't even remember what I'd said. I just remained standing in the middle of the room for a while, feeling like I needed to work at focusing my eyes in some way—make them *see* better— as if that would help to make the situation real, because it didn't seem like it was. The mess around me, the violation of my privacy, seemed bizarre, impossible. And yet it had happened. I found myself running to the door to lock it, as if that could keep me safe, but it was already clear the lock could do no such thing. And it wouldn't turn, anyway; it hadn't just been picked—it had been broken.

I was trying to shove my couch up against the door when my phone rang. It was Jack, calling back. I quickly told him what happened, including the backstory about the letter from the Blue Awareness attorneys and the blue paint splashed across Victor Haberman's storefront office. I think I was beginning to babble about the cemetery and the dog, when Jack finally cut me off.

"Laurie," he said. "Calm down, calm down. First of all, are you all right?"

"Yes," I told him. "I mean, they were gone when I got home."

"You didn't know that," Jack said. "You shouldn't have walked into the apartment alone."

"I didn't think . . . I wasn't thinking."

"Well, thank God they *were* gone. Have you called the police?"

"No. Should I?"

"Of course you should. You've been robbed."

"They'll never believe what happened. Who did this."

"It's New York," Jack said. "They've heard crazier stories." Behind him, I heard some kind of New Age music playing that I recognized as the intro to his show when it returned after a break for the news. "I've got to go back on the air," he said. "But I'm coming over there as soon as the show's over. And call a locksmith," he said just before he hung up.

I did both. I called the police and then went online to find a locksmith with a twenty-four-hour emergency service. They all arrived about the same time—three young men with wary faces: two in blue uniforms, and one in jeans and a leather jacket over a tee shirt decorated with grinning skulls.

While the grinning skulls replaced my lock with a more secure deadbolt, the two policemen listened to my story— the same one I'd told Jack, only I went back even farther to include my telephone call to the radio show and all that had followed. As Jack had said, they'd probably heard even stranger stories, or else were just very well trained not to react to anything they were told with even the slightest sign of surprise, because neither of them even raised an eyebrow when I told them that the Blue Awareness had to be responsible for the break-in. Then, in the middle of trying to explain just what, exactly, had been stolen, since neither of the policemen had ever heard of a Blue Box, let alone a Wheatstone Bridge, I happened to glance over at a shelf in my living room that I hadn't looked at before and saw a big, empty space between two piles of books.

"My radio," I said. "They took my radio, too."

That really shook me. As upset as I was about the loss of the device I still thought of as a kind of electrical toy, the theft of the radio was even worse because it represented a much more direct and visceral connection to my childhood. I remembered how many times I had listened to it with Avi, how many times it had burped out strange, tinny beeps and hisses that were the voices of satellites—to me, the voices of the stars. And maybe it was because the image of the thin brown dog in the cemetery was still so much with me that I suddenly thought of another dog—Zvezdochka—orbiting Earth in her space capsule so many years ago. It was the telemetry signal of Sputnik 10, the satellite with the dog aboard, that Avi and I had been listening to on the fire escape of the Sunlite Apartments on the night that presented me with the radioman. The loss of the radio made me feel as if little Zvezdochka had just spun off into the cold wilderness of infinity, never to come back. *That's not what happened,* I told myself. *Stop it, stop it, stop it. You're making it worse.*

So I forced myself to focus on my voice, on what it was saying to the young policemen with blank, carefully composed faces. I told them about the radio—that it was actually more like a ham receiver built from Haverkit parts. Then I had to explain what a Haverkit was, since it was something they had never heard of.

Finally, everyone left. I put the new key to my new lock on my key ring and then started to clean up my apartment. Nothing was broken—the intruders had been oddly careful about that—but it seemed like every single thing in the place had been taken from its rightful place and tossed somewhere else. Maybe I didn't own a lot, but the disarray still looked monumental to me. I picked a random corner of the living room to start with and mechanically began to put things away.

I was so deep in some automatic pilot state that when the buzzer near my door went off, announcing that there was someone downstairs, I almost jumped out of my skin. I went to the intercom and asked who it was, expecting anything from alien invaders to more policemen, but it was Jack. I had completely forgotten that he had told me he was coming over when he finished his show.

I buzzed him in. Realizing that I had completely lost track of time, I glanced at my watch and saw that it was three A.M.— Jack's program actually had another hour to go. He must have put on a tape for the last segment and rushed all the way from Brooklyn to my end of Queens.

I let him into the apartment and he took a quick look around. "Jesus," he said. "They really ransacked the place."

"I've been trying to straighten up," I replied. "But I don't think I've made much progress. I keep finding myself wandering around holding things I thought I'd put away."

"Yeah, well. This is a pretty shocking thing to come home to," Jack said. "It's going to take awhile."

~ 116 ~

Awhile for what? Until I felt less like I was going off the rails? Because that was how I felt right now. Really, really shaky.

"They took the radio," I heard myself say to Jack.

"What radio?" he asked.

I realized that I had never told him I had Avi's Haverkit receiver. "My uncle's," I said. "The Haverkit receiver he always used."

"The one from the night on the fire escape? You still have that?"

I nodded. "I did. But I'll probably never get it back."

"No," Jack agreed sympathetically. "The cops will send someone to the Blue Awareness headquarters in Manhattan but they won't get anywhere. No one ever does, with them."

"Monsters," I said, feeling a surge of deep rage.

"They can be," Jack replied. "But at least they're gone for tonight and I doubt they'll be back." He looked around the room then and noticed that my couch was still near the door. "I see you were setting up the barricades," he said. "How about if I stay here tonight? Would that make you feel better?"

It made me feel a little ashamed, actually—I was not used to needing anybody's help to get through even the worst situations. But since he had offered, I realized that yes, it would help a lot if there was someone else in the apartment overnight besides me. It would be daylight in just a few hours but still . . . I didn't think I was quite ready to tackle the monsters by myself if they came back, even though Jack was right—it was unlikely.

We pushed the couch back where it belonged. I gave Jack some sheets to cover it, and a blanket. Then he took off his shoes, stretched himself out and said good night. I think he was asleep in a few minutes. I lay down in my bedroom and didn't expect to be able to sleep at all, but I did. Not restfully, though; for the rest of the night, I was fighting blue meanies in my dreams or running away from faceless robbers without finding anyplace to hide.

I finally got up around nine. In the living room, I saw Jack stirring as well. I made coffee and toast while Jack got up and washed.

As we ate breakfast, he said, "Are you going to be all right?"

"I don't know," I told him honestly. "I don't know what I'm supposed to do next."

"You're supposed to do whatever will help you let go of this."

"That's the problem; I don't know what that is. Half of me wants to call the lock guy back, tell him to put half a dozen bars on the door and just sit in here and hide, but the other half wants to go punch somebody in the nose."

"Like who?" Jack asked.

"I could start with Ravenette. It's about time someone gave her a black eye."

"Should I apologize about all that again?" Jack asked. "I still feel responsible."

"It's my fault as much as yours. I didn't have to tell her about the Blue Box. It's just that she seemed so . . . arrogant. I hate people like that."

That made Jack laugh. "I bet there are a few other categories you could add to that list."

"Yeah, probably," I agreed. "I'm not exactly a big fan of people. Most people, anyway."

"We seem to be getting along," Jack pointed out.

"Well, now we are," I agreed.

We lingered over our coffee for a while. An hour later, as Jack was finally getting ready to leave, my doorbell chimed.

I froze. My mind ran a warp-speed checklist of who could possibly be ringing my doorbell without having to be buzzed in downstairs, and I came up with exactly nobody. Jack glanced over at me and seeing what I suppose was a look of abject fear on my face, went into the kitchen, picked up an old iron frying pan—probably the only potential weapon he could find—and went to the door.

He peered through the peephole and then turned back to me with a perplexed look on his face. "It's a woman in some kind of head scarf," he told me. "She's holding a baby. And there's a man in a suit."

"Sassouma," I said, with relief. "It's my neighbor."

I didn't know who the man was, but I told Jack to let them in. Sassouma smiled at me but then settled herself and the baby on my couch. Whatever the purpose of this visit, it was apparently going to be explained to me by the stranger who was with her—who had brought with him yet another unexpected guest, a small, thin dog the color of dust.

For a moment, I thought the dog was Sassouma's, but then I realized that it was a little larger than the animal I sometimes saw with her children. And this one also had another feature that differentiated it from hers: it had an odd, almost wedge-shaped head. When it looked up at me, which it did immediately upon entering the apartment, it regarded me with dark, glittery eyes. And, it occurred to me, that much like the dog I had encountered in the cemetery—the elusive Buddy—it seemed to be sizing me up.

I finally turned my attention away from the dog, and took a good look at the tall, dark-skinned man of indeterminate age who accompanied my neighbor. There seemed to be quite a contrast between the image he presented, which was all business—the suit, the serious demeanor that almost seemed to precede him into my living room—and the fact that he was holding the leash of a peculiar-looking dog.

Everybody said hello, and the man introduced himself as Dr. Carpenter. I got the feeling that he was not in a good humor. Well, that wasn't my problem; I had enough things to deal with already.

I asked Dr. Carpenter to sit down, which he did, stiffly, on a kitchen chair that had somehow wandered into the living room during what I was now thinking of as the ransacking of my apartment. Jack and I sat down, too, as did the dog. Sooner or later, someone was going to have to start talking about something, and it was going to have to be Dr. Carpenter, since apparently he and Sassouma had some sort of errand they had come to carry out.

Finally, Dr. Carpenter cleared his throat and began an explanation. "Sassouma asked me to come here," he said. "You know her English isn't all that good, so she would like me to speak for her."

Admittedly, my neighbor and I had only interacted on a sporadic basis—and that was generally when I was doing some small thing to help her out, like lending her the space heater—but when we did, we seemed to be able to communicate well enough. So, I was surprised that she felt she needed some sort of middleman to help her say whatever it was she needed to convey to me. "Is there something wrong?" I asked, since the first thing that came to mind was that somehow the goons who had broken into my place had caused some trouble for her, as well. But that turned out not to be the case.

"Sassouma heard people in your apartment last night when she knew you were at work," Dr. Carpenter said. "She guessed that they were thieves but she was afraid to call the police. She believes that you will understand why."

I did understand, and I said so. Dealing with the police for any reason was about the last thing she and her family needed, since their immigration status was likely not something they wanted to draw attention to. I certainly didn't blame Sassouma for that and would have been horrified if anything had happened to anyone in her family because of me. That wasn't because I was any kind of sweetheart—I surely wasn't—but because my old hippie self still suspected that karma might yet turn out to be an operating principle on this particular plane of existence and I wouldn't want anything like people being deported to be on my particular Akashic record.

So I tried to smile at Sassouma, though I still felt a little too shell-shocked to be completely genuine about it. Turning back to Dr. Carpenter, I said, "The burglars left more of a mess than anything else. They didn't even really take very much. Just some old electronics," I added, thinking I was being generous in downplaying the real effect that the break-in had had on me. Besides, there was no reason to explain what the electronics were; the story was too involved and wouldn't have meant much of anything to my visitors.

"Well, Sassouma feels very guilty. We are both Dogon people," said Dr. Carpenter. "For us, caring for one's neighbors is very important."

"I'm sorry," I said. "Dogon? I don't know what that means."

Surprisingly, it was Jack, not Dr. Carpenter, who answered me. "They're from Mali," he said. Jack was suddenly sitting forward in his chair, looking very interested, though I didn't find his information very helpful.

Dr. Carpenter, however, nodded in agreement. "Yes, exactly," he said. "But to clarify, I've been in this country for many years. I took my degree at Columbia University," he said. "And now I teach there. French literature." He seemed to relax a little now that he had established his credentials with us, as if we might have thought something less of him were he not a university professor. I stifled my instinct to explain that he was talking to a bartender and a guy who interviewed people on the radio about how they've seen signs of the end times in the grill marks on a cheese-melt sandwich. He probably had us both outclassed by a mile.

Now that he had more properly introduced himself, Dr. Carpenter also revealed his relationship to my neighbor. "Sassouma's husband is my cousin," he said. "As the eldest in the family, I am, to some degree, responsible for them."

I thought that his qualifier—"to some degree"—further helped to explain why he seemed unhappy to be here. He was carrying out some kind of familial duty that he would have preferred not to be required of him.

"In any event," Dr. Carpenter continued, "Sassouma has asked me to perform a task for her, which is why I am here.

This dog," he said. "As my cousin's wife has requested, I have brought it for you."

Up to now, the dog had been so quiet and the conversation so odd that I had pretty much forgotten about the animal. But the moment Dr. Carpenter mentioned him, the dog, which had been lying flat on the floor—as flat as the floorboards, I thought—sprang to attention. And again, looked straight at me.

Now I understood what this visit was about, or at least I thought I did. Because she felt bad about not calling the police last night, Sassouma was trying to make it up to me by getting me a watchdog. Not that this dog seemed particularly suited to that job. He certainly seemed alert enough, but otherwise, he hardly seemed like a substantial presence.

"Well, that's very thoughtful," I said, "but I don't think I really should have a dog."

At last, Sassouma spoke. "But this *is* your dog," she said. "Yours," she repeated, gently but firmly.

"I'm out so much," I told her. "At work. He'd be alone most of the time."

"He will wait," she said. "He is a Dogon dog."

Everyone—Jack included—now fixed their eyes on me as if something very significant had just been said, something grave and serious that I should have understood. But I didn't. True, the dog did seem like a somewhat strange creature with its wedge-shaped head and its way of looking at me as if we'd met before, but otherwise, I couldn't see anything special about it. So it was a Dogon dog. So what?

Perhaps Dr. Carpenter knew what I was thinking because he said, "We have very few of them here. And Dogon dogs don't take to everyone. This one, however, seems to be willing to live with you."

Really? I found myself wondering. *Had they asked him?* Because it almost sounded like just that kind of conversation had somehow taken place.

Dr. Carpenter handed me the leash, which at first I managed to avoid taking from him. "I really don't think it's a good idea," I said. "I mean . . ."

I was about to give all sorts of reasons why I didn't want the dog but Jack suddenly interrupted me with a discreet elbow in my rib. "Laurie," he said, speaking slowly and deliberately. "Take the dog. Say thank you and just take it."

There was something in his tone that made me pay attention. He wasn't making a suggestion, he was issuing some kind of urgent directive. "Okay," I said, speaking to Jack but really addressing everyone. I took the dog's leash and he came to sit beside me. He tilted his wedge-shaped head to look up at me once more and then stretched himself out on the floor again. In my mind, I now decided that there was another difference between him and Sassouma's dust-colored dog: this one was somewhat darker. He was really the color of a shadow.

"Thank you," I said, and then asked, "What is his name?"

"His name is yours to decide," Dr. Carpenter replied.

Well, he wasn't a puppy, so surely somebody had called him by some name previous to his sudden appearance in my life. But if so, apparently from this moment on, that name was erased and I was supposed to come up with something with some resonance for me—and, I assumed, for the dog.

A list of dog's names went through my mind: *Pepper, Petey, Benjy, Bullet*—I was relying heavily on old TV shows and movies. But none of them seemed to suit this particular dog.

"I'm going to have to think about it," I said. A look of concern passed across Dr. Carpenter's face, so I added a qualifier. "I'll come up with a name today."

That seemed to be a satisfactory, if temporary, resolution to the matter. "Very well then," Dr. Carpenter said. He rose from his chair as did Sassouma, still holding her baby, who had slept through the entire visit. "The dog will alert you to any further dangers," Dr. Carpenter added. "And he will be loyal to you."

"Thank you again," I said to Dr. Carpenter. "And thank you, Sassouma."

She beamed at me as she followed her cousin-in-law out the door. As soon as they were gone, I locked the new dead-bolt, which slid into place with a comfortingly heavy click. Dog or no dog, I wasn't taking any chances.

Still, I couldn't help but turn my attention to the dog, who remained stretched out on the floor. Jack, I saw, was looking at him, too.

"I feel like I've just been inducted into the Knights of the Round Table or something like that," I said. "He will be loyal to me? I mean, I would hope so, but he's just a dog."

"Not exactly," said Jack. He bent down to pet the dog, who barely reacted to him. "I've never seen one of these before," he said to me.

"One of what?"

"A Dogon dog."

"Oh yeah," I said. "Why did you look so freaky when you heard that?"

"You really don't know who the Dogon are, do you?" Jack said.

"Never heard of them."

"Well, like I told you, they're from Mali. That's in West Africa." Seeming to address the dog directly, he said, "I wonder if that's where you were born."

But the dog, right now, was paying no attention to either one of us. He closed his eyes and appeared to drift off to sleep. Jack though, became pretty animated as he launched into an explanation about Dogon lore, which seemed to be something else he had picked up from a guest on his show who had written a book about Dogon culture.

He told me that the core belief of the Dogon was that somewhere back in the dim mists of time, alien beings had come to Earth and had stayed for a brief while in some kind

~ 124 ~

of encampment near where the ancestors of the Dogon people lived. The visitors told the Dogon that they came from a universe that they described as being *next* to ours. Apparently, they were able to cross back and forth between the two using an entry point—a kind of bridge in space—near the star Sirius.

"That's it?" I said. I wasn't impressed. I had watched enough late night cable TV to have seen a dozen programs—more—about the beliefs of various tribes and indigenous people all over the world. Lots of them had interesting ideas about dream worlds and alien visitors and spirits who lived in the sky.

"No, that's not it," Jack said, sounding annoyed. "If you'll just let me finish . . ."

"Go ahead," I said. "Tell me a story."

He frowned at me, but proceeded to explain that even before the aliens arrived, the Dogon had been interested in the stars and other objects—comets, meteors, the starry white river of the Milky Way—that they saw in the heavens every night, and had compiled rudimentary star charts for themselves. Perhaps because they took note of this interest, the alien visitors revealed a secret about the night sky that the Dogon didn't know: the great, bright star Sirius has a companion star, a white dwarf that is tiny but immensely dense. The white dwarf and the great star are so closely aligned in space that their mutual gravitational pull causes them to be constantly exchanging gases with each other. The Dogon were frightened by their visitors, who they described as being aloof and rather unpleasant, so they were surprised that these strange beings had bothered to share any kind of special knowledge with them. The Dogon decided to mark the occasion by giving the secret star a name that had meaning to them. They called it Digitaria, after a tiny seed indigenous to their territory. Over time, they seem to have incorporated its story of faithful companionship into many of the ceremonies marking important milestones in Dogon culture such as births, marriages and deaths. What is perhaps most controversial about this tale, Jack said, is that Digitaria is invisible to the naked eye. It can't be seen without a telescope—in fact, no one else knew about it until an astronomer using a telescope discovered the white dwarf in 1862. And no photograph had been taken of this star, which is now officially known as Sirius B, until 1970. Though current-day astronomers scoff at the idea that the Dogon knew about Sirius B—Digitaria— generations before they did, the fact remains that the Dogon people have hand-drawn star charts dating back hundreds of years that show it positioned near its larger companion. And their "Digitaria" ceremonies also go back many centuries.

As I listened to all this, I was able to fit a little piece of my own into the story. I had spent too many nights waiting at bus stops, watching the progress of the seasons mapped out in the slow movement of the constellations across the great, dark grid of the sky, not to have been curious enough to look up their names. And because of that, I knew what other name Sirius went by. Orion, the hunter, with the Three Sis- ters stars in his belt, was accompanied all night by two star- marked hunting dogs, Canis Major and Canis Minor. Canis Major—the Great Dog—contains Sirius, which is also called the Dog Star.

Then I said the words aloud. "Sirius is the Dog Star."

"Right," said Jack. "Now you're getting it. But there's more. The Dogon say that when the visitors came from the universe they described as *next* to ours, the one with an entry point near Sirius, they brought dogs with them. Or anyway, some kind of companion being that seemed like a dog. When they left, they took all these—well, for the sake of argument, let's call them animals—with them, except for one, which had become attached to a Dogon boy. The boy wouldn't part with his pet and the animal wouldn't leave the boy, so it was allowed to stay. The dogs that the Dogon have now are sup- posedly descended from that animal and the camp dogs that lived with the Dogon people, but they aren't like any other dogs in one other respect: they have very few offspring. A Dogon dog may only have one or two offspring in its entire lifetime. So they're relatively rare. And the Dogon never give them away to anyone. I didn't even know there were any in the United States."

We both now looked over at the flat little dog lying at my feet. He seemed suddenly to be aware that he was the object of our conversation because he opened his eyes and rose to his feet. He stretched and then jumped up to sit beside me on the couch. He looked at me, blinked, and leaned against my side. With the weight of him against me, I was surprised by how substantial he seemed to be; he looked like he was made of thin sticks and that odd wedge-shaped head, but he didn't feel that way. He felt heavy, and he felt strong.

I put my arm around him and he leaned even harder. "Hello, Digitaria," I said.

Jack laughed. "That's a good name," he said. "Your secret companion."

"Not so secret," I said. "But very quiet, don't you think? He's barely made a sound since he's been here."

"More thoughtful than vocal," Jack said. "A good quality in people—and in a dog."

"I guess I'd better go out and get him some food," I said. "Want to come?"

"No, I'd better get back to Brooklyn," he said. "I've got a lot of material to go over for the show tonight."

I asked how he was going to get home and he told me that he'd driven here last night—which explained how he'd gotten to my place so quickly—and had parked his car a few blocks away. As he was getting his things together and putting on his coat, he paused to give me an appraising look. Then he said, "You seem a lot better than when I got here last night."

"I do feel better," I said, agreeing that my mood seemed to be settling. The sense of craziness I had been feeling since I'd walked into my ransacked apartment last night was definitely dissipating. I still had a lot of putting-things-back-where-they-belonged to do, but the task seemed less impossible now. Another few hours' work and everything would be back the way it was—almost.

But then something occurred to me. Jack was already out the door, so I hurried after him and caught him on the stairs.

"You left something out of the story," I said to him.

"What's that?" he asked.

"You didn't tell me what they looked like. The visitors."

I waited to hear what I thought was inevitable: the words *shadow, faceless, flat,* but Jack had no such description to offer. He said, "As far as I know, the Dogon never passed on a description. But they do seem to have some sort of collective memory of what they sounded like. Mostly, they hissed."

I paused before responding. Jack remained on the stairs, waiting.

"That's was Gilmartin's description too, wasn't it?" I said finally.

Jack shrugged. "I'm just telling you what's been told to me."

He raised his hand, signaling a brief wave good-bye, and then continued on his way.

I went back to my apartment and got the dog. He trotted along beside me amiably enough, so I took him for a walk to the nearest bodega and bought a few cans of dog food. I hadn't asked what he ate—though as I thought about that on the way back home, I realized that I probably would have gotten the same nonanswer as I did about the dog's name.

In my apartment, I put some water in a bowl and scooped some of the canned food into a dish. The dog walked over to the dish and immediately started eating, so I left him in the kitchen while I went to the bathroom to begin getting ready for work. A little while later, when I stepped out of the shower, the dog was sitting on the bath mat, waiting for me.

I patted him on the head, dried myself off, and went into the bedroom to get dressed. He followed me and sat patiently while I pulled on a pair of jeans and a shirt. Then he followed me out to the living room, where I gathered up my jacket.

I had started to feel anxious again and very tired. I really shouldn't have gone to work, but if they were going to get another bartender out to the airport, I would have had to call in hours ago, and I hadn't thought of it, so I felt responsible for showing up. *Why?* I asked myself. It wasn't like anybody who signed my checks—people at the corporate headquarters in Cleveland—would ever feel responsible about me. But I decided that it was going to help me to stick to my usual routine, and so I unlocked my massive new deadbolt and started out the door.

But before I left, I stopped to give the dog another pat on the head. "Digitaria," I said, "guard the house."

His eyes seemed to glitter even more brightly. He really was a small dog, thin and narrow. But as I looked down at him, with his wedge-shaped head tilted slightly to the side as if he were listening, processing my directive, I had a definite feeling that if anyone so much as tried to get back into my apartment tonight, he would eat them alive.

When I finally got home from work around two A.M. on that first night I had the dog, I was surprised to find him sitting just about where I had left him, facing the front door. I told myself that of course he hadn't simply been waiting there all night; probably he had heard me at the door and the sound of my key in the lock had brought him back to what he seemed to regard as his post. Later, when I went to bed, the dog jumped in as well, settling himself at my feet. Since my two small rooms were set up like a railroad flat, you could see through the bedroom doorway straight through to the front door of the apartment and the dog had positioned himself so that he was pointed right at that door. He kept his attention focused there as sharply as if he were looking at it through a nightscope. I found this very comforting. I hadn't expected to be able to sleep very well, and I didn't, but each time I woke up, the fact that the dog was there was reassuring enough to allow me to drift off again.

So I got used to him, but more than that, I quickly grew fond of him. I'd never had a dog before but even so, I was pretty sure that as dogs go, this one was unusual. For example, he rarely made a sound. And though I had bought him some dog toys—rawhide bones and a ball—he didn't seem much interested in playing. He liked walks, the longer the better, and he liked to be let off his leash to run around at the edge of the marshland near my bus stop where he could chase seagulls, but that seemed to be enough activity for him.

All he seemed to want other than his daily exercise was to sit next to me, or to lean against my feet—in other words, to be where I was. And every night when I came home from work, I found him sitting at the front door, waiting for me. And he continued to sleep at the edge of the bed—or at least, I assumed he slept sometimes. Those times when, for whatever reason, I woke up in the middle of the night, Digitaria always seemed to be awake, too. And he was hypervigilant. Any noise in the hallway, even Sassouma and her family or other neighbors passing by, sent him running to the front door. He didn't bark but simply stood at alert, staring at the door until whatever sounds had disturbed him finally subsided. And then he'd march back to bed and curl up in exactly the same position he'd been in before, but with his eyes open, glittering in the darkness.

During the next few weeks, Jack checked in with me once in a while to be sure that nothing else had happened, but each time he called I was able to tell him that nothing had. That was both good and bad; good, because it meant no more threatening letters and not even a hint of anyone trying to get back into my apartment for any reason. Not that—at the time, anyway—I thought there was anything left that could be of any value to anyone in the Blue Awareness. Bad, because the police were clearly not going to do anything about the break-in. I called once and was told they had indeed talked to a representative of the Blue Awareness, who said my claim that they were responsible for the theft of my property was not only absurd, it was also an egregious example of the religious persecution that they were often subject to. It was pretty clear to me that as far as the NYPD was concerned, that was the end of that.

I missed listening to the radio so, eventually, I bought another one, but even though it had world-band capability, it was still a poor substitute for what I'd lost. Avi's radio had been a kind of magical portal for me, able to pull in distant stations and mysterious broadcasts in foreign languages from the far-flung outposts of the world. Low-watt stations boosted by the Kennelly-Heaviside layer of the ionosphere, booming shortwave frequencies sailing over the curve of the Earth—picking up these broadcasts was something that was exciting to me, as I guess it must have been to Avi. I couldn't exactly explain it, but even if I didn't understand most of what was being said, when it was late at night and I was tuning in a station drifting in from Siberia or the Seychelles, I felt like I was listening to strangers whispering their secrets, which made them not really strangers anymore. And I liked listening to the marine-band chatter of ships approaching the New York harbor or waiting in the deep-water channels outside the Jersey ports. Hearing the clipped, stentorian tones of the news readers on the London-based BBC or the cheery discussion programs on the Voice of America—which anybody with a decent world-band set like the one I'd bought or even a backyard antenna could pick up—wasn't quite the same thing.

One night, it occurred to me that maybe I could find some interesting stations on the Internet. There was certainly a lot of online music from all over the world that could be accessed, but though I listened for a while, I couldn't develop any real enthusiasm for what I was doing. Maybe it was because there was no challenge to locating or hearing these stations—click a hyperlink, open a media player and you were instantly connected to clear channels emanating from Prague or Gdansk—and there was no surprise at what you could or could not tune in on a given night. Listening to online music didn't depend on how the troposphere was feeling from one hour to the next or on seasonal temperatures or the reflective qualities of the cloud layer above the Sargasso Sea. And you rarely heard the sound of a human voice unless it was some robotic tone repeating the station's call letters.

But there was a different kind of voice I found on the web that did interest me. In fact, I developed a kind of obsession with it for a while because it was like listening to the greeting of an old friend. Actually, *friends* would be more accurate because, as Jack had once told me, Sputnik—the original satellite and all its successors—was online.

The sound of the satellites' telemetry signals had been digitized and posted on various websites. I first found them by accident, on a website devoted to the history of both Russian and American satellite launches, but once I did, night after night when I came home from work, I clicked open the files and listened in. All the recordings sounded pretty much alike, but of course, my favorite was Sputnik 10, which was the satellite that had once had little Zvezdochka aboard. Zvezdochka, who got home safely. Night after night, I sat in my living room, with my own dog leaning against my leg, listening to the scratchy, metallic *ping, ping, ping* of Sputnik's telemetry signal, faint but steady as a distant heartbeat. There was something about the sound that I found comforting.

The telemetry recordings were on my mind one night at work a couple of weeks after I got the dog. I was pouring beer for an order that had been placed by the waitress I was working with that night and, at the same time, wondering what other kind of interesting historical recordings I could find online, when my attention was diverted by some kind of commotion outside the bar. It was always pretty dark in The Endless Weekend, but quite bright outside in the wide walkway between the bar and a row of fast-food restaurants across the way. Looking out into the square of lighted space that was my view of the outside area, I saw a crowd of photographers walking backward. The corridor pulsed with the lightning-like flash of their cameras, and then the swarm of men and women quickly passed out of my line of sight. A few moments later, behind a phalanx of bodyguards, the object of their attention came into sight: a slight man, dark-haired and intense-looking, wearing a suit that looked as sharp-edged as a razor. Surprisingly, he stopped in front of the bar and then, even more surprisingly, turned and headed in.

The waitress was still standing near me, waiting for her order, and when she saw who was about to enter the bar, her eyes widened and she took a step back, as if she wasn't worthy of being in the presence of the man who was, apparently, about to become our customer. "Ted Merrill," she breathed. "I don't believe it."

But indeed, it was Ted Merrill, mega movie star, who was now entering The Endless Weekend, accompanied by his entourage. He took a seat at the bar—near the end, where I was standing—while his three bodyguards and a few other assorted members of his party arranged themselves at a nearby table. As they did, the scrum of photographers returned and positioned themselves outside the bar where they continued to snap pictures.

I placed two mugs of draft on the waitress's tray and practically had to push her away from the bar to go serve the pair of businessmen who were her customers, though they, too, were staring goggle-eyed at our unexpected visitor. In contrast to the star-struck trance that everyone else seemed to be in, I was feeling a little weird about the appearance of Ted Merrill in my particularly unremarkable workplace. There was absolutely no reason I could think of for him to have stopped for a drink in this specific bar—except for the fact that I knew him to be a prominent member of the Blue Awareness. In fact, he was probably their most visible and vocal spokesman. I had seen him talking about it often enough on the TV gossip shows. *Of all the gin joints in all the towns in the world,* indeed. What was he doing here?

I walked the few steps over to him and asked what he'd like, while the waitress scurried back to take the drinks order from his group at the table. He showed me the grin that was always referred to as "Ted Merrill's famous smile"—and in person, I had to admit it was dazzling—and then asked for a complicated cocktail. It took me a few minutes to mix it up, and while I was adding crushed ice, I heard him ask one of his bodyguards for a pen.

When I brought him the drink, I saw that he was doodling something on one of our napkins, which had a printed border meant to look like confetti. He tasted the drink, pronounced it delicious, and smiled at me again.

"I hope I'm not causing you too much trouble," he said, gesturing toward the photographers. "At least they know enough to stay outside."

"We're happy to serve you," I said.

"Well, I'm happy to be served," he replied. He leaned forward a little, just enough to suggest that he was about to tell me something meant only for my ears. Because I was on my guard, I registered this move as a trick, one meant to imply an immediate intimacy between the great movie star and the lowly bartender. "I was in the mood for just this," he said, taking a sip of the jewel-colored drink I had prepared for him. "I'm having a late dinner with some very sober-minded people and I thought I needed something wonderful first. Something edgy and beautiful. And prepared just right."

If he was trying to make conversation, he was actually doing a poor job of it. I thought he sounded false, even silly, though I guessed that the glittery chatter was another ploy—this one intended to disarm me in some way.

"Then I hope it's just what you needed," I said, playing along.

"Oh, it is," he told me. "But it's just one thing. One thing out of many."

Now what did that mean? I wondered. Because I had a strong feeling that it meant something, that every word Ted Merrill had said to me since he sat down at the bar was freighted with subtext. All I could do was wait for him to decide when, and if, he was going to make himself any clearer.

As it turns out, I didn't have to wait long at all. The next thing he said was, "There are a lot of different things people need. Special things, sometimes. Don't you agree, Laurie?"

Was I really surprised that he knew my name? Not really, though it did give me a chill. And when he lit up the megawatt smile again, it seemed decidedly menacing. I had the sudden thought that if I had my dog with me I could have told him to take a bite out of Ted Merrill's leg. I wasn't exactly sure how I would have conveyed the message, but I was sure that Digitaria would have received it, and just the thought of my little shadow-colored pet digging his incisors into Ted Merrill's shins emboldened me.

"No, Ted," I said. "I don't, really. Myself, I don't feel in need of anything special. Why do you ask? Do you?"

"Oh, maybe," he said. He downed the rest of his drink, then picked up the pen again and resumed doodling on the napkin. "I find that it's hard to be specific about what I might need these days. But sometimes, someone gives me something and it turns out to be exactly what I needed at a particular moment."

"Do things like that happen to you a lot?" I asked.

"You know," he said, "they seem to. I guess I'm just lucky."

He finished whatever he was sketching on the napkin and then held it up to examine his work. "Not bad," he said. "How about if I sign it and give it to you as a present?"

I didn't reply, but apparently, that wasn't necessary. He placed the napkin on the bar in front of him and added an elaborate signature. Then, he lit up his smile again, this time making it a little lopsided, which also brought out a web of crinkles around his eyes. The smile was beginning to seem like it led a life of its own, cleverly deploying itself in many different, useful versions. This was clearly the endearing version, one that had won countless fans. I, however, was not among them.

Ted Merrill put a hundred dollar bill on the bar and pushed it over to me, along with the napkin. "Time to go," he said. "But it's been nice talking to you, Laurie." He tapped his finger on the napkin. "I hope you'll keep this as a souvenir of our time together."

As soon as he got off the stool, the members of his entourage all stood up and made ready to leave with him. Each one seemed to have assigned places and they formed themselves into a kind of human exoskeleton that surrounded the movie star. Then they all walked out together, moving as a unit.

Once they were gone, the waitress came back to join me at the bar. She was a young, pretty girl with very long hair dyed the color of ink; in her black uniform, she seemed to only partly emerge from the darkness of the bar. I focused on the pale disk of her face, a little moon bobbing in the nearby shadows.

"Wow," she said, seeing the money on the bar. "The guys at the table only left me a ten."

"I'll split it with you," I said.

I was actually tempted to give her the whole thing, since I had a feeling that the money came wrapped with an invisible helping of very bad vibes. But I didn't have much time to dwell on that idea because the waitress was now examining with a studied interest the sketch on the napkin Ted Merrill had left behind.

"Well, look at that," she said.

"What is it?" I asked her, since I hadn't yet glanced at what Merrill had drawn. I didn't really have a lot of interest in some doodle he'd signed—just more bad vibes as far as I was concerned.

But I'd asked, and so she showed it to me. The drawing on the napkin seemed to depict a kind of ribbed cone lying on its side, spilling out a variety of things that I took to be apples and peppers and maybe a small pumpkin or two.

"I guess he's no artist," the waitress said, "but you can see what it is."

I certainly could. It was a cornucopia.

I asked the waitress to spell me for a moment and carried the napkin to the back, where our lockers were, folded it carefully and placed it in my shoulder bag. Then I did my best to put a mental shield between myself and the last half hour so that I could finish the rest of my shift. The less I thought about Ted Merrill and the message he'd drawn for me on the napkin the better off I was until I could call Jack. Because that was my plan, to call Jack. I couldn't think any further than that.

When I finally got off work, I dialed Jack's number as I was heading down the road at the far end of the airport that ran between the warehouses where the food service trucks dropped off their pallets of packaged meals. He didn't pick up, but I hadn't expected him to since he was still on the air at this hour, so I left him a message and kept on walking in the direction of my bus stop. It was a cool spring night, netted with stars.

He called back when I was on the bus, just as we were passing by Flushing Meadow, where there was a lake that looked like black glass. Tiny red lights seemed to skip across the lake's dark surface like bursting bullets, then disappear, then suddenly sizzle back into view again; but this was an optical illusion, the reflection of the blinking airplane warning lights that topped the high-rise apartment buildings on nearby Queens Boulevard, which were right under the flight path leading to the airport.

"Guess who came into the bar tonight?" I said. "Ted Merrill."

"Oh?" Jack replied. For a moment he sounded puzzled, as if he were wondering why I had bothered to call him about this, but he quickly made the connection. "*Oh,*" he repeated. "I gather it wasn't a coincidence?"

"I don't think so," I said. "For one thing, he knew my name. For another . . . well, he drew me a picture, on a napkin. He even signed it."

"A picture of what?" Jack asked, sounding like he already knew he wasn't going to like the answer.

"A cornucopia," I said. "In other words, a horn of plenty."

There was a long pause in our conversation. My bus had passed the lake now, and was turning off the parkway into the residential streets of Queens where the monolithic ranks of apartments gave way to rows of small brick and stucco houses leaning one against the other, and all shut up against the night.

Finally, Jack said, "They've got the radio. Now they want the antenna."

"That's what I thought," I replied. "But why?"

Jack fell silent again. The bus rolled on through sleeping neighborhoods, past shuttered stores and empty streets.

"Well," he said finally, "maybe when your intruders broke into your apartment, they were after the Blue Box, but once they saw the radio, and saw that it said Haverkit—just like your box—they knew to take that, too. Or someone told them to look out for it. The Blue Awareness considers itself to be a religion and religions have sacred objects: maybe Avi's Haverkit radio is one of those things. Only it's missing an important component: a very unusual antenna."

"I still don't understand. How would they know about the radio?"

"Remember I told you that Avi and Howard Gilmartin had some kind of relationship way back when? Well, before it fell apart over the Blue Box thing, Avi and Howard likely exchanged alien encounter stories. Howard saw something—someone—tinkering with his radars. Avi had a niece who told him that she saw a very similar figure years later, adjusting the tuning dial on his radio receiver . . . and don't argue with me right now about whether or not that actually happened, okay?"

"Okay," I agreed. I wanted to hear where this was going.

"So let's say for a while, at least, Gilmartin and Avi were kind of friendly. Collegial, at least. You have to bear in mind that they had something else in common: whatever else these guys were, at heart, they were both ham radio operators. Hams love to talk about their equipment, love to compare the parts they use, the quality of the parts, who builds them, stuff like that. And of course, one of the main things they always focus on is the kind of antenna they use, the kind the next guy uses, what kind of reception they get, what's the best time of night to send and receive broadcasts using what kind of antenna. The fact that Avi had constructed a horn of plenty antenna—one small enough for an amateur to use, because back then, the only ones that anyone knew of belonged to observatories and you needed a flatbed truck to haul them from one place to another—that would have been a fascinating piece of information. So if he shared it with Howard Gilmartin . . ."

Now, I couldn't help but interrupt. "So what if he did? That would have been more than thirty years ago, Jack. And maybe the Blue Awareness doesn't think Howard is dead, but really, we know he is."

"Yes, but his son isn't. And from what I understand, Raymond Gilmartin has studied every scrap of information about his father's life, every document, every memoir. Whatever went on between his father and Avi—good and bad—you can bet Raymond knows about it. And you did tell Ravenette that you've got a device she thinks—no, *believes*—is a Blue Box, because she can't imagine how anyone but an Aware trained to use one to scan a devotee would have a Box. But Raymond knows how—he knows that Avi Perzin built it. Well, if Ravenette is a Second-Level Aware, she's certainly got access to the only person who's ever been awarded First-Level status, and that's Raymond. So put all this together, Laurie, just like Raymond probably did. It's not hard to figure out who your uncle's niece is—I did it in about ten seconds. To begin with, Perzin isn't exactly the world's most common surname. Now add in the fact that Haverkit was the only manufacturer thirty, forty years ago that was producing high-quality electronic and radio kit parts and it's more than likely that whoever was in your apartment was told to look for

~ 140 ~

anything that said Haverkit—after all, if you've got Avi's Blue Box, there's a chance you've also got his radio, no? And then whammo; right on your shelf, there it is. Think about it, kiddo: you gave them all the clues they needed."

Jack was right. I might as well have drawn them a map to my apartment, handed them the keys and told them to look around. "Crap," I said, which seemed to sum up exactly how I was feeling about this.

"So back to the antenna," Jack continued. "I'm sure these days, on the web, you could certainly find the plans for building a small enough horn of plenty antenna to make the radio work the way they want it to—meaning, to be able to draw in signals outside our atmosphere. But I guess they don't want any antenna—they want the original."

"But I don't have it. I've told you that. My father cleaned out Avi's apartment after he died. I took a few things, like the radio and the box, but that's it. I never even saw the antenna."

"All right then," Jack said. "Let's tell them that. Exactly that."

"How?"

"I'm going to call Ravenette. As I said, she's got to have something to do with the creep show they seem to have given you a starring role in. Or at least she'll know who to pass the message to, and I'm guessing that person's name is Raymond."

"You don't have to call her for me. It's a good idea, but I could do it myself."

"Sure you could," Jack said. "But we're friends, and friends don't let friends deal with the Blue Meanies by themselves." He paused for a moment and then repeated, "Friends. That's what we are, right?"

"Sure," I said. "I thought we cleared that up."

"You're right," he replied. "We did. So now, a couple of friends are going to wake up a psychic who seems to have a bunch of friends of her own. Nasty ones."

I stayed on the line while Jack dialed Ravenette's number. Once it began ringing, he conferenced me in. When she answered, though, she didn't sound like she'd been in dream-land. Busy, sleepless—who knew why she sounded wide awake. But Jack decided that he did.

"So you're up," Jack said after telling her who was call-ing. Then, not waiting for her to reply, he added, "Of course you are. You're a psychic. You knew that we would call."

Ravenette ignored the jab. But she did pick up on the fact that Jack had implied he wasn't the only one on the call. "We?" she said. "Who's *we*?"

"Laurie Perzin is on the phone with me."

"Oh really? Well what do you want?"

I thought she sounded annoyed, but in a fake sort of way. There was a note of caution behind her bravado. Jack must have picked up on this, too, because he wasted no time in going after her.

"So tell me something," he said. "Why is it that you and your buddies can't do anything in a normal way? Everything has to be weird and mysterious, right? Or downright threaten-ing. And when even that doesn't work, you send your movie-star poster boy to play games for you. Did it ever occur to any of you that you could just pick up a phone and say *Hello, I'd like to talk to you*? Isn't that a lot easier than breaking into someone's house? And don't tell me you don't know what I'm talking about."

"I did talk to Laurie," Ravenette said smoothly. "I'd be happy to talk to her again."

Exasperated, I finally broke into the conversation. "I'm on the phone," I reminded her.

"Oh, yes. Yes, you are. Well, Laurie, how are you doing, dear?"

"Come on, Ravenette," Jack snorted. "Can we just stop this? Laurie doesn't have the antenna for the radio. She hasn't even seen it since she was a kid. So you're just going to have to make contact with your alien overlords some other way, okay?"

"Now I *am* going to have to tell you that I don't know what you're talking about."

"Please. I know the backstory, Ravenette. But maybe it'll make you feel better if I rephrase. If the aliens are our ancestors, I guess you're just going to have to wait for them to call you instead of the other way around because Laurie can't help you out there. So maybe we should get off the line. They could be dialing in at any moment."

"Don't mock what we believe, Jack."

"What you *believe*," Jack said acidly, "is that you're the only ones who know the truth and that makes you special. Smarter than everyone else, so you can do whatever you want *to* anyone else. Well, you know what that really makes you? A bunch of fanatics. A cult. You've just got more money—and a better public relations operation—than most."

I could hear the controlled fury in Ravenette's voice as she said, "So that's what you really think, is it, Jack? Then I guess you won't be inviting me on the show anymore. Such a pity. I do so love taking those piece-of-shit town cars you send to drive me all the way to the ass end of Brooklyn to that palatial studio of yours. Really, I'll miss the star treatment. I'll rue the day. But good luck with all that, Jack. The show, I mean. You'll need it." And then she hung up.

The bus had now arrived at my stop. Still holding the phone to my ear, I waved good night to the driver and descended the steps. The bus pulled away—a glowing box of light disappearing down the dark road—leaving me standing alone by the chain-link fence that separated the bay and its bordering marshland from, to use Ravenette's term, the ass end of my particular urban landscape.

It was a mild night, pretty enough, with a sharp slice of moon overhead and the salty smell of deep water riding in on the currents, so I stayed where I was, leaning against the fence as Jack and I finished our conversation.

"I'm sorry, Laurie," Jack said. "I could have handled that better. I just lost my temper with her."

"It's an easy thing to do," I told him. "I know. Believe me."

"But I probably just made it worse."

"Well, I think you just dropped yourself into the blue soup with me. So to speak."

At least that made him laugh. "What?" he said.

"She likes to make threats. They all do, I guess. What was that she said? Good luck with the show? I don't exactly think she meant it."

"No, probably not. But I guess we'll just have to wait and see what happens next. If we're lucky, nothing will. And if we're not, we'll deal with it."

"Maybe I'll just have to find another fire escape to climb out on and ask whatever shadow is lurking around to intercede. If I can find him."

"I thought you didn't believe that," Jack reminded me.

"You know what? It's late, I'm tired, I've had a weird night and a long ride home. I'm liable to say anything right now."

"Okay," Jack said, "Let's leave it on that note. Good night," he said.

" 'Night," I replied, and clicked off my phone.

I crossed the road and started to walk down my street, past the locked body shops and garages. As usual, a big rig was parked on the block, though someone had made more of an effort than usual to hide it. Beyond the sodium glow of the streetlamps, I could just make out the dimmed-down running lights of the Peterbilt cab nosing out of the end of an alley beside a scrapyard. As I walked by the truck and approached my building, I happened to glance up at my window and thought I saw a pair of twitching ears framed behind the dark square of glass. Since Digitaria was usually positioned by the front door when I came home, I wasn't surprised that he was waiting for me, but that he had figured out that he could stand up on his hind legs and watch out the window for me was something new. It made him seem anxious, peering out into the night like that. I quickened my step and was in the building, up the stairs, and unlocking my front door just a few moments later, greeting my dog with a pat on the head. In response, he uttered a soft yip.

It was the first time I had ever heard him make a sound. "You can stop worrying now," I said to him, since I realized that having lingered outside to talk on the phone had made me later than usual in getting home, and perhaps that had disturbed him. Maybe I was attributing to him qualities of mind and heart that he didn't have—he was, after all, just a dog, not a person watching a late-night clock tick off the time that a friend should be home—but I assumed that all people who owned pets did that. And so I patted him again.

~X~

Over the next couple of weeks, I noticed that my dog—and he was definitely my dog now, as bonded to me as I had become to him—seemed to remain in a heightened state of anxiety, or at least alertness. He was eating less and often, in the night, jumped off the bed to pace back and forth between the bedroom and the front door of my apartment. And every night, when I came home from work, I would see him in the window, ears twitching above his wedge-shaped skull, seemingly poised to leap through the glass and come looking for me if I didn't get home exactly when I was supposed to.

I began to worry about him a bit, so decided it was time to take him for a checkup. When I'd gotten him, I'd been so overwhelmed by everything that had happened—the break-in on the previous night and then the visit from my neighbor and her cousin, the somewhat grim professor of French literature, Dr. Carpenter—that it had never even occurred to me to ask questions like whether or not the dog needed vaccinations or anything like that. So I made an appointment at a nearby veterinary clinic, and brought him in on a quiet Tuesday afternoon when I was off from work. The vet, a Dr. Tyner, who turned out to be a serious young guy with lots of snapshots of his four-legged patients in the waiting room, earnestly shook my hand after an assistant ushered me into an exam room. Then the doctor took a good, long look at my dog and asked his name.

When I told him, he asked me to spell it and then carefully corrected a mistake in how his assistant had entered it on the chart she had started for Digitaria.

"That's an unusual name," he said.

I didn't want to try to explain the whole story—visitors from the interstellar neighborhood of Sirius and the dark star that was its invisible companion star seemed like a bit much for a first visit to a vet's office—so I just said that it was a Dogon name, and explained that the Dogon were an African tribe.

"That makes sense," Dr. Tyner said. "He has the look of a pariah dog. He's narrow, and has that curled tail."

I probably looked like I was not happy to have my dog called a pariah, and that made Dr. Tyner smile. "It's not an insult," he said. "It just means that they're hardy animals. They live with nomads and tribespeople who follow their herds. When life's hard for the people, it is for the dogs, too."

As he spoke to me, Dr. Tyner was examining Digitaria, who he had hoisted up onto an examining table. All the while, the dog kept his eyes focused on me. And I got the message: he was only enduring this going-over for me, because I wanted him to.

"Well," Dr. Tyner said, "we'll give him the regular inoculations, but otherwise, he seems fine. In fact, he seems like a particularly hardy fellow. He is a little thin, but that may be natural for him."

"I think he's been anxious," I said. "I mean, he's been pacing a lot."

Dr. Tyner gave me an inquisitive look. "Have you maybe been upset about anything lately? Sometimes dogs pick up on how their owners feel and start acting the same way."

"My apartment was broken into a couple of weeks ago. That's actually how I got the dog. Someone gave him to me."

"So he's a watchdog," Dr. Tyner said. "Has anything else happened since you got him?"

I thought about Ted Merrill and his big, threatening smile, but didn't think I could explain that to the vet, either. "No," I said. "Not at home."

"So, Digitaria," Dr. Tyner said to my dog, who was still standing on the metal examining table, "did you hear that? You've been doing your job, so you can relax a little. I'll even tell you something that might help. Most bad people are afraid of dogs, so just the fact that you're around is a good thing for your friend Laurie." And then he patted Digitaria on the head.

I left with a receipt for the $125 I had put on my credit card to pay for the exam, but the cost was balanced somewhat by an appreciation for the vet's good humor about my concern that the dog was acting a little odd. And I liked that Dr. Tyner talked to him the way I had found myself talking to Digitaria almost from the beginning, as if he understood me, which meant it was reasonable to speak to him in pretty much the same way I did everybody else. Never mind that I knew there was a much more logical case to be made that, other than vets, the people who talked to their dogs as if they understood every word probably were mostly old ladies, or else lonely souls and other odd types.

In any case, maybe the dog did understand Dr. Tyner's reassurances—at least, I decided to believe he did—because Digitaria did seem to calm down after visiting the vet. Though he kept up his nightly vigil at the window when I was due home from work, the pacing back and forth between the bedroom and front door stopped, and he was even eating a little more. Sometimes he even wagged his tail when he saw me opening a can of his food and since generally, he wasn't much of a tail wagger, I took a kind of silly pleasure in thinking that I was making him happy.

During these few weeks that I later thought of as a brief lull in our lives, an interlude between my visit from Ted Merrill—which I had started thinking of as the Night of the Big Smile—and what came next, Jack and I kept in touch.

Whenever we could arrange it, we met in the city for lunch. He liked to eat somewhere in the Village, where we had both lived at different times when we were younger. Afterward, we sometimes went for a walk around the neighborhood, and Jack and I both took turns pointing out to each other where shops or businesses we remembered used to be but weren't anymore. From the far west side, near the river, where the Socialist Workers Party had had their headquarters and turned out political tracts on mimeograph machines, to radical bookstores and chess clubs and coffee bars, Jack, in particular, seemed to have a geography in his head that had been overlaid by a new grid of streets, new buildings, and a new millennial affluence that had turned old neighborhoods into fashionable quarters, unaffordable to most of their original residents. But he didn't seem overly nostalgic about any of this, just interested in how time and change fought with memory to establish precedence. Which was more real: the Village he remembered—more gay than straight, more hipster-friendly than home to fashionistas, more hole-in-the-wall than penthouse in the sky; or the one where we often had to make a reservation at some tiny restaurant on Bedford Street or Jane or Great Jones or Little West Twelfth because the rich and famous (or just plain rich) were edging us out of all the places that people like Jack and I used to take for granted as being ours?

One morning, though, Jack phoned me so early—early for me, anyway—that he woke me up, and asked if we could have a late breakfast. I had to be at work in the afternoon so I wasn't eager to travel all the way to the Village and then navigate my way by subway back to Queens to catch the AirTrain out to Kennedy, but Jack suggested something else. He wanted to meet at a diner off the Grand Central Parkway. I knew the place because it was near the strip mall where Victor Haberman had his office. On my bus ride to work every day, I still passed my very-much-ex-attorney's office (I had received a registered letter from him, copied to the Blue

Awareness's attorneys and about half the senior administrative managers of the group listed on their website officially resigning from my "case") and knew that it had taken weeks for him to clean up the mess that had been left by the blue paint that had been smeared all over his windows, door, and even the sidewalk.

An hour later, I caught the bus heading toward the airport, but got off before my usual stop, right across the street from the diner. It was a hazy morning, the weather almost summery, but this was hardly a spot to appreciate the mild season. Stuck on the edge of the parkway, between Flushing Meadow Park, with its shallow ponds and rusty barbeque pits, and the seemingly mile-high rows of balconied co-ops squeezed together on the boulevard stretching toward the city, the diner had the feel of a place sitting uneasily on a temporary foundation. Everybody inside seemed anxious, gulping down coffee and singed toast in the rush to get from one place to another. This was just a stop on the road when you were in-between destinations and ready to hurry on.

Jack was sitting at a booth near a window that presented a view of the traffic speeding past on the parkway and in the distance, planes lifting themselves off the tarmac at Kennedy and angling upward into the sky. He had a plate of eggs in front of him that he wasn't eating, and an empty coffee cup.

When I sat down across from him, Jack offered me a quick greeting and then, almost immediately, started explaining why he'd wanted to meet. Something had happened.

"The company that syndicates my show is called Coast-to-Coast Radio Networks," Jack began. "I knew they'd been working on a merger or a sale for a year now; a number of media conglomerates seemed interested, and as far as I was concerned, it would just mean a change in the name on my contract. But two days ago, I got a call from a friend on the corporate side who told me there's a new bidder and they're offering a ton of money. Make that a ton-and-a-half. So you know who suddenly wants to buy the Coast-to-Coast Radio Networks?"

I sighed. "The Blue something, right?"

"Blue Star Communications," Jack told me. "Both the president of the company and the chairman of the board are Awares. So, I don't think it's a coincidence that Blue Star's single condition for going forward with the purchase of Coast-to-Coast is that, once the deal is done, they drop my show. Meaning, kick me off the air."

"So now you're going to suffer because of me."

"Laurie," Jack said, "we can go back and forth about who dragged who into this mess, but one thing I know is that this part of it is all my own doing. I've gone out of my way to make them angry."

"I still can't believe it," I said. "Because I won't give them a radio antenna I don't even have, they'd go to these lengths to . . . what? I don't even understand what the point is of going after you."

"Ravenette warned us they would."

"I haven't forgotten that. It still seems pretty extreme."

Jack gave me a wry look. "I take it you haven't been listening to the show. I told you, I haven't exactly been trying to placate them. I've had a lot of ex-Awares on lately, and they've been pretty outspoken about the trials and tribulations of being a member of the Blue Awareness if you're not high up the ladder. Or in favor with someone who is. Most of the people who've talked to me on the air have spent their life savings, or went deeply into debt, to pay for what the group calls Awareness training—all that Blue Box stuff, and more— and then were harassed nearly to the breaking point when they finally left. I guess Raymond Gilmartin isn't too happy about my having them on the show where they can spill the blue beans, so to speak."

"Do you think Raymond himself is after you?"

"I doubt that anything the Blue Awareness does happens without his say-so. And this is how they are, this is what they do. It's bad enough if you're just a regular member and turn against them. But if you're someone like me—someone with a public platform—I guess they view that as a real threat. So I'd say we're way beyond their issues with you now. Way beyond."

I looked out the window, into the dusty haze of sunshine that had spread itself across the sky, all the way to the horizon. We were almost alone in the diner now. This was the dead time, the half hour or so before morning rolled over into afternoon when no one was ready to sit down and eat lunch yet, or grab more coffee. One waitress was outside taking a cigarette break; another was sitting at the counter, slowly going through a pile of receipts.

"What are you going to do?" I asked.

"I'm flying out to LA this afternoon; that's where Coast-to-Coast has its headquarters. I've got a meeting scheduled tomorrow with the head of programming. I want him to tell me to my face that they're thinking of dropping my show. It can't be anything financial because I bring in plenty of ad revenue and as far as I know, they don't have any trouble selling my commercial slots. But just in case this Blue Star deal does go through, I've also got a meeting scheduled with the World Air satellite people. They might be interested in carrying my program," he said. Suddenly, a kind of lopsided grin appeared on his face. "I hadn't thought of it until now, but I guess that's a little weird—given the context. A satellite radio company might just save the day."

"Well," I said. "Maybe Avi's pulling some strings somewhere."

"A ghost with influence? He'd make a great posthumous guest for the first satellite show."

I drank some of the coffee that had been brought to me before the lull and started picking at Jack's plate of cold eggs. "All this is totally crazy," I said. "I wish there was a way to just . . . I don't know. Make it all go away."

"Too late," Jack said. "You can't un-know things."

"Sometimes I wish I could."

"Yeah, sometimes we all wish that. But maybe it's better to be . . ."

I couldn't help myself; I finished his sentence for him. "Better to be what? Aware?"

He laughed. "Okay," he said. "Yes. Aware. But promise me you won't go over to the other side while I'm away, all right?"

"I don't think you have anything to worry about," I replied.

Jack had driven to the diner but had decided that he didn't really want to leave his car at one of the public lots at the airport, so he asked me to do him a favor by taking care of it for a few days. I said sure, so he paid the bill and then I rode with him to the airport, where we said good-bye and I took over the wheel. I drove the car along the looping roads that ran around the outskirts of the terminals to a distant spot I knew, near the huge sheds where salt and snowplows were locked up during the warmer months. There was an employee parking lot here, where I was able to leave the car and then catch one of the airline courtesy vans back toward the main area of the airport. I was early for my shift, so I sat around in the back of the bar for a while, near the lockers, reading a book. It was a spy novel and I had been absorbed by it, but suddenly it just couldn't hold my attention anymore. Compared to my own life, the spy's problems seemed easily solvable. Make a few well-placed phone calls. Shoot someone. Or else say, *I give up.* Or maybe, if it seemed like it would work better in certain circumstances, *I give in.*

TWO DAYS later, I had a rare Saturday off. I woke up feeling restless—something that seemed to be happening to me more and more lately—and wandered around my apartment for a while, picking things up and putting them down somewhere else. I was sort of hungry but sort of not. I thought that if I took the dog out for a while I'd work up an appetite, so I put on his leash and led him out of the building. We wandered up toward Queens Boulevard, where I bought some breakfast concoctions at a McDonald's and then walked back to my neighborhood.

It was a mild day, but overcast. I didn't feel like going back inside, so I sat on the stoop, sharing the food I'd bought with my dog. After a while, one of Sassouma's children—a boy of around fourteen—came out of the building, walking the family's little dust-colored pet. I said hello to the boy, who solemnly smiled back at me. A moment later, Digitaria turned his head and pointed it upward, seeming to sniff the air above the other dog, which did much the same thing, as if both animals somehow occupied a larger space than their actual size would suggest. Then, without any further interaction between them, Digitaria went back to eating part of a biscuit while the other dog quietly followed his owner away, down the block.

I watched them go and then returned to my own thoughts, which, much like my earlier behavior in my apartment, went from one thing to another without lighting anywhere. The problem was that I still felt like I couldn't settle down. Eventually, it occurred to me that since I had Jack's car, maybe Digitaria and I could go for a ride somewhere. Maybe the beach, I decided. My last visit to Rockaway, odd and unhappy as it was, had been months ago—long enough to use my talent for dissembling to pretend it hadn't happened. Besides, I suddenly had a strong yearning to go back, which I decided meant that my happy memories of summers at the beach were reoccupying their rightful place in my mind, which seemed like a good thing to me. When I was a child, I had liked gray days at the beach almost as much as sunny ones. Days that were slightly gloomy were tailor-made for reading or just sitting on the boardwalk, watching the waves stretch themselves toward the shore and then slowly slide back, as if into a great, gray bowl, pulling shells and pebbles with them. Besides, I had recently read in the newspaper about how, after decades of neglect, urban development was finally coming to Rockaway, though the area targeted for gentrification was much farther up the peninsula from where my family used to spend their summers at the Sunlite Apartments. Two or three miles away from that desolate spot, condo developers were putting up new townhouses, building gated communities that were supposedly going to bring this old working class getaway back to some semblance of its former respectability. Why not go see how that was coming along? At least, it would give me something to do with the restless energy that, so far, had been the animating feature of my day. And because I had the car, the dog could ride along with me. On pet food commercials I'd seen on TV, people were always taking their dogs for walks along the beach. Both the people and the pets seemed to enjoy it; maybe we would, too.

I gave the last bites of my breakfast to Digitaria and then led him to Jack's car, which I had parked a few blocks away. After I unlocked the passenger-side door, he jumped right in and faced forward, giving every impression that he was familiar with the idea of car rides. I slid into the driver's seat, turned the key in the ignition and tuned the radio to a station that was playing some hard-line rock and roll.

"We're going to the beach," I said to my dog. "You're going to get to chase some seagulls." At the sound of my voice, Digitaria turned to me, but then quickly went back to looking out the window. "So here we go," I said, as I eased the car out of its parking spot and headed toward Woodhaven Boulevard, which I could follow to Cross Bay Boulevard and out across the causeways and bridges that led to Rockaway.

It was a drive of about forty-five minutes. The last part of the trip took us across a toll bridge that grabbed onto the peninsula right in the middle, on the bay side. Turning left would lead me to the streets where I had spent my summers. Turning right took me in an unfamiliar direction, up toward

~ 155 ~

the northern end of the peninsula which, even years ago, had always been the more affluent area.

At the termination of the bridge, I took the unfamiliar turn to the right. At first, as I drove along, I saw what I expected: a few surf shops, some bars and restaurants, the usual street scene of a seaside town. But then, finally—as if the photos I had seen in the newspaper had sprung into life—I found myself driving past block after block of newly erected town-houses painted the color of foam, decorated with trim work in sandy hues. Some of the buildings were shingled like a glossy magazine's vision of coastal cottages, some bristled with balconies and faux widow's walks. It certainly didn't look like the ruined neighborhood I had encountered last winter, nor did it in any way resemble the Rockaway I remembered from childhood. This was something new, something created to fit a new reality, new people, new money. I felt like a complete stranger here, completely out of place.

There were no spaces available to park along the street— signs warned nonresidents away—so I turned around and drove back toward the more commercial area, where I found a parking spot about a block from the beach. I clipped Digitaria's leash back on his collar, got out of the car and led the dog toward the boardwalk.

In just a couple of weeks, when the summer season officially opened, lifeguards would be stationed at regular intervals along the sand and police cars would be patrolling the boardwalk, so I would never have been able to take Digitaria down to the beach because dogs were officially not permitted. But at this time of year there was no one around to object, so we crossed the boardwalk and went down a wooden ramp to the sand.

Since the day was cool and windy and the sky was overcast, there weren't very many people on the beach, though an occasional group had set up lounge chairs and umbrellas and were playing cards or just chatting. Other people—some singly, some in pairs—were stretched out on towels, reading or listening to the radio. It was a pleasant scene and I felt more at ease here. Now, finally, I was glad I had come.

Digitaria didn't seem so sure. He let me lead him onto the beach but then sat down before we'd gotten halfway to the shoreline and stared out at the ocean, which I suppose he'd never seen before. He tilted his head from side to side as if examining this unexpected vista from every possible angle.

He must have finally decided that this new environment was not threatening, because he soon raised himself off his haunches and trotted down to the water. He began—at first tentatively and then eagerly—to splash around at the edge of the waves as they rolled in and out, growling low in his throat. I assumed he was playing some sort of chasing game with the tide, and unclipped his leash to give him more freedom to run around.

But after just a few minutes of carefree play, he suddenly stopped where he stood, and became absolutely still. I could see his body tense as the chilly seawater bubbled around his feet. Slowly, he turned his head to the left. He sniffed the air. His eyes glittered.

And then, as if a tightly wound spring inside him had been released, he took off running. This happened so fast that he quickly became a vanishing object, already passing the first of the wide stone jetties that separated different sections of the beach from each other, before I reacted. I started running after him, calling his name as loudly as I could. As I ran, people turned their heads to stare at me. One man, thinking to help me, ran toward the dog and tried to grab him, but Digitaria just changed course, swiveling away from the Good Samaritan and sprinting straight up the beach, away from the water, finally disappearing under the boardwalk. He was now running free on the streets. My heart was pounding from running and it was only because I was almost out of breath that I didn't break down into tears. I was sure that I would never see my dog again.

I didn't know what to do, but some part of my brain had kicked into override mode and I found myself running again, this time heading for the car. I found it without even consciously thinking about where I had parked it, got in and started the engine. My first organized thought since I had seen the dog take off down the beach was to drive around, looking for him. What else could I do?

So I drove up and down the streets in an ever-widening grid, stopping to ask people if they had seen a small, thin dog with a tightly curled tail roaming around anywhere. Everyone said no, so I kept driving. I drove for half an hour, and after that, half an hour more. The afternoon was getting later, the weather turning unseasonably cold. And then it began to rain.

Sheets, buckets, pails of water, rain was pouring from the sky. Streams of water formed along the curbsides; rain pooled in potholes and spread across the asphalt roadbed like a watery veneer. For a few minutes, the rain started to come down so heavily that I couldn't see well enough to drive, so I pulled over and let the engine idle.

Then, finally, I did start to cry. To the core of my being, I felt incredibly sad, terribly lonely and completely bereft. I remembered reading once—in the magazine TV Guide, of all places—that maybe it wasn't a good idea to make television shows and movies about pets who are lost or in some kind of trouble because small children tend to identify with small animals in dangerous situations. At that moment, sitting in Jack's car, imprisoned by the rain, that was exactly how I felt—like I was a helpless child and Digitaria was an extension of me, wandering lost and frightened in the rain. I seemed to be reexperiencing every feeling I'd ever had about abandonment, about being estranged from my family long ago, about being on my own for most of my life and too often living near the edge of the economy, supporting myself but just barely, about needing to take care of myself because there was no one else to help me. All of that got mixed up with my terrible sense of responsibility for having lost the dog and the imminent prospect of having to abandon my search and leave him alone in a world where he would face hunger and cruelty and loneliness. I cried until I had the dry heaves. I cried until I just didn't have any tears left. I cried until I felt I had cried for everything bad that had ever happened to me in my whole life.

And then, suddenly, as I was leaning back against the car seat with my eyes closed, feeling exhausted as I listened to the rain continuing to pound on the windshield, an image came into my mind. That's the only way I can explain it. Maybe there was a reason I had thought about the *TV Guide*, because it was like a screen had been turned on somewhere in some viewing theater in the back of my brain and a scene was being projected in a little bright, white square of light. The scene was made up of pixels of memory and intuition, little bits of experience and dreams and stories. It had a fire escape in it and a small dog orbiting Earth in a satellite and my uncle in his worn-out old suit, showing me how to turn the dial on a radio. Before the scene faded away, I had an idea of where Digitaria might be.

The rain was finally beginning to let up just a little as I eased the car back into the street. I left the condos and surf shops behind, heading down the peninsula on the badly torn-up road that ran between the elevated train tracks and the boardwalk—if you could call it a boardwalk, here, where many of the wooden slats were warped or missing and the beach beyond had been overrun by salt grass and tall stands of sea oats. Now, I was driving up and down the same ruined sidewalks, passing the same empty lots that I had passed by last winter. This was a no-man's land of litter and rubble and it was going to take a long time for urban renewal to march its way down to this lonely area and reclaim it with bulldozers and backhoes. It had the look of a place that intended, almost deliberately, to continue its decline. The buried foundations of old bungalows, the piles of rotting, painted planks that used to be stairs and porches seemed more like archaeological relics than urban debris waiting to be replaced with upscale versions of what used to be.

Peering through the rain, I kept watch for the dog as I passed the remnant of each cross street, but I didn't expect to find him yet. I just kept driving until I reached the corner where, up the block, I could see the squat brick box that was the shell of the Sunlite Apartments, framed on either side by the blackened trees that I remembered from the last time I'd been here. The rest of the landscape around me was flat, overgrown with tangled weeds.

I stopped on the edge of the road across from the Sunlite Apartments and turned off the ignition. I sat for a moment, listening to the near silence that now contained only the sharp ticking of the rain on the car's hood and the occasional rattle of sand and pebbles as a gust of wind blew by. Then I opened the door and stepped out into the wet world.

And there he was. My dog, Digitaria. My entire self—blood, spirit, bone—felt flooded with relief.

The dog was sitting on his haunches, on what remained of the sidewalk outside the entrance to the Sunlite Apartments. Previously, I hadn't paid much attention to the entrance of the building, but now I did notice that the front door of the building was gone. That made it possible to see inside, but because it was growing dark, from where I stood on the street, I couldn't pick out any specific structures that might remain. Perhaps some part of the internal staircase was still standing, perhaps some of the apartments were intact, though surely long since claimed by mold and rot. It was impossible for me to know if the dog had tried to get inside, but whatever explorations he might have made were over now and he was simply sitting in the rain, looking at the building and occasionally tilting his head from side to side.

As I walked up beside him, he acknowledged me by moving closer and then leaning against my leg, the way he did at home. I picked up his leash, and wrapped it firmly around my hand. He turned his head and stared at me with those dark, glittering eyes.

I tugged on the leash but he didn't seem to want to move. He turned back to face the building and then, suddenly, let out a loud yip—a high-pitched, disturbing sound that was something like the noise he'd made when I had come home late, but more urgent. The sound seemed to linger in the night air until the wind swept it away.

After a few more moments of staring intently at the gaping hole where the front door of the building had once been, the dog finally let me lead him back across the street to the car. He jumped in and moved over to the passenger seat. Once I slid into the driver's side, the dog managed to maneuver his body so that he was lying flat across the seat with his head in my lap. Soon, we were driving back across the bridge and Digitaria was fast asleep. A few times as I was driving, he continued to make that yipping sound, and though it was much softer now, coming from somewhere deep in his sleep, it still made me wonder just what it was that he might be dreaming about.

"A pedophile?" I said to Jack. "*That's* what they think you are? And they actually think they have some kind of evidence for this?"

"You don't need evidence nowadays," Jack said. "You just make accusations. And then you repeat them on some listener's blog and before you know it—wham. Tried and convicted. Oh, yes—and did I tell you I might also be a drug dealer, a rapist and possibly the Antichrist? The Pope himself might issue an encyclical denouncing me because I promulgate degenerate theories about the sex life of the saints."

"Well, you did have on that medium who claimed to be able to channel Joan of Arc and apparently she and one of her soldiers did not have a totally chaste relationship."

Jack let out a long sigh. "Great," he said. "*That* was one of the shows you tuned into."

It was a warm Sunday night. In just a few days, the weather had shaken off its late spring chill and turned almost sultry. Jack and I were sitting at a table outside a restaurant on Seventh Avenue South, in the Village and he was telling me about his trip to Los Angeles, which clearly had not gone very well.

"But you told me they've been carrying your show for years. They know you. Why would they believe things like that?"

"Because there's money involved. Blue Star Communications seems to have limitless amounts of it and they're telling my bosses that they want to buy the company but won't honor the contracts of anyone who's morally unfit."

"The Blue Awareness has an issue about morals? Maybe they can just hook you up to a Blue Box and cure you of your degenerate tendencies."

Jack frowned at me. "Yeah, well. They didn't offer me that remedy. All they're going to do is buy out the rest of my contract, which just had a couple of months to run on it anyway, so they make out like bandits and I'm screwed."

"But you're going to sign on with World Air, right?" That's what Jack had told me when he'd called me to arrange getting together tonight. Ostensibly, we were meeting so I could return his car to him, but I had also assumed that we were going to have a celebratory drink to toast the World Air deal. Now the situation seemed a lot less worthy of a celebration.

"I don't have a choice," Jack replied. "I have to say, though, I'm not as thrilled with what they're offering as I thought I'd be. I mean, I thought they'd offer more. The deal on the table is two hours, from midnight to two A.M., five nights a week, on what they call their alternative talk channel. The problem is that my listeners aren't exactly the kind of people who subscribe to satellite radio. There's a big difference between what comes to you free, over the air, and something you have to not only pay an annual fee for but also have to go out and buy some special equipment to even get involved in listening. Would you do that?" he challenged me.

I thought about it for a minute. "I might," I said.

"Yeah, you might. But then, you're a radio freak."

"Am I?"

Finally, Jack laughed. "You don't know that? Boy, have you got your uncle's disease. Same as I do. Everybody else is watching TV or surfing the web, but people like you and me . . . I don't know. There's something about turning on that little box and hearing voices come out of the air. It's kind of tied up with nighttime, right? And for a lot of people, with working. People driving trucks and cabs, guys working night shifts . . ."

"Bartenders," I added.

"Exactly. Night people. Strange, angry, weird, bored, curious, sure they're being duped by the higher-ups who really control the levers of power . . ."

Now he had me laughing. "Well, we are, aren't we?"

"Of course. Probably since the beginning of time. What's scary, though, is people like Raymond Gilmartin having that kind of power. What is he but a rich guy who's running a cult empire based on a bunch of science fiction books? Just my luck, they decided to diversify into media. And then picked me as a target."

"Maybe you should be flattered," I suggested. "They apparently think you have some influence."

"I doubt it, really," Jack replied. "I don't think Raymond Gilmartin and his Blue Awareness disciples can distinguish between who's just an irritation and who's a real enemy. To them, everyone who isn't with them is an enemy."

Now he was sounding gloomy again; his few moments of lightheartedness had quickly fled. It was surprising to me to experience this side of him. Up until now, I had thought of Jack as a kind of unrepentant optimist. But even for him, apparently, there were a limited number of bright sides of life he could find a way to look on.

We parted around nine o'clock. He went to collect his car, which I had parked a block or so away, and I headed for the subway. When I got home, Digitaria, as usual, was waiting by the door. He was used to getting a walk at night, so I obliged him, putting on his leash and leading him downstairs.

Except for the one furtive truck lurking in an alley with its running lights on, the neighborhood was deserted, almost silent. I led the dog down to the end of the block, meaning to cross the street and walk him along the chain-link fence that bordered the marshy shore of the bay.

Just as I stepped off the curb, a van came careening down the block. I heard the sound off to my right and pulled the dog, who was a few steps ahead of me, back to the safety of the sidewalk. Holding tight to his leash, I moved back a couple of feet and waited for what I assumed was some kind of crazy drunken driver to pass by.

Only, that wasn't what happened. The van came to an abrupt halt right in front of me, deliberately blocking my path. For a moment, I still thought that what I was confronting was just an impaired driver—until two men stepped out of the back of the van.

I knew immediately that this was a very bad situation, but was frozen in one of those moments where your eyes register what's happening but your brain refuses to respond by initiating any kind of useful action. I saw the men walking— no, running—toward me, but did nothing. The dog, however, experienced no such hesitation. He reacted before I did.

I heard a sound come out of him that was bone-chilling— a growl that ended in yet another version of his strange, high-pitched yipping. This sound was clearly meant to be interpreted as both a warning and a challenge. I felt him stiffen at the end of the leash and then, in an instant, he pulled at the strap so hard that it ripped in half. The next thing I saw was Digitaria rushing at the two men.

He stopped just before he reached them, standing straight and still, with his tail coiled behind him like a hook. He bared his teeth and continued to emit his strange warning sounds. My thin shadow of a dog suddenly seemed deadly mean.

I hadn't noticed it before—that frozen-brain blindness, I guess—but the two men had obscured their features by wearing yellow ski goggles, which gave them a bizarre appearance. Focusing on that for just a moment, whatever part of my mind was still logically processing information sent me a question: *yellow* goggles? Couldn't they have found some that were blue?

But logical thinking was once again overcome by the kind of panic that takes away your sense, your breath and your voice. I watched them advance toward the dog, thinking they meant to walk past him to get to me. I knew I should at least start screaming, but I couldn't seem to remember how.

Instead of moving toward me though, the men turned to the dog. One of them was holding a rope with a loop at the end. With a quick motion, he attempted to slip it over Digitaria's head, but he never got the chance because, in an instant, the dog went into a frenzy.

Yowling like a mad thing, he leapt at the man with the rope and locked onto his arm. Then he let go and leapt at the other man, who had a box cutter in his hand. The sudden, terrifying notion that he might actually kill my dog brought back my voice. I started to scream for help.

That must have been what summoned another pair of men, who came running from behind the truck that was parked in the alley. One had a tire chain in his hand and the other was carrying an iron crowbar.

At this point, one of the two men in the yellow goggles had gotten hold of the torn piece of Digitaria's leash that was still attached to his collar and was trying to drag the dog into the van, but each time they pulled at him, he spun around and sank his teeth into an arm, a leg, a hand . . .

My rescuers looked like the guys I see around the airport all the time—the ones out on the runway, or in the back lots, loading cargo or driving big, dented vehicles that haul things or move them or clear them away—tough, burly guys with scraped hands and meaty faces. But they moved quickly; in an instant, it seemed, they had positioned themselves between me and the men in the ski goggles.

The confrontation between the ski-goggle guys and the men from the truck was over almost before it started. As the truckers approached, one of the goggle men weakly waved his box cutter around, but all that got him was a solid whack with the tire chain that quickly brought him to his knees. The truckers soon had both attackers pinned against the side of their van, weapons raised as if they were going to lop off their opponents' heads in some grisly, slasher-movie fashion, using the chain and crowbar. Instead, they dragged them around to the back of the van, ripped open the doors and tossed the two men inside. Then, after slamming the doors shut, the guy with the crowbar banged on the back of the truck so hard he left a visible dent.

I hadn't realized that there was someone else in the van, but my rescuers must have seen him. Immediately, whoever it was gunned the engine and the van took off down the street, quickly disappearing into the darkness. In the silence that followed, I could hear the sound of water lapping against the rocks at the edge of the marshy shore just yards away, beyond the chain-link fence.

It was suddenly quiet; the dog had stopped yowling. Then he turned, ran a few steps and leaped into my arms. He was a small dog but still too big, really, to hold like that, and surprisingly heavy. And he was covered with blood—his, the attackers, I didn't know. He was panting like he couldn't catch his breath.

I couldn't hold him, so I had to put him down. Immediately, he went into his characteristic stance of leaning against my leg. The truckers, who had waited in the road for a few moments, watching after the fleeing van, now walked back toward me. They were grinning, as if the minifight they'd just engaged in had turned out to be an unexpected pleasure.

One of them looked over at me and said, "You're the bartender, aren't you?"

I nodded. "I work at the airport," I said.

He nodded. "Don't we all?" he replied, which brought a loud guffaw from his companion. I decided to treat the remark as philosophy; I couldn't imagine it would do any of us any good if I could suddenly place my rescuers, put them in a uniform and picture them working some late-night shift on one of Kennedy's back lots, loading and unloading crates of valuable goods that sometimes got misplaced.

Still chuckling over his friend's joke, the second man said, "So, bartender, are you okay?"

"Yes," I lied. And it was a lie, a big one. The shock of what had just happened was really beginning to hit me now. I was shaking inside, feeling wave after wave of fear, anger— and worry about how badly hurt the dog might be.

"You know, if you'd ever like to sell that dog, I might be interested," the first of my two new friends said. "Did someone train him to fight like that?"

"I don't think so," I said, looking down at Digitaria, who continued to lean against my leg. "But maybe."

I thanked the men, and they good-naturedly waved at me as they walked away. It was when their backs were turned toward me that I saw another van come around the corner— but this one posed no danger. It was a black vehicle commonly called a dollar van. These illegal, low-cost vans and black cars regularly prowled the outer borough neighborhoods where regular taxis were never to be found. I flagged it down and climbed in, hauling my dog with me.

The van already had three other passengers who all just shoved over on the bench seats to make room for me and the dog. I told the driver where I wanted to go and sat back, clutching the dog's leash. No one said a word about the fact that the dog was covered in blood. I assumed that I probably had his blood all over my clothes now, too.

The van weaved its way through the local streets, letting passengers off in front of different houses, all with unlit windows and the look of structures somehow sagging beneath the dark weight of the night. I recognized these places—they were, in a way, the modern-day equivalent of the Sunlite Apartments—rooming houses for immigrant families, where a lot of people lived together in a few small rooms. At some point in the journey, I realized that the van driver had the radio on. He was listening to a talk radio program being broadcast in Spanish. I couldn't understand what was being said but I could make out two distinctly different voices, one edged with sarcasm, the other sounding incredulous, like neither believed what the other was saying. It was the kind of radio Jack and I had been talking about earlier—could it be that was just hours ago? Late night radio—radio for the workers, the up-all-nighters, the sleepless and the strange.

I was the last to be dropped off. That was how it worked with these black vans: the last one in was the last one out. It probably wouldn't have mattered if I had a knife stuck in my side; I had to wait my turn. When it finally came, I gave the driver a few dollars and then led the dog into the vet's office I had taken him to some weeks back. I remembered seeing a sign in the window saying they offered twenty-four-hour emergency service, and even though it was now past midnight, they were indeed open. I wasn't sure how badly the dog had been hurt but I had brought him here because I didn't want to take any chances.

Through the glass door, I could see a young woman sitting at the desk, leafing through a magazine. I buzzed to be let in and led Digitaria into the quiet office.

Seeing the dog striped with blood, the girl became instantly concerned. "Poor doggie," she said. "What happened to you?"

I almost started to tell her, but the story was just too complicated and much too long. Instead, I said that I had been mugged, adding. "The dog jumped at the two guys who came at us and I think they may have cut him." I saw her reaching for forms that I knew she was going to hand me, so I stopped her. "We were here just a few weeks ago. Perzin," I told her, spelling my name. "We must be in your system."

She turned to her computer, found Digitaria in her records, and then led us into an examining room. There were no other patients in the office tonight, she said, so the doctor would be with us in just a minute.

As we waited, Digitaria leaned against my leg again. I looked down at him and saw that his eyes were closed. It was possible that he was even asleep.

The vet did come in very shortly. He was a different doctor than the one I'd seen when I was here before but similar in manner and appearance: young, efficient, sympathetic. I told him a more detailed version of what had happened, and he lifted the dog onto a metal examining table.

"He's got a bad cut on his leg," the vet said. "I think that's where most of the blood came from. I'm going to have to put in a few stitches, but I think he'll be fine."

"He kind of went crazy," I said. "It was pretty amazing."

The vet patted the dog on the head. "You're a very good boy," he said to Digitaria. "I'll bet the other guys are in much worse shape."

As he began to work on the dog, the vet asked me if I'd called the police. I hadn't even thought of that; everything had happened very quickly, and once the attackers had been chased off, my main thought was about getting help for Digitaria.

"I guess I should do that," I said.

The vet told me I could sit outside while he stitched up the dog, so I left the examining room. The girl stayed with them, so I was alone in the front room. It was nearly one A.M. now, and very quiet. The phones weren't ringing and even the traffic outside had slowed down. The only sound that interrupted the peace was the ticking of a wall clock shaped like a black cat wearing a rhinestone-studded collar. Its long plastic tail swished back and forth with the beats of the second hand.

I got out my cell phone, thinking about how I was about to tell the police another crazy story, but before I could dial a number, it rang. The sound was startling because it was so unexpected. I almost dropped the phone as I fumbled to flip it open. I thought that maybe it was Jack—as if he somehow could have learned what had happened to me—but the number displayed on the phone was one I didn't know.

"Hello?" I said.

A man's voice responded. The tone was smooth, but slightly urgent. "I hope you're all right," the voice said to me.

"Who is this?" I asked.

The reply was without hesitation. "Raymond Gilmartin."

I had to take a moment to process that information. *Raymond Gilmartin? Really?* For whatever reason, what came into my mind at that moment was the title he had been referred to by in the threatening letter I'd received about the Blue Box: *Chairman of the Board of the Religious Technology Center of the Blue Awareness.* Well, I had a pretty good idea of what the Chairman wanted to talk about. And I wanted to talk about it, too. In fact, just as I was in the middle of more or less accusing him of attempted murder, he cut me off.

"Laurie," he said, using my name in a way that implied a familiarity I immediately resented, "please let me assure you that no one I know tried to hurt you." His voice was smooth, his tone measured, supremely confident.

"Okay, so we're going to play a word game. They tried to hurt my dog."

"Why would anyone do that?"

"You tell me," I said.

My question was met with silence. This was another game, one of control. He wasn't going to respond to me unless he felt like it.

I probably should have hung up the phone, but at the moment, my self-control wasn't any match for his. I was too upset. "Why are you calling me?" I demanded.

As it turned out, that question he did have an answer for. "I'd like to meet you," Gilmartin said.

I glanced at my watch. "It's nearly one o'clock in the morning and you're calling me because you'd like to meet me? Seriously?"

"I'm often up late. I hear that you are, too."

"Well, right now I'm up late because I'm in the vet's office where my dog is getting stitches because we were attacked by a pair of lunatics wearing ski goggles. Sound like anyone you know?"

Gilmartin didn't miss a beat; he just added a note of concern to his voice. "I hope the dog is all right," he said. "Why don't you bring him with you when you come by?"

"Come by where?" I replied. "And who says I'm agreeing to meet you, anyway?"

"Sometimes things get out of hand," Gilmartin said. "Don't you find that happens? I mean, as life goes on. But I think if we met and talked for a while, we could repair some of the damage."

"The damage? Do you mean everything you did to me? The break-in, the blue paint, the attack tonight—did I leave anything out?"

Gilmartin completely ignored what I'd said. "The damage piles up," he said, continuing his own train of thought. "You went to see one of our members, Ravenette, for help. She feels very badly that she couldn't convince you to let her advance your state of Awareness. That's why I'm calling. That's why I'd like to see you."

"Just about everything you just said is a lie, and you know it."

"Come by tomorrow," he said smoothly. "Seven o'clock." Then he gave me an address on the Upper West Side of Manhattan. "Damage can be repaired," he said. "It's just a matter of understanding our true nature and doing some real work on ourselves."

"What a revelation," I said, but Raymond Gilmartin had already hung up the phone.

A few minutes later, the vet led Digitaria out to the waiting room. He had a bandage on his leg and looked a little scraped up, but as soon as he saw me, he began tugging on the new leash that the vet had attached to his collar. Dragging the vet with him, he pulled himself toward me and then, as if settling himself in for the night, leaned against my leg and closed his eyes.

"He certainly seems strong enough," the vet said, handing the leash over to me. I handed over my credit card and started calculating how many overtime hours I was going to have to work to pay for this. The damages did indeed pile up, though maybe not the way Raymond Gilmartin had meant.

In fact, this whole thing was getting so complicated I thought it might be better if I tried to explain it to some cop in person, using my wounded dog as exhibit A. I left the vet's office and flagged down another dollar van, asking to be taken to the local precinct. I thought the driver was going to refuse—there were already other passengers in the van and it was clear by the looks I got that none of them wanted go anywhere near the police station—but eventually, he dropped me off in the part of Queens where the court buildings were. This wasn't exactly where I'd wanted to go, but I didn't complain because I guess it served as a compromise. Here, at least, the driver could pick up more fares since it was the hour that night court was closing down and people who had to be there—thieves, burglars, drunks and assorted mischief makers, along with their relatives who came to bail them out—would be looking for rides.

The entrance to night court was around the side of the Queens Criminal Court building. The structure looked more imposing under the high summer moon than it did during the day when office workers and high school students on class trips ate their lunches on the wide flight of stone steps leading up to what otherwise seemed like just another hulking, boxlike building squatting on the dark bedrock of central Queens. Now, as the last of those who had business in the court climbed into the cruising dollar vans or simply walked off into the night, it was like being on a deserted movie set. Leading the dog, I walked past the complex of now-shuttered municipal buildings that included the court and a surrounding host of fortress-like brick edifices that housed lawyers and bail bondsmen. The police station was at the end of the block.

Inside, the first officer I saw told me I couldn't bring the dog into the station. When I explained what I was there for and that there was no way I was going to leave the dog tied up outside, he finally sent me to another floor to talk to someone. I had to wait for a while, sitting on a hard bench while Digitaria slept at my feet. When a detective led me to his desk half an hour later—a big, beefy man with an unmistakable Jersey accent—he listened to me with considerable attention, but I knew that the more I talked, the crazier my story sounded. It even sounded that way to me: stolen radios, African dogs, the possibility that the Blue Awareness was targeting me for a reason I wasn't sure I understood anymore. (Could this, really, now all be about a radio antenna? Seriously?) I didn't think that even the fact that there was a report on file about what I insisted was the related break-in at my apartment made me sound any more credible. I also told the detective about the phone call from Raymond Gilmartin, and though that seemed to pique his interest just a little after I explained who Gilmartin was, I didn't think even that was going to get me very far. I left the police station half an hour later with what sounded like a half-hearted promise that the attack would be investigated and a copy of yet another police report. Outside, I started looking for another roaming dollar van to take me home.

When I finally walked back into my apartment, it was almost dawn. I stripped off my clothes and more or less fell into bed. The dog jumped up after me and despite everything he'd been through, took up his usual post at the end of the bed, facing the front door. Digitaria was still on duty.

When I woke up a few hours later, there was a moment when I couldn't recall whether I had to go to work or not. I felt exhausted and groggy, and was greatly relieved to finally remember that this was one of my days off this week.

I had breakfast, fed the dog and then took him for a walk. I had some qualms about leaving the apartment, but I had to get over my reluctance because the dog had to go out. He exhibited no such hesitation but patiently waited by the door for his collar and leash to be put on, as usual.

Outside, I noted that the truck that had been hiding in the alley last night was gone and so were the men who had helped me. In the light of day, everything that had happened seemed unreal. I wanted to go on feeling that way, to compartmentalize enough to not think about last night, but I wasn't very successful. When I returned to my apartment, I finally tried going back to sleep for a while, doing my best to block out not only unwelcome thoughts but also the noise of a weekday morning in automobile alley. Today, in particular, it sounded like somebody was deliberately grinding the gears of a dozen rust buckets right outside my window, or crunching up cars in some evil car-killing machine.

I did feel a little better when I woke up again in the afternoon. I sat on the edge of the bed for a while, thinking about what I should do. Digitaria watched me, with his head tilted to the side.

Finally, I picked up the phone and called Jack. "So listen," I said, "what are your plans for tonight?"

"The usual," he said. "I have to go on the air later, so there's stuff I need to go over. I've got an ex-navy fighter pilot who says he was tailed by UFOs a couple of times when he was doing bombing runs over North Vietnam."

"Can you reschedule him? Play a tape or something?" I said. "I mean, what difference does it make? They've already fired you. You'll be gone in a couple of weeks."

On the other end of the phone, Jack was silent for a few minutes. Finally, he said, "Okay, Laurie. Why don't you tell me what's happened now?"

And so I did.

~XII~

"**I** still can't believe he actually called you," Jack said. "Raymond Gilmartin doesn't talk to actual *people*. Supposedly the only human beings who see him live and in living color are the celebrities. The Ted Merrill types. The hoi polloi only get to see taped messages from him now and then."

"Well, it should be an interesting visit," I replied.

"And you'll really bring the dog."

"He suggested it."

"Well, I wish someone had suggested to me that I bring some sort of weapon. Or maybe at least left a note behind—you know, the kind of thing that says, 'If I don't come back, look for DNA evidence at the Blue Awareness Center on Riverside Drive.'"

"We do have a weapon," I said, patting the dog's head. We were in Jack's car, just passing over the Fifty-Ninth Street Bridge, and Digitaria was sitting next to me on the passenger seat. He was looking out the window, his dark eyes fixed on the passing scenery blurring into the summer twilight. "He's already got two bad guys to his credit."

Jack frowned. "I thought he needed some help."

"He never stopped fighting," I said. "It was really something to see."

Jack and I both fell silent then. He concentrated on navigating the river of traffic and I tried to make myself as still as the dog was now, just watching the other cars rush along beside us, the lights coming on in the tall apartment buildings

~ 176 ~

along the east side of Manhattan. I had no idea what was going to happen tonight but I had a feeling that cultivating an inner stillness would be helpful. Maybe that was some old hippie idea still rattling around in my head or something I'd heard recommended on some TV program about creating a better you. Either way, given the circumstances, it seemed like a useful thing to do.

It took almost as long to get crosstown from the east side to the west as it had to drive all the way from my place in Queens, where Jack had picked me up, to Manhattan. Once we reached Riverside Drive, we started looking for the address Gilmartin had given me, which turned out to be a townhouse on a quiet, curving block facing the Hudson. Miraculously, we found a place to park just a block away. Then we walked back to the townhouse, a four-story edifice of white stone with a columned portico. There was a brass plaque on the gate that barred entrance to the walkway leading to the massive front door. The plaque had no name on it, just the street address.

I pushed the button on a nearby buzzer, announced who I was, and shortly, Jack and I were let in. The front door was opened for us by a pleasant-looking young woman dressed in the kind of fashionable suit and slacks that anyone her age would have worn in any business office anywhere in the city. She led us to an elevator—an old-fashioned contraption with velvety wallpaper that barely held the three of us, plus the dog—which we exited on the top floor. As we walked down a carpeted hallway, our guide made small talk, telling us that the building had been converted from a gilded-age private home to an embassy for one of the Central American nations, which had sold it ten years ago when it had been converted yet again to serve as the New York center of the Blue Awareness; there were similar headquarters in Los Angeles and Miami. This particular building had offices, conference rooms, and a large auditorium on the first floor where seminars were sometimes held. Tonight, she said, there were no events on the schedule, but a number of staff members, like herself, were working late. And of course, she said, Raymond and his assistants were always here until all hours. There was, she continued cheerfully, always so much work to be done.

"Sure," Jack whispered to me, when she moved a few steps ahead of us to open the door to a room at the end of hallway, "lives to be ruined, plots to be plotted . . ."

I put my hand on his arm, which I hoped he read as a signal to cut out the sarcastic remarks. I was still trying to stay in my zone of stillness; I didn't trust myself not to have an instant reaction of hostility to anything Raymond Gilmartin had to say, but that wasn't what I wanted. The instinct that had warned me to quiet myself in the car was now telling me to be smart about this encounter. I wasn't at all sure what Raymond Gilmartin wanted from me, but I didn't think I would find out by being antagonistic.

The young woman opened a door, ushered us into an office and then left us alone. Jack and I were now standing in a large room that had tall windows curtained with heavy fabric in a deep purple color. That was the only vaguely magisterial characteristic about the décor, which was otherwise very businesslike. There was a wide desk that held a computer with two screens, a leather couch, some chairs, a simple area rug on the floor bordered in the same purple as the drapes, a low coffee table that held a silver carafe on a tray along with half a dozen water glasses. Bookshelves lined one entire wall; I walked over to look at the titles and saw that several shelves were taken up by Howard Gilmartin's novels and non-fiction writings. The majority of the other volumes focused on a host of esoteric subjects including spiritualism, mysticism, time travel, alien abduction, reincarnation, Egyptian beliefs about the afterlife and the complete works of Edgar Cayce. If these were really Raymond Gilmartin's books, he was apparently interested in ideas that were outside the boundaries of his own religion, which I thought was somewhat surprising.

In fact, the selection of books could have served as resource material for Jack's nightly lineup of guests. I said as much to him, but he didn't seem to like the comparison.

We were only in the office for a short time before the door opened again and Raymond Gilmartin entered the room. Another surprise—he was alone. I had expected a retinue: lawyers, bodyguards, some entourage of hangers-on. But there was no one. I also expected him to seat himself behind his imposing desk but, instead, he walked over to the couch and gestured for us to join him in this more informal part of the room.

As we arranged ourselves in the chairs and the dog settled himself against my leg, I had a moment to study the leader of the Blue Awareness. He was, I thought, in his midforties, somewhere near my age. He was thin, blade-like in his movements, with dark hair, dark eyes, and a serious demeanor. He was dressed in a charcoal-gray suit, with a matching tie. He struck me immediately as a man without humor, an individual who exuded a sense of great calm when in reality, inside himself he could not rest. I had been feeling so edgy myself lately that perhaps I was simply identifying someone who was in the same state—although certainly, he had a great deal to do with my uneasiness, while I couldn't imagine that I had any influence on his.

He poured us all a glass of water and then sat back against the couch. "I appreciate your coming here," he said to me. And then he added, "I see you've brought a friend."

"You know Jack Shepherd," I told him.

"Do I?"

"Sure you do," Jack said, with mock cheerfulness. "I'm the guy whose life you're trying so hard to ruin."

Gilmartin frowned. "Why would I do that?"

"I have a radio show, *Up All Night*. At least I did, until your company bought out my distributor. Anyway, I've had a lot of ex-Awares on lately and they've been telling on you."

"I can't imagine what there is to tell," Gilmartin said. His voice was measured, calm.

Jack wagged his finger at Gilmartin. "Oh, come on now. You people do some pretty crazy stuff. You rough up members who try to leave; sometimes, I hear, you kidnap them and keep them locked up in some reeducation camp out in New Mexico. You encourage Awares to separate from even close family who won't join your group. You send members' children to special schools where you teach them that everything every normal school teaches is false doctrine and only Awares know the truth about the world, which is that we're all asleep, we believe in false prophets, the only real one being your father, Howard, who is . . . what? What is it that you people say about him? Oh yes, he's sailing around the world solo, writing a new book, expanding on Awareness Doctrine even though he would be way over one hundred years old now. He must be one hale and hearty guy. And he's due back soon, I hear, along with the aliens who are our true ancestors, the shadow men from beyond our universe . . ."

Gilmartin waved his hand, as if he were bored. "That's enough, don't you think? You don't know anything about us. Or about me or my father. In any case," he continued, "I don't remember inviting you. So perhaps you might temper your behavior just a bit."

I actually agreed with him. Jack's outburst had taken me completely by surprise. I knew he was angry at Gilmartin, but it had never occurred to me that he would behave like this. Maybe it should have, but it didn't. If anything, I had expected him to be the voice of reason here, the grown-up, but that wasn't how things were going. And this wasn't at all how I wanted the meeting to begin.

But Jack stayed on the same track. After Gilmartin's admonition, he seemed to rear back, as if he had been struck. "Listen, you jerk . . ."

"What is it you want?" I asked Gilmartin, deliberately interrupting Jack. If this meeting devolved into some kind of name-calling fiesta, I wasn't going to learn anything I needed to know in order to get my life back to some semblance of what it had been before all this craziness started. "You've got my radio and the box my uncle built," I reminded him. "Let's just not pretend that you don't. The horn of plenty antenna is long gone as far as I know, so I couldn't give it to you even if I had it. There's nothing else that connects us, so why do you keep after me? I mean, you had a pair of goons try to take my dog away from me last night. What were you going to do? Try to trade him back to me for the antenna? I told Ravenette that I don't have it. You're going to have to believe me because it's the truth."

"I would never have told anyone to do anything that would harm that dog," Gilmartin said.

"Oh really? Two men in ski goggles came out of a van and tried to grab him."

"That had nothing to do with me."

I closed my eyes for a moment and took a deep breath. There were a few things I could do at this point: get angry, like Jack; burst into tears, which part of me felt like doing; or keep going round and round with accusations and denials. None of these was a useful path to follow; none would get me any relief. So I tried something else, I tried, simply, to be human.

"Mr. Gilmartin," I began . . .

"Raymond."

"Okay, Raymond—just tell me how to make all this stop. How we can arrange things so you go your way and I go mine. I can't live my life waiting for the next crazy thing to happen."

"No, of course not," Gilmartin said. He took a sip of water and then leaned forward. "And so you see, there is something that connects us—because we believe, as you so clearly do, that no one's life should be chaotic and unpredictable. Once we understand our true nature and devote ourselves to getting closer to it, everything improves. Our work, our relationships . . ."

"I guess my true nature is to be a pain in the ass," Jack said, unable to keep quiet any longer. Then he pointed at me. "And don't think this one is a pushover, either. Still waters run deep and all that."

I was actually beginning to find Jack annoying, and to feel that he was working against me. I knew he probably couldn't help himself for behaving the way he was and it was probably my own lack of empathy that hadn't permitted me—perhaps until this moment—to really understand the depth of his fury. Perhaps there were other factors at work, too, but he was still reeling from being forced off the air. It didn't matter that he had a deal in place to relocate his show; he had been bested by people he didn't like—and didn't respect—and because of that, he couldn't contain his anger.

Jack's remark, however, had no effect on Gilmartin. He simply ignored him and continued to address himself only to me. His next comment, though, involved the other member of our little visitors group. "Your dog," he said. "He is interesting looking. A little darker colored than they usually are. Am I right? I mean, he is a Dogon dog, isn't he?"

"Yes," I replied. I was surprised that he had identified Digitaria's origins. "How did you know?"

As was apparently his habit, Gilmartin didn't reply to questions until—and if—he felt like it. So, instead of answering what I'd asked, he had a question of his own. "Can I pet him?"

This was an even stranger question, I thought. I wasn't sure if it was a tacit admission that last night did involve the Blue Awareness, and Gilmartin was well aware that the dog could be aggressive, or if he was simply—in his own weird way—being polite by asking permission.

"All right," I said. Then I looked down at my dog. "Be nice," I told him.

Gilmartin got up from the couch and approached the dog slowly. Then, bending down, he gently touched the dog's head. He patted Digitaria a couple of times, while the dog mostly ignored him.

"What's his name?" Gilmartin asked me.

"Digitaria," I told him.

For the first time, Gilmartin almost smiled. "Is it really?" he said. "That's extremely interesting. Extremely." He stood up and started walking toward the bookcase. "I want to show you something," he said.

He reached for an object that was on a high shelf and carefully carried it back to us. Handing it to me, he said, "Look at this. It's very old."

What he had given me was a rock—a heavy, solid object with a smooth black surface. I saw that it had a carving on one side, and held it so that Jack, who pulled his chair closer to mine, could see it, too.

Holding it in my hand, I had no doubt that the rock was old, just as Gilmartin suggested, or perhaps even ancient; it just had that feeling about it. So did the pictograph that had been carved on its surface. The carving was simple, but that somehow made it appear even more powerful. Under a diagram of dots and lines that I couldn't identify, three beings stood together, The first seemed to be a human, rendered as a kind of genderless line drawing. The second was also humanlike in that it appeared to have arms, legs and a head, but it was hard to identify where the boundaries of the figure stopped and plain rock surface began because this being was made up of tiny lines, like scrapes, so that it appeared to be more of a blur than a solid shape. Between these two figures stood the third being, a small dog, thin and compact, with an angular head shaped like an anvil and a tightly curled tail.

As soon as I focused on the figure of the dog, what had happened last night suddenly made a different kind of sense to me. Digitaria wasn't meant to be traded for anything—not even the horn of plenty antenna. He was important all by himself. "This is why you wanted my dog," I said to Gilmartin as I pointed to the little dog scratched into the rock.

"I told you, I never even suggested to anyone that they try to take your dog from you," Gilmartin replied.

"Really? Then let me get this straight. Breaking into someone's apartment to steal stuff is okay. But stealing a dog is off-limits?"

"Even the detective who got in touch with us earlier today thought that accusation was reaching a bit. I believe they might actually be under the impression that, with all these complaints you've been making, it's you who's harassing us."

So, great. Now I knew that while the police report I had filed last night had resulted in some kind of action, once again, the outcome was going to be that absolutely nothing was going to happen.

"So now what do I have to do, Raymond? Worry that every time I take the dog for a walk some fanatic is going to try to snatch him from me?"

"I can't imagine why you think that," Gilmartin responded, pronouncing each word carefully. "The only thing I can tell you is that sometimes, people become overzealous in their desire to fulfill another person's wishes. But, at least hypothetically, one can explain to those people that they have gone a bit too far."

That, I gathered, was meant to reinforce what he had said earlier, that trying to take my dog from me had nothing, specifically, to do with the Blue Awareness. Maybe the men involved were Awares but they were acting outside the boundaries of Blue Awareness teachings, or any direct instructions from their leader. I wondered if Gilmartin thought this would make me feel better about what happened—or at least, somehow better about him.

"How did you even know I had the dog?" I asked, as a very creepy thought formed itself in my mind. "Have you been watching me?"

"No one has been watching you," Gilmartin replied. "I am, however, sometimes in contact with Dr. Carpenter. He told me that he had given you the dog. He knows I want one and it seemed to please him to tell me that, while he won't give or even sell me a Dogon dog, he had just handed one over to you."

"I don't understand," I said. I really was completely puzzled. "What does Dr. Carpenter have to do with all this?"

Gilmartin held out his hand to receive the stone back from me. He gave it a thoughtful glance and then looked back at me. "In Mali," he said, "where the Dogon live, this carving would be a national treasure. My father bought it years ago, before there were laws about the purchase and export of cultural heritage items. I hear there is only one other like it, and that's in the national museum. I've offered to make an exchange with Dr. Carpenter: this sacred object for a Dogon dog."

I understood this explanation to mean that Raymond was further underscoring how civilized he was. Even when he did want to trade for something he desired he was open about it, transparent. Well, I was willing to accept that idea—but only up to a point. I could imagine that Dr. Carpenter was in a different category than me; he was a person to be respected, someone with a position, a professional reputation. Who was I? A bartender. Dr. Carpenter could make trouble for Raymond Gilmartin. I, apparently, couldn't even get a New York City cop to take me seriously.

Now Raymond continued with his litany of complaints against Dr. Carpenter. "No matter how much I offer him—relics, money—he refuses me. He just doesn't like me. I suppose it's because we think very differently about . . . well, many things."

Jack, who had been mercifully quiet for a while, now jumped back into the conversation. "Well, who *would* think like you?" he demanded. Then, turning to me, he said, "Have you figured out what our friend Raymond here is doing? He's collecting touchstones—or trying to. The radio, the antenna, even your dog. I'll bet he believes that if he can get his hands on the objects that influenced his father's writings he can get closer to . . . well, to be honest, I'm not sure what he wants to do." Addressing Gilmartin again he said, "Are you trying to bring them back? The boys from the Wild Blue Yonder? You believe the visitors who came to the Dogon are the same beings that Laurie calls the radiomen. The beings your father described as looking like shadows—like that figure carved on the rock. The ones who made the same kind of sound your father described. They hissed at the Dogon—and your dad. I'm right, aren't I?"

Without even waiting for Gilmartin to reply, Jack went on, spitting out his words. "So what do you do? Sit here and rub your hands over the rock hoping to summon them? Or do you and Ravenette hook yourselves up to Blue Boxes and try to channel them? Wait," Jack said, with a sarcastic little cackle, "I've got another guess: you were going to use Avi Perzin's old radio and antenna to broadcast a message telling them you've found their lost dog."

"You know what?" Gilmartin said. "I think I've had enough of you now. You spend so much time trying to defame us, you've lost your own way."

"My *way?*" Jack sputtered. "Who are you to bring up anything like that? I've already told you; my *way* is to go to work every night and talk to people. Yours is to try to stop that."

"So you say," Gilmartin replied. "At the moment, however, you happen to be right. I do want you to stop talking. In fact, I want you to get out of my office."

Suddenly the door opened. I had no idea how Gilmartin had signaled for her, but the cheery young woman who had led us to Gilmartin's office was now standing in the entrance, looking much more officious. Her smile was gone and her posture was stiff.

Jack stood up, but he wasn't about to leave just yet. "Sure you don't want to duke this out on my show? Come on," he said. "Mano a mano." Then he directed a sardonic smile at Gilmartin. "You did know I still have a show, didn't you? I start in a couple of weeks on World Air. Unless you're planning to buy all the communications satellites, too—though come to think of it, maybe that would be better for you than a dog. They'd be like Blue Boxes, circling Earth. You could set them to send signals that would have everyone's engrams running wild. Think of the power you'd have."

"Good night," Gilmartin said quietly. And then he looked at me as if, anticipating the next thing Jack was going to say, he wanted to see every phase of my reaction.

"Let's go, Laurie," Jack said. It sounded like an order.

It was actually the dog who turned his head first, reacting, I guess, to the sound of my name. That gave me an extra moment to think about my response. All the while, I was very conscious of Raymond Gilmartin, and how intensely he was looking at me.

"Not yet," I finally said to Jack. "I'll meet you at the car in a little while."

I saw the color rise to his face. He hadn't expected me to refuse to follow him and, clearly, that was adding to his anger. Without saying another word, he stalked out of the room. The young woman followed after him, closing the door behind her. Now I was alone with Raymond Gilmartin.

He made no comment about Jack, but finally broke his stare. Once more, he looked down at the rock. Touching a fingertip to the diagram above the heads of the carved figures he said, "Do you recognize this? It's the constellation Canis Major."

He was right. I recognized the Great Dog who hunts with Orion, since I had seen the constellation so many times, at night, waiting for the bus to take me home from work.

"And here's Sirius," he said, pointing to the largest dot in the diagram. "The Dog Star. You can't see it, but there's another tiny pinprick next to Sirius. That's its companion star, Digitaria."

Once more, my dog tilted his head, this time, perhaps, to acknowledge his own name.

"Do you think that's where they came from?" Gilmartin suddenly said to me. "I mean, where they entered our universe? From someplace near Sirius?"

"I don't know," I said, surprised by the question. "I don't even know that they're real."

"But you've seen them. Or at least, one of them."

I heard something in his voice that I struggled to describe to myself—longing, maybe. Or envy. Perhaps, I thought, this was the real reason he had wanted me to meet. And I thought something else, as well. That however I might characterize these feelings, they were what had kept me here even as Jack had stormed off. I thought that Raymond Gilmartin was strange and definitely dangerous and yet, somewhere within myself, I had identified an unexpected sense of sympathy for him. On some visceral level, I understood him, or at least, something about him, because as much as we were different, there was something we had in common: we had both been left a legacy that was rooted in the experiences of another person. He had his father, I had Avi. Gilmartin had embraced his inheritance, even enlarged and expanded it, while I had dismissed mine—forgotten it, almost completely— until it had come back to me. Or been given back to me. Certainly not in a way I would have chosen—robbery, assault. The Blue Awareness had a decidedly peculiar way of making friends—but at the moment, I found myself in a forgiving mood. Maybe it was because I understood the feeling of being haunted by things you didn't understand while pretending that you weren't haunted at all, that you were in control, sure of yourself and unassailable in your beliefs and all the decisions you had made about your life and its direction.

"The radiomen," Gilmartin said, perhaps unconsciously using Jack's description to prod me, since I had fallen silent, lost in my thoughts. "You saw them."

"As you said, just one. Maybe."

"They left us unfinished," Gilmartin said. His voice, now, was as soft as a murmur. "There is some process, some . . . metamorphosis we are supposed to go through to reunite with them. We come close . . . all the work we do here is leading us closer to them. I'm sure of it. But there's something missing, something else. Something that we still have to reach for. Search for."

"Did you think that *I* knew what that was? Because I don't. Believe me, I don't."

"Nobody seems to," Gilmartin said sadly. Then I saw him glance over at Digitaria again. And again I felt, from this man, an almost palpable sense of longing.

"He's just a dog," I said, answering a question that had not been asked of me, but I knew what it was, all the same. "Nobody's ever come looking for him—except those men last night."

"I don't think you have to worry that anything like that will ever happen again," Gilmartin said.

"All right," I told him. "I'm going to accept that. From you."

"But if someone . . . someone *else* did come looking for him? Or anything like that? I mean, if you had any idea that he . . . *they* . . ." Raymond shook his head, as if he simply couldn't speak anymore. His sudden silence added to my increasingly keen awareness of how strange a conversation this really had become. Neither of us was saying anything directly, but each knew exactly what the other meant.

"Do you really think that's possible?"

Raymond Gilmartin closed his eyes for a moment. When he found his voice again, he said, in a whisper, "I have been waiting all my life."

What else could there be to add to that? I sat quietly in my chair until he opened his eyes again and then said good night. Digitaria reacted as I stood up, planting himself solidly on his legs and waiting for the next signal about where we were going. I tugged on his leash and led him out the door.

The cheerful young woman who had so quickly turned into a dour functionary was nowhere to be seen, but I was able to find my own way out. Instead of taking the elevator, I led the dog down a wide, winding flight of carpeted stairs. On the ground floor, I found myself back in the reception area where we had started, a brightly lit and high-ceilinged hall where presumably the grand family who had once lived here greeted their guests. But now, except for a different young woman sitting on an ornate bench in front of an even more ornate mirror with a gilded frame, it was deserted. The young woman smiled when she saw me, then rose to punch in some numbers on a keypad next to the front door and let me out into the street.

It was a balmy evening. I walked down the block and crossed at the corner, heading to where Jack had parked the car, but it was gone. I thought, for a moment, that I had made a mistake but then reminded myself that we had parked near a fire hydrant, and Jack had said something about needing to make sure that he was far enough away not to be in danger of getting a ticket. Well, there, right in front of me, was the fire hydrant but the car now occupying the spot we had taken was not Jack's, and he himself was nowhere in sight.

I hung around for a few minutes, unable—or maybe simply unwilling—to accept what had happened, but finally, I had no choice. Apparently, Jack was so angry that he had driven away and left me behind. It was a particularly unkind and thoughtless thing to do because I had the dog, which limited my travel options. He wasn't allowed on the subway or on a bus, which meant I had to take a taxi. That was going to cost a fortune if I had to flag down the yellow taxis that cruised up and down Manhattan. However, there might be one other possibility; but to see if my hunch was right, I had to get out of this high-rent neighborhood.

So I started walking uptown, leading the dog. I was a little worried about him, concerned that he'd be tired since he was still pretty banged up, but he seemed to be doing fine as he trotted beside me, swiveling his head now and then to take in some new sight or odor. It took about fifteen minutes, but eventually, the blocks began to get a little less tidy, the buildings less grandiose, and there was more street life around, more people, music, restaurants.

It was amid the noise and traffic—more or less hidden in plain sight—that I found what I was looking for. With few exceptions, the unspoken rule in New York was that gypsy drivers and dollar vans kept to the outer boroughs and weren't supposed to operate in the heart of the city, But they were always around; you just had to know how to identify them, and I did. Here, at the edges of an edgy neighborhood, I spotted a black car with a certain hard-bitten look about it slipping, like a black ghost, in and out of the stream of traffic. I flagged it down and climbed in beside another passenger who didn't even glance at me or the dog as he jumped in after me, fitting himself into a space between my legs and the door. We soon crossed the bridge over the East River and began driving through the back-door neighborhoods of Queens, dropping off the other passengers and picking up new ones. Apparently, as seemed to be my luck lately, my stop was going to be last. I expected the dog to fall asleep, lulled by the movement of the car, but he didn't. He stayed awake all through the long drive, alert and watchful. Once in a while he would lift his head to look up at me and I could see his eyes glittering in the dark.

I waited until the next day and then called Jack to straighten things out. He didn't answer so I left a message, and then another one in the late afternoon before I went to work. When he still hadn't called back the day after that, I decided that I wasn't going to chase after him. If he wanted to hold on to what was obviously some huge grudge against me for not following him, then so be it. We weren't teenagers who had to test each other's loyalty. If he decided to get back in touch, I'd talk to him. If not, well, a chapter in my life seemed to have closed when I left the Blue Awareness headquarters and if Jack Shepherd was part of that chapter, I didn't think there was much I could do. I didn't leave any more phone messages. The summer days went on.

Toward the end of July, every day seemed to grow warmer than the one before. Temperatures, the TV news reported, were soaring to record highs. When I walked the dog in the morning, by the fence near the bay, I took to carrying a bottle of water with me. Digitaria never seemed to mind the heat but I did, and often found myself trying to cool off by splashing water on my face. Later in the day, waiting for the bus under the hot city sky was an endlessly uncomfortable experience. I kept the small air conditioner in my bedroom running on a timer so that when I returned at night, at least one room in the house was habitable. Once I did get home, I would change into shorts and a tee shirt and then take the dog out again. It was actually quite awhile before I could leave the house at night without worrying about being outside with him in the dark, but finally, my anxiety began to subside. Time passed and there were no more incidents. I traveled back and forth to my job through the hot, pale days, walked the dog beneath a harvest moon that rotated through its phases, disappeared, and then showed up again, looking like a thin, bright scimitar hanging low on the horizon. Amazingly, it would soon be fall.

Every morning I woke up expecting to feel fine—after all, except for the fact that I now owned a strange little dog, my life was pretty much back to exactly how it had been before I had called in to Jack's radio show. But I didn't feel that way. I couldn't quite identify it, but some part of me felt empty. Somewhere deep inside myself there was something I wanted, but I couldn't say what it was. Now, during the day, my thoughts were often foggy. At night, my dreams became unsettled, though I could never remember what they were about. I would wake up and see the dog at the end of the bed, sleepless, as he always seemed to be in the darkest hours of the night, and listen to him breathe. It was like listening to a shadow breathe. A little gray ghost.

On a Sunday when I didn't have to work, I took the dog out in the morning intending to walk no farther than we usually did. It was already hot, and I wanted to get back into the air conditioning as soon as I could. But despite what I thought were my own firm intentions, at the point where I normally would have pulled on the dog's leash to turn him around and head back home, I found that I had changed my mind and instead, continued on, heading toward a neighborhood about half a mile away.

For quite a while now, an old church around here had been undergoing renovations. The last time I had gone shopping at a nearby supermarket, I had noticed that the ever-present scaffolding around the church had finally been taken down and a sign outside proclaimed that there would be a number of celebratory events to mark the conclusion of the building's restoration. This particular Sunday, there was going to be a blessing of the animals and, though I wasn't aware that I had consciously thought of it before, I realized that I now had a particular destination in mind. I was on my way to have my little Dogon dog blessed by a priest.

A Catholic church was about the last place I thought that I belonged, so I felt more than a little bit uncomfortable as I lined up on the sidewalk outside the church behind a couple of dozen other people, including families with children who also had brought their pets to be blessed. Many had dogs on leashes, but some were holding cats or birds in cages, or a variety of small animals such as hamsters and gerbils. A few people had even brought lizards and snakes.

I couldn't remember what the church had looked like before, but it had emerged from its scaffolding with a surface of dark, rough stone scoured so clean that it seemed freshly quarried. Topped by a small bell tower, the building seemed to belong to some bare western landscape, not this busy urban neighborhood, with its mix of ethnic-food shops and brick-faced apartment complexes.

Around noon, the church doors opened and people began to file in with their pets. I could hear music playing inside and the soft, pleasant sound of murmuring voices.

The line moved slowly, so it took about twenty minutes for me to make my way past the front door. My first reaction was to be relieved that it was cool inside. It was also pleasantly dim in the candlelit interior, where an orderly procession of people and animals—myself and Digitaria included—was making its way down the center aisle of the church toward a priest, flanked by several servers, who was quietly blessing each animal presented to him.

When it was our turn, I found myself facing the priest, a gentle looking man of middle age, wearing some sort of white vestment that bore an elaborate cross stitched on its front panel in maroon and gold thread. Despite the smile he gave me, I was still feeling very out of place and not quite sure what I was doing here. Maybe it was just another symptom of the vague anxiety that had gripped me lately that I thought it would be a good idea to have the dog blessed. Or maybe I was just developing a belief in some kind of otherworldly magic, even religion. Even if it was not my own.

Just as the priest seemed ready to bend down in order to lay his hands on my dog and deliver the blessing, he unexpectedly paused for a moment and addressed me—something I hadn't noticed him doing with any other pair of pets and owners.

"Isn't that an African dog?" he asked me.

"Yes," I replied, startled that he recognized this.

"When I was younger, I spent some time in Mali," he explained. "I was in the Peace Corps. We visited the Dogon tribal area once, and I saw dogs like that. I thought they tried not to let anyone outside their own people have one."

"You're right," I said. "He is a Dogon dog." And lest the priest think I had somehow acquired him in some nefarious way, I added, "He was given to me. By a professor at Columbia," I added, as if that certainly put matters on the up and up.

"Well, my friend," the priest said, looking down at my dog, "you've come a long way. Peace be with you."

And then he murmured a prayer. He almost seemed to be speaking privately to the dog, who closed his eyes when the priest touched him. I couldn't hear all of what the priest recited, but I did catch these lines: *Bless this animal. May it carry out the function it has been given, and may it aid us to think of You, its Creator.*

"Thank you, Father," I said, adding the title less because it was respectful to do so, but because—like too many things in my life, probably—I was taking my cue from what I'd learned from watching television. On TV, priests were almost always addressed as Father.

We left the church then and I led the dog back outside, into the heat of midday, where we began the long walk home.

In my apartment, I flopped down on the bed in my one air-conditioned room and turned on the small TV I kept on a dresser. The dog took up his usual place at the foot of the bed and quickly went to sleep. He did a lot of napping during the day; it was at night when he was most wakeful.

I started watching some cops-and-robbers movie, but soon found that I couldn't concentrate. The episode with the priest was bothering me; not in a bad way—I was quite touched by the care he'd taken in blessing the dog—but in the sense that it seemed unusual. What were the chances that in some small church in a nondescript neighborhood in the far end of Queens, I would happen upon an individual—a priest, no less—who could not only identify my dog's origins but knew exactly which African people he was connected to? There was that question to consider, not to mention that I found myself, over and over again, thinking about the words in the blessing that the priest had bestowed, about the dog carrying out its function and, in doing so, helping to bring to mind its creator. As I went back to making what turned out to be another unsuccessful effort to follow the plot of the movie, I found myself, time and time again, looking over at the sleeping dog. His function? His creator? I was pretty sure that no one else who had been at the blessing of the animals earlier—no owner of a hamster or a pug or a parakeet—was wondering about those things as much as me.

EVERY DAY for the rest of the week, I woke up with an idea in my head and each day, the thought of following through on it became more insistent. It wasn't like the idea had formed a logical conclusion of some well-thought-out plan of action; not at all. I just had a feeling that there were things I needed to find out, and very few ways to do so other than the one that had occurred to me, seemingly out of, well . . . the wild blue yonder. However, I had still done nothing when a small event took place that made me think, okay, here's karma at work and karma, when it walks through your front door, probably should not be ignored.

Actually, it was my neighbor, Sassouma, who came into my apartment. It was around lunchtime on a weekday, and she needed help with some forms that her children's school required before classes started up again in a week or so. I filled out the paperwork for her—mostly proof that the kids had received various inoculations and booster shots—but just before she left, I asked her for her cousin-in-law's telephone number. She gave it to me without question, which I assumed meant that it would be all right to call him. At least, all right with her.

Dr. Carpenter did not seem particularly happy to hear from me when I reached him. Apparently, Sassouma had given me his home number, and he said he was too busy to talk. However, he said he would be at the university during the week because he was preparing for the fall semester, and he could spare me some time, if I insisted. No, I said, trying to be nice, I wasn't insisting at all; I was just hoping he could answer some questions I had. When he asked me about what, I answered, simply, that I wanted to talk to him about the dog.

He said that he'd told me everything there was to know about the dog, but I was kind of relentless in my wheedling, so much so that he finally agreed that we could meet. He told me to come up to the Columbia campus on Morningside Heights around one o'clock the following day, which meant that afterward I would have enough time to get back on the subway to Queens and catch the AirTrain that would take me to work. He told me where I would find him, which building, which room, and then, quite unceremoniously, hung up.

I rose at a relatively early hour the next day, walked the dog, got myself ready for work later in the afternoon and then headed for the subway. As usual when I was trying to get almost anywhere in the city, I had to change trains in the middle of my trip, but finally arrived at a stop near one of the entrances to the imposing complex of university buildings just after twelve thirty.

It was a warm, lazy day on campus. Columbia seemed like a city unto itself, with vast paved walkways leading to pillared libraries and lecture halls that look like the ancients might have hewn them out of giant blocks of stone. It was a somewhat intimidating atmosphere for me, but my feeling of being an uneducated slouch was somewhat mitigated by the fact that there were not a lot of students around. It was the week before Labor Day and probably, most people were off trying to enjoy their last few days of vacation before the academic year officially got underway. I, on the other hand, was scheduled to work all through the holiday. I wasn't going to have a day off until the middle of next week.

The building I was looking for felt like it was a mile away from where I had exited the subway. When I finally found it, I had to show identification to a security guard and let him peer into my shoulder bag before he directed me to an elevator that carried me up a few floors and let me out in a wide, quiet hallway where the warm air was infused with the paradoxical scent of both summer and school.

I expected to find Dr. Carpenter in an office but, instead, the room number he'd given me turned out to be a class-room, though one much larger than any I'd known in my aborted high school career. There must have been a hundred empty chairs scattered haphazardly around the room, some with those flat, plank-like arms for resting a notebook on. They looked abandoned, like they'd been unused for a hundred years. Tall windows, the kind that have to be opened with poles, let some light into the otherwise dim room. The floor was worn wood planking; the blackboard at the front of the classroom was blank.

Dr. Carpenter was sitting at a desk in front of the black-board, leafing through a book and making notes on a yellow pad. He did not take any notice of me when I walked in.

I seated myself in one of the chairs nearest to his desk and waited politely for him to acknowledge me. Finally, he looked up.

"So, Ms. Perzin. You managed to find me." He made it sound like he wasn't exactly pleased that I had.

"It's a big place. I had no idea."

He closed his notebook and sat back in his chair. "Well," he said, "now that you're here, what is it that I can do for you?"

I didn't reply right away, reacting, first, to how different he somehow seemed to me than when he had been in my apartment. The change I sensed was subtle but, at least to me, unmistakable. His demeanor was still decidedly off-putting, but he was less stiff, less formal than I remembered. Annoyed to have to give me some of his time, perhaps, but not adding the extra effort of presenting himself in the role he had played when he was in the presence of Sassouma: the wise family elder, called upon to carry out some official task.

"Why did you give me that dog?" I asked. All during my ride on the subway, I had tried to figure out how to begin this conversation, and I had arrived at the gate of the university still not sure what I would say. But the words that had just come out of my mouth now seemed as good as any. At least, they seemed like a start.

"I thought that was clear. It was a favor to my cousin's wife, who is fond of you."

"I understand that. But I'm wondering if maybe something else is involved."

"Like what?" Dr. Carpenter asked, sounding irritable.

"I don't know. That's why I came to see you."

"Is it that you don't want the dog? If so, I'll take him back. They're not easy to breed, so each one is valuable."

"No, I don't want to give him back," I protested, alarmed by the way Dr. Carpenter had chosen to interpret what I was saying. "He's my dog," I insisted, knowing that I now sounded childish and stubborn, but Dr. Carpenter's inhospitable attitude was bringing that out in me. "You said so."

"It was Sassouma who said that, if I recall."

"But you brought him to me."

"I did. As you have pointed out. So I am still waiting to hear what it is you want."

"Is there something . . . some significance about the dog that I don't understand? That maybe you didn't exactly tell me?"

Dr. Carpenter narrowed his eyes. "And why do you think that?" he asked.

"It's what Raymond Gilmartin thinks," I said. "He told me that he tried to get you to give him a Dogon dog."

"I see." The voice in which Dr. Carpenter now spoke to me was still controlled, but perhaps even more icy. "I had no idea that you knew Raymond."

"I met him. Recently."

"Isn't that interesting," Dr. Carpenter replied, and then said nothing more.

Outside, it was a sunny summer day, but here, in this dim room, my vision seemed limited. Though he was sitting just a few feet away from me, Dr. Carpenter almost seemed to be fading from my view and I thought I probably looked the same way to him—like I was on the other side of some great divide, an indistinct figure, hard to focus on, hard to see. Turning away, I glanced toward the windows, which were like bright panes of light framing the boundaries of a different world than the one I inhabited here, in this moment, in the shadowy classroom of Dr. Carpenter.

Finally, he spoke again. "So," he said, "are you going to tell me, or do I have to guess? You're here on behalf of Raymond Gilmartin, aren't you?"

"No," I said. "Of course not." But maybe, in a way, that was true. I had to be honest with myself; something had happened to me when I'd stayed on with Gilmartin, in his office, after Jack had stormed out. It was as if I had caught something from him, some sickness or desire, some obsession that had progressed beyond the empathy I'd felt in his presence.

~ 200 ~

Some need to know about the radiomen. It was part of me, now, the same way it was part of him. And like him, I found myself looking for anything there was to know about them, through any means possible, no matter how oblique.

"Then I'll ask you again. What is it you want?"

The response that came to mind—at least, the way to frame it—was more Raymond's than mine, but I proceeded with it nonetheless. "I want to show you something," I said to Dr. Carpenter.

I stood up then, walked over to his desk and picked up the yellow pad he had been making notes on. I tore out a sheet and using the same pen he'd been writing with, sketched the pictograph that was carved on the rock Raymond Gilmartin had shown me. I pushed the drawing toward Dr. Carpenter and then returned to my chair.

I gave him a moment to study my drawing and then said, "Raymond showed me a stone with that picture on it. He said you knew what it was."

"I've seen it."

"There's a dog in the drawing. It looks like my dog, I think. So I'm wondering, what's the connection between my dog and this picture?"

Dr. Carpenter's reaction was to utter a harsh, derisive laugh. "To *this* drawing? What an idea. Despite what you may think—or what anyone has told you—your dog does not even have a direct connection to Africa. It was born in my house, which is in Montclair. You know where that is?"

"New Jersey."

"The Garden State. Hardly exotic." But then his attitude seemed to change again. He looked down at the drawing and then back at me. All traces of laughter were now gone. "I know what you're really asking me," he said. He pointed to my rendition of the shadowy figure standing beside the dog and the human figure. "It's what everyone wants who has seen these pictures. You want to know if these beings exist. But I have no idea. My field of expertise, as I told you when

~ 201 ~

we met, is French literature. It most certainly is *not* extraterrestrials." Dr. Carpenter set his face in an attitude of extreme irritation. "But perhaps you don't believe me. Perhaps you think I'm one of those magical Africans who turns up in Hollywood movies to explain to the white explorers where the lost treasure caves are and what the secret symbols mean that they've found on some long-lost map?"

Now he wasn't the only one in the room who was irritated. "Look," I said, "I don't think you're particularly magical—you're not even very nice—and as for me, I don't really want to explore anything. I was just living my life and all of a sudden it was invaded by these Blue Awareness people . . . they were the ones who robbed my apartment the night before you were there. It was probably Raymond who sent them. So much for your theory that I'm here to do his bidding, right? Later, they even tried to steal the dog. Raymond swears that wasn't his idea, but still . . ."

"I'm not surprised," Dr. Carpenter said, cutting me off. He shifted in his chair, leaning forward a bit and, for the first time since we'd begun this conversation, he sounded animated. "Raymond Gilmartin is an impossible person. Once—once!— I gave an interview about Dogon culture to a student who wrote for one of the university's publications. Unfortunately for me, Gilmartin is an alumnus and read the article. Since then he has given me no peace." Leaning forward in his chair, speaking with intensity, he said, "Let me tell you something, Ms. Perzin. I know all about him." He briefly tapped the crude drawing I had made, touching the shape I had used to represent the nonhuman figure and then quickly withdrawing his hand. "He thinks that it's possible to become like them. To know what they know. That's Gilmartin's dream, isn't it? Well, good luck to him. He has never considered the fact that perhaps—even if they exist—they know nothing.

"Raymond Gilmartin," he continued, "has a rock with some scrapings on it that someone sold his father, telling him it was a great treasure. It isn't. In Mali, in the Dogon lands, there are many such pictographs on rocks, on cave walls, on cliff sides. But this is hardly unique, I think. In every corner of the world there are legacies of such images left by ancient societies. Jackal-headed beings, men with the bodies of lions, mermaids, giants, centaurs. Does anyone today think that creatures like that exist? Or ever did?"

"If that's true—if the pictographs are just so much graffiti to the Dogon—then why wouldn't you let Raymond have one of your dogs? He probably would have paid any amount of money you'd asked for."

I kept pushing this point because I just couldn't give up on the idea that there had to be something important hidden within Dr. Carpenter's refusal to permit Raymond Gilmartin to even purchase a dog that had been given to me for free. But Dr. Carpenter wouldn't concede that this was so. In fact, he seemed to take the suggestion as an affront.

"Because I didn't like him, Ms. Perzin. And I have no interest in promoting his fantasies."

Dr. Carpenter turned to look toward the window, where a block of dusty summer sunlight seemed to sit on the sill like a package someone had forgotten to bring inside. When he faced me again, the professor seemed almost weary. He let out a sigh—something I probably wasn't meant to hear—and said, "The men from the stars and the dog who stayed with a little boy. In Mali, in the Dogon lands, it's become the national myth and look what it has led to," he said, shaking his head. "Crazy people become fixated on the animals. And for the rest of us, for the Dogon, even if we leave Mali behind, we don't seem to be able to live without these damn dogs. It's as if we feel compelled to have them."

These damn dogs. That small outburst seemed almost amusing to me, and I was grateful for it. At last, something in this conversation didn't seem like armed combat. But the moment passed quickly and almost immediately Dr. Carpenter's forbidding persona reassembled itself. "Well?" he said testily. "Is there anything else or may I be permitted to go back to my work?"

I didn't think that I deserved to be treated so dismissively. So perhaps I was just being stubborn, but I wasn't ready yet just to get up and walk away. Besides, I had something more to tell him.

"I took the dog to be blessed by a priest," I said. "It was actually kind of an accident. But maybe that's the point. I happened to walk into a church in the middle of Queens and found the one priest—I bet you, the *one* priest in the entire city—who had been to Mali, to the Dogon lands, and could recognize that I had a Dogon dog."

"Well, that's what they say, isn't it? God moves in mysterious ways."

"Who brought up God?" I demanded, feeling just as prickly as Dr. Carpenter sounded. But then I remembered—the priest did. He had referred to the Creator in his blessing. And that was what had been on my mind all along, what had compelled me and brought me here. *Bless this animal. May it carry out the function it has been given, and may it aid us to think of You, its Creator.* I was about to repeat these words to Dr. Carpenter when he spoke first.

He said, "You aren't a believer?"

"I don't know," I said. "I don't think so."

Dr. Carpenter made a small gesture toward my drawing although this time, he didn't even deign to touch it. "Then you have something in common with your friends here. In all the pictographs I have ever seen that relate to this myth—and I have seen hundreds—there is no depiction of a deity. None. So if you have come to me seeking some sort of spiritual guidance, then I really do have nothing to offer you."

"I came here," I repeated once more, as firmly as I could, "to ask you about the dog."

"Then asked and answered," Dr. Carpenter said. "He is a pet."

That was it; that was clearly all Dr. Carpenter had to say. He returned to reading his book and would not look up from it. I knew that I could sit there for the rest of the afternoon, but he wasn't going to engage with me anymore. It was time for me to leave.

And so I said good-bye and walked out of the room. I retraced my steps down the hallway and took the elevator back to the lobby. The classroom upstairs had been warm, but not uncomfortable; downstairs, however, it was sweltering. The security guard, sitting in front of a huge, rattling fan, once again checked my ID before letting me leave the building. I was glad to get outside, where there was something of a breeze.

It was a long way back to the subway, but I was still going to be early for work. I bought a newspaper and read it as I first waited on the platform for the subway, then rode out to Queens where I transferred to the monorail that took me out to the airport.

I had an hour to kill before I had to get into my pseudo-hipster outfit and turn myself into the cheerful bartender welcoming the traveling public to The Endless Weekend. I had finished the paper, so I sat by one of the gates for a while, watching airplanes lifting themselves up into the sky.

All the while, of course—even when I had pretended to myself that I was deeply absorbed in every column inch of news, gossip and opinion in the paper I had read so assiduously—I was going over and over the conversation I'd had with Dr. Carpenter. I tried to replay it in my mind but it was already slipping away, as conversations tend to, even the most intense. But while I could not repeat to myself every word we'd spoken, every exchange, the general sense of what Dr. Carpenter had to say to me remained strong. He had clearly told me that in essence, he had nothing of any importance to share with me—or that he wished to share—except that Raymond Gilmartin was deluded and I was chasing a myth.

Well, maybe. I might even have let myself be convinced of all that except for one particular point that nagged at me. Even if I accepted that everything Dr. Carpenter said was correct, particularly about the insignificance of the picture that I had reproduced for him, he had misled me about something. Maybe deliberately, maybe not. Or perhaps the fault was mine and I had just misunderstood his implication. I thought he had meant that because there was no god of any kind represented in any of the pictographs to be found in the Dogon lands—or on the stone that Raymond had shown me—then it was likely that the shadowy beings did not believe that one existed. But it wasn't the visitors from the stars who had recorded the encounter by scratching pictures on rocks and cliff walls; it was the Dogon people. Dr. Carpenter had said so himself. And since they could barely communicate with their visitors, how did they know *what* the people who had pointed out the Dog Star to them actually believed in? Other, of course, than a need for the companionship of dogs.

~XIV~

Was it a mistake to have gone to see Dr. Carpenter? Maybe, I concluded as I thought about it over the next few days, because I didn't feel any better after visiting him. In fact, I felt worse. He had been cynical and unpleasant and left me with the impression that he thought my questions were stupid. Delusional. But since even his dismissive attitude had not chased them from my mind, the only result was that now I felt even more confused. And I felt that the way forward— wherever I was headed—had become even murkier.

I became depressed, edgy, far out of my comfort zone, which was to know exactly what I was doing day after day, and why, and where I was supposed to be. I did not, for example, think of myself as the kind of person to ask for the blessings of priests. I did not entertain the ideas of New Age crazies, which—until I had met him, and maybe still—was exactly what I considered Raymond Gilmartin to be. I did not wonder about the function of dogs or their relationship to a creator. And since I was now doing all these things, I began wondering about myself. Though I was capable of holding two ideas in my mind at the same time—for example, that the world was exactly what it appeared to be while, at the same time, maybe there were inexplicable things going on beyond the human line of sight—the balance seemed to be shifting, and I was concerned about which way it was going. Granted, I had been flirting with a lot of strange ideas these past months, but now I was afraid there was the potential that they might take over my life. I was fighting it, but you never knew. And if they did gain more than just the foothold they currently had, what would become of me? Would I wake up one morning and decide that joining the Blue Awareness suddenly made sense? Or maybe I would become religious, or dedicate myself to some alien-hunting group. In other words, little by little, I was beginning to lose trust in myself, in the inner control I had learned to depend on to keep me going. Maybe I lived at the margins of the economy and sometimes struggled to keep my head above water, but so far, I had managed. It had taken me long enough, but I had created some stability for myself. What would happen if I put all that at risk? It did occur to me that maybe I already had.

To some degree, I could distract myself from these thoughts at work—the baseball playoffs were underway and since the Yankees had made it to the postseason, pennant fever was cranked up to an eleven out of ten at The Endless Weekend—but once I got on the bus to head home, everything came back to me. On those long, late-night rides, I did a lot of deep breathing and hummed the great *Om* to try to center myself, but since I didn't know where that center was, I was mostly unsuccessful. At home, I ate too much and watched infomercials, pretending to myself that nut choppers and oxygen-infused cleaning solutions would make my life better. And then I went to sleep, to the world of haunted dreams.

I dreamt about the dog, Zvezdochka, the little star orbiting Earth. I dreamt about Buddy, the dog who had come to me in the mausoleum. I dreamt about the dog scratched into a rock, standing between a human and something that was not a human being. In my dreams, all these dogs visited me—even Zvezdochka, safely landed on Earth and stepping out of her capsule—and I would pat them on the head, greeting each in turn. And then I would wake to see my own dog, my sleepless shadow, positioned at the edge of the bed. Many nights now, when I woke, I saw that, instead of watching the door, Digitaria was watching me.

I began making mistakes at work, which had never happened to me before. I mixed the wrong drinks, I rang up the wrong prices, I gave the wrong change. This scared me, maybe more than anything else, because no matter what had ever happened to me in my life, I had always been able to put those things aside when I was at work and concentrate on what I had to do. Deeply rattled by the fact that I seemed to have lost my ability to leave myself behind when I was at work and act the part of the carefree bartender, I began to make a conscious, concerted effort to focus on every order I got, every transaction I had to process. And I thought I was making some headway until I had an encounter with yet another dog.

It was at the end of my shift. Most of the TVs in the bar were tuned to the sports wrap-up programs and I had announced last call. I started wiping down the bar and stacking glasses in the back. The shops on the other side of the concourse were also closing, pulling down their security gates. The woman who ran the luggage store opposite the bar waved to me as she headed down the concourse toward the exits at the front of the airport.

A few minutes after her figure vanished from view, I suddenly saw something run past the front entrance of The Endless Weekend. Looking out from the dark bar into the overly bright light that bathed the corridor outside could be disorienting, so at first I thought I had been mistaken. But then, whatever it was flashed by again, going in the opposite direction. My mind was having some trouble processing what my eyes had apparently seen, maybe because I couldn't quite believe it, but when the streaking image—something gray and lean—ran past again, what had just been a vague impression sharpened into unmistakable clarity. A dog was running back and forth outside the bar.

I didn't have to think about what to do next; my response was automatic. I stepped out from behind the cash register where I was checking receipts and walked into the concourse. At this late hour, with so few people around, the sharp, artificial light made everything in sight—the areas around the arrival and departure boards that no one was looking at, the rows of empty seats by the unmanned boarding gates—seem even more deserted. And unreal.

In the brief time it had taken me to cross from the darkness of the bar into the bright corridor, I had decided that what I'd seen must have been a police dog that had gotten away from its handler and was running around the airport. It didn't matter to me that this explanation made no sense because these dogs never did things like that—unless, of course, one of them was chasing a criminal, and if that was the case, then probably I should have gone back into the bar, pulled down our security gate and told the waitress and our last few customers to hide under a table. But instead, I simply stood in the corridor, under the bright fluorescent light, and waited. I didn't see the dog just yet, but I had a feeling he would come back.

And soon, he did. I looked down the long corridor, toward the area where the screening machines were, and saw nothing—not even the personnel who should have been manning the equipment, no matter how late at night it was. But when I looked the other way, in the direction of the departure gates, I suddenly saw the dog, sitting on his haunches, in a carpeted area under a row of blank television screens.

As if he had simply been waiting for me to notice him, he now stood up and started walking toward me. When he was close enough for me to get a better look at him, I could see that he looked like a small greyhound, a dog as narrow as a bone.

It took him less than a minute to pad down the length of the bright, empty hallway, where not a security guard, not a member of the overnight cleaning crew, not even one wandering traveler seemed to be in sight. The dog came right to me and sat down again. Then he raised his head to look at me with dark, glittery eyes.

I didn't want him to be there. I didn't want to think about why he was. And most of all, at that moment, I didn't want to touch him. But then, how can you not pet a dog that walks right up to you and looks you in the eye?

So I patted him on the head. "Hello," I said. But what I was thinking was, *Who sent you?*

Just then, the waitress I was working with that night, a young woman named Kim, walked out of the bar and stood beside me. She had a blonde ponytail and a tattoo of a butterfly on her wrist—the perfect Endless Weekend girl.

Gesturing at the dog, she said, "Where did he come from?"

I think it was at the same moment that we both noticed the dog was wearing a collar. Kim bent down to look at the tags hanging from the collar, but as she did, the dog whipped his head around to face her and growled.

"Whoa," she said, stepping back. "Maybe there's something wrong with him. We should call security."

But I knew there was nothing wrong with the dog. The problem was that the wrong person had approached him. "Let me see if I can find who he belongs to," I said to Kim.

Then I crouched down to get a look at his identification tag. With me, the dog didn't seem to object. I read the information etched onto the little bone-shaped tag attached to his collar and learned that his name was Dax and he belonged to someone named Kelly Branigan.

Was that a man or a woman? Human or alien? *Stop that,* I told myself firmly. *Just start looking.*

"Would you hold the fort for a few minutes?" I said to Kim, and then began walking down the corridor, toward the departure gates. I glanced back at the dog just once, and he immediately started to follow me.

I continued heading down the row of gates near the bar; none of the boards behind the desk had departures listed except one at the far end of the terminal, which showed a flight leaving for LA at six A.M. A young man, with long hair and lots of rings on his fingers, was asleep on a bench near the gate, his head resting on a backpack. Beside him was a dog kennel, with its wire door pushed open.

I reached out to shake the young man awake, and as I did, the dog darted past me and slipped back into his kennel. I thought immediately of a dog in a capsule, as if Zvezdochka had decided to appear before me in another form.

"What?" the young man said, opening his eyes. He looked at me and then glanced over at the sign above the gate. I saw the confusion on his face turn to relief. "Wow. I got scared there for a moment. Thought they'd called my flight." He couldn't have been more than nineteen or twenty, and had a friendly smile.

"You've got a couple of hours," I told him.

"Yeah, I guess. They canceled the red eye and booked me on the morning flight. They said I could crash here until boarding time. Is that still okay?"

"If nobody's telling you to move, I guess so," I said, "but I'm not with the airlines. I'm the bartender from The Endless Weekend. Your dog paid me a visit."

"My dog?" he said, sitting up. "Dax?" He looked over at the kennel, where the dog had stretched himself out on his side and appeared to be quite comfortable. Reaching over to touch the open latch, the young man looked totally flummoxed. "Hey boy," he said, "how did you do that?" The dog yawned and turned over.

"Well, I guess he's not talking. Did you bring him back?"

"Yes," I said. "When they come to get the kennel, maybe you should make sure somebody ties that latch closed with a rope or something."

"Thanks. I will. And thanks so much for looking after him. I don't know what I would have done if he'd gotten lost."

"Well, I have a dog," I said, invoking what I supposed was the universal empathy of one dog owner for another.

I watched as the young man locked the kennel and checked the latch to make sure it was secure. Then he lifted the backpack off the bench and placed it so that it leaned against the kennel door.

"That thing weighs at least thirty pounds," he said. "Hopefully, that'll do the trick until morning."

The dog now appeared to be sound asleep. He was even softly snoring.

"What kind of dog do you have?" the young man asked me.

"A Dogon dog," I replied. "Do you know what that is?"

"Never heard of them," my new acquaintance said cheerfully.

"Well, mine looks a little like yours."

"Huh. That's interesting. Mine came from a shelter. He's just a mutt. But he's a great traveling companion. Over the past couple of years we've been all over together. Europe, Canada, South America. We're on our way back from Spain now, heading home for a while."

Other than the fact that he was waiting for a West Coast flight, the young man didn't offer any information about where, exactly, home might be. And I wondered how he managed to travel around with the dog as easily as he seemed to be suggesting, since many international destinations had strict quarantine laws about bringing in pets, even temporarily. Those issues aside, how did he manage to afford his wanderings? Was he a student? A con man? The eccentric heir of a family fortune?

I might have asked, except that my new friend kept chattering on and, meaning to or not, he ended up answering my unspoken question. Sort of, anyway. "Actually," he said, "I don't think I'd be able to get anywhere without Dax. I hitchhike wherever I go, but just about nobody will pick up a guy, a traveler, standing alone on the road. Because I have the dog with me, though, they know I'm okay. I mean, bad guys don't travel around with dogs, right? So Dax is like my ambassador. My intermediary." He tapped the top of the kennel and the dog responded with a sleepy yip, "Don't you think dogs do that? Act as a go-between, sometimes. For example, you and I would never have met if Dax hadn't gone exploring." He smiled at me, looking as pleased as if, instead of having a passing encounter, we had just made a connection that would last a lifetime. "What's your name?" he asked.

"Laurie," I told him.

"Laurie," he repeated. Still smiling, he added, "And something with a P."

I nodded. "Perzin,"

"Yup, I knew there was a 'z' in there, too." He laughed. "Well, that's weird. I mean, I don't usually get any psychic vibes or anything like that."

"It happens," I responded quietly.

"I'm Kelly, by the way."

He held out his hand and I shook it. Then Kelly stretched himself out on the bench again, replacing his backpack with his jacket, which he balled up to use as a pillow. "I'm going to try to nod off again for a while," he said, and tapped the kennel again. "We've still got a long trip ahead of us," he said.

"Okay. Good night," I said. I started to walk away but turned back for a moment, meaning to add something like, *Safe travels*, but he had already closed his eyes. I walked back down the deserted corridor to the bar. The last of the customers were gone and Kim had pulled down the security gate, but I could see her sitting at a table, counting her tips. I called to her, and she let me in through a side door.

"Well?" she said. "Did you do your good deed? Did you find out who the dog belonged to?"

"Yes," I said. "I did."

And then I checked my watch. We still had to wait for the night manager to come and count out the register, but I was thinking I might take off a little early tonight and leave Kim to deal with him. It had become apparent to me that there was something else I had to do.

"Now? You want to come over now?"

"Yes, now."

"It's after midnight."

"You're up, aren't you? I can be there by one thirty."

"So what? Why would I even want to talk to you?"

"We don't have to talk. I want you to do a reading for me."

"That's even more ridiculous."

"Call Raymond," I said. "Ask him if you should do it."

"You want me to wake up Raymond Gilmartin. At this hour."

"Yes, I do. Tell him it's about the radiomen. Tell him that you and I are going to talk to them tonight. One of them, anyway."

It was a tense conversation, but I knew what the outcome would be. I knew it before I had even dialed Ravenette's number and got her on the phone. She was beyond annoyed, but as soon as the phone call ended I was so sure that she was already dialing Raymond that I didn't even head in the direction of my regular bus stop but instead exited the terminal and walked toward the far end of the taxi rank, where the gypsy drivers hung around even though they weren't officially allowed to join the lineup of yellow cabs with city medallions.

As I expected, I was offered a ride. I made a deal with the driver for what I wanted, which was to take me to my apartment, wait a few minutes for me while I went upstairs, and then head directly into the city. I was already in the back seat of the car when my phone played the chiming tones that meant I had a call.

"All right," Ravenette said, sounding like she had to clench her teeth to get out that one word. "But just because Raymond said so."

"You can tell him everything that happens."

"I intend to," Ravenette said.

"I'm on my way," I told her and clicked off the phone.

The car pulled up in front of my apartment house in less than half an hour. I jumped out, ran into the building and hurried up the stairs. As soon as I opened the door, I saw Digitaria sitting, as usual, just inside, waiting for me to come home.

He nudged my leg—his usual greeting—and waited to be petted. I gave him a couple of quick pats and then put his leash around his neck. He was expecting a walk, so he waited patiently while I dashed into the bedroom and grabbed the small stash of emergency cash I kept hidden in my bureau drawer. I thought it would be just enough to pay for the ride to Manhattan and, later, get us back home.

I led the dog down the stairs and out the front door, where I loaded him into the car. He didn't seem at all disturbed by the change in our usual routine and, instead, leaned against me, sitting like another watchful passenger. The car glided down my block and then turned toward Queens Boulevard to join the luminous stream of traffic heading off into the night.

We pulled up to Ravenette's building just about the time I'd told her I would arrive. I paid the driver and stepped out of the car, pulling Digitaria along with me. Late as it was, there was still plenty of foot traffic around. The restaurants were still busy, the local bars were still open. A young, pretty girl in a silver skirt walked by me and stopped briefly to scratch Digitaria's ears.

"Cute dog," she said dreamily, and then walked on.

I rang Ravenette's bell, and when I got no answer, rang it again. Finally, she buzzed me in.

"Okay," I said to Digitaria. "Here we go."

We rode the elevator up to her loft, where she was waiting for me on the same low couch where she had waited the last time I was here. The few lamps that were lit in the huge loft illuminated only the area where she was sitting, so that she seemed to be positioned at the edge of a vast pool of darkness.

She rose when the elevator let us out and said, almost immediately, "The dog?" There was something about the way she blurted that out, some familiarity that made me realize she knew all about the time when the two men had tried to steal Digitaria. Being reminded of the episode was going to make me upset all over again, so I was just going to have to try to get past it.

"There's a reason you brought him?" Ravenette continued.

"There is," I told her.

She waited, studying my every move as I led the dog into the circle of light and seated myself on a chair. Digitaria took his place against my leg.

"But you're not going to tell me."

"I'm not sure myself about what I'm doing. We're probably going to find out together. So let's try, okay? Truce?"

She picked up a cell phone from an end table near the couch and said, "I want to call Raymond again."

"Why? You'll have more to tell him after."

"After what?"

I answered her the best way I knew how. "I told you. I want to talk to the radioman. I know you think he's an engram but I think he might be . . . well, something else."

"Oh, so now you suddenly need my help?"

"Will you listen to me, please? The first time we spoke, you told me about a being who looked like a shadow sitting in a room. In a boarding house. You said he was upset, that

~ 218 ~

he was telling me to be quiet but pointing out the window, at the fire escape."

"That is an image created out of a disturbance in your own mind," she said impatiently.

"You can go on saying that all you want, but the room was my Uncle Avi's. And it was me outside on the fire escape. We were listening to satellite signals."

Maybe Ravenette already knew this part of the story, maybe not. I couldn't tell by her expression, which remained unfriendly. Nevertheless, I continued.

"I'm not exactly sure how I'm supposed to ask this," I said, "but can you find him again? The radioman? Or channel him?"

"I'm not a medium," she said.

I was exasperated by her response. I wasn't here to debate the fine points of what one kind of paranormal practitioner did as opposed to another. "Fine," I said. "Whatever it is you do."

"Whatever I *do*?" she said, sounding deeply affronted. "Are you suggesting that I'm a fake?"

"No. Just the opposite. That's why I'm here."

She shot me a suspicious look. "You're serious."

"I am." And then I added, "Please."

That seemed to help—along with the fact that she was likely under instructions from Raymond Gilmartin to do what I asked. "All right," Ravenette said, "let's see if I can find out anything."

She sat down again and took a moment to calm herself. Then, she fixed her green eyes on me. I thought we were going to have some sort of staring contest but almost immediately, she let out a sudden gasp. "Oh my," she said. "I see him. In that same room. He's like a gray shadow sitting on the bed."

Well, all right. Evidently, it was time to begin. There were things I needed to know.

"Ask him if he's the one sending me all the dogs."

For a moment, Ravenette was silent. The strength of her presence in the room seemed to dim; it was almost as if the essence of whoever she was had gone away.

And then, suddenly, *something* returned. A sharp hiss came out of Ravenette's mouth. It was a threatening, alien sound, high-pitched and raspy that seemed to hang between us in the air, like an invisible snake.

I almost felt afraid to breathe, but when I did, Ravenette was back with me. "That's his answer," she managed to tell me, though she was clearly unsettled.

Her voice was trembling and I got the sense that she was in totally new territory. Whatever she actually did as a psychic, whether her "contacts" were real or imagined, what she was experiencing now was something completely new for her, and it was apparent that it was frightening for her. But not for me. For the first time in days—weeks—I suddenly felt focused. I felt like myself, which probably had something to do with my anger flooding back, my one reliable weapon against all attacks. It might go missing from time to time, but it always found its way back to me, or I found it. *So,* I heard myself thinking, *what the hell was this thing hissing at me for? I thought he wanted me here.*

It is likely, at that moment and with that thought, I didn't actually recognize the personal Rubicon I had just crossed: in my mind, whatever that being was in my uncle's room, he had become real. In what sense *real* I probably couldn't have said, but it was the right description. And I knew who he was, who he had always been: my radioman. The shadow I had met on the fire escape all those years ago. And that's why, unlike Ravenette, I wasn't afraid. Not at all. I had known him too long.

"Well, hiss back at him or something," I said to Ravenette. "I'm not here because I want to be. I came here because I think he wants something from me, but he's going to have to give me some help because I don't know what it is."

Ravenette gasped again, like someone in the throes of genuine shock. "Laurie," she said, speaking my name softly, like she was whispering something she didn't want someone else to hear. Like for the moment, we were on the same side. "We have to be careful, I think. This is different from last time. He's angry. *Very* angry," she said.

"I'm a little pissed off myself. You can tell him that."

"I don't have to tell him," Ravenette said. "He can hear what you're saying."

"How? How does he hear what I'm saying? Through you?"

"Not exactly."

"Then what?"

Ravenette opened her mouth as if to speak, then closed it again. She seemed to be struggling, reaching for words. "I don't know how to explain. I've never encountered this before. He's here. Sort of here. Here, but in a parallel place."

Well, wherever he was, there was one thing we had in common. One way to bridge the divide—or at least, that was what I hoped.

I looked down at Digitaria, meaning to tap him on the back so he'd stand up, but I didn't have to. He was already up on all fours, staring straight ahead. He was on high alert, nose twitching, eyes wide.

"I brought a friend of yours," I said, addressing myself to Ravenette, but not really—that much I knew. Ravenette herself had now closed her eyes. She was so still that she genuinely appeared to be in some kind of altered state.

"You like dogs, don't you?" I continued. "You brought them here. Something like them, anyway. Right?"

Ravenette grimaced, and once again, that strange, high-pitched hiss emanated from her mouth. She opened her eyes and stared straight into mine as if she were desperately trying to hold onto the reality of me, of the lamp-lit room, the world—this world—itself. "It's all right," I whispered. I wasn't sure if that was true, but I didn't spend any time wondering about it. Instead, I pushed Digitaria forward, toward the couch where Ravenette was sitting. He took a few tentative steps and cocked his head sideways, a look I knew well. He was thinking about something, trying to figure something out. Then, slowly, he began to wag his tail.

He sat down beside Ravenette and leaned against her leg.

"Okay?" I said. "Better now?"

Ravenette nodded but said nothing. After a few moments, the dog stood up again, shook himself and trotted back to me. He remained watchful, but apparently at ease.

"Where is it?" Ravenette said suddenly.

"What?" I asked.

"The Haverkit. That's what he wants. He needs. He needs the Haverkit," she said emphatically. "He says that's what it was called."

"The radio? It was stolen."

"Not the radio!" Ravenette screeched.

"The what? Does he mean the horn of plenty antenna? Does he want that, too? I've told everybody who will listen that I don't have it anymore."

She shook her head. "No, no, no, no, no. Not the antenna. It's the wrong thing. He says to tell you that's the wrong thing."

"Okay," I said, thinking about all the chaos that had been caused by the search for what a shadow was now telling me was *the wrong thing*. "Then I don't understand what the *right* thing is. Does he mean the radio?"

Impatiently, Ravenette shook her head. "No, no, no, no, no," she said again, sounding even more irritable. "He wasn't even supposed to be listening to the radio. He just wanted to hear the signal. When you saw him on the fire escape—he wasn't supposed to be doing that. That's why he was telling you to be quiet . . ."

"Not because he was worried about my uncle seeing him."

"No. Because he wasn't supposed to leave his post."

"His post?"

"His job, his job!"

Sometimes Ravenette was speaking in her own voice and sometimes it was inflected with a strange, high-pitched tone that grated on the ear. It was unnerving, but I couldn't let that distract me.

"What's his job?" I asked.

I didn't get a direct answer. Not yet. Instead, Ravenette spit out an angry question. "Why did Avi take it away?"

"I'm sorry," I said helplessly. "I still don't know what *it* is."

Again, no answer. "He says he doesn't want to talk to you. You're just . . . all he can find. At least, I think that's what he's saying."

"All he can find?" I took a guess at what he meant. "He's been looking for Avi, is that it? Well, Avi's dead. Does he understand what that means?"

Ravenette was silent for a moment. When she spoke again she said, "He does but . . . time is different where he is. Maybe death is, too."

"Then channel Avi for him and tell him to leave me alone." I stood up, as if to leave, and Ravenette hissed again. "That's not going to work with me," I said.

I knew that I was taking a chance by being so confrontational, but I didn't think I had anything to lose. I needed answers and so far, I hadn't gotten them by being nice. At least, relatively so.

To my relief, the tactic quickly seemed to work. "Wait," Ravenette said, holding up her hand as a sort of stop signal. I didn't think she was even aware that she was doing this; the gesture seemed forced, mechanical. "He says to remember that it was you who contacted him."

"I called into a radio show," I replied. "I was half drunk."

Ravenette—or the radioman she was speaking for—paid no attention to me. "He is very angry," she said, pronouncing each word with grim deliberateness, as if there was any possibility that this particular communiqué hadn't gotten through

~ 223 ~

to me yet. And then, after a pause, she spoke again, this time sounding puzzled. And she was speaking for herself. She said, "Laurie? He sounds . . . desperate, too."

"Desperate? And he thinks I can help him?"

"Yes, you," she said, snapping back into the strange state in which she seemed to be only partly in control of herself. "He repeats that he needs the Haverkit. 3689D. 3689D," she said suddenly, seeming, now, to be slipping more deeply into the grip of her alien counterpart. I finally sat back down as she closed her eyes once more and cocked her head to the side in the same way that Digitaria often did. "These numbers must be important. 3689D. 3689D. He keeps saying them over and over again."

"I don't know what that means."

She held up her hand again; this time, she wanted me to stop speaking because there was more she had to tell me. "He's showing me a vast network of . . . energy waves? Maybe radio waves? I'm not sure what it is. But there are stations all across the galaxies. Many galaxies? Millions? Here and . . . *there*. This universe and others. *Theirs*, he says. And others." She shook her head. "I'm not sure of the words, exactly. But he has a job to do; he has to remain at his post. It's just a small part of the grid but still . . . still . . . his part of the network isn't functioning. He can't broadcast without the Haverkit. He can't send out the signal. He hasn't sent a signal in years. Our years. So much time has been wasted! Why did Avi remove 3689D? Why why why why why?" The strange screeching sound had once again inserted itself into Ravenette's voice. It was very difficult to listen to and it was becoming more and more insistent. "Give it back," the alien voice said over and over again. "3689D. 3689D."

"Ravenette," I said, trying to summon her back from the trancelike state she had fallen into. When she didn't respond, I spoke louder, and then louder still, calling out her name. Finally, I reached out and shook her. She blinked, and seemed to focus on me.

"What is he talking about?" I asked her. "What kind of signal is he supposed to be sending out? Do you understand what he means?"

She nodded. "They're sending out a message."

I had a moment where all the monster movies of my childhood flickered across my memory and I thought of huge robots stomping out of flying saucers, alien insects invading the Earth. Faceless, soulless beings with ray guns lurking in the gas clouds just beyond the edges of our solar system, waiting for the signal that it was time to start the attack.

"What kind of message?" I made myself ask.

"It's hard to believe."

"Just tell me. What are they broadcasting?"

"Prayers," she said incredulously. "Encoded in a signal that's sent out into . . . the infinite. He says they send it through the Watering Hole, whatever that means. Laurie, Laurie. They're sending out prayers."

"Prayers?" I couldn't quite believe what she was saying. "*Prayers?* You mean like . . . to God?"

Ravenette seemed to be listening to whatever she was being told.

"Yes. To God."

"Why? I don't understand."

Slowly, she shook her head. "He can't answer that. He doesn't know."

"Because he's just the radioman," I said, mostly to myself. But someone else had heard me.

"Yes," Ravenette responded. "That's all. He's just doing his job. He's been doing it for . . . for . . ." She stopped speaking and then finally, started again. "There is no word to describe for how long." Her eyes opened wide, as if she were trying to see out from somewhere deep inside herself, and then closed again. A moment later, in the alien-inflected voice that I found so disturbing, she began droning "3689D, 3689D," until I couldn't stand it anymore.

I grabbed her arm and shook her again. "Ravenette," I said. "Ravenette."

The response I got was that vicious hiss, even louder and more ferocious sounding than before. It stopped abruptly and Ravenette seemed to recoil, as if she had been shoved backward. After a moment, her body posture changed, her features seemed to change, to become less rigid, and she expelled a long breath. "He's gone," she said. "He won't talk to you anymore. It's like . . . like he slammed a door. And he won't open it again."

"What door?"

"The door between us."

"What does *that* mean?"

The only image I could create out of what Ravenette had said was literal—like the door to Avi's room being slammed shut. Or at least, the version of Avi's room where the radio-man seemed to be waiting. Waiting for someone to give him back whatever it was that could be identified by the numbers 3689D.

Ravenette didn't answer. Instead, she suddenly sprang to her feet. Now, she was the one who was agitated. She started wandering around the room, moving in and out of the circle of light. "Is *this* who they are?" she said. "Is *this* who we are supposed to strive to become? Howard Gilmartin promised that when we met them again, they'd be higher beings than us, better than us, and instead, they turn out to be these . . . these creatures?" She continued to pace, and as she did, she continued to voice her apparently deepening despair. "They don't care about us. They're completely indifferent to our existence."

"They?"

"There are others," she said vaguely. "They're not with him. I mean, they're not here. Not exactly. I told you that." Her voice trailed off. She seemed unable to find a way to add any further description.

"But the room you described to me. It still exists. At least, the building it's in still exists. Is he there?"

"I don't know," Ravenette said. "I don't know, I don't know, I don't know. And what difference does it make? Nothing he said makes any sense. What is all this . . . this idiocy about prayers?"

Like a wheel turning, I could almost see her trying to think her way back through everything that had just happened in order to return to where she had started, which was in a place that definitely had nothing to do with prayers. From what I knew about the theology of the Blue Awareness—if it could even be called a theology—the concept of a universal creator would have been an anathema. After all, the goal of becoming "Aware" was to expand your consciousness in a way that would eventually allow you to evolve to the same exalted level of mind as the alien beings who were our true ancestors. Why would you pray to them when your aim was to *become* them?

Suddenly, she stopped her pacing and whipped around to face me. "This is all your fault," she said. "I don't know how you tricked Raymond into thinking that you could be trusted, because you're sick. You're damaged, deranged. I told you when we first met: this . . . this gray *thing* is a creation of your own perverted mind. It's an engram, a manifestation of the pain and anger inside you that keeps you chained down to a miserably low level of consciousness. That's what I made contact with—not a living entity but some kind of projection of your own neuroses. Someone needs to lock you up for about a year with a Blue Box and a trained Aware to help you rid yourself of this insanity. *You're* the one who wants there to be some great big fat God off in the ether somewhere, waiting to receive prayers he might or might not answer a billion years from now. My guess is probably not, because there is no such thing. There is no God, Laurie, there is only mind. Only consciousness. The way to the infinite is through becoming Aware, rising through the levels of consciousness to the higher planes. Once we achieve that, we will deserve to join the beings who left us here. To join with them, to understand their minds and therefore, the true nature of the universe."

"Ravenette. I didn't say there was a God. *He* did."

"I don't believe that. It's you—all this is coming from you. There's no other explanation."

After making this declaration, Ravenette began screaming at me to leave, to get out of the loft. She was working herself into a rage, repeating to me over and over again that my mind was perverted, my spirit too dangerous for her to be around for another second. I was just rising to my feet when she suddenly lunged at me as if to literally push me toward the door.

But she had forgotten about the dog. Lying at my feet, he had seemed to be fast asleep, but in the moment that Ravenette came toward me, he jumped up and positioned himself between us. Then he began to howl, producing the same threatening, high-pitched yipping that I remembered from the time that we had been confronted by the men in the blue van. It was worse than a growl, more frightening because the sound seemed to enter your body and make your blood sizzle. And, I realized, it now carried with it an even more familiar marker: the same high-frequency tone that had distorted Ravenette's voice when she was speaking for the radioman. Or, as she had now decided, when she was speaking for my supposedly dangerous engram.

The dog stopped Ravenette from advancing toward me, but she continued to demand that I leave. There was no point in staying, anyway, no point in trying to talk to her any further. I took hold of the dog's leash and tried to lead him away, but it took all my strength to get him to move. He bared his teeth and continued to howl at Ravenette until I finally managed to pull him into the elevator.

He calmed down when we were back on the street, but then he started panting and couldn't seem to stop. I hadn't even yet started to process everything that had just happened but my first thought was that I'd better get Digitaria some water before he keeled over. It was about two thirty in the morning now—but two thirty in the morning in New York—so there were still plenty of places open. There were half a dozen people hanging around outside a bar down the block and across the street, a brightly lit minimart had its door wide open.

I was about to step off the curb and head toward the store when I felt someone brush past me. I turned around and saw the same girl in the short silver skirt that I had encountered earlier. She had an odd look on her face. When I'd seen her before, I'd thought she seemed dreamy, but now . . . her eyes seemed vacant, her features slack. I thought she probably wanted to pet the dog again but I wasn't in the mood for that right now, so I moved away from her. Turning back in the direction of the minimart, I once again went to step off the curb but somehow—and seemingly, impossibly—there was the girl again, standing right in front of me.

"Excuse me," I said, as I went to walk around her. But as I did, her eyes grew bright and her body seemed to stiffen. My dog had an immediate, but completely unexpected reaction to the change in her body language: he stopped panting and began to wag his tail.

The girl in the silver skirt, however, paid no attention to him. She stepped in front of me again and pushed her face close to mine. Then, opening her mouth wider than seemed humanly possible, she let out a long, high-pitched hiss.

~XVI~

*S*o listen, sister, do damaged, perverted engrams generally manifest themselves in other people? Do they hiss
at you when you're walking down the street? I so much
wanted to go back up to Ravenette's loft, grab her by the
throat and start screaming at her myself that I almost turned
around and rang every intercom button on the door until
someone let me in. But what would be the point of getting
into a debate with her? The reality of the only world she
would accept was the one described by the beliefs of the Blue
Awareness, so arguing with her would have been a waste of
time. Besides, what would I be arguing for? The existence
of an alien being in some parallel universe who had seemingly lost some piece of equipment that he needed to send
prayers out into infinity? It sounded crazy even to me, but I
was at the point—far past it, really—when I had no choice
but to accept that it was so. Perhaps more than anything, it
was the way the dog was reacting that made it impossible
for me to come up with any other explanation. On some
level, somewhere deeply encoded in the flesh and chemicals
of which he was made, he was recognizing the presence of
another being, a consciousness that was familiar to him. And
that consciousness had communicated its purpose, or at least,
what it perceived its purpose to be. That much seemed clear.

But it was also extremely bizarre. Aliens, prayers, perhaps
even the existence—or the search?—for God himself. How
was I supposed to incorporate all this into what I understood

my life to be? How was I supposed to get on the bus in the afternoon, spend the night in an airport bar mixing up Cosmos and then go home to watch the late night infomercials knowing that behind some sort of screen—some divide between the reality I could see and something else I could not—things were going on that I simply could never comprehend? The tiny glimpse I had been given of that other reality, which could even be one of many, of an infinite number, was just enough to make it impossible for me to use my most powerful survival tool: the ability to compartmentalize, to deny what I did not want to know about. Or else to simply run away, as would have been my instinct when I was younger, because there was no "away" that I could get to. Not only was there no longer a hippie trail to follow (maybe there was still some commune, some network of crash pads somewhere, that welcomed forty-plus-year-olds, but I had no idea how or where to find them), but even if there were, I had a feeling that now, whether I was walking down a rural road in the back of beyond or wandering on a city street, I would hear that high-pitched, sizzling hiss come out of the mouth of a driver passing by in a car or a child on a swing. Or maybe a hawk swooping down from the windy sky. I would hear it until I helped the radioman get what he wanted, even if I had no idea what that might be.

All of this, all these thoughts and images, flashed through my mind as the girl in the silver skirt slowly turned away from me and drifted slowly down the sidewalk, as if nothing had happened. I watched her go for a moment, trying to collect myself. I looked around to see if anyone on the street had reacted to her bizarre behavior, but no one seemed to have paid her, or me, any attention. It was just another late-night scene in the city, another weird interaction that came and went.

After a while, as if I were on automatic pilot, I continued on my way to carry out the interrupted errand that I had set for myself. I crossed the street to the convenience store, where I bought a bottle of water and let the dog lap some out of my cupped hands. Then I took his leash and started walking, looking for a cab.

I thought I might find some gypsy cabs cruising around this neighborhood because it was home to a lot of after-hours clubs, but at this time of night, the drivers working these streets would be looking for high-end fares; I'd never get one to take me home for what I could afford to pay. So instead, I hailed a regular yellow cab and asked him to take me to Queens. I was already in the back seat with the dog next to me when the driver told me forget it, get out, he wasn't crossing bridges or heading off into the outer boroughs. I knew why—for a metered cab, the trip back would turn out to be a waste; no one would flag him down to get back to Manhattan. But it was also illegal to refuse me and I wasn't in the mood to play.

I leaned forward and spoke through the opening between the panels of the plastic barrier that was supposed to protect the driver from thieves and crazies. "Look," I said in the darkest voice I could come up with, "I am not a nice person and this is not a nice dog that I have with me. Either just drive the damn cab where I want to go or I'm going to take off his leash. He will be through the partition and in your lap in about ten seconds and I promise you won't like it."

The man glared at me in his rear-view mirror, but I saw his glance slide over to the dog and then, muttering to himself, he threw the flag on the meter. The cab moved forward.

It was nearly four A.M. when I let myself into my apartment. I stripped off my clothes and got into bed, finally letting myself feel how exhausted I was. As I pulled a blanket over myself, the dog took his usual place at the end of the bed and with his head facing the door, began his customary nighttime vigil. Almost immediately, I fell asleep.

But I didn't sleep for long. I awoke just a few hours later knowing exactly what I had to do, because I had to do something. I just couldn't go on living my life waiting for new dogs to show up—as if I needed any more intermediaries to bring me messages—and strangers to hiss at me, or worse (what "worse" meant I had no idea but didn't think I wanted to find out) if I did not at least try to provide what the radioman wanted. But to do so, I needed help.

I took Digitaria outside, and as I walked him, I dialed Jack's cell phone. It went directly to voice mail so I tried the studio line, but that was also picked up by an answering machine that announced I had reached the *Up All Night* show on World Air. That at least answered a question I hadn't thought to ask myself: was Jack still working out of his Brooklyn studio even though he was now doing his show for the satellite service? Apparently, the answer was yes. I started dialing his cell phone again but then I thought, *The hell with this. What am I wasting my time for?* I pulled on Digitaria's leash and marched back home.

I fed the dog and then left my apartment again, heading off to the subway. I got on with the morning commuters and rode out to Brooklyn. I hadn't been on the train during a morning rush hour in—well, forever—and it was a kind of disorienting experience. I wasn't used to traveling with such a well-dressed crowd. Squeezed in among the suits and dresses and crisp fall jackets, I felt like a trespasser from another world in my jeans and hoodie. And in a way, I suppose I was.

When I changed trains, the crowd thinned out because I was now traveling away from Manhattan. I stayed on all the way out to the last stop on the line. When I emerged in Brooklyn, the air was chilly with autumn and tinged with the smell of river water. I headed off toward Red Hook, walking along, block after block, under a high mackerel sky.

Arriving at Jack's building, I didn't let myself hesitate. I pushed the buzzer and was rewarded with the sound of Jack's sleepy voice asking who was at his door.

"It's me," I said. "Laurie. I need to talk to you."

Silence followed. I tried to control my impatience as I waited for Jack to consider how mad he still was. Weeks and weeks had gone by since we'd last seen each other at the Blue Awareness townhouse. Despite all the unreturned phone calls, it was hard for me to believe that he really continued to nurse a grudge against me. Maybe it was hard for him, too, because, when he finally replied, he seemed to be wavering a little.

"About what?" he asked.

About what? That was a complicated question. I decided to start with a simple answer. "I need to know what a Haverkit 3689D is."

"A what?"

It was a little disconcerting to be having this conversation over an intercom, which added crackles of electricity to our already tinny-sounding voices. I hoped we weren't going to have to continue this way much longer.

"What?" he repeated.

In frustration, I slapped the button on the intercom box and said, "Jack. For heaven's sake. Just please let me in."

Another few moments passed and then the buzzer emitted a scratchy bleat. I let myself into the building and went up to Jack's studio. He greeted me in a bathrobe and sweats. Instead of a hello, he acknowledged me with a kind of grunt and then waved me toward the kitchen.

A coffeemaker was gurgling away on the counter. He poured himself a cup and, sighing heavily, settled himself in a chair by the kitchen table. Both pieces of furniture looked like they had been rescued from the street eons ago.

"You know," I said, gesturing at the coffeemaker, "I got up early, too."

"That's what you have to do when you want to ambush people," he replied.

I picked a mug off a rack on the counter, poured myself a cup of coffee and seated myself at the table. "How long are you going to keep this up?" I asked him. "I mean, being pissed off at me?"

"I don't know. Indefinitely seems like a nice target date."

"Because you're what? Nine years old? Somebody disrespects you on the playground so you hold a grudge for the rest of your life?"

"Is that what you think happened?"

"It *is* what happened."

I didn't really want to discuss our meeting with Raymond Gilmartin and the way Jack and I had parted that night because so much had taken place since then. I felt like those events were part of some distant era that was already far behind me. But apparently, we were going to have to get it out of the way before we could go on to anything else.

"Look," I began, "I'm not saying I don't understand how you feel. I can be pretty good at holding grudges myself. But if it makes things any better, I apologize for not backing you up with Raymond Gilmartin. I really do. Maybe I should have walked out with you. But . . . I don't know. I had to hear him out."

"Why? He's even crazier than I thought. And dangerous."

"I'm not defending him, I'm defending myself. I'm in the middle of something I barely understand, so cut me some slack, okay? I haven't known who to listen to or what I'm supposed to do."

"And now you do?"

"I think so, yes."

He regarded me with a look that radiated skepticism, but I knew he was going to give in. "All right," he said finally. "Tell me."

And so I did. I told him everything, from my meeting with Dr. Carpenter to my late-night encounter with Kelly, the traveler, and his dog, to last night's turbulent visit to Ravenette. A couple of times, he made me go back over what she had told me about the radiomen broadcasting prayers.

When I was finished he let out a long, low whistle. "Yikes," he said.

That seemed to express just about everything there was to say. "Exactly," I agreed.

But now what? Were we going to go back to being reasonable people? Maybe even friends? It seemed maybe so, because Jack got up then and poured us both some more coffee, which I took as a kind of a peace offering. I accepted the mug without comment because all I wanted at this point was to get back to the real reason I had come here.

"So," I ventured, "what's a Haverkit 3689D?"

"I really don't know," Jack said.

"Well, I can at least tell you one thing it's not. It's not the horn of plenty antenna. He—the radioman—made that very clear."

Jack shook his head. "So everybody's been chasing the wrong thing."

"Not me," I reminded him. "Not you."

"Oh, I don't know," Jack said. "In the great, wide scope of things, that's probably open to interpretation."

"But that's not where we're looking. In the great wide scope of things."

"Nope," Jack said ruefully. "More like the Twilight Zone. But come on," he said, gesturing toward his office. "We can try to find out what a Haverkit 3689D might be."

We went over to his computer, where he sat down and opened a browser. As I watched him, I realized that it hadn't even occurred to me to search the Internet, which just reinforced how hard it was for me to find logical ways to think about the situation I found myself in. But it was better, anyway, that Jack was doing it. If what we were looking for was some kind of radio equipment, which was my best guess, then it was more likely Jack would have a better idea of what to search for and where to look than I did.

He bounced around from site to site for a while until he finally exclaimed, "Got it." He had navigated to a website that was devoted to collectors of the various electronic parts and equipment that the long-out-of-business Haverkit company had made. Pointing to a rectangular metal box that looked like it belonged on a rack of computer parts, he said, "Your friend is looking for a repeater."

"Which is what?"

"It's a device that amplifies the range of a broadcast signal by repeating it from one source to another."

I thought about that for a moment and something clicked. I told Jack, "Before she flipped out on me, Ravenette said that the radioman was describing a huge broadcast network that covered . . . well, she said galaxies. Many galaxies. It can't be possible that one Haverkit repeater could help boost a signal that much?"

"Of course not," Jack explained. "These types of repeaters were meant to be used by amateur radio operators trying to extend the range of their broadcasts over relatively finite distances. But sometimes, repeaters like these were used as the hub of what's called a linked repeater network. With that kind of system, when one repeater is keyed-up by receiving a signal, all the other repeaters in the network are also activated and will transmit the same signal. So if there is a chain of repeaters waiting to hear from this one . . ."

"Just this one?"

Jack shrugged. "Maybe. If that's how the network is set up."

"So why doesn't whoever gave the radioman his job just ship him another one? Send him a replacement for the hub repeater?"

"I don't know," Jack said, though he seemed to have a guess. "Maybe," he said, "for something to exist where the radioman is, it also has to exist here. If it disappears from where we are, it disappears from where he is, too. Or maybe the supply train from his home base—wherever it is—only shows up once a millennium."

"Do you think that's funny?" I said to him.

"I think this is a very strange conversation," Jack replied. "I'm just going with the flow."

Something else suddenly occurred to me. "You know," I said, taking another look at the repeater that was still displayed on Jack's computer screen, "I don't remember *ever* seeing Avi fiddling with something like that."

"It wouldn't have been something he would have carried back and forth with him, like the radio. It would have been permanently installed somewhere, on high ground." Then, pointedly, he added, "Like a roof, for example."

I closed my eyes for a moment, picturing Avi and me on the fire escape of the Sunlite Apartments, listening to the pinging sound of Sputnik's 10 telemetry signal—and then Avi, frowning, as the radio suddenly went silent. *Laurie,* he'd said, looking up at the roof, *I have to go fix something . . .*

Still there was something that puzzled me. "Why would Avi even need a repeater?" I asked Jack. "He was just listening to satellite signals on his receiver. He wasn't broadcasting."

"Well," he replied, "he sort of was."

Jack asked me to give him a minute and left the room but was soon back, carrying a brown accordion folder. I thought I remembered seeing it months ago when he had told me about the ghost signals, but it turned out that this was a different folder. And it held some very different material.

As he sat back down at the desk and started taking papers out of the folder, he said, "So, I have to tell you that when I did the original research about the ghost signals, I also used the Freedom of Information Act to get whatever I could on Avi, too. I had to know if there was anything . . . well, off about him."

I realized that he thought I might have been upset by the fact that he had been digging into Avi's life, but I wasn't. At this point, I just wanted to hear the rest of the story: *what* was Avi broadcasting? And why?

"Was there anything strange about what he was doing?" I asked.

"No," Jack said. "Not at all."

I looked down at the papers he was pulling out of the folder. They were color photocopies of documents that looked vaguely familiar to me. I had a feeling that I had seen them before, but I couldn't remember where, or when.

"It turns out that Avi was a member of a Distance Listening Club," Jack said. "You never heard him mention anything like that?"

"No," I said. I started leafing through the dozens of documents that Jack had now laid out on his desk and realized that they were copies of what looked like postcards from foreign destinations—some familiar, like Paris and Moscow, but others from places with odd names like Tannu Tuva, or breathtakingly distant, like a town in Tasmania. There was also one from what appeared to be a weather station in Antarctica. Some were in English, some in languages I couldn't recognize, let alone read.

Suddenly, something focused in my mind; a clouded memory became clear. "I *do* remember these," I said. "Avi kept these—the originals—in an album that he used to let me look at. All he ever said was that people had sent them to him."

"People did send them to him," Jack told me. "They're what's called QSL cards. In radio lingo, that's a code meaning, 'I confirm receipt of your transmission.' If you were a DX-er, which is what distance listening guys were called, you'd send a signal on the short or medium wave band to another DX-er in some distant location, and then the two of you would exchange these QSL cards to confirm that you'd received each other's broadcast. Some of the cards were very colorful, some had pictures, some were just plain, typed confirmations. From the 1950s up until about the time he died, Avi was apparently a very active member of a Distance Listening Club that had members all over New York. And that's probably why he maintained a repeater out at Rockaway Beach. It may not even have been his, but it's also likely that he shared it with everyone else in range. Repeaters are often used by large networks of amateur radio types."

Interesting as all that was, it still didn't explain why copies of Avi's QSL cards had turned up in some government file. I asked Jack about that and he explained, "It was the Cold War era. A lot of these cards are from countries behind the Iron Curtain. Maybe some federal agency kept records of correspondence that went back and forth between the United States and countries they thought of as problematic."

"Antarctica?" I said, holding up the copy of the QSL card from the weather station, which included a series of call signs and a drawing of a penguin with a big smile on his face. The happy bird was wearing a striped scarf around his neck and on his head, a set of oversized headphones.

Jack shrugged. "It was just the job of some guy at a government desk to intercept these things and make copies. He probably didn't even know where Antarctica was."

"Can I have these?" I asked Jack.

"If you really want them, sure."

I did want them. I was feeling a little nostalgic about these lost-and-now-found postcards, but looking at the penguin again, I was still a little puzzled.

"I can't really imagine that anybody needed to worry about Avi. I doubt that he was sending secret messages to the Communists. Or to penguins."

"No, of course not," Jack said. "And I think they actually gave up on worrying about him pretty quickly. But maybe somebody else heard him and decided to piggyback on his repeater. Remember the story I told you about Howard Gilmartin's encounter with the gray man on the radar tower during World War II? What if he—and your radioman, and however many others there are—well, what if they were stationed here?" Jack's voice had a note of incredulity in it even as he confirmed, for himself, that he had come up with the right terminology. "Yes, I guess they're stationed here. So what if these guys were always trying to find some way to boost their signal? I guess at one point they were trying to use radar towers—where one of them ran into Gilmartin, senior—but eventually it turned out that, of all things, the Haverkit repeater in Rockaway worked best. Maybe because of the thin, cold air out at the beach. Maybe the fact that it was always kept in good working order. Maybe the moon, the tides, and good luck. And maybe," Jack said, speaking more slowly now, as if he were thinking through every word, "they'd been trying for a very, very long time to find just the right place to link up their network to get the maximum distance out of their signals. Maybe one of the places they tried was in Mali, a couple of centuries ago."

I finished his thought for him. "When one of them left behind a dog."

"I guess that could be."

"And the signals they were trying to send out . . ."

"Were the ghost signals. The prayers. They wanted to send them as far out into space as they could."

"Where there are more repeaters to send them even farther. Or—just like Ravenette said—a vast network of energy waves."

We both fell silent for a moment as we considered the fact that perhaps we had just stumbled upon the solution to the mystery that had plagued Avi, but in which he had also, however unwittingly, apparently played a role. On many levels, this scenario was difficult for me to accept.

"I don't know," I said to Jack. "It seems a little primitive, doesn't it? I mean, they're using radio waves and a repeater built from a kit you could order from the back of a catalogue? Shouldn't they be using interstellar wormhole-piercing light rays or something like that?"

"You're asking me?" Jack said. "I haven't got the slightest idea *what* they should be using. But I guess radio makes sense. That's more or less what astronomers have always expected to hear if another civilization ever decided to make contact, for example. Radio is an easy technology to discover.

And if you keep boosting radio waves with a repeater, then they can probably travel through space for an infinite distance, for an infinite amount of time."

I picked up another one of the photocopies and examined it, and as I did, I had the sensation, real or imagined, of feeling a little light go on in some tiny compartment in a cabinet in the storeroom of my memory. The picture of the card I held in my hand showed a jolly-looking, bearded leprechaun in a green jacket, wearing pointy green shoes, with a big grin on his face. The only unusual thing about the otherwise familiar depiction of this particular creature of folklore was, like the smiling penguin, that he was wearing a pair of oversize headphones that covered his ears. Above his head, in bright green letters, were written the words, "Hello from the Emerald Isle." Looking at this fellow, I felt like I was gazing at the face of a long-lost friend, because I remembered him. This had been one of my favorite postcards in Avi's album. For the longest time, I had no idea that the Emerald Isle referred to Ireland. I thought it was a special place you could visit where bright green gems would wash up on the beach like seashells.

"What do you think happened to the repeater?" I asked Jack.

"Who knows? If it was up on the roof of . . . what was that place called where you used to go?"

"The Sunlite Apartments."

"Right. So maybe if it was on the roof of the Sunlite Apartments, Avi did take it down at some point—maybe to repair it. Or maybe, after your mother died and your family stopped going out to Rockaway, he just relocated it and let someone else in the DX club maintain it. Or it was destroyed in a storm and no one replaced it. All we really know, I guess, is that it isn't where it's supposed to be anymore. At least, where it works for your radioman."

All this time, Jack had been standing next to me, watching as I paged through the photocopies of the QSL cards.

Suddenly, he lowered himself into a chair and said, simply, "Wow."

"What?" I asked.

He shook his head. "I guess it just hit me," he said. "I talk about this stuff all the time on the radio. Aliens, alternate universes, you name it. But that's just . . . talk. This is real, isn't it?"

"Tell me it isn't," I said, "and I'll try to believe you."

"I can't," Jack replied, "because I've got this picture in my head now. I think your friend is a member of another distance listening club. Only in his club, the members' idea of distance is . . . well, a lot farther than ours. And there's something else." Jack pointed at the computer where the image of the Haverkit repeater was still displayed; a black rectangle with silvery metal mountings hovering in cyberspace. "This is a D model, 3689D," he said, emphasizing the letter that ended the model number." That means *duplex*. A duplex repeater uses two radio frequencies. The designated output frequency retransmits a signal, but there's also a frequency dedicated to recognizing an incoming signal. In other words, it seems like your radioman and his—well, what should we call them? Friends? Colleagues? Fellow workers? Whoever they are, they seem to be hoping for an answer."

That was about the first thing either of us had said this morning that actually didn't seem so peculiar to me. "I guess that's what everyone expects when they pray."

A sort of faraway look came over Jack's face, like he was trying to find a clear line of sight from a distant spot where he really had to focus in order to see what was ahead. Finally, he said, "You want to give it back to him. The repeater."

"If I don't, he'll never leave me alone."

"And you have an idea of how we would make this hand-off?"

"I think so. I think you just gave it to me. You said, 'maybe for something to exist where the radioman is, it also has to

~ 243 ~

exist here.' Well, what if the opposite is also true? He's in a room that exists wherever he is but I know where that room exists here. The building where we stayed in Rockaway is still standing. So . . ."

Jack nodded, understanding what I meant. We had both already accepted so many bizarre ideas as possibilities—even facts—that I didn't really have to explain this one any further. "Okay," he said and turned back to the computer. He started jumping around different websites again, going from auction sites to online electronics stores to message boards filled with technical information about radio parts. He spent some time scrolling through these and then announced, "I can't find a duplex Haverkit repeater anywhere. But I have another idea. Maybe I could build one. I mean, they were kits; they were meant for people to put together themselves. I think I can buy most of the parts and probably even an old schematic."

"You really think you can?"

"I should be able to. I told you a long time ago, Laurie— I'm a radioman myself."

It only took Jack about fifteen minutes to find a blue-print for building the repeater on a site that archived Haverkit manuals, and he soon became absorbed in looking for the parts. Some components he was able to find, some he left messages about in chat rooms for radio buffs, asking if he could substitute one thing he couldn't locate for another that he could. I sat beside him for a while, watching him as he went about his online search, but then I decided to go home. I hadn't had much sleep; I was tired and I was supposed to work that evening so I wanted to go back to my apartment and try to nap for a while.

We said good-bye, clearly back on our old, steady footing. Jack said he'd be in touch and I headed out, meaning to start off on the long walk to the subway. But maybe just out of mental exhaustion, or maybe something else—who knows?—I found myself wandering in the opposite direction, toward the waterfront, which was just a few blocks away. Here, the landscape was dominated by huge cranes meant to lift containers on and off the barges that floated them in from the huge ships anchored somewhere off in deeper water, though few were still in operation. Rust was creeping up the steel feet of these monster-like structures; rot had pulled down whole sections of the nearby piers that stretched into the water of the oily shipping channel.

I sat down at the edge of a dock supported by moss-covered pilings. Mindlessly, I looked off toward the towers of Manhattan, standing like a cluster of shadowy obelisks against a backdrop of vast white sky. It was a cool day, neither summer nor fall, with no wind, no clouds, and seemingly, no sun, just that sheet-colored sky, stretching from horizon to horizon above the calm, colorless water.

Suddenly, without even having to turn around, I knew there was a presence standing behind me. Not a person, but a presence. And I knew what it was.

I didn't move, but waited for it to show itself. After a few moments, I heard it move. I expected it to come face me, but instead, it sat down beside me and leaned against me in a familiar way.

For a little while longer, I kept my gaze fixed on the black obelisks across the water. When I finally turned my head, I saw that sitting next to me was a reddish gold-colored dog with a narrow muzzle and a narrower body. It had thin ears that stood up straight from the back of its tapered skull and a long tail that curved at the end like a whip. I had watched the occasional dog show on television so I thought I knew what kind of dog this was: a pharaoh hound. Hardly the kind of dog that would be wandering by itself around a deserted Brooklyn dockyard. Hardly a stray—but then, I didn't for a moment try to convince myself that it was.

The dog leaned against me even harder. I nodded to acknowledge his presence, which I decided to accept as a kind of peace offering, and said, "I am going to try to help him. But you might tell him to be a little nicer to me."

The dog turned to look straight at me with dark, glittering eyes. Then he stood up, shook himself, and ran off toward the horizon, toward the edge of the white sky.

~XVII~

The days went on. I slept, I got up, I walked my dog, I went to work and then came home and went through the cycle again. I was in a strange state, a kind of suspended animation, in which few sensations seemed to get through to me. Instead of being in the world, I felt like I was walking along a corridor just outside, seeing everything through a kind of filmy curtain. Sometimes, drifting through the motions of work or riding the bus or walking down the street, my mind would clear for a moment and I would be able to focus on what I was involved in and it would occur to me that maybe I had gone crazy. Maybe I was deluded. Maybe I was imagining things. Dogs were bringing me messages? An alien sitting in a room that was not really a room—not in this world, anyway—was waiting for me to give him back the lost component of an interstellar radio network? Beings who were not human were consumed with sending prayers into space in order to speak to God? Maybe instead of wasting my money on rent and food I should ask Jack to watch Digitaria for a while and check myself into some sort of clinic.

But it was actually Jack's phone calls—he spoke to me now almost every day—that kept me tethered to the strange reality that was now the framework of my life. He was making progress building the repeater, and actually seemed to be enjoying himself, as if he, too, sometimes forgot the real purpose of his task. We talked about that one night, late, when he was off the air, and agreed that it was hard to hold the idea in mind of what we were really doing; the subject came up in the context of a surprising piece of information he wanted to share with me.

"Guess who wants to come on the show?" Jack asked.

"I can't guess," I said. "I just got back from work a little while ago. I'm too tired."

"Raymond Gilmartin."

That was a surprise—and it certainly got my attention. "Why?" I asked. "The last time you suggested that, he threw you out of his office."

"You haven't been listening to my show, have you?"

I hadn't because once I found out how much it actually cost to buy the special radio you needed to listen to the satellite service, as well as to pay the subscription fee, I decided that I could live without it. I was kind of embarrassed to admit that to Jack, though. So, hemming and hawing, I said, "I've been meaning to sign up for the service, but . . ."

"Never mind," Jack said. Maybe he'd guessed at the reason I wasn't listening in or maybe he was just being nice—maybe both—because he immediately offered a way to fix what, to him, must have seemed like a problem that needed an immediate solution. "I'll get you a radio and pay for the service. I should have at least one loyal listener."

I said thanks and then waited for Jack to circle back to the subject of Raymond Gilmartin, which he did, almost immediately. What he told me was interesting, but I still didn't think it explained much.

"I've been after them—the Blue Awareness—ever since Raymond kicked me out that night," Jack said. "Well, before, of course, but that just made me . . . oh, let's say, it made me even more pissed off. So I've had lots of ex-Awares on, and they've been pretty frank in revealing just about everything they know about the movement. I have to say, they've told some very interesting tales about Raymond, in particular. Apparently, he's revised a lot of the Awareness doctrine to make it more to his liking. Howard Gilmartin was a grandiose, narcissistic paranoid, but the picture I'm getting is more of someone who wanted to play out his fantasies than a man who was deeply invested in having people create a cult around him. It's Raymond who built a small group of followers into a worldwide movement. I've actually had on a number of people who joined the Blue Awareness when Howard was alive and left during Raymond's tenure as the movement leader. They all say that Raymond is totally inflexible; you can't disagree with him or question him in any way. For example, did you know he was the one who came up with the idea of engrams and Blue Boxes? He really believes that he has a duty—a mission—to make people adopt his beliefs."

Though I hadn't known these specific details, overall, I didn't think the information was all that surprising. It seemed to go without saying that Raymond was picking and choosing from his father's ideas then adding in his own to create a religion that suited his own strange view of the world and what lay beyond. But just as obviously, he was doing a very good job of it, because, from what I knew—and despite all the disgruntled followers Jack could find—people seemed to be joining the Blue Awareness in record numbers. So why bother to go on Jack's show? Why give Jack that satisfaction—and the buzz it might create for his program? What was in it for Raymond?

I asked Jack that question and he said, "To be honest, I don't care. Though I imagine he thinks he can get the better of me, just like he did last time."

Oh boy, I found myself thinking. *This is some guy thing. Jack Shepherd lost a fight with Raymond Gilmartin and now he wants to get back at him, no matter what.*

"You're not going to mention the repeater, are you?"

"Jesus, no," Jack said. "Not to Gilmartin. That story is for later."

Later? What did he mean? "Wait a minute," I said. "You never even asked me about that. I wanted you to help me—not to talk about . . . well, about *anything*. Not on your show." The idea made me panicky. My life was already weird enough without hearing it discussed on the radio. Helping shadow men send prayers out into the distant universe—that didn't sound like how the ideal Endless Weekend employee should be spending her spare time. If the story got out, I could easily guess how quickly I would get fired.

"I would never mention your name," Jack said.

"Oh, great. That makes me feel so much better."

"Stop worrying, Laurie. Everything will be fine."

"That's what they say in the movies just before the psycho killers show up."

Jack sighed. "We've got enough going on, don't you think? Don't bring up psycho killers."

After we hung up, I went to sleep, got up the next morning, and the cycle of days began again, though after that phone call with Jack there was one big change in my life, and that involved my dog. Digitaria now seemed to be on edge all the time. For the first time since he'd been with me, I had to restrain him from lunging at people in the street whose look I guess he didn't like. And at night, keeping his vigil at the edge of the bed, he'd sometimes make that odd yipping sound, but softly, as if he were talking to himself. *You totally are crazy*, I said to myself the first time I had that thought— *Digitaria is talking to himself*—and then rolled over and went back to the broken, fitful sleep that now characterized my nights.

Raymond Gilmartin was scheduled for his on-air talk with Jack about a week after I first heard that he was going to do the show. I was very nervous about what direction their conversation might take since the last thing I wanted to hear was either of them mention my name on the radio. Ravenette had found me that first time with very little trouble—who knew what other kinds of crazies might be moved to invade my life if they heard anything about my connection to what was undoubtedly going to sound like some kind of alien invasion?

I tried to put Jack and Raymond out of my mind for a while, and it helped that I had to work on the night of the interview. I managed to keep myself occupied by tracking the sports scores and suggesting elaborate mixed drinks to customers; making Singapore Slings and Mai Tais kept my hands busy and my thoughts engaged with inconsequential tasks.

But afterward, after the bar had closed down and I was waiting for the bus on the service road that separated the food service parking lots from the marshland edging Jamaica Bay, I couldn't keep my attention focused on trivialities anymore. Looking up into the night, I saw that Orion and his hunting dogs were climbing back into the ink-colored sky, making their return from their summer hiding place below the horizon. Recognizing these constellations led me immediately to locate Sirius, the brightest star in the sky, which is pinned to the snout of the Great Dog constellation. Along with its lesser companion, the Minor Dog, Canis Major faithfully follows Orion the hunter throughout the seasons, never leaving his side. I tried to imagine the companion that belonged to Sirius itself—Digitaria, the invisible other, the dwarf star bonded to its massive twin by the bonds of ancient, interstellar forces. But that's all it could be: imagination. Sirius is a bright dot in the sky, but a single point of coldly burning light is what it must remain to any Earthbound observer. The human eye, unaided by a telescope, cannot see that Sirius has company. It is impossible.

With Orion and his fierce pets on the ascendant, these were still the supposed dog days of summer, but it was actually late in September, and the night air was cool. I had brought a hoodie with me, rolled into a ball and stuffed into my shoulder bag, so I pulled it out and zipped myself into it, hoping the bus would show up soon.

It finally did, though the ride home seemed to take forever. Once I got to my block, the usual scenario was playing itself out: a long Diamond Reo was parked up against the wall of an alley near my house, its running lights on and its engine idling softly. Two men were unloading cartons from the back. I knew they were not the pair who had helped me out last summer, when the men in the yellow goggles had tried to steal Digitaria—I had never seen those two workers again. Tonight, I barely even glanced at the guys pulling swag from the truck as I walked on toward my building.

I unlocked the vestibule door with my key and started up the stairs to my apartment. As usual, it was long past midnight, but as I opened my door, I heard my neighbor's door open as well. I waited while Sassouma walked down the hall toward me, carrying a small FedEx box.

I wasn't all that surprised that she was awake, since she sometimes came home very late from the convenience store where she worked. I assumed that she had retrieved the package from the hall where the FedEx deliveryman had left it, but I had no idea what it might be until she handed it to me and I saw that the label had Jack's return address on it.

As we chatted for a moment—I asked about her children and her husband, and she answered as best she could with her limited English—Digitaria came out into the hallway and she patted him on the head. Down a few doors, I could hear her little dog barking for her to come back, so we said good night and I went inside.

Before I took Digitaria outside for his walk, I opened the package and found that it contained a radio, a small one, about the size of an old-fashioned transistor, but much sleeker looking. It was slate gray in color and had an array of buttons under a small, gray screen, and I quickly realized that it was the satellite radio Jack had promised to get for me. I'd forgotten all about that, but now, here it was. Jack had once called me a radio freak, and he was right—that was one thing I certainly had in common with Avi. This was a completely new kind of radio, and as soon as I had it in my hands, I was intrigued.

The radio came with instructions for activating it, which involved a phone call to a twenty-four-hour customer service line, and in a few minutes, I was able to push the On button and watch as the radio lit up and the screen displayed a scrolling menu of more than a hundred channels to select from.

One thing the radio did not have, though, was a speaker; to listen to it, you either had to plug it into a stereo system or listen with headphones. I tuned the radio to a station dedicated to playing classic hits of the sixties, then rooted around in my top dresser drawer until I found a pair of earbuds, which I plugged into the radio, and soon I heard the Beatles singing *yeah, yeah, yeah,* as if they were inside my brain. Not bad. Not bad at all.

I found Digitaria's leash and led him outside for his walk. In the short time I'd been upstairs, whoever was responsible for unloading the Diamond Reo had finished their work. The truck was gone. The street was otherwise empty, so it was just me, the dog, the music in my head, and the starry pictures of men and beasts drawn on the night sky.

Maybe it was just the music, but for the first time in a while, I felt like I was coming back to myself, like my spirit— whatever that was—had been absent from my body but was beginning, gingerly, to fold itself back in. I felt calmer, a little stronger, a little more centered. So, as I walked, I found myself putting aside my aversion to hearing what Jack and Raymond might have to say to each other. After all, Jack had promised to keep the focus on the Blue Awareness, and what difference did it make to me, really, if he and Raymond went at each other about that? Besides, Jack never spent his entire show talking with only one guest; the odds were that I had already missed Raymond's segment and Jack was on to some other topic, like the existence of poltergeists or which lost civilization might have built the Bimini Road.

But like everything else, lately, what I didn't want to happen was exactly what did: as I tuned through the stations, I suddenly heard Jack's voice. He said something I didn't quite catch, and received an answer from his guest who was, unmistakably, not a poltergeist hunter or anyone else but Raymond Gilmartin. The radio provided a clear, finely modulated sound, which made me focus on the quality of the voices speaking to me through the headphones. I hadn't noticed it before, but now, listening to Jack and Raymond, I realized the two men's voices presented as much of a contrast as their personalities: Jack's was rough, but tinged with irony—very New York—while Raymond's was polished and smooth, the voice of someone who gave a lot of speeches to attentive audiences.

As I listened, though, whatever good humor Jack projected quickly vanished. He kept pushing Raymond to talk about specific issues that ex-Awares had brought up on his program, such as the accusation that the Blue Awareness was set up to extract escalating fees from members for seemingly endless Blue Box sessions, which were required for rising from one level of "Awareness" to another, meaning, to have more and more of what Jack characterized as Raymond's "bizarre doctrine" revealed to them. But Raymond dismissed all that as complaints from disgruntled individuals who were also, possibly, mentally ill. They needed more Blue Box sessions, Raymond suggested, not fewer; and then left that issue entirely to defend Blue Awareness doctrine, which, he said was based on irrefutable truth—and you could hear the capital "T" in that word as it rolled out of his mouth.

By the time he got to this point in the conversation, I was climbing the stairs back to my apartment. Once inside, I unclipped the dog's leash and as he sat beside me, I listened to Raymond describe, in his own words, how one ascended to the Wild Blue Yonder.

He repeated what I already knew, but put it in a way that I had not heard before. He said that humanity was stuck in a low level of evolution. That an alien race—ancient, brilliant, god-like in their knowledge and abilities—had seeded the universe with beings meant to develop, over time, into equally god-like creatures, capable of straddling the many dimensions of time and space and becoming equal partners with their creators. But we humans had forgotten this history, had lost our way and rejected our destiny because we had become too enamored of the corporeal world, of material pleasures and what Raymond called "idiotic pastimes," such as sports, climbing the corporate ladder, and dieting—he was particularly opposed to diet fads because, as he explained, if you spent enough time having your engrams analyzed and "cleansed" by Blue Box sessions, your body would always remain fit and healthy.

But he reserved his harshest criticism for what he called "the stupidest pastime of all," which was religion—at least any religion based on a belief system other than the tenets of the Blue Awareness. As Raymond spoke, his voice remained smooth as oil, but I heard something else in it: the visual image came to me of little fires burning around the edges.

"The mistake people make," Raymond said, "and they have made it for centuries, is in thinking that something we call 'God' exists outside ourselves. Nothing could be further from the truth. In reality, the universal awareness we seek through religion—through begging for the intervention of some kind of Big Daddy who exists apart from us—is what keeps us in the dark. It's what keeps us ignorant. The elders—the beings who brought us here—already have all the knowledge, all the understanding needed to be truly alive, to truly understand the nature of consciousness and the forces of infinity. This is what they seeded within us. Now, they are simply waiting for us to evolve, to become their partners in roaming the universe. In understanding and even transforming it. They are waiting for us," Raymond repeated emphatically. "But we've forgotten that. Instead of growing into the infinite, we've grown more deaf, dumb and blind with every generation."

Then there was silence. It was an unnerving experience to just sit and listen to the dead air settling like dust in my earphones. But I knew that Jack was deliberately creating silence—the one thing you never hear on the radio—because he wanted to make everyone uneasy, Raymond and his listeners alike.

Finally, Jack responded to Raymond by posing a set of questions that he had clearly been leading up to throughout the interview. "What if you're wrong?" he asked. "I mean, totally wrong? What if the aliens—given that they really are here, that they even exist—aren't interested in us at all? Never were? Never had anything whatsoever to do with the presence of human beings on Earth? What if they don't care if we live or die? Evolve or disappear? If that's the case, what's the point of the Blue Awareness? Wouldn't you just have to . . . well, give up? Disband?"

Jack had sworn not to mention what I'd told him and while technically, he hadn't, I felt he was skirting the edges of his promise to me. And while I had no way of knowing whether Ravenette had revealed the same information to Raymond, I had a feeling that Jack and Raymond were now interacting on two levels: they were conducting a conversation meant for the consumption of their radio audience, but they also were having a deeper, more personal argument. I could imagine them, now, speaking to each other through clenched teeth.

"That's ridiculous," Raymond said.

"Why?" Jack asked. "For about forty years, I've been talking to all kinds of people—scholars, archaeologists, writers, historians, even men and women who've had abduction experiences—and it seems that our concept of alien life interacting with ours always hinges on them meaning us well, trying to teach us things we don't understand, or else doing us harm. Sticking probes down our throats—or elsewhere." Jack chuckled at his own innuendo, and then went on. "But I'm just wondering, what if they're as confused as we are about . . . what it all means? You know? Why we are here?

Who put us here? Who put *them* on whatever planet—in whatever dimension of time and space—they come from? In other words, who do you think they pray to?"

"There is no need to pray to anyone," Raymond said, sounding cool again. Calm and collected. "What we need is to develop the universal spirit within ourselves. To nurture it while driving out the painful memories and internalized messages that prevent us from evolving toward the infinite."

"In other words," said Jack, "we're supposed to be performing spiritual surgery on ourselves."

Raymond seemed to like this analogy. "In a way, yes," he replied. "That is what you can accomplish with the Blue Box, if you dedicate yourself to it. In fact," he said, "I have an invitation for you. If you can spare some time—let's say a week or so—we have a retreat upstate where you could work with a trained Blue Box counselor. I'm sure it would do you a great deal of good—and change your mind about us. About the Awareness."

Jack chuckled again. "Maybe I will take you up on that offer," he said. "In the meantime, I think we're coming to the end of this segment, so let me thank you, Raymond Gilmartin, for visiting us at *Up All Night.*"

Raymond replied with a string of muttered niceties I knew he didn't mean, and then some spooky, space-age kind of music came on. A few moments later, Jack was back on the air, announcing that his next guest was an expert on Kennedy assassination conspiracy theories. I wasn't interested, so I turned off the radio.

I puttered around my apartment for a while, folding laundry that had been waiting to be put away and doing other minor chores. As I worked, I allowed myself to feel some relief at the fact that whatever remained of my privacy still seemed to be intact—at least, I hadn't heard my name mentioned on the show—when the sound of my telephone ringing jolted me out of what ended up being a very temporary sense of calm.

"I'm finished," I heard Jack say as soon as I picked up the receiver.

"What?" I didn't understand what he meant.

"The repeater," he said. "I'm finished. I didn't get a chance to call you before the show went on the air."

I hadn't expected to hear this. I think I had been telling myself that it would be many more weeks—even months—before Jack finished constructing the repeater. More time to stay in a sort of in-between zone where nothing had to happen.

"I thought you were calling about Raymond."

"The segment is over," Jack said.

"I know," I told him. "I heard you."

"Well, I'm glad, because I have an idea."

I carried the phone into the kitchen and drank some orange juice from the carton. The dog, of course, followed me. I put the juice away and patted him on the head.

"Laurie. Are you still there?" Jack asked impatiently. "I have another guest on in a few minutes."

"I'm here, I'm here. What's your idea?"

"I want to ask Raymond to come with us when we take the repeater out to Rockaway."

"This thought just came to you tonight?"

"I've been mulling it over for a while, but tonight just kind of clinched it for me. Raymond Gilmartin is so sure of himself—and he's so deluded. Showing him the radioman would just blow him out of the water."

"That's not the point of what we're doing. And even if we actually see the radioman—if he comes to get the repeater—that may just reinforce Raymond's belief that he's some sort of emissary from our . . . what? Our ancestors? Creators?"

"I don't think so. Raymond Gilmartin is such a narcissist—among other things—that he'll expect your friend . . ."

"He's not my friend." How many times had I said this to Jack?

"He will expect your *shadow* to shake his hand and tell him to keep up the good work. Or at least give him some sign of recognition. After all, he's made it *his* life's work to try to emulate these beings."

"Don't you think you're being a little vindictive?"

"That's because my engrams are in serious need of repair. You heard Raymond."

I walked back to the bedroom with the dog still at my heels. Outside, in the street, a car went by, and I could see the reflected glow of the headlights moving in bright bars across my living room ceiling.

"You know," I said to Jack, "this may not work. Nothing may happen."

There was a brief silence at the other end of the phone, but a different kind of silence than the dead air on the radio. This void pulsed with questions. Finally, Jack asked one. "Do you really think that?"

"I don't know," I replied. "There's still a lot of room in this story for it all to be some kind of fantasy."

"Whose?"

"Mine. Yours. Ravenette's. Raymond's. The list goes on."

"I'm going to invite him, Laurie."

"It's a mistake," I told him. But he had already hung up the phone.

WE DIDN'T do anything right away. Partly because I was working a lot—one of the other bartenders had quit without notice, and I ended up working a week straight, with no time off—and partly, I think, because Jack was having a fine time continuing his campaign against the Blue Awareness and wasn't ready yet to hold out a flag of truce, even a fake one. Almost every night on his show, one of the guests was either an ex-Aware or someone who had produced some kind of exposé—a book, a documentary—about the Blue Awareness. What he was doing made me uneasy so I stopped listening to Jack's program and I told him so. He didn't try very hard to change my mind about that.

But one night, when I was at work, the waitress I was working the shift with answered the phone near the bar. She said a few words that I couldn't hear because of the constant babbling of the televisions, and then held out the receiver to motion that the call was for me. I shook my head—I was too busy with customers, at the moment, to go to the phone—so she wrote down a message for me and then went back to her tables.

A few minutes later, I read the message, which the waitress had scribbled on a cocktail napkin. I wasn't surprised that it was from Jack, since I couldn't imagine who else would call me here. It seemed that he wanted me to listen to the show later, specifically, the segment that began at one thirty.

So a few hours later, I was back in my own neighborhood, walking Digitaria while I once again listened to the *Up All Night* show through my set of earphones. I planned to give Jack maybe five minutes; if he had on another troubled ex-Aware, I still wasn't interested. My focus right now was not on the Blue Awareness and how they screwed people over on the path to the Wild Blue Yonder, where all would be revealed—or not. I had other things on my mind.

And tonight, apparently, so did Jack's guest. When I tuned in the station, I heard the tail end of a question Jack was asking—something, I thought, about Howard Gilmartin—and then I heard him address his guest as Rabbi Friedman. The next thing I heard was a man's voice that sounded a bit frail, but genial. He said, "Well, yes. I knew Howard. We were very friendly, in fact—at least back then. We served together on a carrier in the South Pacific. That was quite awhile ago."

"Almost sixty years," Jack agreed.

"True. But my memory is still pretty good." This assessment was accompanied by a laugh that was full of self-amusement.

"I understand something unusual happened to you, on your ship."

"Yes, I guess you could say it was *very* unusual. It changed my life, as a matter of fact." Again, the rabbi laughed. The sound was soft, soothing, like he was telling a joke about himself, a joke he liked to repeat and hoped that everyone listening to him would appreciate.

A few moments later, he continued with his story. "I was the Morse Code operator, so I worked in the radio shack with Howard. We were in the South Pacific, in the thick of the war, so as you can imagine, it was a very tense time. We saw a lot of fighting—a lot. I wasn't particularly religious in those days, but there was a nondenominational chapel on the ship that I used to go to once in a while. I had been to Hebrew school, you see, and I still remembered how to pray in Hebrew, so sometimes I did. That helped a little."

"Helped?" Jack broke in.

"Well, I was scared, you see. Sometimes I wasn't so much, but sometimes I was. And when I was, I went to the chapel and prayed. One night . . . oh, I guess I got lost in what I was doing—just thinking more than praying, actually—but after a while, I thought I felt someone sitting beside me. I turned, but I didn't see anyone. So I went back to my prayers but then the feeling returned. The feeling that someone was with me. This time, I didn't exactly turn to look, but I kind of glanced to the side and out of the corner of my eye, I saw something. Someone. The silhouette of a man . . . well, of a person, anyway, but flat and gray. No real face, no features, but . . . a living being. Well, *that* was certainly something I should have been scared of, but somehow I wasn't. I wasn't at all. I felt that the best thing to do was just to go back to my prayers. And so I did. I started praying pretty seriously. And as I did, I felt the shadow person slip his hand in mine. And then he began to cry. I mean, I couldn't see him crying or hear him or anything like that, but I knew that's what he was doing."

"Well . . . wow. What can I say? That's a pretty strange encounter you're describing," Jack said.

"It would certainly seem to be, wouldn't it? But . . . well, whenever I tell this story, it still doesn't feel that way to me. I mean, when I think back."

"Do you tell it a lot?"

"Oh yes. I'm very open about it. As I said, it's a very important experience for me. Anyway, I know I should have felt that something truly bizarre was happening, but I didn't, you see. The . . . person? I always call him a person though I suppose he wasn't. Well, I sympathized with him because it was like I could feel some of what he was feeling. I mean, I got the sense that he had a job to do, just like me, and he was trying to do it. And, also like me, he was far from home and he wasn't sure if he was ever going to get back."

"Do you think that's why he was crying?" Jack asked.

"Oh, no. That wasn't the reason. He was crying because we were in the presence of God."

Jack made a noise in his throat that came through the radio as a kind of gulp. I was surprised that he sounded surprised; I assumed he knew what his guests were going to talk about, so he should have been familiar with the story the rabbi was telling. But maybe he hadn't heard all these details. Maybe he had been thrown off guard.

He soon recovered enough to ask another question. "Is that what you thought, too?"

"No. But I guess I had started praying so fervently that the other radioman believed I was in touch with some sense of God that he wasn't. That he couldn't find."

"You knew he was some kind of radioman."

"Oh yes. That was his job. He was setting up some kind of radio network. I know how odd it sounds, but that's what he was doing. His . . . people, I guess you'd call them—well, his people are broadcasting prayers. All through the universe. They're hoping that someday, in some way, God will reply. You know, find a way to let them know He hears them. That

He's . . . somewhere. And He's listening. That's what all religious people want, in one way or another. At least, in my very humble opinion, that's what I think people want, people who are devout. Or perhaps even people who aren't."

"How did you know what he was doing?' Jack asked. "Your . . . visitor."

"I think he told me," the rabbi said. "When he was holding my hand. Somehow, he told me. There were no words but . . . I knew. I understood."

I was riveted by this conversation. So much so that I found I had wandered far beyond the bounds of the usual route I followed when I was walking the dog. I was near a deserted canal that ran behind the auto repair shops, a polluted scar that remained from the time when small barges were part of the commercial traffic in this area. The struts of a broken crane leaned over the water, looking like a monster getting ready to dip a long, rusted finger into a poison well. This was probably not the greatest place to linger, but I didn't care. I sat down on an empty oil drum and listened as the rabbi continued to describe what had happened to him that long-ago night. Digitaria seemed to simply accept that we were stopping in this unexpected place for a while and made himself comfortable on the ground, keeping close enough to me so that I could feel the weight of his body against my leg.

Jack seemed to have recovered from his surprise about the turn the story had taken and he zeroed in on the narrative, the step-by-step details that the rabbi was recounting. "And then?" Jack coaxed. "What happened after you realized that the radioman was crying?"

"That's really it, all of it, to tell you the truth. Except that, after a while, I felt this sense of pressure on my hand—almost like the person was squeezing it."

"He was hurting you," Jack interjected.

"No, no, not at all," the rabbi replied. "It was just like when you're holding someone's hand and you squeeze it, just before you say good-bye. It's just an extra gesture of contact, of touch between two . . . well, persons. People. So when he did that—my visitor—I just instinctively looked down and saw that what I thought was a hand wasn't really that at all. What I mean is, I *felt* like my hand was intertwined with another but no—laying across my palm was a band of light. Moveable, incandescent light. Whitish, bluish, sort of." The rabbi chuckled softly. "I guess I'm having a hard time explaining myself."

"You're doing fine," Jack assured him, but he sounded a little confused himself.

"He let me see him," the rabbi continued. "At least part of him; the part I was touching. That was what he really looked like, I think. Light. Not filmy or diffuse but . . . well, flexible. Flexible light." The rabbi chuckled again. "That's as close as I can get to a description."

"You never saw his face?"

"No," the rabbi said. "Nothing more than what I've told you. He let me see just that part of him. Another gesture, I guess."

The rabbi continued. "A couple of nights after this, Howard and I were down in the crew's quarters. His bunk was across from mine and for once, all the other bunks around us were empty, which was unusual. On a ship like that, you're almost never alone. So maybe it was just that it was quiet and that we weren't on alert or anything that started us talking. And I just blurted it out . . . about the radioman. About how I'd felt him next to me in the chapel, and he was crying. Howard started questioning me then. He wanted to know exactly what the radioman looked like. I did the best I could to describe him—you know, my impression of a flat, gray shape sitting beside me—and then Howard said he had something to tell me. He said he thought he'd seen the same figure up on the radars maybe a month or so prior. His radioman, though, had acted very differently than mine. He had made some sort of awful noise—it sounded threatening, Howard said—and made it very clear that Howard was not to come near him."

"Did you ever tell Howard what else you saw? That you actually got a glimpse of what the radioman *really* looked like?"

"But I didn't—not for sure. I just saw that band of light."

"Even that? You didn't tell Howard?"

"What would have been the point? Howard's experience was so much different than mine; his was angry, confrontational. I didn't want to make it seem like I had been given a gift that had been withheld from him."

The rabbi sounded philosophical, which didn't suit Jack's style of questioning, so he tried to find a way to elicit a more definitive answer. "Given your different experiences, do you think that you and Howard actually met the same, uh, person?"

"I don't know," the rabbi responded. "And I don't know that it matters, really."

"But they—or he, if it was the same radioman—acted so differently."

"Well, we all act differently, don't we, at different times? I mean, even the most confident, aggressive person can have a moment of vulnerability. Especially if you're around someone who you think will be sympathetic."

"And you were."

"I guess you could say that. But you could also say that what happened to me was a turning point, so if I gave the radioman a moment of comfort, what he gave me was . . . well, a purpose to my life. I didn't know it then, but that's what happened. After the war, I tried different things, different jobs, but I was very unhappy. Eventually, I realized that what I wanted was to feel what the radioman *thought* I felt that night, in the chapel. I wanted to feel the presence of God. And so . . . well, eventually, I enrolled in a Jewish theological seminary and became a rabbi."

"Who has stood in the presence of God?"

The rabbi's gentle laugh seemed to soften the bluntness of Jack's question. "We all do that, whether we know it or not. Let's just say I have been trying to be deserving of that awareness."

"To coin a phrase?"

The rabbi laughed again. "No, no, it certainly wasn't me who had anything to do with Howard coming up with that name. The Blue Awareness." I could almost picture Rabbi Friedman shaking his head in amusement. "Well, I suppose it's *what* we're trying to become aware of that matters in the end."

Jack went on questioning him. "Did you and Howard Gilmartin keep in touch after the war?"

"No," the rabbi replied. "As a matter of fact, after the night we talked about the radioman, he barely spoke to me again. The fact that we'd had such different experiences seemed to drive a wedge between us—at least from his point of view. I think he was already trying to, well, let's say *process* what had happened to him." Another chuckle punctuated that last part of the story and the rabbi said, "You can tell I've had some psychology training, right? Well, the point is that I imagine he was already thinking quite differently than I was about what had happened to us both."

"Do you think he was jealous of you?"

"For having some lost soul cry on my shoulder? I hope not."

Since that line of questioning wasn't producing the kind of fireworks that Jack was clearly attempting to ignite, he tried another angle. "Let's focus in on Howard Gilmartin a little more specifically, on what you know about him from personal experience. Am I right about the fact that there was no desert, no secret radar installation, no black ops outpost called the Wild Blue Yonder? I want to remind our audience that those are the experiences that Gilmartin said led him to create the Blue Awareness. Rabbi? What do you have to say about all that?"

"Actually, those were stories Howard wrote after the war. I read some of them. They weren't bad."

"But that's what they were, right? Just stories? His real encounter with the radioman was on your ship, up on the radars, and it scared him. Just about scared the life out of him, I'd say. And on top of that, he wasn't given any secret knowledge, he wasn't entrusted with any supposedly lost information about the origins of human beings."

"Do you mean, did he ever tell me anything like that? No," the rabbi admitted, but he sounded reluctant to endorse even this implied suggestion that Howard Gilmartin was an outright liar. He obviously didn't give any credit to Gilmartin's ideas but it just didn't seem to be in his nature to directly criticize his old comrade in arms, either.

"I have one last question," Jack said, though this turned out to be more of a barrage than a single query. "Tell me, honestly, do you think the being that you met in the chapel was real? In other words, do you think there are aliens on Earth? Here, on this planet, right now? Do you think they're abducting people—you know, I'm sure, there are hundreds, maybe thousands of people who claim to have had abduction experiences. Do you think others are encountering the same beings you and Howard did, or is something else at work here? Maybe there are different races of aliens that have visited, or are visiting our planet. In light of all those possibilities, where do you think that leaves the Blue Awareness and its followers?"

"I couldn't begin to speculate about any of that, Mr. Shepherd," the rabbi said. "All I can do is refer you to Shakespeare. As the bard said, 'There are more things in heaven and earth, Horatio, than are dreamt of in your philosophy.'"

I could almost hear Jack grinding his teeth in frustration. He was doing everything he could to stir up controversy, but instead, he was getting poetry.

And he got something else too: the sound of a dog barking.

This time, it was Jack who reacted with laughter, though it sounded forced. "I guess you can tell we have another guest in the studio tonight," he said, addressing his audience. "Rabbi Friedman brought his dog with him. What's his name, Rabbi?"

"We call him Sammy, but officially, his name is Samson. Samson the bulldog," the rabbi said. "And he's usually very quiet. My apologies."

"No need," Jack said. "We've got open phone lines here. We welcome all opinions—human and otherwise."

Both Sammy's interruption and Jack's comment may have been unplanned, but they provided an opportunity to end the segment on a light note. Jack said good-bye to his guest and then the same spooky, synthesizer-generated music that had signaled the end of Raymond Gilmartin's appearance on *Up All Night* began to play.

I turned off the radio and, almost immediately, my cell phone rang. Of course it was Jack, who said the next half hour of his show was a taped segment, so he had time to talk. "What did you think?" he asked.

"He seems like a very nice man," I said. "The rabbi."

"That's not what I meant," Jack said impatiently.

"I know."

"So?"

I sighed, loud enough so that Jack could hear me. I wanted him to. "So? You want me to tell you that you proved Howard Gilmartin was a phony. Maybe you did—a little—and maybe you didn't, but we both know what you really wanted is to get some sort of rise out of Raymond by mocking his father—but I don't know *why*. What are you doing, Jack? Daring Raymond to come with us when we take the repeater to Rockaway? It's not enough just to ask him, if you're still so dead set on doing that?"

"I did ask him. And he did say yes."

I was so taken aback by this response that it more or less shut me up. I did give more than a passing thought to arguing with Jack about how counterproductive his behavior seemed to me, but I knew it was an argument I would never win because Jack was clearly getting a great deal of satisfaction out of whatever game he thought he was playing with Raymond. We ended up just having a long, complicated conversation about when we could make the drive out to Rockaway. When was Jack free, when was I, what days had Raymond said he would be available? The whole exchange seemed unreal to me, like we were planning some innocuous shopping excursion or a trip to the movies. We settled on the following Sunday afternoon, just a few days away.

Later, at home, when I finally got myself to bed, I was prepared for a restless night, but it was Digitaria who seemed unable to settle down. He kept jumping out of bed and then getting back in again. I thought he was thirsty, or hungry, but he wasn't making any detours to the kitchen where his water bowl and food dish were; instead, he kept padding back and forth between the bedroom and the front door.

There was no way I could pretend not to understand what was going on. Though all I wanted was to plunge back into the depths of a dreamless sleep and not think about the reasons for his restlessness—there were too many of them, all disturbing—it was clear to me that my dog was on high alert.

It was a rain-washed afternoon, blustery and dark. I felt chilled even though I was wearing a jacket, so I asked Jack to turn on the heat in the car as we inched along the Belt Parkway, headed out toward the Rockaway Peninsula. Digitaria was sitting in the back seat along with the Haverkit repeater, assembled from the parts that Jack had managed to acquire. It was wrapped in an old quilt meant to protect it during what I was beginning to think of as a ride to nowhere, because that was where we seemed to be going: nowhere fast.

The traffic was horrendous; there were multiple accidents and endless congestion caused by rubbernecking drivers trying to get a look at the smashed vehicles and trails of shattered glass. We had hoped to be out at the beach before dark but that wasn't going to happen now; we were in the decline of the season, when the days seemed to close themselves out with a grim immediacy that brooked no negotiation with the light of afternoon. The fall horizon was already serving up the night's cold slice of moon.

The only benefit I saw to the fact that we were way behind the schedule we had set for ourselves was that we might not meet up with Raymond. We were almost an hour past the time that Jack said he had told him we would be waiting outside the Sunlite Apartments. Jack had tried Raymond's cell phone, but it went straight to voice mail so I was hoping that by now, he had just given up on us and gone home.

The closer we got to Rockaway, the more uneasy I became. I couldn't sort out which thing was bothering me the most: the combustion that might result from Jack and Raymond meeting outside of the controlled environment of Jack's studio or Raymond's office, or the idea that a shadow man might really show himself to me on the grounds of a deserted building where I used to live. Or maybe it was the fact that I could hear my dog panting feverishly in the seat behind me. If there had been enough room, I knew he would have been pacing back and forth.

Finally, not far ahead, I saw the sign that said, "To the Rockaways." Once we made it down the off-ramp, the traffic cleared up and there were no more delays. We followed a road that led through a series of small communities built on the canals that fed into the bays whose waters washed in and out of the ocean with the tides. Then it was over one last bridge, and we were—I was—back in Rockaway, heading down the peninsula to the vacant lots and broken sidewalks that were now the domain of the Sunlite Apartments.

As we went deeper and deeper into this desolate area, Jack kept asking me if I was sure I knew where we were going. I simply said, Yes, I am. Keep driving. Occasionally, we passed an old summer bungalow, half collapsed into a street that had been taken over by beach sand. It was too dark, now, to make out the deserted boardwalk just a few blocks away and the sea beyond, but even with the car windows closed, I could smell the salt tang in the air, or imagined I could. Deep water, seaweed, fish, sharks, the bones of whales. I could conjure up pictures for myself of what was out there, past what I could see.

Finally, we came to the right block. I told Jack to turn and we slowly drove along what remained of the blacktop, between the rows of thin, blackened trees that had grown up in this sandy soil. And then there it was: the squat brick building with its crumbling wedding cake fretwork, its missing doors and broken windows.

"Here?" Jack said. He sounded incredulous, but I couldn't imagine what else he was expecting. I had told him the building was long abandoned, the neighborhood a ruin.

Out of habit, he was careful to parallel park at the edge of the blacktop, as if some municipal authority might still be concerned with the observance of local traffic rules. When he finally turned off the motor, I got out of the car, and my dog quickly followed me. He stood close by my side, his ears twitching as he looked up at what remained of the Sunlite Apartments.

"That's right," I said to him. "You remember, don't you? You were here once before."

Jack, walking up behind me, heard what I said and asked, "What are you talking about? Why would you have brought him here before?"

I was going to explain about my excursion to the beach last spring—in his car, as a matter of fact—when he had gone out to California, and about how Digitaria had run away from me and found his way to this same spot, but before I even started speaking, something distracted me.

"Look," I said to Jack, pointing down the street, where I suddenly saw the blindingly bright headlights of a huge Suburban with blacked-out windows sweeping toward us. The vehicle pulled up behind Jack's and the driver cut the motor. When the headlights finally dimmed, I noticed that there was another vehicle easing itself into line behind the Suburban. It was a blue van.

"Not good," I whispered to Jack.

"Relax," he replied. "It will be fine." But I was not reassured.

We watched as the back door of the Suburban swung open and Raymond Gilmartin stepped out. As if he had come to keep a business appointment, he was wearing a dark suit and tie, just as he had been the last time I saw him. As he carefully smoothed out his clothes, another familiar figure exited the vehicle: Ravenette, dressed in some sort of faux hippie-chic dress that seemed to have been sewn together out of black scarves. They both, I thought, had the look about them of people harboring a deadly intent they did not want you to know about—not just yet.

I waited to see who would come out of the blue van, but no one did. It stayed tucked in its spot, behind the Suburban, with its lights off. It reminded me of the trucks parked in the alleyways in my neighborhood. The blue van looked like it was hiding.

"You're late," Raymond said, frowning. "We've been driving around, looking for a place to get coffee."

"Miles," Ravenette said, waving her hand as if to dismiss the blight around her as a personal affront. "We had to drive for miles."

"Nice to see you, too," I said to her.

We spent a moment glaring at each other and then I turned to Raymond. My intention was to be a bit more civil to him, but he didn't give me the chance. He drank the dregs from a paper coffee cup and then tossed it on the ground.

"So now that we're all here, let's get on with this, shall we?" Raymond said. "I understand you have some sort of ritual you intend to carry out."

He had addressed that last remark to me, in a tone so cold, so distant, that it made me feel pretty bad about him. Bad in a lot of ways, including the fact that he, too, apparently intended to behave like a jackass. It was disappointing. I wanted to think better of him but now, there seemed to be no reason to think much about him at all.

"There is no ritual," I told him. "I'm just going to try something. Actually, I got the idea from Ravenette."

She turned to Raymond and spit out a declaration of anger. "I told you that was what she would say."

"Never mind," Raymond replied.

Right after that, I thought I saw her make some sort of motion toward the blue van, but Raymond caught her arm and stopped her. This worried me and I wanted to make Jack aware of what she'd done, but he had already gone back to the car to get the repeater. When he returned in just a minute or so, he had removed the blanket, so it looked like he was carrying a big radio tuner—a squat black box bristling with wires and dials.

He put it in my arms and then stepped back, as if the thing might pose a danger to anyone around it. "Okay," he said. "It's all yours."

It was dark now, fully nighttime. The rainy wind had blown itself out but inky clouds had placed themselves between us and the stars. The only illumination came from down the block. The one remaining streetlight in this whole area burned with a dim insistence as if sheer will, not electricity, was keeping it on.

Did I really have a plan? No. Just a feeling, just a guess about what to do. I walked across a path of rubble toward the wide, empty darkness where the front door of the Sunlite Apartments used to be, with my dog following me almost step for step. The building stood before me in two realities: the crumbling brick structure that I could see now, and the memory of what it had been in those summer days. I played on the wedding-cake balcony outside the rooms where the adults cooked dinner, dealt out a hand of cards and listened to one of Avi's radios spin out the sentimental ballads that were popular in those years.

I put the repeater down in front of the doorway and waited. I waited for what seemed like a long time. Nothing happened. I was wondering if I was going to have to try to climb the rickety fire escape, when I suddenly heard Raymond's voice coming from behind me.

"Well?" he said impatiently. "Is that it?"

I looked down at the dog, who was staring intently into the empty doorway. I was still thinking that something might happen when the dog suddenly turned around and began to growl. The sound ended in the kind of high-pitched yipping that I remembered from that last time we had been in the vicinity of a certain blue van.

And indeed, as I turned, I saw the side panels of the van slide open and two men emerge. They were young, trim, wearing jeans and hoodies. I tried to picture them in yellow goggles but quickly realized that it didn't matter whether these were the men I had encountered before or not. They were generic people, Blue Awares, Raymond's followers. They would do whatever he wanted them to do and I knew that whatever he wanted them to do right now was not going to be anything good.

Jack was standing near Raymond and Ravenette, but looking toward me. He didn't see the two Awares until they walked right up to him. They had some sort of small, bulky objects in their hands; for a moment, I had the wild—though maybe not crazy—thought that they were holding guns. But no, that's not what they were: I had watched enough episodes of cop shows on TV to recognize a Taser when I saw one in real life.

I watched as Jack finally realized what was happening. I was not totally surprised by his reaction. He laughed.

"Really?" he said to Raymond. "Who do you want to take prisoner? Me or the alien?"

"There is no alien," Raymond said. "No radioman. Ravenette tried to tell Ms. Perzin that. You're both in need of serious help. Counseling. We're going to try to give it to you."

"You're kidding, right?" Jack said. "You couldn't kidnap a dog, so now you're going to try to kidnap human beings?"

Raymond shrugged. "The event you're referring to wasn't authorized. This, however, most certainly is. However, it's hardly a kidnapping. It's an intervention. I am convinced that your hatred for the Blue Awareness is evidence of deep-seated engram damage. The problems and disappointments you've had in your life have become like a cancer affecting your mind, your ability to think clearly and to reason. We're going to help you overcome all that. I told you about our retreat center upstate and everyone who listens to your show heard you say that you'd consider going. Well, now you are. It's a wonderful facility; we have wonderful, caring Blue Box counselors . . ."

"Who also do wonderful things with sleep deprivation, hallucinogens and other nifty therapies, right? I've heard all about what goes on at your retreat centers," Jack said.

"Everything the counselors do will be designed to help you. You'll be able to change your outlook, the whole trajectory of your life."

"Listen to me," Jack said. He sounded firm, even reasonable, but the look on his face was beginning to rearrange itself into one of alarm. "I can't just disappear. It doesn't matter what I said on the radio. People will look for me."

The answer to this statement came from Ravenette. "You're going to send everyone an e-mail," she told Jack. "Something witty and persuasive. That's exactly the kind of person you think you are, right? Well, we'll do you a favor. We'll help you keep that fantasy going for a while. And that blog they have you writing on World Air's website? Every week, you'll post an update on your progress."

"This is crazy," Jack said. "Don't either of you realize that?"

"What about you, Laurie?" Ravenette said to me. "Do you think this is crazy? Because basically, that's what I think is wrong with you, too, and we're going to help you get better. Heal you."

"And you think no one will miss her, either?" Jack interjected.

"The vice president of the company that owns Endless Weekend is Aware," Raymond said. "He understands how important it is that Ms. Perzin go through counseling with us. Ravenette really does feel that your friend is in imminent danger of having a breakdown."

I was listening to all this with the same sense of duality I had about the Sunlite Apartments. I understood what Raymond and Ravenette were saying they were going to do but there was also a part of me that found it impossible to accept that it was actually going to happen. Not because they couldn't do what they said but because I couldn't really believe that they wanted to. Because if they did, it meant that *they* believed in what they said they did—really believed—and that seemed unimaginable to me.

And so—at the wrong time, in the wrong place—I had an insight about myself: there was a part of me that actually envied Raymond Gilmartin. Which was why I had been so willing to cut him some slack, empathize with him when all the evidence that I should do nothing of the sort was overwhelming. The fact that he believed in something, had some sort of deep faith, was a feat impossible for me to achieve. And I felt the lack of that, felt it over my lifetime, felt it enduringly, achingly. In that respect, even Ravenette was better off than I was. It was an awful revelation. I couldn't accept the reality of someone else's faith in anything beyond themselves because I didn't have any myself. Perhaps that's why I had finally allowed myself to believe in the radioman's existence, to be willing to grant the possibility that he might actually be waiting for me in the Sunlite Apartments—because I wanted him to be.

But I didn't have a lot of time to dwell on these thoughts. No matter what I did or did not believe, I had to face the fact that Raymond and his followers intended to herd Jack and me into the van and drive us off into some sort of blue oblivion. And there was no way that I could see to get away from them. The men standing beside Raymond and Ravenette were blocking the path to Jack's car; we'd never be able to get to it before they got us. And trying to run away wasn't an option either; where was there to run, in the middle of all this desolation?

I was still desperately going through a mental list of escape routes and coming up with nothing useful when, suddenly, I became aware that my dog had fallen silent. The insistent growling and yipping that he'd kept up since the two Awares had exited the van had stopped. And he had turned away from all of us now, pointing himself toward the ruined board-walk and the sea beyond. He kept staring in that direction as the crescent moon pulled itself out from behind the ragged, night-colored clouds, allowing me to see the ramp leading down from the boardwalk to the street. At first, it looked like just some bare boards lit by the moon's weak light. Then, a moment later, that empty space was no longer empty at all.

Dogs were coming down the ramp. Dozens and dozens of dogs. And they were coming from the other direction as well, running up the street toward the Sunlite Apartments. Dogs were also coming through the vacant lots, picking their way between the brambles and the trees. Dogs seemed to be coming from everywhere. Silently, soundlessly, they began to converge in front of the building until there was a line of dogs—hundreds of dogs, small ones, huge ones, and every-thing in-between—packed tightly together, forming a barrier between me and the other people standing in the broken street in front of the Sunlite Apartments.

It was an astonishing sight. Amazing. And as I tried to understand what I was seeing, I began to pick out a few famil-iar figures in this giant pack of dogs. Or at least I thought they were familiar; perhaps I was just mistaking one dog for another. But I really did think I saw Sassouma's dust-colored Dogon dog among the pack. And Buddy, the dog who had visited me in the mausoleum where Avi was interred. And Dax, the dog from the airport. A particular bulldog stood quite near me, and I had a feeling that he would have answered to the name Samson. Near him stood the golden-red pharaoh hound. And though I did not see her, I was sure that some-where in the pack was another dog whose name I knew: Zvezdochka.

Of all of us, it was Raymond who finally spoke. "How did you do this?" he asked me. His voice had softened; his whole demeanor had changed. Now, he seemed more like the man who had once said to me, *I have been waiting all my life.*

"I didn't," I told him.

"Maybe he did," Jack said.

Slowly, almost imperceptibly, Jack raised his hand and pointed toward the door of the Sunlite Apartments.

I turned back around so that I was facing the darkness that filled the empty doorway of the ruined building. But now, a piece of that darkness seemed to have detached itself and began moving toward me. The darkness had a humanoid shape, so that it was like watching a shadow walk by itself.

And then, when it was about twenty feet away from me, it stopped. It was hard to see, hard to be sure that what I was seeing was actually there because it—the shadow—seemed blurred around the edges, as if, at any moment, it might lose whatever substance it had and be absorbed back into the night. It had no face, no features, no real structure to its arms or legs or torso. It was just a thin shade that barely stood out from the darkness draped all around. I knew who this was and so, though I should have been, I was not afraid.

I pointed to the repeater, which sat on the ground nearby. "That's it," I said to the being that I knew as the radioman. "The Haverkit. That's what you wanted."

Suddenly, from behind me, I heard a soft click followed by a momentary flash of light. Someone had a camera and was trying to take a photo.

The radioman's reaction was swift. Though I saw no mouth that could have produced a sound, somehow, from somewhere inside itself, the figure before me emitted a long, loud, angry hiss.

And then it strode forward, moving faster than I could have imagined possible. It was still hissing and now, as if I were the individual responsible for the camera flash—the one it was angry at—it was coming straight at me.

~ 279 ~

Can a shadow hit you? Kill you? Drag you into the neth-erworld? I barely had time to think before it was just a step away from me.

And then, suddenly, my dog stepped between us. He was facing the radioman and his spiral-curled tail was wagging slowly. Digitaria was offering a greeting to someone he knew. Someone he remembered.

Immediately, the radioman stopped moving forward. The edges of his shadow-shape seemed to waver so that it became even harder to see him. But he was there, right in front of me. I knew it. I could feel it. So I did the only thing I could think of; I also offered a gesture of greeting, one I had tried before—though last time, in Ravenette's loft, I had left it to the dog to calm the radioman by himself. This time, I shared the effort. I bent down and patted the top of my dog's head.

And then, the flat, gray figure of the radioman became more distinct. Slowly, he bent forward as well, reached out his hand and began to pet Digitaria. Our hands brushed, and as they did, I felt the slightest quiver, as if the space in which we touched had become charged.

Quickly, the radioman withdrew his hand. He pulled him-self up to his full height, which was about the same as mine, and stood in front of me, like a cut-out figure composed of night and darkness. He was completely still, completely silent.

And then I saw him. It was for just a moment, but I really *saw* him in the way that the rabbi had described what he had seen, only more completely. Suddenly, gone was the humanoid shadow that Howard Gilmartin had described, that I remembered. Instead, just as if a switch had been turned on, positioned before me was a kind of thin, flexible stalk of bluish-white light with a round nimbus at the top—a head, perhaps, if the bright, vertical stalk was a body. Inside the nimbus were three round, black spots: eyes and a mouth, maybe, if such a being was in need of those.

The stalk seemed to sway from side to side for another moment, just long enough, I realized, to make sure that I really registered what I was seeing. Like the rabbi, I was being given a gift. The flat, human-shaped shadow was how this being hid himself. What he was allowing me to see was how he looked without that protection.

But in the space of a breath, the light disappeared. The darkness rearranged itself into the shadow that lived inside my memory.

I thought that was it, that the most extraordinary moment of this extraordinary experience was over. But I was wrong. It wasn't—not quite yet.

As the shadow once again took shape, the radioman lifted his hand and extended one long, gray, human-seeming finger, which he raised to his lips—or where his lips would have been if what was once again his flat, gray face had features. It was a gesture I well remembered, and of all the ways I could have reacted, the one I would never have expected from myself is exactly what I did. I laughed. And I laughed because I knew how he meant it: not as a warning to stay silent but as a kind of joke between, well, not old friends, but at least two individuals who had passed this way before.

And then, in an instant, moving so swiftly that all I really saw was a blur, the radioman snatched up the repeater and strode back through the doorway of the Sunlite Apartments. He was gone.

As soon as his figure had disappeared into the empty doorway, the dogs began to disperse as well. As quickly as they had come, they left, running down the street, through the vacant lots. Some of them went back up the ramp toward the boardwalk and for a brief minute or so, I could see them, framed against the night sky, heading off to wherever they had come from.

And then we were alone again, the human beings who had witnessed what had just transpired: Jack, Raymond, Ravenette, the two Awares, and me. And one last dog; the one who stayed behind when the others left. Digitaria.

I saw, now, that there were actually two people who had cameras: Jack and Raymond. They both looked poised to take pictures, but it seemed that since the radioman had lunged at me, neither of them had made a move. They both appeared to be frozen in place.

But that changed in an instant. Jack looked at the camera he was holding and, as if he suddenly remembered what it was, mumbled something about getting a picture and ran past me, into the building. Raymond ran after him.

Ravenette stood with the two Awares. Her mouth was open and she seemed, temporarily, to have forgotten how to speak. The young men with her were still clutching their Tasers, but made no move to use them as I moved past them and began to walk away. The dog padded after me as we headed down the street. I didn't want to wait for Jack and Raymond to return from what I knew would be their fruitless hunt for a photograph of the radioman. Perhaps they needed proof that what they had just seen had actually happened but I didn't need anything like that. For now, I just wanted to get away. I didn't want to talk about anything. I didn't want to hear or make apologies or explanations. And I didn't want to find out what anyone planned to do next. I didn't care.

It was a long walk from the beach to the town, which appeared to be closed up for the night. The pizza parlors, dollar stores and bodegas were all locked. Most were hidden behind security gates. This was not a safe place to be; I knew that, but I also knew that I was in no danger. Nothing bad was going to happen to me tonight.

And I knew what I would see next: a black car gliding down the empty street. And that was exactly what happened; a cruising gypsy cab appeared from around the corner of a side street. I flagged him down and climbed into the back seat with my dog—and for once, I had the car to myself. There were no other passengers aboard.

The driver asked me where I was going. I told him and he named a reasonable price, so I said fine, sat back and closed my eyes. I didn't open them again until I felt the car slow down when we were pulling up to my building.

As I got out of the car, followed by the dog, I saw my neighbor, Sassouma, heading down the block, heading home from her job. I said hello, and we walked upstairs together.

To get to my apartment, I had to pass hers. As she said good night to me, she unlocked her door and I could see inside, to the small living room, where one of her young sons was sitting on the couch with the family's dust-colored Dogon dog.

"Bad boy. You should be in bed," Sassouma scolded her son, though her tone was more fond than angry.

The boy said nothing to his mother, but I saw his gaze wander toward Digitaria. At the same time, he pulled his dog toward him and began, gently, to pet it.

I said good night and unlocked my own door. Once inside, I saw the light blinking on my answering machine and I knew it was Jack. I would call him back eventually, but not just then because I still didn't want to talk. I had powered off my cell phone somewhere on the ride back from Rockaway so I left it turned off and took the further step of unplugging my landline. As I carried out this small task, my dog padded off to the bedroom. I followed after him and watched as he jumped up and arranged himself in his usual place at the foot of the bed. But instead of sitting there, eyes open, nose pointed at the door, he curled up and almost immediately went to sleep.

I left him there and went back to the living room, carrying my laptop. I had no intention, yet, of going to sleep myself. Instead, I started trolling the Internet. There were a number of sites I wanted to visit.

I spent the next couple of hours going back and forth from one site to another, dozing sometimes, but mostly just sitting, just waiting. Eventually, around dawn, I found the first sign of what I was looking for on the site of a university in Australia with an array of radio telescopes that systematically analyzed the radio waves emitted by celestial objects. This was one of the places that Avi had received a QSL card from. Using the photocopies Jack had given me, I had been able to make a list of every one of them. Years ago, long before there even was an Internet, someone at the university had been a distance-listening partner of Avi's and had corresponded with him by postcard. Now, I only had to wait a few hours to find out what they had heard on the other side of the world. Several times a day, the university posted a log of signals it picked up from the array, along with a summary to aid amateur astronomers and students, and scrolling through the notes, I read that an anomalous signal had been picked up from a French satellite as it passed over the Atlantic Ocean. It wasn't a routine telemetry signal from the satellite to its terrestrial base but, rather, seemed to be originating from an Earthbound source. What made it particularly unusual—what flagged it as something very different from any kind of stray signal being accidentally picked up by the satellite—was that its origin was deliberately masked so as to be untraceable. It was clear, however, that the signal was specifically aimed in such a way as to use the satellite as a booster to send it farther out into space. Confirmation of the signal was requested from other listening stations and additional review was recommended.

I knew immediately the radioman was back on duty. He had gotten the Haverkit repeater hooked up and put his network back online. The ghost signals—the alien prayers that had been silent for so long—were being sent out again, toward the stars.

There was a hyperlink embedded in the log notes about the strange signal. I clicked on it and the media player on my laptop automatically opened itself up and prepared to play the file. The program had a screen feature set to create a sort of psychedelic display timed to the beat of whatever music it was playing, but since the file it was retrieving was not music, it seemed to hesitate, briefly, before it pushed out a handful of colored pulses. I watched them slowly blossom and disappear as the audio finally kicked in.

And there it was: the faint, echoing heartbeat of my old friend Sputnik. I knew that it wasn't really Sputnik's telemetry signal I was listening to but the pulses that were carrying the radiomen's message. Perhaps their signal contained a code or perhaps that was what their language really sounded like. I was sure that I would never know, but it didn't matter to me. I couldn't understand what they were saying but I knew what they meant: that they were still searching for whoever—or whatever—had created them. And though it wasn't a concern of theirs, what they were seeking was the creator of human beings, too, as well as all the other beings that likely shared the vast universe with us.

At some point in the morning, I must have dozed off, because when I woke up, Digitaria was beside me. I took him out for his walk and then went back to the couch and resumed listening to the signal.

In the early afternoon, I turned my cell phone back on and, almost immediately, it rang. Of course, it was Jack.

He didn't even say hello. The first words out of his mouth were, "Have you heard it?"

"Yes," I said, knowing exactly what he meant. "I heard it."

"Amateur radio networks all over the world are picking it up and so are the big observatories with radio telescopes. Actually, I should say, picking *them* up. It's not just whispering at the Watering Hole; there are more than a dozen ghost signals on different frequency bands. It's like the whole radio spectrum has lit up."

"So it's big news."

"It will be for a while," Jack agreed. "But since I'm assuming—just like before—that nobody will be able to figure out what the source of the signals is or what they mean, eventually most everyone will decide that they're some sort of anomaly and go on to other things. That will leave the usual suspects—the alien hunters and conspiracy guys—to come on my show and tell me all about what they think is going on."

"And you're not going to tell them that you know the truth?"

"I didn't even get a photo, Laurie."

"No. I didn't think you would."

"So what am I going to do? Tell them that I built a repeater out of old Haverkit parts so I could give it to a shadow who wants to find God? I can't do that. I'd sound crazy—and I'm supposed to be the cool head, the objective host who gives the unexplainable phenomena crowd a place to come and work up a sweat."

I made a mental note of what Jack had just said: he'd called the radioman a shadow—no mention of the bright, slim being that had revealed itself behind the shape of darkness. Evidently, only I had seen the radioman in his real form. I knew Jack well enough by now to be sure that if he'd even glimpsed anything other than the shadow, he would have been dissecting the experience, going over and over it with me. Then was I going to tell him what I had seen? Maybe, but not now. That was a conversation for another day, another time.

"What about Raymond?" I asked.

"Well, we didn't exactly kiss and make up but we went our separate ways without incident, as they say. We both lived to fight another day." Then Jack laughed. "The Blue Boxes are going to be working overtime to soothe the angry engrams that he and that vampire queen are going to be dealing with while they try to fit your radioman and his behavior into Blue Awareness."

"Ravenette is a psychic, not a vampire." How odd, I thought. I actually felt a little protective of her. Almost fond, as if she were already fading into the background of how *my* thoughts were arranging themselves around the events of last night.

"I stand corrected. I got my alternative lifestyles mixed up."

"You know what, Jack?" I said. "I actually have to get ready to go to work."

"Can't you call in sick or something? You must be exhausted. Have you even slept?"

"Not much, but I feel fine. I really do."

After adding a promise to Jack that I'd call him later—or maybe tomorrow—I got off the phone, took a shower, and went through my usual routine of having something to eat, getting myself dressed, and taking the dog for a walk. After I brought him back to the apartment, before I left again, I gave him a pat on the head.

Standing at the bus stop a few minutes later, I saw the moon high up in a corner of the afternoon sky. Planes from the airport where I was headed were pulling themselves up into that same late autumn sky, headed out over the ocean. Down the block on the road between the garages and the bay, I could see my bus come lumbering toward me. Everything was the same as it always was, except that it was not.

And what was not, was me. I was different now than I had been yesterday, different when I got home last night than when I had left. And the difference was irrefutable. I felt the way I thought I must have felt when I was a child, crouching beside Avi on the fire escape, watching him tune around the dial on his radio. I felt energized, awake, alert—and deeply curious, although there were some things I already understood. I suppose it had taken last night to make them clear to me, but they were certainly clear now.

I knew, for example, what Avi had wanted, probably all the years of his life. Avi, who had never traveled more than a few miles from home, wanted his radios to connect him to distant places. And my friend Jack, so consumed with revenge lately, really just wanted to go on listening to people tell him stories about things going bump in the night. Dr. Carpenter wanted everything that he considered nonsense having to do with strange dogs and ancient visitors to stop being any concern of his. Raymond Gilmartin simply wanted to be right, and Ravenette wanted him to be, too. The rabbi who owned the bulldog wanted enlightenment. And the radioman simply wanted to do his job.

And me? What did I want? I could answer that question in the few moments it took me to climb onto the bus, take my seat, and let it carry me to work under the pale light of the afternoon moon.

What did I want? Maybe to believe what I had denied for longer than I could remember: that life could be something other than just a series of days and weeks and years to get through. Slog through, with my head down and eyes averted. Instead, it could actually be interesting, rich with possibilities. It could even be mysterious. Very mysterious. It could keep me up all night, thinking. Wondering. Listening. It could make me want to keep tuning around the universal dial, trying to find out what I might hear. What I might encounter.

What did I want? There was no doubt about that now.

What did I want? I wanted more.